The Redneck Riviera

"Honey, it's not like when I was growing up here in the 50s. Myrtle Beach
was a quiet, friendly, family beach place
back then. Now it's turned into the
Redneck Riviera."

> — Estelle Simmons,
> forty-year Myrtle Beach resident

Other books by the author:

Love By Mail

Local and Family History in South Carolina

The Dictionary of South Carolina Biography

*Mary's World: Love, War, and Family Ties
in Nineteenth-century Charleston*

As literary collaborator:

Safe House, by Edward Lee Howard

Patriot Dreams, by Lt. Col. Robin Higgins

No Time for Tears, by Dorris R. Wilcox

Stopping the Train, by Edwin B. Martin, Jr.

Death by HMO, by Dorothy Rose Cancilla

The
Redneck Riviera

A novel by

Richard N. Côté

CORINTHIAN
BOOKS

Mt. Pleasant, S.C.

First Edition. First printing, September 2001.

Publisher's Cataloging-in-Publication
(Provided by Quality Books, Inc.)

Côté, Richard N.
    The Redneck Riviera: a novel / by Richard N. Côté. – 1st ed
    p. cm.
    ISBN 1-929175-17-5 (trade hardcover)
    ISBN 1-929175-34-5 (trade paperback)
    I. Title
    LCCN 2001091644
    1. Mothers and daughters—Fiction. 2. Myrtle Beach (S.C.)—Fiction.
    I. Title
        PS3553.O763785R44 2001   813'.6
                                                 QBI01-700720

Jacket design © 2001 by Rob Johnson Design
Back cover photographs © 2001 by Richard N. Côté
Author portrait by Mary Ingalls Côté

Corinthian Books
an imprint of The Côté Literary Group
P.O. Box 1898
Mt. Pleasant, S.C. 29465-1898
(843) 881-6080
www.corinthianbooks.com

Contents

This book is dedicated to every mother who is willing to risk everything — even her own life — to save a loved one who is headed down the path of self-destruction.

Even though South Carolina's Redneck Riviera is quite real, this story is a work of fiction and is solely of my own creation. However, it is not a "formula novel." It evolved from a myriad of sources and encounters with real people and real events in and outside of the Myrtle Beach area. What's real? What's not? You decide. That's the fun of it.

I am indebted to the reference librarians of the Chapin Memorial Library, Myrtle Beach, for their assistance. At Corinthian Books, the skills of Diane Anderson, Margaret Grace, and Georgianne Francis Batts were invaluable, as were the insights of Dra. Maria Cordova and Rose M. Tomlin.

I also want to thank Sherry, Brooke, Sarah, Jennifer, and Robin in Myrtle Beach, and dancer-entertainers "Peaches," "Destiny," "Isis," "Natasha," "Monica," "Veronica," "Melissa," "Kayla," "Georgia," "Nadine," and "Leah" for sharing with me so candidly their real-life personal experiences in Redneck Riviera strip clubs. Thanks also to Guy Schmidt at the U.S. Office of National Drug Control Policy for the extensive information on clandestine d-methamphetamine labs and meth production techniques and hazards.

Richard N. Côté
Mt. Pleasant, South Carolina
August 22, 2001

1

High Cotton

Murrell's Inlet, South Carolina
Early May

Y*ahoo! Life rocks!* Dolly Devereaux's heart raced as she fluffed her platinum blonde hair and checked her blue eyeliner in the bathroom mirror. Outside, the light mist of rain from the gray clouds above did nothing to dampen her spirits. *Nothing,* she thought, *is going to get me down today. Yesterday I was an employee, a drone, a seven-dollar-an-hour sales clerk. Today I'm the store manager, the boss, the queen bee of Fantasia Lingerie Store #23 in Myrtle Beach.* Recalling a phrase she'd learned from her grandmother when she was just a baby growing up in rural Darlington, Dolly grinned and thought, *Honey, you's in high cotton now!*

She couldn't believe how casually the lingerie chain's district manager had made the announcement to her and the other employees the day before. Maybe it wasn't a big deal for him. After all, he supervised thirteen stores in three states. Wanda, the previous manager of Dolly's store, had quit without warning just two days ago, and he had to make a quick replacement. "What the heck," he probably thought to himself. "Take the blonde. She's the oldest, and she can't do any worse than the last one."

It might have been a routine decision for him, Dolly thought, *but it sure was a big deal for me. Yesterday I was working by the hour with no benefits. Today I have health insurance, sick leave, and in three more months, a 401(k). What the hell is a 401(k)?* she thought when he told her, never letting on for a minute that she had no idea what it was. *Who cares?* she thought, smiling. *It's a benefit, it's free, and nobody else in my family ever had one.*

For Dolly, life in the North Myrtle Beach mobile home park where she spent her teenage years had centered around earning money after school to help her mother, Anne, with the cost of food, rent, electricity, and dodging the hands of her mother's succession of boyfriends. The "trailer trash," as the city kids called her kind, didn't spend much time worrying about 401(k) plans. But now, at the age of 36, her years of hard work and overtime had finally paid off. She had finally made it out of the trailer park and into the middle class. She was a manager. She was on a roll. She hoped the promotion wouldn't cause trouble with the other three girls. But if it did, well, she was the manager now and they'd just have to live with it.

Dolly swung her long, dancer's legs into her rusting blue Honda Civic and slammed the door shut, hoping the passenger side window wouldn't jump out of its track again. She pulled out of the SeaVue Apartments parking lot in Murrell's Inlet, turned left, and headed north toward Myrtle Beach.

As she pulled onto King's Highway, as U.S. Highway 17 was known locally, a long, silver gasoline tanker sped by on the left, shrouding her car in a light-brown fog of rain, dirt, and road oil. Her windshield wipers, long overdue for replacement, smeared the thin brown soup across the windshield, making it even harder to see. *Tomorrow,* she thought, *I might celebrate the Big Event by taking the car into the shop for some maintenance. Heck, maybe I'll even splurge for some overdue dental work.* The pay raise would bring her nearly $200 more a month. She was rich! Or as close to rich as any member of her family had ever gotten. She knew that she couldn't give up her waitress job at Captain Willie's yet, but the thought of the extra money from her day job made her head spin. *Maybe it's even time to move up from Budweiser to Heineken's.* But she quickly reconsidered. *Nah. I like Budweiser.*

As she drove towards the store, thinking about how she'd handle her first day as manager, Dolly scarcely noticed the non-stop blur of signs and billboards that lined both sides of King's Highway. The entrance to Murrell's Inlet was the unofficial southern boundary of what the business community promoted as the family oriented, fun-in-the-sun and golfing heaven known as the "Grand Strand." To local wags and far-away travel writers it is known as "The Redneck Riviera."

A two-hour drive north of Charleston, South Carolina's Redneck Riviera is a forty-mile-long strip of coastline that ran south from the North Carolina state line and includes Little River, North Myrtle Beach, Myrtle Beach, and ends at Murrell's Inlet, ten miles south of Myrtle Beach.

Each year, the region hosts twice as many visitors as the entire state of Hawaii. On a typical summer day, nearly a half-million people enjoy its wide, clean beaches and fill its 60,000 hotel rooms, 200+ tennis courts, 100+ golf courses, amusement parks, theaters, mini-golf courses, factory outlet stores, seafood restaurants, bars, and two dozen strip clubs.

Civilization — as most traditional South Carolinians conceive it, anyway – starts a couple miles south of Murrell's Inlet at Brookgreen Gardens. The historic former rice plantation and its magnificent outdoor statuary is the first pearl in an unbroken chain of natural beauty that lies to the south of the neon, plastic, and T-shirt shops of the Redneck Riviera. Further south lies 150 miles of the state's greatest natural treasures, including South Carolina's legendary rice plantations, the incredible eighteenth- and nineteenth-century architecture of Charleston, and the lush sea islands, which stretch down to the beautiful historic town of Beaufort.

Heading north from Murrell's Inlet is another story. The closer Dolly got to Myrtle Beach — Ground Zero for rampant commercialism and tacky excess — the harder it was to tell one Redneck Riviera community from another. The endless procession of nearly identical beachwear and T-shirt shops was evidently designed with the assumption that no addition of more fiberglass sharks, neon lights, or chrome could possibly be bad for business. The countless tourist traps that lined King's Highway formed a continuous commercial blur. When a boyfriend took her for a weekend rendezvous at a romantic nineteenth-century bed-and-breakfast hotel in Savannah, Dolly began to realize that the Myrtle Beach area lacked some of the finer things in life. She immediately upgraded her aspirations another notch.

On King's Highway, the traffic, signs, and billboards increased in density the closer she got to the center of Myrtle Beach. In bright colors and pulsating neon, they all hawked the wares and services of the Redneck Riviera.

The Pirate's Cove Gift Shop – Welcome Canadians –Free fireworks with purchase – Liquidation Sale – Up to 80% off – Beach Breeze Souvenirs – Myrtle Beach towels $5 / 2 for $9 – The Pussycat Lounge – Girls, Girls, Girls – Bikers welcome.

Will Melissa show up for work on time today? Dolly wondered. Melissa, the twenty-year-old girl who was hired a few weeks before, had been coming in late and tired for the past several weeks. *Just like I did when I was eighteen, out of control, and dancing till 2:00 A.M. at the Wild Canary Lounge,* Dolly thought. Dolly had always been the mother hen of the lingerie store, looking out for the younger girls who worked there. She was particularly worried about Melissa. The day before, Melissa said she was burning up, but her skin was cold and clammy. Shaniqua, another young clerk, said Melissa was taking medication for a migraine, but Dolly knew better.

Oh God, don't let it happen to this girl, Dolly thought, recalling a night she'd spent years earlier, holding the trembling body of a fellow eighteen-year-old stripper as she came down hard and fast from a bad heroin high.

Water Melons $2.00 each – Ice – Peaches – Corn – Beachwear Outlet – Free Myrtle Beach decals - 48-item seafood buffet – All you can eat, $14.95 – Casino cruises – Las Vegas-Style Gambling – Two cruises a day – Horsefeathers, a Gentlemens' Club – Beautiful Women – wet T-shirt contest Tuesday nights – Saturday Night Football – Ladies Welcome.

Ladies welcome. Yeah, right. Like some fifty-something golfer from Toronto or the Rust Belt is going to bring his wife, fiancée, or girlfriend along to watch him get a hard-on while he slips dollar bills into the g-strings of teenage girls with silicone boobs. In the eight months that Dolly had worked the strip clubs after her divorce, she occasionally saw a woman come in with a man. *Not many qualified as ladies,* she thought.

On the left, just past the Pancake Palace Restaurant, a thirty-foot, round-bellied fiberglass Buddha smiled enigmatically at the mini-golfers who putt-putted their way across the green plastic grass. Across the street, a happy mermaid holding crossed Canadian and American flags rode a huge fiberglass killer whale, poised as if plunging into the blue-dyed water of yet another miniature golf course.

Harriet is the one most likely to be jealous, Dolly thought. *She's been at Fantasia almost as long as I have, and she's been kissing up to the district manager for months.*

"WATCH OUT!" she yelled as a big blue Oldsmobile with Ontario license plates cut across her lane without warning. She leaned on her horn, but the balding driver in the Hawaiian print golf shirt paid no attention and drove on. He was obviously intent on enjoying the annual Canadian-American Days festival. Each year, it lured thousands of snow-weary Canadians south when the Grand Strand's Atlantic beaches — still frigid by local standards — were seductive when compared to the gloomy weather north of the U.S. border. The timing of the annual event fit in with frost-bitten Ontario's school holiday was no accident.

Wouldn't that be just my luck?, Dolly thought. *Yesterday, I'm a clerk. Today, some golf-obsessed Canadian tourist almost totals me before I get the chance to enjoy my first day as a manager.*

The traffic was light — nowhere near as bad as during the main tourist invasion that started on Memorial Day weekend, when all the theme parks and attractions officially opened for the summer.

One mile to go. How will Melissa and Shaniqua take it? They both wanted the manager's job. They'll probably figure I got it because I'm so much older, she thought.

A paunchy, long-haired biker on a chromed-out, candy-apple-red Harley Softail cruised by, his sunglasses, black T-shirt, and graying ponytail dripping water from the rain. The back of the shirt read, "If you can read this, the bitch fell off."

How does he do it? Dolly wondered as the driver guided the massive motorcycle with one hand, holding onto a large nylon mesh bag of groceries with the other. Gunning the engine, he flashed her a big, gold-toothed smile as he thundered down the road.

Here we go again, Dolly thought, remembering that Myrtle Beach Spring Bike Week, an annual spring invasion of 150,000 mostly white Harley Davidson motorcyclists, followed by a second week of 100,000 mostly black speed bikers, was only days away. The biggest challenge, she knew, was that the bikers' largest swap meet — five acres of T-shirts, jewelry, leather goods, and performance parts vendors and twenty acres of parking for tens of thousands of bikes – was headquartered at Inlet Square Mall, just a few blocks from her apartment. At her lingerie store, Bike Week was great for business. The biker crowd loved to shop for sexy leather and lace, but the crush of motorcycles would add an hour to her usual fifteen-minute commute to work.

King Kong Golfland – Live turtles – Every item $1.00 – Papa Primera's Pizza – Large 4 toppings $10.95 – T-shirts R Us – Free Sand Dollar (with purchase) – Myrtle Beach mugs 3 for $5 – Swimwear – Fantasia Lingerie and Novelty Shop – Where Lace and Heaven Meet – Welcome Canadians.

As if on cue, the sun broke through the clouds as Dolly turned into the parking lot next to Fantasia. She drove behind the store to the staff parking area. When she arrived, her heart nearly burst with joy. There, at the back door, stood Melissa, Shaniqua, and Harriet, each with a big grin on her face. They posed on both sides of a shiny new metal sign. It read, "Reserved For Manager." Hand-lettered below, in flaming-red glitter nail polish, was the name, "Dolly."

Dolly yanked the keys out of the ignition and ran to the girls. "Congratulations, Dolly!" said Melissa, giving her a big hug.

"Way to go, girl!" said Shaniqua, who kissed her on the cheek. "You deserved it."

"You're the best," said Harriet, smiling, though her heart was breaking at having lost the promotion.

The foursome walked happily into the store, talking about the sudden change in management with their hands and eyes as much as with their lips.

"It's gonna be soooo cool!" said Melissa. "Wanda was a real witch."

"Now we're gonna run this place right," said Shaniqua. Dolly was in heaven. She truly liked her co-workers and had been praying that they wouldn't be jealous.

"Ok, ladies, let's get this show on the road," Dolly called to the chattering women. "We've got shelves to stock and displays to clean. Melissa, open that case of vibrators and get 'em priced and on the shelf."

"Where do the vibrators go?" Melissa asked. Dolly and the other women glanced at each other and spontaneously broke into uncontrolled laughter.

With a wicked grin, Dolly asked, "You're twenty years old and you don't know where the vibrators go? You grow up in a convent or WHAT? Don't they sell AA batteries in your part of town?" Melissa turned red. The other women convulsed with laughter. Dolly knew it was going to be a good day.

2
Doc Something-or-others

Fantasia Lingerie Store
The same day

By noon, the shop was clean and looking sharp. The glass door, windows, and shelves sparkled. The sex lubricants were all carefully restocked and arranged, one flavor per row. All of the X-rated videos were dusted and arranged by sexual performance specialty or fetish. The racks were full of new fantasy lingerie, ready for all of the local clients and tourists. The peel-away dance outfits and six-inch, strobe-light heels were arranged by color and size for the local strippers, who were among the store's biggest spenders.

Just after lunch, Shaniqua answered the phone. "Fantasia Lingerie, where lace and heaven meet. Can I help you?" Within moments, her smile evaporated and the tone of her voice dropped. "It's her," she called to Dolly.

Dolly didn't have to ask who "her" was. "Hello, Mamma," Dolly said in a sinking voice. "I just got a promotion. I run the shop now. I'm pretty busy. Can we talk after work?"

"Dolly, this is your mother talking to you," said Anne Doolittle. "You'll just have to take a few minutes out of your busy life and talk to me. It's important."

Dolly knew the tone of her mother's voice. There was no use arguing. "OK, Mamma, what's the subject today?" It was a perfunctory question, as both women knew from long experience.

"It's April, Dolly. What on earth are you letting your daughter wear those crazy clothes for? Those big, black, steel-toed shoes she's wearing belong on a construction worker, not my granddaughter. And the red shoelaces don't make them a bit prettier. She's seventeen years old, almost eighteen now. Why can't you get her to wear some decent shoes?"

"The girls don't dress like you did to go to the prom forty years ago, Mamma. A lot of women wear big, black, ugly shoes these days. Those are Doc Something-or-others. I think they look awful, but she used her own money to buy them. She told me a lot of the girls wear them."

"And what about the long-sleeved shirts and sweater vests? Don't girls wear blouses anymore?"

"Those are Fred Perry shirts, Mamma. April's friends all wear them. They're considered very stylish among her friends."

"And the haircut? How can any girl cut half her hair down to the skin and let the rest grow? She's always wearing some kind of cap to cover the bald top. It doesn't make any sense. She looks like some weirdo from the wrong side of another planet."

"It's just fashion, Mamma. Give her a break. She's going to be a senior in high school this fall. Remember my tie-dye days in high school? Remember the 70s, when Bobby had hair longer than mine? You didn't seem to mind strange hairstyles on my brother. What's the problem now with April's?"

Anne Doolittle wasn't done with her grilling. "She looks so sad and pale. Did you stop feeding her? Is she spending too much time at Kenny's? I don't like that new girlfriend of his a bit. I don't think either one of them can cook past opening a can."

"I feed her, and I love her. I keep a close an eye on her, Mamma, but I can't run a prison. I don't like Kenny's lifestyle or choice of friends any more than you do, but April wants to see her father, and he has joint custody."

"I don't see why you let her go over there at all," Anne said. "Kenny hasn't improved a bit since they arrested him for the marijuana thing ten years ago."

"April lives mostly with me now, Mamma. I don't let her go

over there without permission, but I have to stay legal with the joint custody order. Yes, Mamma, he's a jerk, but Kenny is April's father, and she wants him to love her."

"What about food? She's thin as a rail. Don't you ever feed her?"

"You know darn well I feed her, but she just doesn't want to eat much, and I can't put a funnel down her throat. And anyway, I was a little scrawny when I was her age, remember? I wanted to look like Barbie."

"What about her skin? Doesn't she ever go out in the sun?"

Dolly was losing her patience. "Yes, she goes out sometimes. But the girls don't wear a lot of makeup like they did when I was growing up, Mamma."

Dolly was happy to hear the doorbell ring as a middle-aged couple walked into the store. She knew that her mother could hear it, and the sound of business relieved her of the guilt she felt at cutting her mother off. "Look, Mamma, I have customers. I gotta go."

"You can take care of them, but what about visiting us once in a while?" Dolly gritted her teeth. *Mamma, you're not getting my vote for Mother of the Year, either*, she thought. "I gotta go now, Mamma. Say hi to Henry for me."

"Why don't you come by on Sunday, Honey?" her mother asked, knowing the answer in advance.

"I'll try, Mamma. Gotta go. Bye." Taking a deep breath, she shoved the guilt and ghosts of her childhood back into their dark caves and tried to think of happier things. Dolly shook her head quickly as if to throw off bad thoughts.

Thank God for Chrissie, Dolly thought. A few hours and a few beers with her best friend at her favorite club was just the kind of attitude adjustment she could use that night. *And who knows?* she thought. *This week already brought me a big promotion. Maybe it's finally time for Mr. Right to show up, too.*

3
The Child Within

Murrell's Inlet
Friday night

Now for some step exercises! Left up, right up, left down, right down. Left up, right up, left down, right down. Left up, right up, left down, right down. Left up, right up, left down, right down." Dolly wiped the sweat from her brow as the exercise video rolled towards its end. *Four more minutes to go*, she thought, *but the hardest four.*

"All right ladies, it's time to tone those abs. Down on the mat and arch your back. It's time to rock and roll."

Chrissie Beasley, Dolly's best friend, watched the workout with studied disinterest as she licked the bright-orange cheese puff crumbs from her fingers. "Why do you torture yourself like this every day, Honey?" she called out as Dolly rocked back and forth on her stomach.

Dolly gritted her teeth. *I'm gonna kill her. I'm just gonna kill her one of these days*, Dolly said to herself as she locked her fingers behind her neck and lifted both legs slowly off the floor in a reverse crunch. *I look at a bagel and put on five pounds. She eats ice cream by the pint, wears size 4 jeans, and never gains an ounce.*

The video instructor moved along, never missing a beat, "Roll over now. Time for some leg lifts. Up and one and two and three and down and one and two and three and up and one and two and three and down and one and two and three and. . . .”

"What?" Dolly called out over the pounding disco beat.

"Why the workout every day? You always look great."

"Ever hear of a millionaire marrying a fat girl?" Dolly replied, feeling the burn in her hamstring muscles. "That's why I work out. Dating is a competitive sport, and I want to win."

"All right ladies, you're looking good. See you again soon," said the blonde Hollywood exercise model as the screen faded to black. As soon as the video stopped, Dolly heard the hard rock music pulsing through her daughter's bedroom door. Dolly opened it and looked for April.

Inside the darkened room, a black light filled the space with an eerie purple glow. When she saw the shaft of light from the opening door, April quickly shoved the small mirror under the bed and returned to her thoughts.

Dolly turned on the overhead light and walked over the strewn clothes and shoes to the far side of the bed, where April was sitting on the floor, her back against a dresser. Above April's bed hung a poster showing shaved-head rockers wearing black leather bomber jackets and black boots as they belted out a song. The headline read "Skrewdriver." Dolly reached over to the stereo, turned down the volume, and said, "Honey, don't play that stuff so loud. You'll go deaf, I swear."

"Yeah, Mamma," April said without looking up.

"Now listen to me, Honey," Dolly said. "I'm going to take a shower and go out with Chrissie for a couple of hours. We'll be at White Lightnin'. Don't go out, and don't let anybody come over here, either. Turn that music off and hit the books. You know you have a chemistry test in school on Monday. Do you have your homework done?"

"Almost finished," April replied automatically, knowing that she had no intention of bothering with homework at all that weekend — or any weekend. Chemistry was her best subject. She knew she could ace the test without hitting the books.

"OK, Honey, I'll see you soon. Be good, stay out of trouble, and finish your homework."

April nodded silently.

Dolly walked over to her daughter and kissed her on top of her head. "I love you, Sweetie," she said. As soon as Dolly closed the door, April picked up the headphones of her CD player, put them on, and turned the volume up to 10.

Dolly called to her friend. "I'm gonna hit the shower and then we can head out, Chrissie. Give me ten minutes."

"Yeah, right." Chrissie rolled her eyes and gave her a mock dirty look. She knew Dolly wouldn't leave the house until every detail of her makeup, hair, and clothes was perfect. She flicked the remote control of the TV and settled into the living room couch.

Across the hall in her bedroom, Dolly stripped off her sweat-soaked exercise suit, leaned into the tub, turned the water to warm, adjusted the shower head to needle spray, and stepped in. *I sure don't want to wind up like Mamma,* she thought as she poured shampoo into her hands and lathered up her hair.

She knew her mother had been dealt a short hand and lived a hard life. At sixteen, Anne had married Robert Manning, a poor, hard-working young Darlington County farmer, and their family arrived quickly. He adored his wife and children and they all repaid his love. If the truth be known, Dolly was his favorite. He always paid special attention to her little stories and calmed her childhood fears.

His favorite saying was, "You're never poor if you have food on the table." To make that happen, he worked the hot, dusty to-bacco fields six days a week, from before dawn until well after dusk. Their modest lifestyle went through a wrenching change when Robert died from a tractor rollover accident when he was only twenty-six. Anne was heartbroken. Seven-year-old Dolly was devastated.

For Anne, being the mother of six children and the wife of a poor tobacco farmer was hard enough, Dolly knew. But being the mother of six children and the widow of a poor tobacco farmer with no insurance was infinitely worse. A young widow with a large family and few skills, Anne was hard-pressed to keep herself and her children fed. During the harvest season, she worked as a clerk in a Darlington tobacco warehouse. At dusk, she went home and started seamstress work and clothing alterations. Although she worked late into the night, the two jobs barely kept body and soul together. Dolly grew up in a household so poor that she and her brothers and sisters only wore their store-bought clothes to school and church. The moment they returned home, they had to switch to home-made.

As she turned in the shower stall and the pulsating water jets hit her chest, the memories of childhood flooded her mind. Dolly didn't blame her mother for all of her problems. She blamed her problems with men on her breasts. By the time she turned fourteen, her breasts were those of a well-endowed full-grown woman.

She remembered the men who came to see her mother. God! How could she forget the men, the endless succession of men. Perhaps it was the loneliness born of isolation in their dusty tobacco village that led her mother to sleep with nearly every man who came along.

Some of them were kind; some of them were not. Some of them treated her mother well; others abused her. But the one characteristic they all shared was their heavy drinking. And when they drank, they all made the same choices. They either beat her mother up, dragged her directly into the bedroom, or came after Dolly. She outwitted or outran most of them, but by the time Dolly was sixteen, the only kind of sex she hadn't had was sex with someone she loved.

That's why she fell so hard for Kenny Devereaux. He was sweet, kind, and gentle in a way that reminded her of her father. She remembered their first kiss as if happened yesterday. She was sixteen and a junior. . . .

"Hey, girl, you growin' fins and a tail in there?" yelled Chrissie. Dolly snapped out of her trance and turned off the water.

"Keep your shirt on, Chrissie. I'll be out in a minute," Dolly said as she quickly toweled off, blew her hair dry, pulled on a thong and a bra, and opened the closet.

Tonight it's black and white, she quickly decided. After she finished her makeup, she pulled on a pair of black, straightleg jeans, a long-sleeved white silk blouse with pearl buttons, a pair of wine-colored Western boots with a white filigree inlay, and a black ladies' Stetson. Her blonde hair cascaded over her shoulders and flowed gracefully down the shimmering, delicately trimmed blouse. Dolly smiled as she checked herself in the mirror. "Yup," she said to herself. "That works!"

"Well, well, well, what do we have here?" Chrissie smirked, waving a glossy magazine under Dolly's nose.

"Gimme that! None of your beeswax, that's what," Dolly said as she made a grab for the magazine.

"Gee, Dolly, do you have a beautiful twin you never told me about?" Chrissie, said with a laugh as she raced around the couch, trying to keep Dolly from grabbing the magazine. "She sure looks like you!"

"GIVE ME THAT!" Dolly yelled.

"I'm 5'6" with long blonde hair, ice-blue eyes. . . ."

"You're gonna be sorry!" Dolly shrieked as Chrissie read Dolly's ad in the singles' magazine.

Chrissie raced around the room, fending Dolly off with one hand as she held the magazine with the other. "I am a sweet, cheerful, and sensitive woman. I crave affection. I love kissing, hugging, and holding hands. I love walking on the beach or in the woods. I want a man who really knows the meaning of love and romance, one who can treat me with respect and kindness. A best friend and soulmate; the man of my dreams."

"Whoo-ee!" Chrissie yelled to her fighting-mad friend. "If you find him, see if he's got a brother for me!" With a disgusted look, Dolly gave up the chase. Chrissie collapsed into the sofa, giggling wickedly as she continued reading aloud.

"My hobbies are reading, horses, and hockey. I love nature. Spending time with my daughter is precious to me. I love country music. I am 36, but I feel more like 21. I am in touch with my inner child. I love to do spur-of-the-moment things. I have a lot of energy when I am excited about something new. I believe in being best friends before lovers. I would love to hear from you."

"So I put an ad in the classifieds, so what?" Dolly asked as she retreated to the bedroom to put her earrings on.

"Nothin', Sugar. It's a real pretty ad. I hope Prince Charming answers it. But let's hit the road. You may find him that way — and I hope you do — but I'm putting my bet on the good ole boys at White Lightnin'."

"Bye, Honey," Dolly yelled through April's door, but she got no answer. Over the last two years, Dolly had become accustomed to her daughter's dark moods. She sighed, then turned and left with her friend.

Behind the bedroom door, April retrieved the mirror, poured a small amount of crystal methamphetamine powder onto it, and divided it into two narrow rows with a single-edged razor blade. Using a short straw, she quickly inhaled one line into her left nostril, then the other into the right. The rush of energy and pleasure started within moments, and her heavy, day-long depression lifted. Two minutes later, she heard the horn, grabbed her black leather jacket, slipped out her bedroom window, and ran out to her boyfriend's car.

4
White Lightnin'

The dusty parking lot was almost full as Dolly slipped her Honda into a slot on the side of the building, twenty yards away from the main entrance to White Lightnin', Myrtle Beach's favorite country-western club. She was on a manhunt and didn't want her rusty car to spoil the manicured image her carefully chosen outfit projected. Dolly surveyed the lot like an auctioneer scanning the crowd for potential bidders. It was full of cars and pickup trucks — mostly pickups — of every description, but a Jaguar sedan, a BMW 535i, a Porsche Carrera T-top, a Lexus, and a Mercedes 450 SL convertible caught her eye. *Not bad for a Friday night,* Dolly thought.

Chrissie's tastes were more domestic than import. "Hey Dolly. Check out the Silverado!" Chrissie yelled, pointing to a meticulously waxed pickup truck. "Brand new. Platinum metallic. Moon roof. Performance package. Full leather. Rosewood trim. Six-speaker Bose premium sound system. That cowboy can put his boots under my bed anytime."

"He's all yours, Cutie," Dolly said. "I'll go for Mr. Mercedes anytime." The doorman at White Lightnin' touched the brim of his hat in greeting. "Evenin', Miss Dolly, Miss Chrissie. Nice to see you again."

"Thank you, Sam," Dolly replied. "How's Nancy and the kids?"

"Just fine, thanks." She gave him a friendly once-over, from his hat to his black, Tony Lama Longhorn boots. "If the boys inside look half as good as you do, Honey, we're gonna have a fine time tonight!"

"Don't break too many hearts, girls," he said, waving them in. The women walked past the blue bug zapper lights that flanked the door. A pleasant, familiar little chill ran through Dolly as she walked into to her favorite hangout. Although it was a large club, she knew most of the people there, by face, anyway. White Lightnin' was part of a happy extended family she didn't have outside its four walls. Here, people kept an eye out for her and made sure nothing bad happened. She belonged here. She liked the place. She could have three beers, dance three hours, and go home alone without feeling lonely. Or, if she decided to let a handsome cowboy get lucky. . . .

"Where do we start tonight?" Chrissie asked. "The bar, the pool room, or the dance hall?"

Ahead, the bar was full of smiling faces, cowboy hats, dress jeans, and narrow-toed boots. It was already lined two deep with animated bodies who were ordering, talking, smiling, flirting, or dodging unwanted passes.

To the right in the dance hall, a hundred well-dressed urban cowboys and cowgirls — and a couple dozen rednecks from the sticks, in T-shirts and baseball caps — danced in perfect formation to a lively line dance.

To the left, a green sea of pool tables buzzed with the whispers of flirting singles and the click of pool balls on their way to their destinations. A brawl inside, which broke out when one player spent too long admiring the cleavage of another's girlfriend, was just the normal spice in the soup of the place. The brawl was over in less than a minute, and no one paid any serious attention to the temporary distraction.

"Let's get a beer and then check out the pool room," Dolly said as they walked in.

The back bar featured a large, green-and-white neon sign with a thunderbolt roaring through the bar's name, "White Lightnin'."

A brass plaque under the epoxy-covered surface of the heart pine bar marked the place of each barstool. One read, "Drink Till He's Cute." The next said, "I'm the guy your mother warned you about," and another read, "I'm not as think as you drunk I am."

"Evenin' ladies. What'll it be?" asked the tall, muscled bartender. On one arm, he sported a red-and-blue flag tattoo. Below the flag appeared the Marine Corps motto, "Semper Fidelis" – "always faithful." On the other arm was a heart-shaped tattoo enclosing the name, "Susan." From his smile and the way he looked at them, Dolly guessed he was probably faithful to both The Corps and Susan, whoever she might be.

Dolly felt jealous of Susan. Faithful was not a word Dolly would use to describe most of her boyfriends. She made it clear to them that she was a one-man woman and expected the same in return. Somehow, it never worked out that way. Dolly took a deep breath, cleared the shadows of her failed relationships from her mind, and turned on her electric smile. "A Bud, please," she told the bartender.

"Lone Star for me," said Chrissie.

Dolly picked up her longneck and clinked it against Chrissie's. "Bring on the cowboys," she said, as the two of them toasted and looked forward to a night full of old friends, new hopes, good country music, and a lot of dancing.

Dolly and Chrissie moved from the bar to the entrance of the dance hall. On the stage, a popular local band was just starting its second set for the night. With his great girth held in check by a two-inch-wide brown leather belt and an enormous Confederate belt buckle, his graying hair pulled back in a ponytail, and his deeply tanned face filled with wrinkles, the good-natured fiddle player looked like a cross between Willie Nelson and Charlie Daniels. Three musicians playing banjo, guitar, and an electric autoharp rounded out the twangy quartet. A tall, long-haired redhead in a red-and-black blouse and gold-embroidered vest added a honey-sweet, Flora-bama flavor to the songs.

The band broke into a romantic Western waltz. The redhead sang, "May I have this dance for the rest of my life. . . ?" Chrissie turned and whispered Dolly's ear, "You're off to a fast start, Honey," as a tall, tanned man in gray snakeskin boots, jeans, and a black Western shirt and hat approached from her right. "Evenin' ladies," he said. "My name's Ron." Turning to Dolly, he said, "Would you like to dance?"

5
Myrtle Beach High

Myrtle Beach
Friday night

Twenty-three-year-old C.B. "Cue Ball" Correlli ran his fingers up and down his red braces — April called them "suspenders" — until he corrected her — and tapped his black, steel-toed boots on the floorboard as he waited for April in the street behind her apartment building. When she jumped into his car, she kissed him and ran her hand over his shaved head. It was smooth as a cue ball — and the source of his nickname.

"Hi," he said. "How's my girl?" April wrapped her arms around him, kissed him again, and said, "Let's get the hell out of here." C.B. handed her a pill wrapped like candy. April greedily took a swig of his beer, swallowed the Ecstasy tablet, and unwrapped a chocolate lollipop. Then C.B. reached under the seat of the car. Pulling out a thin, clear plastic wand, he bent it into an arc, and it made a small crackling sound. Immediately, the crystals inside the wand glowed an eerie, psychedelic green. April laughed and bent another wand; it turned a bright, fluorescent pink. The Ecstasy magnified the colors a dozenfold.

"Party time," C.B. said as he put the car into gear and popped the clutch.

"Where's it goin' to be tonight?" April asked.

"We'll know soon," C.B. replied. April smiled at him, leaned

21

her head on his shoulder, and waved the wands in front of her dilated pupils, enjoying the rush of energy that surged through her body.

In a few minutes, his beeper went off, and C.B. punched the numbers into his cell phone. "Yo," he said to the caller, then listened for the brief instructions. "Cool," he said, hung up, turned the car around, and drove north toward Myrtle Beach. Ten minutes later, he pulled into the driveway next to an unlit, deserted building off King's Highway. In the headlights from his car, the fading sign nailed to the boarded-up window of the former T-shirt warehouse said, appropriately, "Fire Sale. Everything must go." Ignoring the scorched front of the darkened building, which had suffered a small but smoky fire the year before, C.B. drove behind the building. There he parked among the fifty or so other cars whose owners had also just gotten directions to the rave. Its carefully guarded location changed weekly and was announced by beeper to the rave community only minutes before the action started. The system worked well. Myrtle Beach raves were seldom discovered by the police.

Outside the back door of the building, a 6'5", 270-pound, heavily muscled bouncer with a massive chest, narrow waist, yellow/red/green Mohawk, seventeen pierced earrings, an eyebrow ring, a tongue stud, nine tattoos, and wraparound, yellow-lens sunglasses passed judgment on the mass of teenagers and twenty-somethings who flocked to the door. His name was Thud, and he never smiled. He worked out pumping iron four hours a day, seven days a week at a local weight-lifting club and steroid saloon. A nod from Thud and your money got you in. A grunt from Thud and you were on your way elsewhere. Everyone knew that if you were stupid enough to give him any grief or tried to argue your way through the door, his name was the sound you'd make when he decked you with one punch. Few people were that stoned or stupid.

C.B. nodded in respect, passed Thud a twenty and an eight-ball of crystal meth, and escorted April through the door. A wall of sound assaulted them as they entered. At the front of the building, every crack through which light could pass had been covered with cardboard and taped. To the left stood trash barrels full of ice-cooled beer. On the right, a DJ cranked out high-energy music fed into massive amplifiers, loudspeakers, and subwoofers powered by a gasoline-fueled electric generator. Red strobes and white laser lights illuminated the room, lending a disconnected, psychedelic, time-warped feeling to everything that happened there.

The sound level was mind-numbing – which was exactly the desired effect. Talking was far beyond impossible. Everything was communicated through sight, motion, touch, and the exchange of money and drugs. Two hundred bouncing, writhing, supercharged dancers filled every square inch of the place. A half-dozen carefully screened dealers openly dispensed marijuana, Ecstasy, crystal meth, PCP, LSD, heroin, and almost any other drug du jour for twenty to fifty dollars a hit.

Like most serious drug dealers, C.B. didn't partake or deal directly. He paid for a beer and took in the sights, while his fellow Skinhead, Skank, dispensed the goods and collected the money. April, with the full rush of the meth and Ecstasy roaring through her, wanted only to dance. Her heart pounded. The sweat poured out of every cell of her body. Every light was surrounded by a bright, shimmering, multi-colored, crystalline halo. C.B. dumped a glass of ice water over her head to cool her off. April didn't even notice.

The rave was already filling the warehouse with bouncing people waving lights and sucking lollipops. The Ecstasy stimulated their enhanced perception of light; the lollipops lessened the damage from the tooth grinding that the Ecstasy produced.

In the middle of the frenzied crowd of dancers, a girl staggered over to April and yelled something unintelligible into her ear. It was Wendy Hickson, her eighteen-year-old fellow Skinhead and friend since grade school.

"Where's C.B.?" she asked in a dreamy, slurred voice.

"What?"

"Where's C.B.? I gotta get some more stuff."

"By the beer."

"What?"

"Over there, by the beer, talking to Suzi," April yelled into her ear.

"I love you," Wendy mumbled as she staggered off through her psychedelic haze to find her lover/dealer.

"I love you, too," April replied in a slurred voice, her head spinning from her own chemical cocktail. She immediately returned to her frantic dancing, oblivious to the fact that Wendy had draped herself over C.B. As he drank his beer and talked to his friends, Wendy patiently waited for him to finish talking to their fellow young roommate, Suzi Vetter.

"Suzi, I can't do this forever, you know that," he said to her. "Here's three tabs. Sell two of them to your friends for me and the third one's free for you, OK?"

"Sure, C.B., whatever you want," Suzi said, her eyes aglow in anticipation of the Ecstasy rush soon to follow.

An hour after the first beeper message went out, the warehouse was packed with high-energy, writhing bodies. Thud – a true man of steel – was now turning away all comers, despite the endless and escalating offers of sex, drugs, and money he was offered to get in.

After two hours of frantic dancing, the alarm on April's watch went off. She groped her way through the bouncing, human maze of light-stick-waving dancers in search of C.B. "I gotta get home now," she told him. "My mother is gonna be coming home soon. I gotta be in bed when she gets there."

"I know, Baby," C.B. said. "Just a few minutes and we'll go. I'm waiting for two friends," he said with a wink. April knew what he meant. C.B. hadn't yet made collections from two of his distributors.

In about ten minutes, she stumbled back to C.B.'s car, her clothing soaked with sweat from the drugs and non-stop dancing. "Dolly's gonna kill me, C.B. I was grounded tonight. You've gotta promise to take care of me if she finds out."

"Don't worry, Honey, I will. We're family. No matter what, we're family. You, me, Wendy, Skank, and Suzi are W.A.R. Skins. We take care of our own."

Fifteen minutes later, April crawled back through the window of her bedroom and collapsed onto her bed. She stripped off her sweat-drenched clothes, threw them in a heap at the foot of the bed, and climbed in.

Less than two minutes later, she heard the front door open and her mother say, "G'night, Chrissie." April pulled the covers up to her head and closed her eyes, her back to the door. In the mirror, she saw her bedroom door slowly open. Silhouetted against the light from the living room was the unmistakable outline of her mother's body. In a few moments, the door closed. Her heart was still racing from the meth, and the sweat was still pouring out. April threw off the blankets and prayed that the air conditioner would kick in. It didn't. As she lay wide-eyed on her back, her mind raced, and her sweat dripped into the sheets until the sun finally rose.

6
Captain Willie's

Right off the bat, Dolly sensed that something was wrong. The sound of the washing machine running at 9 o'clock on a Saturday morning was unusual to the extreme. It was totally out of character for April, who was usually still in the sack at noon. Dolly opened the top of the machine and saw that April was laundering her sheets and clothes. Another mystery. Since she turned fourteen, April had to be constantly cajoled, prodded, and nagged to change the sheets. She'd gladly leave them on the bed forever if Dolly hadn't insisted on changing them once a week. The load of clothes was also a mystery, since April wasn't any more eager to launder clothes than sheets. Then there was the early hour. . . .

Dolly knocked on April's door, but there was no answer. She knocked again; still no answer. Gently, Dolly opened the door, expecting April to be up and alert, considering the work she'd already started. Instead, she lay diagonally across the width of the bare mattress, dressed only in panties and a soaked T-shirt. A body-length damp spot covered the center of the mattress. *What on earth?* Dolly thought. *Did she have a heavy period and get everything bloody and clean it up with water? Is she ashamed and wanted to hide it?* "Hey, Sweetie, you OK?" she called to April. "Honey? You OK?"

"Yeah, Mamma. Just tired. I want to sleep."

Dolly sat down on the edge of the bed and put her hand on April's shoulder. It was cold and clammy. She gently tugged on her shoulder. "Honey, what's the matter? You have a bad period or something?"

"No, uh, yeah, Mamma. I'm just tired. Let me get some sleep."

The feeling of her daughter's cold, clammy skin alarmed Dolly. She firmly grasped her daughter's shoulder and rolled her face-up on the mattress. The sight made her suck in her breath in fear. April was pale as a ghost — nearly colorless. The eyes that had twinkled like diamonds when April was an eight-year-old were dull and bloodshot; dark circles under her eyes emphasized her exhaustion. She'd been through this with others at the clubs so many times before.

"You were out partying last night, weren't you?" Dolly demanded, knowing the truth all too well.

"I'm tired. I wanna sleep," April mumbled as she rolled over on the bed, turning her back to Dolly.

"I told you not to go out! Where'd you go? Who were you with?" April's head screamed with pain with each of her mother's increasingly loud questions.

"I thought you had to work this morning. I was just doing some laundry to help you out. Gimme a break," April said, and rolled over again onto her stomach.

The phone rang, rang, and rang again. Eventually, it stopped.

"Where were you last night?" Dolly asked again, this time in a louder, more demanding voice.

"No place. Can't I get a little sleep on a Saturday morning? Is there some new law?"

"Don't give me any lip, April," Dolly said as the phone rang again. She knew who it was. She had an appointment with the district manager at 10:00 A.M. to discuss the store's summer promotional plan. She knew she was going to get grilled on sales statistics, customer traffic counts, and sales trends. She didn't want to risk her new promotion by keeping him waiting.

"Hello? Hi, Harriet. Yeah, I know what time it is. Tell him I had car trouble, and I'll be there in fifteen minutes. Keep him busy.

I don't know, show him how clean the place is. Tell him about the couple who got carried away in the dressing room last week. Give him all the details. He likes that kinda stuff. Make 'em up if you have to, but stall him, OK? Gotta run."

"You're grounded until I get home. Got it?" Dolly barked to April as she raced out the door. "Grounded. Stay here. Inside. No visitors. Understand?"

April rolled over and said nothing, her head pounding like bricks falling on a steel drum. Even the noise of a passing car was enough to tear into her head. There was no danger of her getting out of the bed for the day.

The sales meeting went pretty well, all things considered. Dolly had good numbers to report for sales traffic, amount of average sale, and inventory turnover. "I told the girls to think about the customers as a package deal. You know, see what they bought, and always suggest something else that would complement the sale," Dolly said.

The district manager had heard every store manager's success claim a hundred times before. "Give me some examples," he said.

"Well, for the first-time customers, for example, we always suggest trying flavored sex lubricants," Dolly said. "First-timers are often a little shy and embarrassed, and they don't want to admit they're looking for some of the kinkier stuff. The lubricants are good, clean fun. They only cost a few dollars, but the profit margin is high. Since I took over, lubricant sales are up 37 percent — about $200 extra profit a month — so you can see how well my idea is working."

"Hmmmm," the district manager said, looking at the sales-by-category printout. "Yes, I see. Good job. What else have you been able to do?"

"Well," Dolly said, clearing her mind of her personal problems and focusing on the job at hand, "Look at the dance outfits. You'll see that we sold five more in the first two weeks of this month than all of last month combined."

"Is that a fluke, or did you do something?" he asked.

"That's my work," Dolly said with a big smile. "I was a dancer for a few months after my divorce. I know a lot of the girls on the circuit. When I got the promotion to manager here, I called all seventeen of the club mothers — you know, the women who manage the strippers in the clubs. I know most of them and told them that they'd get real good prices if they shopped here."

"Good prices — you mean you're giving discounts?" the manager asked, a quizzical look in his eye.

"You bet I'm givin' dancers a discount. It says in the Fantasia Lingerie Sales Manual, page 17, 'Store Managers are authorized to grant discretionary discounts up to 10 percent to preferred customers who spend at least $200 a year in the store.' Heck, the typical dancer who shops here spends $500 to $800 a year, and some of them twice that. Our basic markup on everything except videos is 200 percent — twice the cost. An outfit we sell for $75 costs us $25. We can afford giving a ten or twenty percent discount to a dancer who spends a lot of money here. A 10 percent discount makes the $75 outfit a $67.50 outfit, but we have only $25 in it. That's $42.50 profit on a $25 cost, or 170 percent markup. We only need an average 150 percent markup to meet all of our profit goals, as long as we do $440,000 a year in gross sales. I only give the discount to the top 5 percent of our customers. About half of them are local regulars, and the rest are strippers. If what I'm doin' holds up, we'll do $600,000 this year." Dolly permitted herself a modest smile, though she felt like the cat that swallowed the canary.

"I like that," the district manager said. "It shows initiative and understanding of the market. Keep up the good work, Dolly. Keep sending in the reports on time every week. See you next month."

He wasn't out the door five minutes before a call came in for her. "Hey, Dolly, this is Ruthie at Captain Willie's. Can you come in early, say, 2:00? Coupla girls called in sick. Yeah, the usual. They probably got fucked up at some bar last night. They said they're sick, but they're probably just hung over. In any case, they ain't gonna show. Be a doll. Come in at 2:00, OK?"

It was already 1:15. Dolly sighed and shook her head. This was the third time in two weeks Ruthie had called with the same request. *Why can't Willie keep reliable help in the place?* she wondered.

And why am I the one who always has to bail him out? Dolly was still tired from last night, not to mention holding down her two jobs. Now April was acting up, and her father was no help at all. April was supposed to go off to study nursing at Horry-Georgetown County Technical College after graduation. Dolly needed the money from her second job to put April through school. "Yeah, Ruthie, I'll come in," she said with a sigh. *Lord, I'm pushing forty. When will it get easier?* Dolly thought.

She dialed April at the apartment, but the line was busy. *Shoot, girl!* she thought. *I need to get through to you. Get off the darn phone.*

Working at Captain Willie's wasn't the pits, and it was certainly a step up from her former night job as a cocktail waitress at The Pink Zone, one of Myrtle Beach's all-nude strip clubs. At Willie's, she at least got to wear decent clothes: white shorts and a navy blue "Captain Willie's" golf shirt.

At the Pink Zone, all the cocktail waitresses wore sparkle stockings, garter belts, pink thong bikini panties, and tight white push-up bustiers with pink laces. Even though the servers — unlike the dancers — were supposed to be totally off-limits to the customers, they still got groped and propositioned almost every night. The hassles came mostly from jerks playing grab-ass, but occasionally, a drunk wanted to see more boob than the costumes displayed and literally took matters into his own hands. A bouncer usually appeared to keep him from doing any serious damage, but fun, it wasn't.

The first time a new server complained to the management about the grabbing and touching, she was told the two basic rules:

1. Never piss off a paying customer.

2. When propositioned or groped, duck it, live with it, or work somewhere else.

The majority of the servers were single mothers or college students paying their own way. The base pay for servers was minimum wage, but a hard-working waitress at the Pink Zone could make $15 to $20 an hour extra in tips. Most of them just gritted their teeth, smiled at the customers, dodged the hands as best they could, and hung in there until closing time.

Dolly rolled into the parking lot behind Captain Willie's at

2:20. Willie's was one of the dozens of carbon-copy, all-you-can-eat seafood places that lined Myrtle Beach's two-mile-long Restaurant Row. Atop Captain Willie's, a simulated lighthouse with a simulated rotating beacon beckoned to passing tourists. Inside, fiberglass replicas of stuffed trophy fish lined the walls of the lobby. In the main dining room, fishing nets were draped on the walls. Heavy ships' mooring lines separated the lobby from the dining area.

Red, green, and blue spotlights sprayed dots of light off a 1980s mirrored disco ball whose motor had burned out several years earlier. Nautical paraphernalia — oars, compasses, barometers, chronometers, and ships' nameplates — were displayed on every supporting beam. The walls were decorated with mass-produced beach scene paintings. At each table, a seashell arrangement framed a small oil lamp. It wasn't much, but if Dolly could get a crowd of non-Canadian golfers, singles, and small families, she could make decent tips there on a good night.

Dolly immediately set to work. Most of the lunch crowd had cleared out, so she went to the empty front section and started to prepare for the dinner hours. Side work was the part of the job every waitress liked least: all labor, low pay, and no tips. First, Dolly collected all of the condiment carriers, condiment bottles, and oil lamps and assembled them on one table. From the storeroom, she brought two-pound cans of salt and pepper, a gallon can of ketchup, a funnel, and lamp oil. For the next hour and a half, Dolly worked on autopilot. First came the ketchup. She opened all the bottles, put a funnel in the first, poured in the ketchup, and moved on to the condiment tray as the ketchup was filling the bottle.

Her mind drifted back to the previous night at White Lightnin' and Ron Pawley. On a zero to 10 scale for looks, he was a solid 8, maybe even pushing a 9. About 6'2", she guessed, maybe 190 pounds. Not muscled, but firm, and definitely not soft. The deep tan showed that he spent a lot of time outdoors, but the 450 SL convertible and the designer shades made it clear that the time he spent in the sun wasn't in a tobacco field.

He said he was in real estate and condos. Showing those to customers would account for the tan. And if he was good at it, that would account for the 450SL and the boat. *So far, so good,* she thought. It was obvious he had plenty of free time because he was a really good dancer, and that only came from lots of practice.

She took the tops off all the salt and pepper shakers, filled them up, and screwed the lids back on. Then she started to refill another jar of ketchup and went to the salt and peppers. When everything was full, she cleaned all the containers with a moist cloth. Next she restocked the sugar and sweetener packets, and refilled the bottles of steak sauce and the oil in the table lamps. Finally, she rolled 120 sets of cutlery in cloth napkins. By the time she had set the tables in her section with condiments, cutlery, and lamps, it was 4:15. The early diners would be arriving at 5:00. She looked around to see how the other servers were doing with their sections.

There were no other girls. She looked over to Ruthie, who gave Dolly an embarrassed shrug. "Will you. . . ?" Dolly sighed in disgust. She picked up her cell phone and tried calling April again. Still busy. With another sigh, she started the entire table-cleaning procedure all over again in the outdoor deck section.

As soon as she settled into the side-work routine again, her thoughts went back to Ron Pawley. *As girl-meets-boy-in-singles-bar-encounters go, that was a pretty good night,* Dolly thought. He was tall and good-looking. He dressed well, smelled good, brushed his teeth, and cleaned under his neatly-trimmed fingernails. When they danced, he held her close, but not too close for a first night.

He asked her on a date that night before they left White Lightnin'. He had suggested a day of cruising the Intracoastal Waterway on his boat, and she accepted. After they exchanged phone numbers, he gave her a nice, long hug — but not too long, and not too firm. And he didn't go for the first-meeting-trophy-kiss. *Yup,* she thought, *this one might be a keeper.*

As soon as she was done setting up the deck section, she made another call to April, but the line was still busy. The first diners for the evening arrived at 5:03. Dolly put on her best "I'm-your-server-and-I-hope-you're-big-tippers" smile and pushed her thoughts of motherly duties and romance to the back of her mind. "Hello," she said to the party of four middle-aged men. "My name is Dolly, and

I'll be your server tonight. Looks like you had a long, hot day on the links. Can I get you fellas something cool from the bar?"

"Sure," said the first man, dressed in khaki shorts, a white golf shirt, and a cap with a red maple leaf over crossed golf clubs. "Whiskey, neat."

"CC on the rocks," said the next.

"Got any Molson or Labatt's?" the third said.

"Sure," Dolly replied. "We stock lots of Canadian beer. We've got Labatt's, Molson, Moosehead, and Karwatha Premium Pale Ale. We also have Guinness, of course."

"I'll have a Molson, my dear. And what are you and your two most beautiful girlfriends doing after work tonight?" he asked. "We have a wonderful night on the town planned, and we'd love you to be part of it."

"Sorry, fellas," Dolly said to the visitors from the North. "I'm afraid we'd all be too tired to be any fun." Dolly had been tempted to say, "Next time, bring your wife and you won't have to hit on the waitresses to get laid," or "I'd love to — but my Mamma doesn't let me date married Canadian men." But, as always, she quickly stuffed the idea. She didn't dare tell the customers what she really felt. She worked hard for a living and needed the tips.

7
The Fourteen Words

SeaVue Apartments, Murrell's Inlet
Saturday afternoon

W hat happened to you after I left the rave last night?"
April asked her friend on the phone. "You were pretty
wasted. Who took you home?"

Wendy let out a small chuckle. "Wasted? It was *you* who was
wasted, chickee-doo. Some guy from North Myrtle gave me a ride
home. I think he wanted to get it on. He tried to get into my pants,
but I wouldn't let him. He was a loser, and I wasn't *that* messed up,"
she said. Both girls laughed.

"Did you get caught?"

"Nah. My parents are out of town this weekend at some stupid sales convention my father goes to every year. He takes my
mother along to get a bigger tax deduction. I think that's the only
reason they had me — to get another tax deduction."

April understood. "Uh, huh," she said. From Kenny, she knew
the emptiness that came from having a father who wasn't there
and didn't care.

"He always brings me some stupid T-shirt with a duck or a
horse on it. It's like, some big deal with him to bring me something. I think it's a guilt thing. He's gone most of the time anyway.
There's always some problem at his stupid office that keeps him
there late every night. I hardly ever see either one of them any-

more. I don't even think they really give a shit, though. What about you? You get busted when you came home? You were pretty wasted, too."

"I beat my mother back by a few minutes, and she never suspected when she came in. But I puked on the sheets and soaked my bed pretty bad, so I washed the sheets this morning, and she knew something was fishy. I guess I wasn't lookin' real good when she woke me up, and she got real suspicious. She told me I was grounded, but screw it. I don't care. I can always hang at my father's place. It's a total dump, and his girlfriend's a pain in the ass, but he doesn't hassle me, and he even gives me weed sometimes."

"Did you hear that they busted the rave about 4:00 in the morning?"

"No way! I can't believe it. What happened?"

"Some kid was all messed up and had a head on right in front of the place when some cops were drivin' by. They saw the accident and started the blue lights. When everybody started running, they knew they had stumbled across something. They busted Suzi and a bunch of other kids for possession and scarfed up all the stuff inside, but that's about it. Rage, Melvin, and Thud all split in time, but they lost all their sound stuff. That sucked big time."

"God, I'm glad I had C.B. take me home early. Is Suzi OK?"

"I dunno. C.B.'s gonna bail her out if her parents won't. I don't think they give a shit since she got busted last month for shoplifting again."

"We're lucky to have C.B. Who else gives a crap about us?"

"Yeah, I know. Hey – you got your reading done for the meeting tomorrow? C.B. wants everybody in the group to know about The Fourteen Words, RAHOWA, and the history of the W.A.R. Skins. Company's comin' tomorrow, and he wants to impress the guy."

"Get real. My head still feels like a garbage can with somebody bangin' on it. I can hardly even stand talking to you. And my body feels like a toxic waste dump."

"You gotta do it, April. You gotta be strong and know the drill if you want to be a W.A.R. Skin. C.B. says we all gotta be ready for the Racial Holy War and know why The Fourteen Words are so important. He says it's us or them. We've got to be ready when Black Bike Week starts next week. It's things like that – an invasion of blacks – that could start the Racial Holy War. He'll be counting on us."

"You're way ahead of me, Wendy. Oh, crap," April said. "I gotta. . . ." and ran to the bathroom. Through the phone, Wendy could hear her gag, throw up, and flush.

"Ooooh," April moaned when she returned to the phone. She fell on the bed, rolled over on her back, and moved her head close to the handset, which lay on the mattress. "I love C.B. and you guys, but I don't give a shit about the stupid Racial Holy War he's always talking about. I don't want to be in any wars with anybody. I just want to get out of my house, out of high school, and live someplace where nobody hassles me."

"You don't even know The Fourteen Words yet, do you?"

"Yes, Wendy dearest," April replied in her most sarcastic tone, "I do. 'We must secure the existence of our people and a future for White children.' But who cares? And who cares about black people, anyway? They usually stay together with their own kind, just like we do."

"Oh, yeah? Then why do all those black speed bikers come down here alone on the second week of Bike Week? The Harley crowd – God-loving, patriotic white people like us – usually bring their wives and girlfriends with them. Those black guys all come here lookin' for white chicks to hook up with. C.B.'s right. Race-mixing is gonna be the death of the white race. Hell, we're already a minority in our own country. Somebody's gotta draw the line. That's why God made W.A.R. Skins like us. If we don't keep the white race pure, who will?"

"Get real, Wendy. Half the white people in Myrtle Beach who don't work in the tourist trade leave town for the Bike Weeks any-way. So who's there for any of them to pick up? Some of the strip clubs even close down for Black Bike Week. I'd never talk to a black guy 'less I had to, but if they don't mess with me, I won't mess with them."

"'Ya comin' to the meeting tonight?" Wendy asked. "One of C.B.'s friends from the Hammerskins is gonna be there. He's a Christian guy. Has his own church. Plays in a Skinhead band. He's got the latest CDs from *Aggravated Assault, Max Resist, Bully Boys,* and *No Remorse.* You can tell your Mom you're goin' to church. I bet she'd let you go to church on Sunday."

April laughed — to the extent that her splitting headache would let her do anything. "I thought their motto was 'When you're a Hammer, everything looks like a nail.' I like punk and ska, but I don't like all the violent öi stuff. My motto is, 'If you don't like 'em, ignore 'em.' Anyway, my mother was pretty pissed about last night. I'll be lucky if she doesn't lock me up until I turn eighteen. Fortunately, that's only three months from now. I'll see what I can do. Bye."

8
Quality Time

Fantasia Lingerie Shop
Two weeks later

You look pretty tired, Dolly," Shaniqua said. "That new boy friend of yours wearin' you out already?" The other girls chuckled. It was a slow time of the day for sales. The tourists were still on the beach, the regulars were still at work, and the new strippers in town for Bike Week had already done their shopping for the weekend.

"Don't worry, ladies, he's not too hot for me to handle," Dolly said with a wink. "I've been in training for years. But it's only our second date."

"You goin' out on *The Love Boat* this weekend again?" Harriet asked, snickering.

"It's not *The Love Boat*, Harriet. Anyone can buy a ticket on *The Love Boat*," Dolly said, sticking her nose high in the air for full effect. "It's open to the public for cruises. The *FunTastic*, my dear, is private. A 42-foot-long private yacht. Full bar, kitchen, private salon with TV and surround sound. Sleeps six — by invitation only."

"Meow," said Harriet.

"Meow," said Melissa.

"Eat your heart out," Dolly said with a grin, flouncing her hair as she walked out the door. "Kenny has custody of April this weekend. Gotta make hay while the sun shines, girls."

"You make hay in the master cabin yet?" asked Shaniqua.

"None of your business, you little nympho," Dolly replied, smiling. "Take care of the place. See you Sunday. I gotta change for Willie's."

Even before Memorial Day, the traditional start of the summer tourist invasion of Myrtle Beach, the Friday night shift was a killer at Captain Willie's. By 6:00 P.M., traffic in the two-mile-long Restaurant Row section of King's Highway between Myrtle Beach and North Myrtle Beach crept along in near total gridlock. Every year, more theaters, theme shows, and amusement parks opened along the Redneck Riviera, bringing with them ever-growing hordes of tourists. The merchants and promoters were already talking about overtaking Branson, Missouri, as the live family entertainment center of the country.

At this rate, pretty soon I'll need a helicopter to get to work, Dolly thought as her overheated Honda wheezed into the staff parking lot, half a block from the restaurant. By the time she walked across the hundred yards of broiling asphalt, she was already sweating hard.

The crush of hungry tourists and the pace of work were exhausting, but the time flew by quickly, and the tips were pretty good. When the crowd finally left for the stage shows, clubs, bars, and strip joints, Dolly was able to take a break and check on April.

Eighteen years earlier, her widowed mother, Anne, nearly had a fit when she found out that Dolly, seventeen, was pregnant. Then Anne got the really bad news: the baby's father was none other than Kenny Devereaux, ten years Dolly's senior.

Dolly had been swept off her feet — and into bed — by an older man, one, she supposed, who could replace the loving, hardworking father she had lost early in life. She got about half of her wish.

Kenny was loving, all right, but a little short in the hardworking department. He was only looking for a pretty young girlfriend who enjoyed good weed, good acid, and good sex anywhere, any time. At the time, Dolly had no problems with that list of priorities. It seemed like a perfect match – until Dolly missed her period, and Kenny found himself in the fast lane to fatherhood.

Anne pressured Kenny to marry Dolly, and he reluctantly agreed. The low-key wedding took place in a small, country chapel near the Doolittle family's ancestral home next to the Darlington stock car racetrack.

Six months later, April Moonchild Devereaux — she had been conceived one night while Dolly and Kenny floated among the stars on a cannabis cloud — made her wet-haired debut into the world. Unfortunately, the duties of raising his girl-child proved to be less interesting and more demanding than those of conceiving her, and Kenny soon departed the domestic scene for one more closely aligned with leisure and raising psychotropic herbs.

A decade and a half later, with April now in her late teens, Kenny Devereaux was still a cheerful, long-haired, bearded, acid-head throwback, trapped forever in The Land That Time Forgot. Like his Hippie contemporaries in the late 60s, Kenny had furnished his single-wide trailer with peace symbols, strings of multi-colored love beads, floor pillows, tie-dye throws for the couch, hand-knotted Indian wall hangings, and a four-hose party bong. On a side table, a small candle burned in front of a framed snapshot of Kenny with Timothy Leary. On the walls, day-glo posters of John Lennon, The Maharishi, and Bob Marley still proclaimed the virtues of peace, love, and *cannabis sativa.*

Unlike the majority of his fellow tune-in, turn-on dropouts of the 60s, Kenny never made the transition from Hippie-dippie-doper into the Real World. Instead, he shifted the evolution of his consciousness into park in the late 70s. He kept body and soul together by working as a part-time motorcycle mechanic in North Myrtle Beach and toured occasionally as a fill-in roadie for the Grateful Dead. The rest of his waking hours were spent acquiring tattoos, raising marijuana in the woods of Horry County, sharing spliffs with the occasional Rastafarian who wandered through Myrtle Beach, and dropping acid with his fellow Deadheads.

His latest girlfriend, Ginger, had added a neo-Nashville patina to his chemically augmented life. She eschewed Kenny's faded jeans and black Deadhead T-shirts for a more colorful fashion statement. Hers consisted of long, red fingernails, hot-pink Spandex mini-skirts, and tight tube tops, which displayed her two most noticeable charms to best advantage.

As soon as she moved in, she took down the poster of the Maharishi and replaced it with a large, dynamic painting of Elvis at the microphone, rendered on shimmering black velvet and framed in deeply carved, imitation-gold-leaf molding imported directly from Mexico. She completed the merge of cultures with the addition of several fake fur leopard and zebra skin rugs and an heirloom lava lamp.

Dolly's call to Kenny caught him toking on the bong and watching a wet T-shirt contest on The Playboy Channel. "Hey, Babe, how's it goin?" Kenny said in a deep voice which sounded like Papa Bear from the Goldilocks kiddie video. "Hear you got a big promotion. Congrats."

"Thanks, Kenny," Dolly said. "Sorry to bother you. I'm just calling to find out how April's doing. Can I talk to her?"

"Sorry, Babe," he replied. Dolly gritted her teeth. "She's not here."

"Where is she, Kenny?"

"I dunno. Out hangin' with her friends, I guess. She didn't say."

"When will she back? I need to talk to her."

"I dunno. She didn't say that, either."

"Dammit, Kenny, we've been over this a hundred times. She's your daughter. Don't you care where she is and what happens to her?"

"Of course I care, but shoot, Dolly. She's almost eighteen. Remember yourself when you were eighteen? Didn't you spend time hangin' with your friends when you were that age?"

A chill ran through her body when Kenny reminded her of that time in her life: pregnant and ready to deliver April. Dolly visualized her daughter doing the things she did in her seventeenth year. It made her want to scream.

"Can't she spend time with her friends?" Kenny continued.

"Who are her friends? What are their names? Where do they live? What do they do together? When will she be back?"

"How should I know?" Kenny said defensively. "They stopped by in a car. She got in. They left."

"So, you don't know who she's with, where they live, where they went, what they're doing, or when she'll be back. Jesus, Kenny. She's your own daughter. Aren't you worried about how she looks? She's been losing weight. She's skinny as a rail, she has dark circles under her eyes, and her skin is as white as paper."

"Whattayamean?" he said. "She looks just like all those high-fashion models in the magazines she reads. Every girl that age wants to look like the models."

"What kind of father are you? Don't you know that girl needs direction, guidance, needs attention? She worships you. Why can't you be as good a father as you are a dope farmer?" Dolly snapped.

Dolly knew the moment the words crossed her lips that she had blown her only chance to get him to pay attention. "Kenny, I'm sorry. . . ."

"Shoot, Dolly, you ain't told me nothin' I ain't already heard from you a hundred times. That's all you care about — bein' in control of every person in the world and blamin' me for your problems. The kid ain't done you or me or anybody else no harm. She's out with her friends like every other teenager in the world on a Saturday night, and I'm the lazy dope fiend who's to blame for it. Well, go take your self-righteous sermon somewhere else tonight, Dolly." Kenny took a long pull on the bong. The smoke slowly curled out of his nostrils. "Ginger and I are spending some quality time together right now, and your lecture ain't improvin' it any. G'bye."

9
FunTastic

Ronald Huntington Pawley, III, was in heaven. Known to his friends as "Ron" and to his ex-girlfriends as "Paws," he beamed with the pride of ownership and the thrill of commanding the *FunTastic's* powerful twin 240-horsepower diesel engines. As he pushed forward the two mahogany-tipped, stainless steel throttles, the sleek sport yacht leaped forward like a scared barracuda, pushing Dolly back deep into the glove-soft white leather seat next to the pilot's chair.

"God, I love that," he said to his beautiful, bikinied passenger. "Idle to full plane in eight seconds flat. That's performance." Dolly slipped her arm through his as the flared fiberglass bow parted the sea before them. She was as impressed with her new boyfriend as he was with his new boat. Ron was forty-five, fit, and tanned. She had a hunch that Ron's performance in bed might just match that of his boat. But her long track record of dating men with flash and cash had taught her to go slowly when entering a new relationship.

Today, she sensed from experience, he'd make the big move. But Dolly was determined to give him just the appetizer this weekend and save the entrée until she'd gotten to know him better. She'd had enough little minnows — the short-timers and one-night stands. She had a new standard now: she was only after a big fish. So far, Ron qualified.

The discreet pulsing of the diesel engines sent a tingle through her skin. The feeling of power was contagious.

"Ron, would you like a drink? I think I have the bar in the salon figured out."

"Sure, Baby, that would be great. I have everything you need for Singapore Slings, Margaritas, Banana Daiquiris and Sex on the Beach."

"You mean you need a glass for that?" she joked.

He smiled. "You need a glass, vodka, Midori melon liqueur, Chambord raspberry liqueur, grapefruit juice, cranberry juice, ice, and cherries for a garnish."

"This boat is amazing. I bet cruise ships don't even stock their bars as well as you do."

Ron chuckled. "I bought it for relaxing and for entertaining my clients. My business can drive me crazy," he said. "This helps me get my sanity back."

His cell phone beeped. "Damn," he said, then answered it. He listened a moment, covered the mouthpiece, and said, "See what I mean? Can you excuse me for a minute?"

Dolly knew this was the signal for her to leave the bridge and move to the salon, the galley, or the rear deck. "Yeah, Baby, how're you doing?" she overheard him say as she walked down the steps to the rear deck. She wondered exactly who he was calling "Baby." *Not competition*, she hoped.

Down in the sculptured cherrywood galley, she looked up the "Sex On The Beach" recipe in Ron's mixology handbook. Ten minutes later, she had completed the complicated procedure and proudly served up two drinks in frosted glasses engraved with the boat's name, *FunTastic*.

"Thanks, Doll," he said with a wink. "To sex on the beach," he said with a wicked grin as he raised his glass. Dolly smiled, clinked her glass, but said nothing about his remark. "Who was on the phone?" she asked.

"Ah, just the wife of a client who wants a condo. Where shall we go ashore for lunch?" he replied. Dolly thought that he'd been awfully chummy with the woman if she was, in fact, the wife of a client. And the quick change of subject seemed suspicious, too. *But,* she thought, *it's a beautiful day, he's a good-looking guy, I'm being treated like a queen on this $250,000 yacht, and why quibble over things I don't know about? I'm not marrying the guy. Yet.*

"Captain's choice," she said, smiling.

An hour south of Myrtle Beach, Ron throttled back the engines and they glided up to Cape Romain, an isolated island wildlife preserve with no inhabitants. Its beaches were pristine; no fires were allowed.

As Ron dropped anchor in five feet of water, Dolly walked to the water-skiing platform on the stern of the boat and dove in. With summer not yet fully in swing, the coastal water was still refreshingly cool. When she surfaced, she saw Ron talking on the cell phone again.

"When?" He pulled out a P.D.A. and checked his calendar. "OK. What's the tee time?" she heard him ask. "How'd the caddie auction go? Got good ones?" he said to the caller, a silly grin on his face. "Make sure they're crowd pleasers. Gotta go. Bye."

Ron saw that Dolly was bobbing in the water a few yards away. He walked to the stern of the boat with an insulated plastic cooler. "Can you get this to shore OK?" he asked her. "Don't worry. It's waterproof. It's OK if a little water gets on it."

"Sure, no problem," Dolly replied, and waded to shore with the cooler. She walked up the beach a few yards and deposited it in the shade of a grove of graceful palmetto trees. Looking back at the boat, she could see that Ron had placed a large picnic basket and a blanket on the ski platform. She watched as he shed his shirt and jumped in the water himself. Reaching up, he placed the blanket on the basket, the basket on his muscular shoulders, and waded ashore.

"And what is a caddie auction?" she asked, though she already knew the answer. Ron gave her a sheepish smile.

"Uh, pretty girls who are working as golf caddies for a charity golf match next month. You know, sit there, look cute, drive the golf carts for the guys. I had to set up a foursome for some clients of mine."

"Do you mean one of the topless golf tournaments like they had last month?" The first try at publicly promoting a topless golf tournament in Myrtle Beach received national attention when the ministers and churches of Myrtle Beach raised a huge stink about the event. The protests made all the national news networks. Community pressure — and the strong opposition to the event by the city fathers — forced the cancellation of the tournament.

However, once the furor died down, the tournament – now with a million dollars' worth of free national publicity behind it — was quietly rescheduled for a month later. This time there was no public notice, and tickets were available only through the local strip clubs – and then only if you knew whom to ask.

Dolly knew. One of her girlfriends had worked at a club that sponsored the tournament. She overheard the DJ at the club tell one golfer, "Topless caddies? Hell, they'll all be so be juiced they'll take everything off." From what she reported, a few lines of coke and a hundred-dollar tip quickly turned many of the topless caddies into bottomless sex toys by the time they reached the fourth hole.

"Well, more or less," Ron admitted. "But it's not illegal, and I have to entertajn these guys. They come down here from New York, New Jersey, and Canada, and if I don't show 'em a good time, they'll buy their condos from somebody else who will."

Dolly wasn't thrilled with the admission, but at least he hadn't lied to her. She was realistic enough to know that showing and selling tits and ass was a basic commodity in the Redneck Riviera.

Dolly set out the blanket under the trees and opened the wicker basket. It was lined with a red-and-white checkered tablecloth and filled with linen napkins and an amazing array of delicacies. Dolly could hardly believe her eyes. The feast included so many new foods that she had to ask what they were: shrimp-salad and smoked-salmon miniature sandwiches; small chunks of ahi – Sushimi-grade yellowfin tuna with soy sauce and Wasabi paste; pink ginger root, sliced paper-thin; a chilled mango-and-peach fruit salad; fresh brioche with brie, Camembert, and Edam cheeses; and for dessert, strawberries dipped in dark chocolate.

When Ron opened the cooler, Dolly saw the label of her favor-

ite French champagne, Moët et Chandon. It was her favorite because it was the only French champagne she'd ever tasted – courtesy of Ron on their first boating date two weeks earlier.

"What's the green paste?" Dolly asked.

"It's Wasabi. Green Japanese horseradish. Cures what ails you,"
he said with a big smile. "Use it in very small quantities until you
get used to it. But once you do, you'll be spoiled forever."

Dolly fumbled with the chopsticks he provided until Ron in-
tervened. "Here's how to hold them," he said, placing his hand on
hers to show her how to hold and move the sticks. His hand was
warm. She smiled. Within minutes, Dolly – the poor country girl
from tobaccoland — was picking up pieces of slippery tuna with
ease. "Take the ahi and dip it in the soy sauce and then in the Wasabi.
Go real easy on the Wasabi. It'll curl your hair if you take too
much."

Dolly picked up a piece of the dark-pink tuna, dunked it in
the soy sauce, and then coated it with the Wasabi paste. Just before
she popped it into her mouth, Ron intercepted the morsel, and it
dropped into her plate.

"What?????" Dolly yelped in surprise.

"The Wasabi. It's the best of the best — full strength, right
out of the tube. Straight from Japan. Not from powder. A tube of
it will power a nuclear aircraft carrier for a year. You picked up a
two-week supply on your first bite. A tenth of that will clean out
your sinuses for a month." He scraped most of the green sauce off
the chunk of fish and handed it back to her. "Try it this way," he
said.

Dolly shot him a puzzled look, placed the fish in her mouth,
and started to chew the succulent morsel. The ahi was delicious —
sweet flesh and a delight on the tongue. The soy sauce was a familiar taste. Then, after three chews, the Wasabi's aromatic vapors
kicked in and made their way into her nasal cavities. It was a sen-
sory experience like no other she'd ever experienced. Her eyes
crossed. She felt as if steam were blowing out of her ears. Her
brain went into overload from over-stimulation. Her mouth didn't
burn — it merged directly with her nervous system, and Dolly
experienced her first culinary orgasm.

"Holy mackerel!" she said, looking at Ron in amazement. "What do they put in that stuff?"

"It's all natural. Just pure horseradish. What do you think?"

Dolly's jaw was still hanging open, her eyes as big as saucers. It was an amazing experience. She had suffered from a stuffed-up head every spring and summer from pollen allergies. But now, Dolly knew, she had the antidote. Her sinuses were totally clear, and she could breathe freely again. She looked at Ron with astonishment.

"Good stuff, huh?" he asked with a chuckle, leaned over, and kissed her. Dolly barely noticed the touch of his lips. She was still somewhere between shock and heaven. With her previous boyfriends, Dolly was happy if they sprang for a steak, fries, and some red wine before they put the make on her. *Whatever other nice surprises this guy's got prepared for me*, she thought, *I'm ready.*

She looked at the *FunTastic*, rolling gently twenty yards offshore. "Tell me more about your business, Ron," she said. "It looks like you've been very successful."

"It's not very interesting, Dolly, but I earn a good living. Condos. The Grand Strand is a real estate salesman's dream. We have everything: forty miles of sun, sand, world-class golf, the Pavilion, waterslides, mini-golf, family oriented reviews and stage shows, seafood restaurants, dance clubs, and nightlife," he said.

Just as he finished his sentence, his cell phone rang. Dolly was dismayed that he had even brought it ashore during their intimate lunch.

"Hi there, beaut . . . , uh, just a minute, please," he said to the caller. "Sorry," Ron said to Dolly. "I gotta take this."

Dolly sighed. *Men*, she thought. *They're all obsessed with business*, recalling a former lover who stopped in mid-stroke to answer his cell phone two seconds before Dolly would have gone over the top. *They never change.*

Ron immediately switched his focus from Dolly to the caller, and briskly walked away to the privacy of the palmetto trees to talk to his . . . who? Her name started with "beaut. . . ," as in "beautiful," which is what he seemed to call every woman. Was it another girlfriend? A daughter? Business partner? Wife? Client? Dolly wasn't sure she wanted to know.

In a few minutes he returned. "Sorry 'bout that," Ron said, a conciliatory smile on his face "Let's see, where were we?"

Well, Dolly thought, *we were about to have a romantic lunch and get a little drunk on the champagne. I was going to lay out in the sun. You were going to offer to put some suntan lotion on me. I was going to unsnap the top of my bikini. You were going to rub the oil all over my back. I was going to get horny and roll over. You were going to see proof of how aroused I was. Then you were going to nibble me all over, slip off the bottom of my bikini, nibble away some more, and then screw me silly. Then I was going to roll you over on your back and return the favor.*

Dolly gave Ron a noncommittal smile. *But those two stupid cell phone conversations with other women in the middle of our romantic rendezvous just torpedoed your love boat,* she thought. *I hope you enjoyed that fancy cocktail I made for you, Ron, because it's as close to sex on the beach you're going to get today. For the rest of this afternoon, all you're going to get is smiles, polite conversation, and plenty of time to fantasize about what you were soooooo close to having all afternoon: me minus my bathing suit.*

10
Voices From the Past

T he Tuesday night crowd was fairly brisk, but not as heavy as the weekend crush. Ron hadn't been thrilled with the rest of their weekend afternoon together. *Lack-a-nookie is the driving force of the universe,* Dolly recalled as she delivered an order. She had once heard Chrissie say to one of her girlfriends, "Men will do anything to get a little."

"What happened, Dolly?" Ron had asked the next time they saw each other. "We'd been having such a good time all morning and then . . . nothing."

"Do you ever take your ear off that damn cell phone?" she said. "And do you ever get calls from men — or just women?"

"Yeah, you're right," Ron admitted. "Sometimes it seems like I don't know how to relax anymore. But don't worry — those were just clients or the wives of clients. Men don't care about the details that go into choosing a condo. They leave that to the women. That's why I get so many calls from women."

Dolly wasn't sure that the answer really addressed the question, but she was mollified and grateful that he'd at least taken the time to explain. Most of her old boyfriends wouldn't have bothered.

"The next time we go out, can you turn that damn thing off?"

she asked in a warm but mildly sarcastic voice. "It kinda throws cold water on things, if you catch my drift."

One look into her big blue eyes and Ron caught her drift quickly. "I won't even bring it with me," he said and wrapped his arms around her. In return, he got a small, but affectionate kiss. She meant it to be a preview of coming events. It worked like a charm.

"How about we run down to Savannah for the weekend? I know a beautiful little Victorian bed-and-breakfast place. We can take a carriage tour, have dinner on the waterfront, catch a little jazz. What do you say?"

"Hey, fella, I have to work for a living, remember?" she said. "And I work almost every weekend."

"Aw, come on. See what you can do."

"OK," she replied. "I'll try to get someone to cover for me. I'm always doing it for the other girls."

He kissed her. "Gotta run. I'll call you."

The cars were starting to fill Captain Willie's parking lot, and the staff was bustling when Ruthie called Dolly to the phone. The look in her eye put Dolly a little on edge. "For you, Honey," Ruthie said, and quickly walked away.

"This is Dolly Devereaux," she said.

"Dolly — er, Ms. Devereaux — this is Detective Capt. Steven Hunt of the Myrtle Beach Police Department. We need you to come to the station. Your daughter is under arrest for possession of a controlled substance."

"What?" Dolly screamed. "What are you talking about, Steve? April's only seventeen. She's at school."

"I'm sorry, Dolly," said her former high school boyfriend, now head of the vice and narcotics division of the police department. "Today was a staff development day. Teachers only. The kids didn't have to go to school. April was arrested on the beach behind the Pavilion with a group of known drug users. She had what we think is crystal methamphetamine and some other drugs in her purse. They're testing them now. She was high when they busted her, and she's coming down fast from whatever she's on. We need you to get over here now."

Dolly mumbled something and placed the receiver back on the hook. Grabbing her purse from behind the counter, she ran for the side door, forgetting to even remove her apron.

11
Cranking Down

Myrtle Beach Police Headquarters

B astard!" April was angry, afraid, defiant, and hungry. She was also coming down fast from a twelve-hour high that had started the night before, tweaking ice — smoking crystal methamphetamine — and using Ecstasy with C.B. Her heart pounded. The green, reinforced-concrete walls seemed to be closing in on her.

"Why didn't you call my father? My mother is going to kill me!" she yelled at the bored jailer, who walked past the holding cell, ignoring her and her friends.

"I want to talk to my father. I want to get out of here."

Her words fell on deaf ears. Few people who saw the inside of a holding cell didn't want to get out. April wrapped her arms around herself as another wave of hot flashes and stomach cramps raced through her slender body. As she looked around the cell at her Skinhead friends, April saw that they were looking and feeling as bad as she was.

Suzi Vetter looked pale as she swayed back and forth beside her on the metal cot, humming random chords from a series of half-remembered songs. Jimmy "Skank" Mullins, who had been kicked off the football team for missing practice once too often, huddled on the floor, depressed. The blood pounded in his veins; his shaking arms were wrapped around his knobby knees; his forehead rested on his firmly clenched hands. Even his steel-toed, ten-eyed Doc Marten boots couldn't keep his feet from shaking. Near the back wall, Wendy Hickson paced back and forth in the cell, constantly looking over her shoulder in paranoia for pursuers who never appeared.

In a conference room near the cell, Detective Capt. Steven Hunt held Dolly's hand as he relayed the information he'd been given by the arresting officers.

"She had three joints of marijuana, an eight-ball of crystal meth and a dozen Ecstasy pills in her purse, Dolly. Those are retail quantities. It looks like she may have been dealing. The other kids had smaller quantities of pot or meth. They've been charged with simple possession. That's a misdemeanor. April will probably be charged with possession of drugs with intent to distribute. That's a felony. Even though she's still a minor, she's in serious trouble."

Dolly couldn't believe what she was hearing. She had been worried that April might be experimenting with drugs, and she was planning to have a big talk with her about it. But April was staying with her father, and Dolly was so busy. She knew that was no excuse, and she shouldn't have put it off for so long, but she had no idea that April was involved in anything like this. When Dolly was in high school, "drugs" meant a little bit of pot and, at the very worst, a couple of hits of acid. Not that she was justifying those things, but crystal meth? Ecstasy? And *dealing* drugs? April? She was too smart for that.

"Was she with C.B. Correlli?"

"Yes, she was. Five of them were arrested behind the Pavilion. A patrolman saw one of them smoking what looked like a drug pipe. They dropped the pipe and ran, but the patrolman called for backup, and they caught the five of them. A search revealed that four of them were carrying drugs or drug paraphernalia. They were arrested for possession of controlled substances. Four — including April — tested positive for methamphetamines. Correlli had no drugs on him and wasn't seen smoking. We had no evidence, so we had to let him go, even though we think he's probably their supplier."

"How is she, Steve?" Dolly asked, fearing the worst.

Steve Hunt paused for a moment, his mind flashing back across the more than twenty years that he had known Dolly. They had lived two blocks apart and met in eighth grade. The relationship was, to put it mildly, slow to grow.

It was instant dislike at first sight for both of them. She thought he was a boring, rigid, small-town jock. He thought she was skinny, stuck-up, and pretentious. For the first year after they met, they avoided each other like the plague.

The ninth grade wasn't much better, but the cold feelings they had for each other began to thaw. She saw how he stuck up for his friends. He saw that the skinny girl was developing some major curves. Of course, so did every other boy in school. But unlike the other boys, Steve — Steven back then — was nice to her. He didn't hit on her and didn't make a big deal about her appearance. She liked that.

In tenth grade, Dolly made the first move. In the spring of her sophomore year, she dropped her books when Steve walked by. It wasn't the most original strategy in the history of getting a boy's attention, but it did the trick. He picked up her books and handed them to her. She said "Thanks," paused, gave him an awkward, noncommittal look, and bustled off to her favorite class: chemistry.

Two weeks later, they started talking during lunch. After another month, they had their first group date, at the Rivoli Theatre. He was still a little intimidated and didn't attempt to put his arm around her. Dolly picked up the slack. She casually dropped her hand so that her little finger grazed his leg. Steve felt as though he'd been shocked by electricity. Two weeks later, they went out alone. That summer they were going steady. By the 4th of July, they were in love and inseparable.

Two years later, Steve graduated from Myrtle Beach High and went off to college in Florida. Dolly stayed to finish her senior year. Despite tearful goodbyes and promises to write, the distance had taken its toll, and by year's end, both of them were dating other people. Steve graduated from college, served six years as a Marine officer, and then returned to Myrtle Beach to join the city police force.

Soon thereafter, he married a nursing supervisor from Georgetown and they had two children. Within three years, he was promoted to lieutenant. Three more and he rose to become chief of the detective division, but the long hours, late nights, and the stress of the job took a toll on the marriage, and the divorce was inevitable. Over the last half-dozen years, Dolly and Steve had crossed paths and exchanged pleasantries, but this was not one of those times.

As she sat in the sterile conference room, Dolly's drained expression reflected her shock. April had two previous brushes with the law, but this was the first serious one. The other two had occurred when April was living with Kenny. Both times she ran off with C.B. and his friends; both times the police found her and brought her back to Kenny's.

Dolly understood why April would stay at Kenny's place. She could do anything she wanted there. He didn't care if she blew off her homework, stayed out late, hung out with strange kids, or drank alcohol. Knowing him, the jerk probably even let her smoke pot. *But heavy drugs?* she thought. *And dealing them, too. When could this have happened? How could this have happened to my own daughter right before my eyes?*

"She's coming down from the meth now, Dolly. She's probably feeling pretty anxious, even paranoid. Meth highs can last up to twelve hours. The side effects can include convulsions, high body temperature, stroke, irregular heartbeats, stomach cramps, and shaking. You need to get her to see a doctor and tell him what she's on. She may be addicted if she's been tweaking the stuff for a while. She definitely needs drug counseling. Maybe a treatment center. The doctors can tell you more."

"Can I see her now?" she asked.

"Sure, Dolly," Steve said. "Follow me."

Dolly reflected on the long road she and Steve had walked since their meeting in eighth grade. He was always the straight arrow, the guy you could count on to be sober and drive you home if you drank too much at a party. Dolly was the one who longed for the bright lights and the one — as a teenager, anyway — who drank too much at the party.

Steve was the one with parents who made him do his homework. Dolly was the one who would do anything to escape the boredom of the trailer and her mother's beer-guzzling boyfriends, whose names seemed to change every week.

Dolly could relate to April in at least one way. She had also run away from home several times, but with Dolly, it was always to seek something better, something nicer, something prettier. April's rebellion was harder to understand. Dolly gave her love, care, affection, and attention. She couldn't understand why April didn't come to her when she was having problems.

Back in the holding cell, the situation was getting tense. "Where's C.B.?" Wendy snapped. "He got us into this mess. Why isn't he doing anything to get us out? I thought that was part of the family plan. We sell, he keeps us out of trouble or bails us out."

April said nothing. Her eyes darted around the cell, looking for something — anything — to comfort her growing fears.

"My parents are gonna freak," mumbled Wendy. "They're gonna beat the crap out of me. They won't even let my older brother have a beer in their house, and he's thirty."

"I'm sick, man," said Skank, as he shuddered and groped his way toward the stainless steel toilet bowl at the back of the cell.

"C.B.'s gonna take care of us, don't worry," April finally said. "We're family. We're Skins. We stick together. We don't judge family members. C.B. will help us. But for now, we gotta help ourselves. Like C.B. always says, we're juvies. They're not going to do anything more than try to scare us. We won't get any jail time. Maybe some probation and community service — pickin' up trash in the city park for a couple of weekends — but I think we can handle that, don't you?"

Weakly, Suzi nodded. Skank said nothing. Wendy said "Sure," her eyes darting from one side of the cell to another, looking for the ghosts who were stalking her.

The clank of the skeleton key in the lock jerked the four teenagers into a single focus. "April, your mother's here," said the jailer. "She posted your bond. Get out of here."

"Go to hell," April yelled at the jailer. "I'm not going anywhere except with my dad. I live with him now, not with her."

Dolly's heart fell into her shoes. *Where did this anger come from?* she thought. "Come on, Honey. We'll get you cleaned up and then we can talk about it."

"Get away from me, dammit. I want to go to Kenny's."

"Kenny's not here, April. He's with his...well, he's just not here. Let's go home."

"I'm not leaving my friends," April yelled, defiantly.

"I can't do anything for them, Honey," said Dolly. "But we are going home now. Or do you want to spend the weekend here?"

April, weak from the drug letdown and lack of food, staggered and fell to her knees. "It's OK, Baby," Dolly said as she helped April to her feet. "I'll take care of you. Let's go." The teenager took a last look at her cellmates and weakly raised her clenched fist to her friends in the universal sign of defiance.

After signing for April's purse and its contents – minus the drugs – from the evidence locker, the two women made their way to Dolly's car.

Good Lord Almighty, how'd she get to this point? Dolly thought. Then the memories of her own drug-laced teenage years came flooding back. Taking a deep breath, she focused her willpower on shoving them back into the dark place while she dealt with April's latest crisis.

Oh, for a long, tender night with Ron tonight, she thought. But she knew that a romantic weekend getaway with her new boyfriend was out of the question for now. *But still,* she thought, *a girl can dream. . . ."*

Dolly had just closed the door on April's side of the car when the unmistakable rumble of Kenny Devereaux's dilapidated, mufflerless '83 Chrysler LeBaron convertible sounded in the parking lot. One tattoo at a time, Dolly's ex appeared from the car.

"Whutzup this time, Dolly?" he asked, trying to focus his red-veined eyes through the marijuana haze. "Why'd the cops bother me? Ginger and I were kickin' back."

"God! No wonder your daughter is doing drugs. You're stoned again, aren't you, you sonofabitch."

"Daddy, Daddy, I'm so glad you're here," April sobbed, and ran to his side. "Take me home, Daddy. I didn't do anything, I promise. The Myrtle Beach Storm Troopers just jumped us all and threw us in jail. We were just talking by the Pavilion."

"Sure, Baby, sure. Whatever you want."

"Kenny, for God's sake, let her come home with me. She's on meth. They arrested her for suspicion of dealing. Look at her. She's a wreck. She's white as a ghost. She needs a shower, a clean bed, and some decent food. I'm taking her home so she can get cleaned up and get some rest. Then I need to take her to the doctor. We can talk about the details later."

"No way, Dolly," April yelled. "I'm going home with Daddy."

"No skin offa my back," said Kenny with a shrug. "Don't much care where she sleeps, so long as she doesn't give me and Ginger no grief."

"Thanks, Daddy," April said as she crawled into the wheezing convertible. "I knew you'd be there for me."

"April, no!" yelled Dolly sternly. "You're coming home with me right now. Now get in this car." She looked at Kenny for some help, some support, some . . . hell, anything except that hazy, nonchalant stare that he always gave her.

"Kenny, please. . ." she pleaded with tears in her eyes. "Instead of trying to be her best friend, be her father for once in your life, dammit."

"That's what I'm doin' Dolly. Bein' her dad . . . takin' her to her daddy's house. I came here to get her, didn't I? What the hell do you want from me?"

"Just go, Daddy. I wanna go home," April said as she stared coldly at her mother. "Home with my *father.*"

Dolly began to cry as she watched Kenny and April drive off. How could she help April with Kenny always there, letting her get in trouble and acting like it was no big deal? Why did he always have to make her look like the bad guy when all she wanted was to love her baby girl and be a good mother?

I'm losing her, Dolly thought. *I just hope it's not too late.*

12
Free Samples

C.B.'s apartment
Myrtle Beach

April was incredulous. "I never thought it would happen like this, C.B.," she said in tears. "I thought my dad was gonna be there for me. He let me come stay with him after Dolly bailed me out. It only lasted two days. As soon as I showed up, Ginger — that bitch who's livin' with him — started giving me grief. Then do you know what happened?"

C.B. ran his hand across his clean-shaven head. He rolled up the right leg of his pants to unlace his red-laced boot, uncovering a large, elaborate red, yellow, and blue tattoo of a lightning bolt on his lower leg. "I can guess," he said as he removed his heavy black boots and tossed them on the floor next to the sagging couch. "But tell me."

"Ginger told Kenny it was her or me. He didn't argue with her for more than five minutes before he told me to get out. ME! He told *me* to get out. Can you believe it? My own father threw me out."

"It's OK, Baby. You'll be eighteen in a few days. You're one of the family now. You can stay here with us for as long as you want. They can't make you do nothin'." C.B. stroked her hair in reassurance. "I bet you're hungry. I'll make you some soup."

C.B.'s place was nothing to brag about. The living room furniture consisted of a worn out couch, an old beanbag chair on the ground that had burst and was spilling its contents on the soiled carpet, an old TV in the corner, and an expensive — and stolen — stereo system resting on top of the TV. Overflowing ashtrays, empty beer cans, pizza boxes, dirty clothes, and every other kind of trash imaginable covered the floor. On the window sill in the kitchen, a small petunia plant barely clung to life in dry soil.

April briefly thought of her mother's apartment, which Dolly kept sparkling clean and filled with plants and flowers. *This place could use a woman's touch,* she thought, *and I'm the woman.* At the time, though, April didn't care what the place looked like, as long as it did not contain the two things she liked least at the moment: her mother and father.

From the outside, the two-story, gray, cinderblock apartment building attracted no attention. It stood unnoticed down an unmarked alley that ran between Loose Lizzie's, a strip club painted hot pink, and Cupid's Play Chest, a neon-lit porno shop on Highway 501. You'd never find the place if you weren't looking really hard for it. It was the perfect place to live when you didn't want to be found. Outside C.B.'s door, Skank had placed an empty STP can on the porch in honor of the group's unofficial name for the place, the "Secret Tweaker Pad."

"Here you go," C.B. said as he handed April a bowl of tomato soup and some saltines.

April managed a weak smile as she sipped a spoonful. She looked around the apartment and noticed a bra strap hanging out of a pile of dirty clothes in the corner. "Does Wendy live here now?" April asked, hoping the answer was no and the bra wasn't Wendy's. She knew that C.B. slept with other girls, but Wendy was her special friend, and April hoped she wasn't one of them.

C.B.'s apartment had been the place April headed to the first time she ran away from her father's trailer when she was fourteen. She had met C.B. through a girlfriend of hers who had turned her on to crystal meth. Within a few weeks, C.B. had become April's lover and meth supplier.

"Yeah," C.B. said, taking a sip of his beer. "She's part of the family; helps me out, you know."

"Sellin' stuff?"

"Yeah, like you. Hands out free samples to the kids. We all gotta do our part. It's the family business, and nobody wants to have to buy the stuff, right?"

April didn't answer. The economics were simple. She knew that as long as she sold a couple of eight-balls of meth a week to her friends, she'd have all she needed for herself for free. If she sold a few more a week, she could easily earn enough money to live on.

All the high school kids in the Redneck Riviera knew which of their classmates — "the druggies," they called them — used pills, pot, or other drugs to get high. C.B. and the other dealers in town targeted the kids when they started the eighth grade. The offer was simple: for six months, any eighth-grader could get free samples of pot or speed any time they wanted it. After that, they either had to buy it or become a dealer and get their own personal stash as a sales commission.

There was hardly any place in the Grand Strand — or any other city, for that matter — where a dealer was more than ten or twenty minutes away. In most cases, the dealers were friends, neighbors, or schoolmates. The only thing that stood between a kid and drugs was what they learned, or chose to learn, from their parents — and what the parents let them get away with.

April remembered her first time smoking pot. Her father was one of several dozen well-organized farmers who raised crops of high-grade marijuana in the subtropical forests and swamps of Horry County.

She was twelve and looking for adventure. Kenny had dozed off while watching TV and toking on his bong. April noticed that the bowl was still burning and out of curiosity, sucked hard on the mouthpiece of the tube and took in a lungful of smoke. The explosive round of coughing that this produced abruptly jerked Kenny and his current girlfriend out of their cannabis dream world. Both broke into a fit of laughter when they saw what had happened.

"Here, Honey, if you're gonna do it, do it right," Kenny said to his daughter. "Just a little bit at a time. Suck it in deep. Hold it there. Then blow it out your nose."

The young girl coughed again, recovering from the initial blast. She wasn't anxious for more of the acrid smoke, but the curiosity that came from the pleasant, dreamy buzzing in her head induced her to take another hit on the bong. Kenny and his girlfriend giggled as his eighty-pound daughter quickly got high. April soon concluded that being high was more fun than being sober. Then she met Wendy, and a whole new chapter of her life opened up.

13
Retro Romance

La Luna Rosa Restaurant
Thursday noon

Dolly felt a chill in her bones as she walked into the little Italian family restaurant down the block from Fantasia on King's Highway. Steve Hunt immediately sensed her tension. "Hey, Dolly. Good to see you," he said.

"Hi, Steve. It was kind of you to meet me on such short notice. I know you're busy."

"No problem. For you, I always have time. I'm starved. What's there to know about the food in this place?"

"I like everything here," she said, looking over the menu absent-mindedly. Dolly struggled with her composure. "God, Steve, I'm a wreck," Dolly blurted out, then burst into tears. She immediately fumbled in her purse for a tissue, embarrassed that she had broken down in the first thirty seconds of the meeting with her old boyfriend.

Steve handed her a handkerchief and put a hand on her shoulder. "It's OK, Dolly. This has to be rough for you. I know that April's been a handful for a while. And now this."

Dolly unsuccessfully choked back the tears. "I've tried so hard to be a good mother to her, Steve. You know, all the stuff that mothers are supposed to do. Make sure they do their homework. Listen to 'em when they break up with a boyfriend. Tell 'em about boys and sex and love and self-respect and all that stuff." Dolly dabbed at her tears, but they continued to flow.

"But I'm losing her, Steve, and I don't know when it started. She used to be such a good kid. She was popular, did her home-work, got good grades, liked sports. Then when she turned thir-teen, it all started to change. The sports were the first thing to go. Then the friends. She started acting depressed and stayed in her room more and more. Then the grades started falling, and she started wearing all these weird clothes and the boots.

"When she was a little girl, she used to snuggle with me all the time and tell me fairy tales and stories about her friends. Now she won't talk to me at all, and she's run away again. Her father said there was a fight between her and Ginger, and April ran off. That was last weekend. It's been four days now, and I don't know where she is. Now she's almost eighteen, and I'm afraid I might lose her for good, Steve." Dolly could barely get her words out between her sobs.

"Any calls or messages?"

"Not a word. I don't even know the names of her friends any-more. I don't even know if she has any friends. For months, she's been shutting herself off in her bedroom. I've tried to talk to her, but it's like she's in a world of her own. I think C.B. Correlli has something to do with all this. I broke up their relationship three years ago, but I know she still wants to see him."

"Correlli is a bad character, Dolly. He's screwed up the lives of a lot of young kids. He's a Skinhead, and the bunch he's in-volved with — the W.A.R Skins — are pretty violent. The White Aryan Resistance is a hard-core, white-power hate group, an off-shoot of the Ku Klux Klan. There aren't very many Skinheads around Myrtle Beach, but they are more or less a basic training group for white supremacist teenagers. The W.A.R. Skins teach kids racial hatred and violence. When the kids hit their late teens or early twenties, many of them move on to the white power mili-tia groups or the Hell's Angels. The HA's in these parts and in North Carolina are pretty heavy into manufacturing and selling drugs, running guns, and prostitution rings. If April is with Correlli, the quicker you can get her away, the better."

"If you know Correlli is a dealer, why isn't he in jail?" she asked.

"He's no fool, Dolly. Like a lot of smart drug dealers, he doesn't do drugs himself. He's never been busted for anything worse than simple possession of marijuana, but we're pretty sure he's running a big drug dealing operation, and he may even be manufacturing. The kids we busted with April last week were all drug users and all friends of Correlli's. If April is running with Correlli, she's in danger."

"She's gone someplace. I filled out a missing person report on Wednesday, but I haven't heard a thing." Dolly reached across the table and took Steve's hand. "Steve, I don't have any right to ask you for a favor, but April is my only child. I feel awful asking. . . ."

"Don't worry, Dolly. I run the vice and drug unit of the police department. It's my job to go after slime like Correlli. I'll do whatever I can for April. When's her arraignment date?"

"Three weeks."

"I hope you can find her and talk some sense into her before then. She's facing charges of possession with the intent to distribute. That could get her twenty years in the Womens' Correctional Institution. If she misses her court date, she becomes a fugitive. She was arrested as a juvenile. When does she turn eighteen?"

"Tomorrow," Dolly replied. "She's going to be eighteen tomorrow. I had a party planned. . . ." Dolly broke into tears again. Most of the customers in the small neighborhood restaurant knew her and looked at her with compassion.

"Well, if she doesn't show up in court on time, they'll issue a warrant for her arrest. She'll be charged as an adult fugitive, even though her original drug charge was as a juvenile. That's really serious. Do you have any idea where she is?"

"I can only guess that she's with Correlli. But I don't know where he lives."

"If I remember right, it's somewhere over on 501 near the strip joints on Seaboard Street. Let me see what I can do." The detective tapped a number into his cell phone. "Hi. This is Steve Hunt. Give me Records, please. Thanks. Hi, Shirley? Steve Hunt. Can you check the last known address of a local drug dealer by the name of John Anthony Correlli. His alias is 'C.B.' or 'Cue Ball.' Yeah. Probably still local. Call me back on my cell. Thanks."

"Correlli's a local offender, so we should have something in a few minutes, Dolly. Do you want me to check out the address?"

"No, Steve. That's very sweet, but I want to do it myself. If she's there, I want to talk to her mother-to-daughter. It wouldn't help now if a policeman walked up."

Steve Hunt's telephone chirped a musical tune. Dolly had forgotten that one of her first fascinations with Steve was his music. For Dolly, who grew up on gospel music and country and western, hearing ballads by John Denver and The Carpenters was a new experience, one which took some getting used to. Three months into their relationship those many years ago, he played "We've Only Just Begun" for her. Dolly thought it was the most romantic piece of music she had ever heard. The evening started out with slow dancing and led to making love all night to the sound of The Carpenters' ballads. Dolly looked into his warm brown eyes and thought, *Why did I ever let this guy get away?*

Steve answered his phone. "Capt. Hunt. Yeah, Shirley. Uh-huh. That's about a block or two from Seaboard, right? That's what I remember. Is there a number? Seven? OK. Thanks." He flipped the phone shut. "Correlli's last known address was a small, concrete-block apartment off 501, down a little alley a couple of blocks from Seaboard. He lives in apartment 7B. The building's behind a strip joint called Loose Lizzie's. "

"Damn! Yeah, I know the place. Scuzzy, low-end redneck place. Lots of hookers. Thanks, Steve. I'm outta here."

"Are you sure you don't want some company?" Correlli is a hardened criminal. He's got no reservations about hurting people."

"No, I have to do this alone. I want her to see I'm there because I love her, not because I'm fronting for the police. If C.B. Correlli is the one who sucked her into all of this, he's going to answer to me."

"I understand how you feel, Dolly, but you concentrate on helping April. You've got to get her back and shaped up before her court date. Correlli is a violent, hardened criminal. The sheriff's department and the Myrtle Beach police are on Correlli's case. You concentrate on April. Leave Correlli to us. He's a menace to the people of Horry County and that's what you pay your taxes for. Here's my cell phone number. Call anytime, day or night. Let me know how I can help. You know you can count on me for anything." He looked deep into her eyes. "We go way back, right?" he asked with a smile.

Dolly reached out and squeezed his hand. "Yeah, Steve, we go way back."

14
Wendy-poo

Cool house, Wendy-poo. Does this place belong to a friend of yours?" April said as they pulled up in the driveway of the luxurious home on Topsail Pointe Drive in Myrtle Beach.

"Of course it does," Wendy answered. "How do you think I have the key and the security alarm code? Would you like the grand tour?" she asked.

"Sure," said April, who had never seen a house so large or elegant.

The girls hopped out of Wendy's BMW convertible, and Wendy unlocked the door. Inside, she punched several buttons on a keypad, and a small red light went out at the same time that the adjacent one turned green. "Entry system disarmed," said the small print below the green light.

Wendy led April to the free-standing circular staircase in the entrance foyer. Above it hung a crystal chandelier nearly six feet wide. "Wow!" April exclaimed. "I've never see anything like that."

"You ain't seen nothin' yet," Wendy said with a grin, taking April's hand and dragging her up the marble stairs. The second floor was no less amazing to April than the staircase.

"God, it's so big," April said. "I've had bedrooms that were smaller than the halls." She marveled at the sideboards, each adorned with long-stemmed fresh flowers. "Where are the owners?" April asked.

"Away in the Bahamas this weekend."

"And it's OK for you to come here when you want?" April asked.

"Well, sure. I worked for them as a babysitter."

"Worked?"

"Yeah, a couple of years ago."

"How'd you get the job? This is a pretty fancy place."

"About the same as my parents' place. No big deal."

"And they let you come here whenever you want?"

"No, silly. I come here whenever *I* want. When I was babysitting for them, they gave me a key and the security code. I copied the key, and they never changed the code.

They entertain a lot. They call one of my friends whenever they leave, and ask her to take care of the place. She and I come over, use the pool, have some parties, drink some champagne. They have a great booze collection. Their liquor cabinet has 200 bottles, and their wine cellar has more than 1,000. They never miss the few we drink. Wanna see the master bedroom? It's got a cool Jacuzzi that overlooks the beach."

April felt a chill — or a thrill — running down her spine.

"I'm thirsty. Let's get some champagne first," Wendy said. She led April downstairs to the wine storage room off the kitchen. Except for the double-glass doors, it was like any other room in the house – only colder. April was amazed when they entered the room. It was the size of the living room in Dolly's apartment. All along the walls lay hundreds of bottles of wine with plastic identification tags hanging from their necks, each bottle resting in its own wooden nesting place. A wine-tasting table with four chairs, a candelabra, and an elaborate cork puller sat in the center of the wine room.

"OK, birthday girl, what shall we have today? French? California? Spanish?"

"What do you mean?"

"What kind of champagne? What country?"

"What do I know about champagne? You choose."

Wendy went to the cooler within the wine room and opened the door. "What the hell," she said. "Let's do some Dom." Wendy pulled out a large bottle of champagne. "It's a jeroboam of Cuvée Dom Perignon Milléseme 1993," she said to April in perfect French. "Whatcha think this baby's worth?" she asked.

"I dunno. It's really big. Fifty dollars?"

"How about seven thousand?" Wendy said with a giggle.

"Whaaaaat?" April gasped. Most cars she'd ridden in hadn't cost seven thousand dollars. She couldn't imagine that a bottle of wine could cost that much money.

"He brags about it to everybody. That one he'd miss. But here's some good stuff he'll never miss," Wendy said as she picked up a bottle of 1997 Dom Perignon. "It's only a hundred fifty bucks a bottle. He has cases of this stuff. Doesn't even count them." April's eyes were plate sized as Wendy dragged her back into the kitchen. When her mother went shopping for wine, she never spent more than eight dollars a bottle, and April had thought that was a lot. The same size bottle of Pepsi only cost two dollars.

Wendy opened the huge brushed-steel refrigerator and took out several cheeses, some butter, and a half a loaf of French bread. She popped the bread in the microwave for a few seconds and retrieved two champagne glasses. When the microwave timer rang, she removed the bread, sliced it and the cheeses, and said, "Dig in."

By the time they had finished the cheese sandwiches and the champagne, April and Wendy were feeling the effect of the bubbles. Then Wendy lit a joint, and the girls had a couple of hits.

"Let's do the pool," Wendy said.

"Hey, I didn't bring a bathing suit."

"Who needs a bathing suit? The place is all ours today," Wendy said. She ran out through the back door of the kitchen and headed for the pool, shedding her clothing on the way.

April wobbled a little from the champagne and the marijuana but quickly slipped out of her shorts, panties, and top; ran across the teak-covered sundeck; and jumped in. The two girls splashed around the shallow end of the enormous pool, laughing and giggling like the teenagers they were. April picked up a Frisbee from the edge of the pool and threw it across the pool to Wendy. Wendy made a flying leap and barely caught it. "How do you throw this thing?" she asked.

"Hold it by the edge and throw it flat," April said. Wendy grasped the plastic saucer and spun it toward April — more or less. She had plenty of power but lousy aim. The Frisbee flew high over April's head and crashed through the kitchen window. Immediately, the screeching sirens of the burglar alarm sounded.

"Oh, shit!" Wendy exclaimed. "The glass alarms. They're on a separate circuit."

"What are we gonna do?" April screamed. "Can you turn them off?"

"I don't know the code for that part of the system," Wendy screamed. "Grab your stuff. They have a private security service. The rent-a-cops will be here in a couple of minutes."

Both naked girls stumbled rapidly back into the kitchen, harvesting discarded clothing along the way. "Get in the car!" Wendy yelled.

"I'm not dressed," April yelled back.

From the front door, Wendy looked up the street. "Oh, shit, here they come," Wendy cried. "Run for the car."

Dripping with water and with only her panties on, April made a dive for Wendy's convertible. Wendy had managed to pull on a tank top — but nothing else. She jumped in, started the engine, threw the car into reverse, and lurched backwards out of the long, curved driveway, just as the security police were entering the other end. The two private guards got an eyeful as the two girls pulled out of the driveway, but their orders were strict: protect the property first, catch intruders second.

"FAR OUT!" Wendy screamed as she wrapped the car around the corner and out of sight of the guards. As each tried to struggle into her remaining clothes, April started to giggle, then Wendy joined in. Soon both were laughing hysterically. By the time they got back to C.B.'s, they were positively giddy.

First, her father had taught her how to smoke pot. Then C.B. turned her on to speed and Ecstasy. Now Wendy had introduced her to the thrill and adrenaline rush of danger. All this and she was now eighteen and living free. *Life*, thought April, *is finally starting to look up.*

15
The Lion's Den

Highway 17 North

What *on earth am I going to say to her that I haven't already said?* Dolly thought as she drove north on Highway 17 past Myrtle Beach Airport. *And what can I tell her that she doesn't already know?* She took the U.S. 501 exit and slowed down, looking for Loose Lizzie's. With the twenty-four-foot-wide billboard sticking up from the center of its parking lot, showing a blonde in a micro-bikini sucking on a lollipop, the club wasn't hard to find. Nevertheless, it took some searching to locate the nondescript gray apartment building Steve had described.

Steve had told her that Correlli was driving an orange '69 Dodge Charger with a Confederate flag on the roof — a clone of the car on the old TV show "The Dukes of Hazzard." When she came to the Charger parked in a small alley, Dolly's heart started to pound. She wasn't sure if she was ready for this, nor was she sure how to handle the situation without making things worse between her and April.

She's going to hate me for coming here, Dolly thought. *But I've got to do this. I've got to save her.* Driven by a desperation far greater than her fear and uncertainty, Dolly took a deep breath and stepped out of the car.

A rusted number 7 hung upside down from the door frame of the old apartment. A knock produced no answer, but Dolly thought she heard some noise from inside. She knocked again and thought she saw some movement from the closed drapes of a window to her right. Gaining more courage, she knocked once more, this time with more persistence. "April?" she called uneasily. "April, can you hear me? This is Mamma. I'm not mad at you, Honey. I just need to talk to you."

Inside the apartment, an emergency conference was underway. "Tell her to get lost," Wendy snapped at C.B.

"All right, Wendy. Lemme take care of this," he retorted. C.B. kneeled down by the couch April was sitting on and looked her in the eye.

"It's bullshit, April," he told her firmly. "She's just saying she's not mad at you to get you out of here. If you open that door, she's just gonna chew your ass for screwin' up and bein' here," C.B. said to April. "You know how much she hates me."

"April, listen to me," pleaded Dolly from outside. "I'm not here to punish you. Just open the door. We've got to talk, Honey. *Please.*"

April felt a twinge of regret when she heard the desperation in her mother's voice. She didn't hate her mom. She really didn't. She just wanted to have her off her back. *Why is she always trying to save me?* she thought. *I wish she'd stop doing this to herself. I never asked for her help.*

"Maybe I should talk to her," she told C.B. "I've always called her when I've run away before, just so she wouldn't worry so much. Besides, if I talk to her, she'll probably leave us alone. She can't make me leave, right? I'm eighteen now."

C.B. placed both of his hands on April's frail shoulders. "April, I've got dope stashed all over the goddamn apartment," he said. "What if there's a cop with her? Think, April. Do you wanna get busted again? Huh?"

"April, you're in trouble with the law, but we can work it out," Dolly yelled as she jostled the doorknob to see if the apartment was locked. "But I need to talk to you. Things could get a lot worse for you with the police if we can't talk. Open the door, April," she yelled as she pounded on the door.

"See, April!" exclaimed Wendy. "She's already been talking to the cops. Dammit! Get her the hell out of here, C.B."

"OK, enough," said C.B. "Wendy, chill out. I'm handling this, OK? I don't need anybody making this worse." C.B. stood up. "I'm taking the stuff out the back door. Skank, gimme your keys, I'm taking your car. Tell the Devereaux broad to get lost."

C.B. ran to the bedroom, pulled out a gym bag full of drugs from under the bed, grabbed another one from the top of his closet, threw all the scales and measuring devices on his desk into the bag, and slipped out the back door.

Outside, Dolly was running out of things to say. "April, I know you're in there," Dolly yelled, not knowing whether or not it was true. "Come out and talk to me."

Wendy looked at April and jerked her head in the direction of the bedroom. "Get in there, April, and close the door. We'll get rid of her." April did as she was told.

Skank went to the door and unlocked both of the deadbolts, leaving the safety chains on. He opened the door a couple of inches and peered through the crack at Dolly. "Go away, lady," he said grouchily. "Nobody lives here but me, and I sure as hell don't know you."

Dolly was confused. The skinny, drawn teenage face she saw through the crack in the door wasn't C.B. Correlli's. *I know this is the right place, though,* she thought, remembering the orange Charger out front. "I need to talk to April Devereaux," Dolly insisted.

"Look, lady, I don't know about anybody named April, OK?" he said as he started to close the door.

Dolly angrily pushed the door back open before Skank could close it all the way. "Listen to me," Dolly demanded. "If she doesn't talk to me, she could go to jail for a long time. If you're any kind of friend of hers, if you care at all about her, you'll let me talk to her." Dolly stared straight into the sunken eyes of the teenager as tears welled in her own. "Please," she begged, choking on her own fear and apprehension.

From inside the bedroom, April had the door cracked open and heard everything her mother was saying. Her heart raced as she trembled with fear — fear of facing her mother after running away but, even more, fear of the possibility that her mother was telling the truth.

Sure, Dolly pissed her off a lot at home, but her mother had never lied to her. Shaking, she slowly opened the bedroom door and walked into the living room.

"No!" whispered Wendy adamantly as she grabbed April's wrist to lead her back to the bedroom.

April shook Wendy's hand off her wrist. "Stop it, Wendy. I mean it."

Shocked, Wendy stood aside and let her go.

April walked towards the door. "Lemme talk to her, Skank," April said with exasperation. Skank stood at the door, motionless, staring at April. "Skank, I mean it. Let me talk to her."

"Shit . . . whatever, April," he sighed as he moved away from the door.

April peered through the door at Dolly.

"April...!" gasped Dolly when she saw her daughter's pale, empty face. "April, Honey, you've got to listen. . . ."

"No, Mamma, you listen," April cut in. "I'm not your problem anymore. I'm eighteen now. Just go away and stop worrying about me. I don't want your help," April proclaimed, attempting to mask her fear with a mask of determination.

"April, you're my daughter. I don't care if you're eighteen or eighty, you're still my responsibility and I'm going to worry. You've got a court date coming up for the drug arrest, and we don't even have a lawyer yet. Get your stuff and come with me. No one here can help you but me. Not your friends, not C.B." Dolly protested.

"I'm not goin' with you, Mamma," April said, her voice devoid of energy or emotion. "Leave me alone. This is my family now, not you."

April's words stung Dolly. "April, don't say that," Dolly said in anguish. "I can't leave you alone, Honey. You're my baby, and you're in trouble. I'm your Mamma, and I want to help you."

"I'm *not* your damn baby any more. I'm *eighteen* for chris-sakes," April insisted. "I have my own friends and my own life without you now, and I can make my own decisions."

"April, are we going to talk through a chained door, or can I at least come in for a minute?" Dolly asked.

April thought a moment. Her mother looked so sad, so frantic. She closed the door, unlatched the chains, and let her in.

Dolly gasped when she entered the apartment. The place was a wreck. Empty beer cans and dirty dishes were strewn all over the dark, dingy rooms. A pungent odor of old food and body odor permeated the place. But it was the sight of April that really shocked her. She was so pale and skinny. Her stringy, uncombed hair fell over her dark, sunken eyes. Her clothes hadn't been washed in days, and they hung on her in a way that made them look like they belonged to someone else — someone bigger, harder, meaner... someone other than Dolly's baby girl.

"We have to get you some decent food and clothes and get you ready for your trial," Dolly said, choking back the repulsion she felt at the rathole her daughter was living in.

"I told you, I'm not going. You can't make me. I'm an ad—"

"An adult, yes, I know April. You're eighteen, but you're not ready to face this on your own."

"How would you know what I'm ready for?" April asked defiantly. "You don't even know me, Mamma. You haven't known me for years. You're always working or hanging out at those stupid clubs or going on some stupid date with those jerks you meet. Don't try to act like you care now, 'cause you're too late," April yelled. "I've grown up and I don't need you. I have all the help I need right here."

"Don't try to act like I care *now*?!" Dolly exclaimed. "All I've *ever* done was care. All I've ever tried to do was make a good life for you. Don't give me this 'you don't care about me crap,' April. You know damn well that's a lie."

"No, Mamma, all you've ever tried to do was make a good life for yourself. The only thing you cared about was that I acted happy so you could pretend like you were a better mother than grandma was for you. Well, Dolly, I hate to break it to you, but it looks like you failed just as miserably as she did. I'm a fuck-up, just like you were, and there's not a damn thing you can do about it now. It's over now, so just go away and stop trying. I'm staying here, with my friends, the people who *really* care about me."

"Honey-child, listen to me," Dolly said. "These people may be your friends, but they are drug addicts. Yes, they need help, too, but my first job is you. If you don't show up to court clean, healthy, and cooperative, they could put you in jail for twenty years."

"Bullshit, Mamma. I was seventeen when I got busted. They're not gonna put a juvie in jail for twenty years, even if I do have to go to trial," April said with a tone of authority.

"A 'juvie,' huh? You're already talking like a jailbird. Someone's been feeding you lousy information, April. You better get that pretty little head of yours screwed on straighter than that. You had a lot of drugs on you when you were arrested. They're not going to just slap you on the wrist with community service for simple possession. They are going to try you as a drug dealer, not a kid who got caught smoking a joint. I don't think you want to spend the next twenty years of your life at the Women's Correctional Institution in Columbia, but that's where you're headed if you don't come home with me, get cleaned up, and get ready for the trial." Dolly took a deep breath and looked at April for some sign that her tirade had had an effect.

"That's bullshit, April," Wendy said. "They can't do that. C.B. said so."

Dolly bit her lip to keep herself from saying anything back to Wendy. "So now you have C.B. Correlli as your defense attorney, do you April? He sure doesn't seem to know much about the law, does he?" Dolly was starting to get angry. Why was April being so foolish? Dolly knew she was smarter than this.

"But there's one thing about C.B. that you can count on· the judge will certainly recognize him. They know he's a drug dealer and that he recruits kids like you and your two friends here to make money for him," Dolly said as she glanced coldly at Wendy and Skank.

"Don't pay any attention to her, April," Wendy interrupted. "She's just on a big control trip like every mother. C.B. will take care of us, you know that," she said forcefully. "And there's plenty of other places we can go."

Dolly shot Wendy an angry glance, then returned to look at her daughter. "So you're going to spend the rest of your life running from the law? Does that make any sense? April, I love you. I just want to help you," Dolly pleaded. "This is your first offense.

You could probably get probation and no jail time if you cooperate. Come home with me so we can start getting all this straightened out," Dolly urged.

April was shaking with fear. "I'm stayin' here, Mamma," she managed to utter, despite her trembling voice and the unmistakable terror in her young eyes.

Instinctively, Wendy and Skank moved closer to her, standing side by side with April, as if to say *It's you against us, lady. She's one of us now.*

"Twenty years in jail, April. That's what you're facing. Think about it. I'll be back tomorrow. I hope you'll come with me then."

With her heart in her throat and tears welling up in her eyes, Dolly turned and walked back to her Honda. She maintained her composure until she got inside the car and slammed the door shut. Then the emotional dam burst, and she sobbed uncontrollably for twenty minutes before she stopped shaking enough to start the engine. She took one final glance at C.B.'s apartment, and reluctantly drove away.

16
Cook Wanted

Detective Sergeant Dan McConnell parked his lanky frame on the steel chair next to Capt. Steve Hunt's desk. "Here's the papers you wanted. So what's up with this druggie, Correlli? We got Skinhead trouble brewin' here, or is Correlli just a dealer who happens to be a Skin?"

"Don't know yet, Dan. But he's definitely into some heavy dealing. Let's see his rap sheet."

The sergeant handed his boss a file folder with a blue tab. "Let's see what we have here," Steve said. "'93: drunk and disorderly. Paid the fine. '95: aggravated battery. Kicked a Japanese golfer half to death outside a strip club in North Myrtle after the guy propositioned one of the girls. The guy never pressed charges, and they were dropped. Same thing again in '96: beat up a drunk black male escorting a white female out of a strip joint on King's Highway in Garden City Beach. Again, no charges pressed. This guy obviously doesn't like race-mixing. Hmmm. '97: arrested in a sting operation at the Blue Moon Saloon for possession of Ecstasy with intent to distribute, but the arresting officer left the force, couldn't be found, and the judge had to dismiss the case. Last month, he was arrested with five known users — probably his dealers — behind the Pavilion, but it turned out that he wasn't carrying, and he was released. He's one lucky sonofabitch. Slippery, too."

"Who's he hang with?"

"He's the head of a gang of W.A.R. Skins, maybe five or six of 'em. Mostly teenage druggies, school dropouts, and throwaway kids from broken homes. All are under 21. You probably know most of 'em. Jimmy Mullins is one of 'em. Street name's 'Skank.' Skinny kid, brown hair, brown eyes. He was a good athlete at Myrtle High until he tested positive for drugs twice and they threw him off the team. He dropped out, and now he spends all day hangin' around the Pavilion. Baggy pants, T-shirts, heavy boots, red laces. He always looks so bummed out that people give him money and food.

"And didn't you book Suzi Vetter for underage drinking once or twice a few years back? Tall girl, a little on the heavy side, dark brown eyes, lots of piercing, henna orange hair, couple of tattoos. I think she's a waitress at some biker bar now."

"Yeah, I know her. Is Wendy Hickson one of 'em?" the detective asked. "I think I saw Hickson with Vetter a couple of times, cruising Ocean Boulevard on the back of a couple Harleys."

"Yeah," Steve replied. "Wendy Hickson, the 'poor little rich girl.' Doc Hickson's youngest. Yeah, Preston R. Hickson, the dentist with the big practice near Briarcliffe Acres. Blonde, blue eyes, long hair. Could have a been a model, but dresses like a cheap whore now. Pierced eyebrow, navel ring, tongue stud.   All her brothers and sisters went on to college, but she majored in shoplifting. How do you figure it? A girl who has a BMW and a platinum VISA card — Daddy pays for both, of course — and she steals clothes and cigarettes, does drugs, and sleeps with a slimeball like Correlli. Suzi Vetter's another mystery. Basketball whiz at Myrtle High until she was a junior, then poof! She starts hanging with the bikers, then with Correlli and snorting meth."

"The guy's like flypaper to kids who are looking for trouble, isn't he?" said the detective. "What about the W.A.R. Skin stuff?"

"From Correlli's rap sheet, he's obviously a hard-core Neo-Nazi White Power freak. But I think he's mostly using the Skinhead mystique — the Nazi tattoos, the steel-toed boots, the black bomber jacket, the violence, the racist talk, and the drugs — as a way to recruit young kids for his drug operation. We've never had much of a Skinhead problem in these parts. White power types, the Hell's

Angels, and what little's left of the Klan, sure. But not Skinheads. I don't think there's twenty of them in the county. I think Correlli brought the Skinhead act with him from California."

"What's the scoop about some new meth lab?"

"We just got word from the Williamsburg County sheriff's office that they've been seeing a lot more crystal meth on the streets there lately. Same thing with Brunswick County, across the state line. Sheriff Nichols there thinks we've got a new meth lab — or maybe two — operating within dealing range of Myrtle Beach."

"Anything else?"

"'Fraid so. We've gotten multiple reports in the last month that the street price of Ecstasy is down from about $25 a hit to about $20. That can only mean one thing."

"Supply is up?"

"Supply is definitely up."

"You think Correlli's part of it?"

"He's originally from Oildale, California, right off the Interstate 5 meth highway from Mexico. According to one of our guys who used to work on a force near there, Oildale's a rough town, full of oil rigs, bars, chop shops, Skinheads, white power groups, and HA's. Correlli's got California and North Carolina Hell's Angels connections, so he fits the meth lab profile pretty closely. The HA's control most of the meth production and distribution west of the Mississippi, but they're doing lot's of business in guns, women, and meth in North Carolina, too.

"The lab we busted west of Socastee last year was a Hell's Angels operation, probably out of North Carolina. We got there about two hours too late to nail anybody or lift any prints. They knew we were comin', evacuated the meth and the critical equipment, and torched the lab. Five acres of forest burned up around the place, too. After the fire, the site was so full of toxic waste that it took the state Hazardous Materials guys two weeks to decontaminate the area. Set the county back sixty thousand bucks just for the HazMat cleanup."

"Was Correlli involved with that one?"

"We don't know."

"What's the next step?" asked the detective.

"Well, for starters, I just put Correlli on my official list of problem children to make miserable. I have two reasons. First, we've got a multi-county meth problem that's growing fast, and he has the obvious connections and record. And second, he's recruited the teenaged daughter of an old friend of mine as a meth and Ecstasy dealer. The first one is enough to make me take action, but the second one makes it personal."

"Where do we go from here, boss?" the detective asked. "Raid his house for evidence?"

"No, he's not that stupid. Any good meth cook makes sure he can't be traced to either the ingredients or the finished product. If we raided the place where he lives, the most we'd come up with is a couple of roaches, and he'd be laughin' in our face again. No, we've gotta develop some other sources of information on Correlli."

"What have we got to start with?"

"Squat, that's what. You got any informants in the HA's that you can squeeze a little?"

"Just one guy. We cut a back-door deal with him on an unlicensed weapon charge a couple of years back in return for information on the HA's who were running a gun supply operation outta North Myrtle. Sellin' stolen army assault weapons from Fort Campbell — RPG launchers and recoilless rifles, mostly — to the militia loonies, remember?"

"Is he still connected with the HA's, or did they burn him?"

"No, I think he's still connected."

"Remind him of his patriotic duty to his native land and see what you can get. Or tell him about our leftover jail time options from the Fort Campbell operation. We need to find Correlli's connection with the meth and where he's getting the other stuff he's selling. If we don't, we could soon have a full-scale drug epidemic on our hands here in beautiful Branson-by-the-Sea."

17
Lost and Found

D olly felt a mixture of dread and delight as she waited for the doorbell to ring. On the one hand, she was not looking forward to hearing the details of what Steve Hunt had found out about C.B. Correlli. On the other, she was grateful for his help. *No, it was more than that,* Dolly thought. *I really like this man. Always did. How did I get distracted? How did I . . . ?*

Her introspection was interrupted by the crunch of tires on the gravel parking lot below. She looked out the window and saw the blue-and-white police cruiser. The bold, black, Myrtle Beach Police emblem on its door flashed in the late afternoon sun as Steve Hunt opened the door. Moments later, her doorbell rang. Dolly fluffed her hair, took off her apron and skipped to the door like a schoolgirl.

Steve was dressed in civilian clothes: a button-down shirt and tweed dress slacks. The tweed brought out the brown and green of his eyes, and Dolly realized once again what a handsome man he was. It finally dawned on her that she had been soaking up his presence for quite a few moments and hadn't said a word.

"Good gracious, Steve, please come in. A cat must have gotten my tongue. Thank you so much for coming by. I know how busy you are."

"I remember your cooking Dolly. And your perfume. How could I possibly refuse," he said as he stepped inside.

For a moment, they were frozen in time — another time, twenty years before, at Myrtle Beach High. When he walked in, neither of them knew what to do, but in moments, it suddenly seemed natural. They embraced like the long-lost friends they were.

"How's it going?"

"Horrible, Steve. I went over to Correlli's yesterday."

"Was he there? What happened?"

"I don't know if he was there or not. A tall, skinny kid, brown hair, big mouth, tried to keep me out."

"That was probably Skank. He's Correlli's go-fer. Correlli always makes sure there's somebody else between him and trouble."

"I wouldn't go away. April finally came to the door. She looked awful: sick and really tired. I know she doesn't want to live like that, but she wouldn't come home with me."

"It's the gang, Dolly. Peer pressure. Correlli's got all of them convinced that they have no friends outside the gang. They think the world is out to get them, that it's them against the world, and that Correlli is the big, strong guy who is going to protect them. What else?"

"I tried to convince her that she had to get straightened out and ready for the trial, or she could end up in prison doing serious time."

"And?"

"And I think it sunk in, but the other two kids were talking her into staying. Wendy Hickson's part of all of this, too. She and April have been best friends for years. She was there convincing April to stay. I couldn't get her to leave," Dolly said, the tears starting to flow.

Steve put an arm around her shoulder. "You did a really brave thing, Dolly. I know how hard that must have been for you. A lot of parents just walk away from their kids when they're this far gone. That's what happened to Skank and a couple of the others who are hangin' with Correlli. Don't give up on her. Kids often go astray, but if they see that their parents are always working for their best interest, setting a good example, they often come around.

Stay in touch with April. Correlli and his gang will try to stop you, but do it anyway. Never give up."

"I'd never give up on April," Dolly said, her tears turning to sobs. "She's made some stupid mistakes, but she doesn't have any bad seed inside her. Her father let her smoke dope at his place when she was twelve. And he let her have boyfriends sleep over with her at his place when she was fifteen. I tried to be there for her all the time, but I have to work two jobs to keep food on the table. I went back to Correlli's place this morning, but there was nobody home."

"What about your ex? Does he contribute any money to raising April?"

"I haven't seen a dime from Kenny in ten years. The family court threw him in jail for a month for non-support, but it didn't change anything. He claimed he was unemployed and had no income, even though he was growin' five hundred pounds of weed a year."

"Sounds like the Kenny I've heard about so much. What about the kids she was with?"

"They looked as bad as April did. Underfed. Black circles under their eyes. Listless. Loud-mouthed."

"Make sure you don't condemn them in front of her. It only confirms their us-versus-the-world feelings. They don't want to be in the condition they're in. They're there because nobody cared about them and never gave them what they needed. Just show April you love her, try to get her to see what's good and what's bad for her, and be there for her. Is there anyone else in the family that she loves and respects? Aunts or uncles? Grandparents? They can often help."

"I'm the only one of my brothers or sisters who has any contact with April. The rest of them all live up by my mother's place in Darlington. They all think I'm stuck up and that I'm better than them. When they heard I got the promotion to store manager, they all figured I was gonna act like the Queen of Sheba and turn up my nose at them. I haven't had a phone call from any of them for some time."

"What about April's grandparents? Are any of them close to her?"

"Kenny's parents are dead. My mother's alive and lives with her second husband in Darlington. April used to be real close to her 'til we moved to Myrtle Beach. But since April's gotten into trouble, Mamma blames it all on me, even though she knows the damage that Kenny's done. Mamma and I, well, we don't talk much anymore."

"Dolly, is there any way you can get your mother involved again with April? You may not be gettin' along with your mother, but if April does, then your mother may be able to help."

Steve squeezed her hand in support. "I can't imagine how hard it must be for you, Dolly. I know how hard you work. Everybody who really knows you, loves you. They all tell me what an idiot I was for lettin' you get away."

Dolly was stunned. Could there still be a small flame burning somewhere in Steve's heart, even after all these years — or was he just being kind?

18
Crystal City

C.B.'s apartment

April sat huddled in a chair in C.B.'s living room, tired and scared. Wendy tried to comfort her. "Don't worry, Honey," she said. "C.B. knows you can't risk sellin' while you're waitin' for trial. We all pitch in here, do what we have to do. We're family. He'll come up with somethin' for you to do."

"When's he due back?" she asked.

The sound of the Charger's muffler was unmistakable. "That's him now," Wendy said.

Skank opened the two locks and the chains and stood at the door with his trademark, goofy grin. C.B. was the coolest guy Skank had ever met, and he tried to anticipate his every need. "Anything you need me to bring in?" he asked.

C.B. gave Skank's stubbly head a friendly pat and snapped his braces. "Yeah. Bring in the food."

Both girls held their places, waiting to be summoned. C.B. nodded to them, and they jumped up and hugged and kissed him.

"April's all bummed out about the court thing," Wendy said.

"Don't worry about it, Baby," Correlli said to April. "I heard it was goin' to Judge Cheever. He's an old geezer who spends most of his time on the bench sleeping. He'll let you off with community service. Who's your mother got you for a lawyer?"

"I don't know, C.B. I didn't want to leave here or go anywhere with her. I'm afraid she'll kidnap me or something. I want to be here with you guys."

"You gotta be practical, Babe. Do the lawyer thing with her. You gotta stay outta jail. But she can't stop you from bein' with us, 'cause you're eighteen now. And we all love you, right?" he said, motioning to the others. Wendy and Skank gathered around her and hugged her simultaneously. April breathed a sigh of relief

"Now listen up," C.B. said. "I already had lunch. Eat your food. Skank, I want you to hold down the fort here. Girls, we have a lot of work to do this afternoon. Wendy, ya feel up to cookin' today?"

"Always," Wendy said, flashing C.B. a mischievous smile.

"Great, I gotta get some supplies. I'll be back in twenty minutes."

"Cook?" said April, eyeing Wendy with curiosity. "Since when do you know how to cook anything?"

"Don't worry, you'll see what we're talking about in a little bit," said Wendy.

April just shrugged and shifted her focus to the food C.B. had brought home for them. She had been on a meth binge since her birthday and hadn't eaten – or slept for that matter – in days. The group wolfed down the burgers and fries and washed them down with strawberry milkshakes, just in time to hear C.B. return. The girls piled into the back seat of the orange Charger, and C.B. headed out U.S. 501 towards Conway. After thirty minutes, he turned off onto a narrow county road and started a long drive through the pine forests. C.B. looked in the mirror with satisfaction. The girls were fast asleep. The less they knew about their destination, the better.

Fifteen minutes more and he pulled up to an unmarked dirt road and stopped before turning in. First he carefully inspected the dirt for traces of footprints or tire tracks. There were none, so he walked to the rusting, galvanized-iron gate and looked closely at the combination lock. The dial was still set precisely halfway between 42 and 43. He smiled. No unauthorized visitors had stopped by. He spun the dials, opened the lock and then the gate, and drove through. He returned to the gate, closed and locked it, drove the

Charger down the dirt road, and turned at two more forks in the road.

In a few minutes, he pulled up behind a small, nice-looking mobile home, complete with yellow plaid curtains and potted geraniums. By the side of the trailer was a shiny black pickup truck with North Carolina plates. The mobile home looked like a little country hideaway for some nature-loving dentist or grocery store manager and his family. That's exactly what it was supposed to look like, in case a hiker or hunter stumbled across it.

"Wake up, ladies, it's time to get to work," C.B. yelled to the girls. "Get the stuff outta the trunk and front seat and bring it in."

Wendy rubbed her eyes and went to the front seat. There she found a propane tank, a kitchen food scale, and box containing clear Teflon tubing, radiator hose clamps, and safety goggles. April popped the trunk and removed four five-gallon red plastic gasoline containers and a box of assorted glassware.

The moment April walked inside the trailer, her jaw dropped. The inside of the mobile home had been gutted, leaving only the back bedroom and a bathroom. The rest of the space was a maze of metal tables and racks full of bottles, tubes, wires, Bunsen burners, and coil condensers. What once must have been the kitchen was filled with drums, cans, bottles, and tanks of chemicals.

A tall, heavily muscled man wearing jeans and safety goggles was pouring a dark orange liquid into a large glass flask. His black T-shirt read, "Fuck you. I already have enough friends."

"Hey, Boomer. How're they hangin?" C.B. called out.

"Hey, C.B. Hey, Wendy. What's the buzz?" he said. "Who's the new chick?" Boomer said without looking up from his work.

"Her name's April," C.B. said. "She's one of us."

Boomer turned to Wendy. "Ready to go to work, Cutie? I got a five-liter batch of chlorephedrine ready for catalytic hydrogenization. I saved it all just for you."

Wendy put on a pair of safety goggles and heavy rubber gloves. "You're too good to me," she said to Boomer, and gave him a kiss on his cheek. Wendy looked at April with a big grin. "Better living through chemistry," she said with a mischievous smile.

"What is all this?" April asked in amazement.

C.B. spoke up. "Crystal meth don't grow on trees, sweet thing. We grow it right here. Ole Boomer here is our head cook."

"And I'm his assistant," Wendy chimed in, grinning ear to ear.

"How come you call him Boomer?" she asked C.B.

"Well, makin' meth is a just little tricky sometimes, ain't it, Boomer?"

Boomer laughed. "Just a little."

"Ole Boomer here had a few of his labs go up in smoke on him," C.B. said, laughing. "After the third one blew up, they started callin' him 'Boomer.'"

"C.B., you know damn well that no lab of mine ever blew up because of me. I know what the hell I'm doin'. It was always some stupid helper that blew the place up," he said.

Then Wendy tugged at April's arm and chimed in. "Remember all the fun we had in sophomore chemistry class? Well, this is the real thing: no experiments, and a hundred times more fun. Makin' crystal meth is soooooo complicated. You wouldn't believe what fun stuff we do here. Welcome to Crystal City!"

19
To April, With Love

Darlington, S.C.

Sitting on her front porch, Anne Doolittle was surprised, if not delighted, to see her daughter's once-familiar Honda coming down the dirt road toward her house. Dolly hadn't made a purely social call in over a year. Anne wondered what the reason for this one was. She knew the list was predictably short: Kenny or April.

"Hi, Mamma, how are you?" Dolly said as she gave her mother a light peck on the cheek.

"That's all I get after not seeing you for months?"

Dolly stepped forward and gave her mother a proper hug. "I'm sorry, Mamma. I've been distracted lately."

"Dolly Devereaux, sometimes you act like you're the only person in the world who has personal problems," her mother clucked. "It wouldn't do you a bit of harm to come see your old mother. . . ."

The roar of a high-powered racecar doing engine tests on the high-banked, oval speedway near the house drowned out the rest of her sentence.

"What did you say, Mamma?" Dolly yelled above the roar.

"I said it wouldn't do you a bit of harm to come see your old mother and stepfather once in a while."

"I have two jobs and a teenage daughter to raise, Mamma. I do the best I can."

"I had no husband and six children to raise, my dear. I know a little bit about work and time. I somehow found time to spend with my mother every week."

"For God's sake, Mamma, she lived right next door."

"Don't you go be takin' the Lord's name in vain, Dolly Devereaux. What we's got is between us. It don't apply to Him."

Dolly felt a sense of anger and frustration rising quickly, just as it always did when she visited her mother. But she quickly swallowed her pride to focus on the most important issue: helping April.

"Mamma, I need for you to stay calm and be very open-minded when you listen to what I have to say today. It's real hard for me to discuss this with you, because you and I have some issues of our own to settle. But this one is bigger than any of them, and more important than either of us. I need your help. Will you promise me that no matter what I say in the next fifteen minutes, you'll listen patiently with your ears open and won't fly off the handle?"

"I never. . . ."

Dolly cut her off in mid-sentence. "Mamma, that's what I'm talkin' about. Before I said two words you were already defending yourself. I need to be totally, completely honest with you, but I can't do it if you're going to jump on me or make a speech before I'm done. Will you listen carefully to me for fifteen minutes without judging me? And then will you think carefully before you respond?"

Dolly interpreted her "harrumph" as a "yes." She took a deep breath and prepared to launch into a description of her dilemma.

"Mamma, April is in trouble with the law. She was arrested two weeks ago with drugs in her purse. She and three of her friends are all in trouble. I bailed her out, and she goes on trial for possession of drugs with the intent to distribute in two weeks. She's being tried as a drug dealer, not just as a kid caught with a couple of joints."

Anne's eyes signaled that she was about to burst—and roast the skin off her daughter, Dolly.

"Take a deep breath, Mamma. You promised to listen and not judge, OK? Two days before she got arrested, she ran away with a boyfriend I told her she could never see again. His name is Anthony Correlli, but they call him 'C.B.' He's 23 and has about a half-dozen younger kids who hang around with him. He's got a rathole apartment in Myrtle Beach. April's living with him and these other kids now. I went to see her, but she wouldn't come home with me. She told me that they're her family now and that she's an adult and can do anything she wants.

"Here's the problem I need your help with: she has to go to trial for the drug possession charges in less than two weeks, but she won't cooperate. She thinks that just because she turned eighteen last week, she can handle everything herself and doesn't need any help. She needs to come home with me, get herself cleaned up, get some food into her, talk to a lawyer, and get ready for court. If she misses the trial date, or shows up looking like a hopeless druggie, the judge is going to throw the book at her, and she could be locked up for twenty years. Twenty years, Mamma. That would make her as old as I am before she gets out of jail."

Anne Doolittle, who started the encounter pumped full of adrenaline, ready to take on her daughter in a guilt-fest, sat slumped in her rocker, speechless. Dolly saw the pain in her eyes and took her frail hand in her own.

"How did this happen?" Anne said, her voice almost inaudible. "How did she get this way?"

"It's a long story, Mamma," Dolly said. "Who can say? I was smoking Kenny's dope and pregnant when I was eighteen. She's doing drugs with her boyfriend — but not pregnant, thank God — now, when she's eighteen.

"When Kenny split after April was born, you and I both raised her. She looked to him as her father, but he wasn't interested. And that stupid judge awarded him joint custody. Joint custody! Like Kenny was somehow going to give his daughter care and nurturing and guidance and education like a real parent! Good Lord! To Kenny, 'joint custody' means giving his daughter joints of marijuana whenever she wants them! He doesn't give a tenth as much attention to April as he does to either his girlfriend or his dope farming!"

Anne was tempted to jump in but restrained herself.

"So here I am, Mamma. April's eighteen now. I have no legal

control over her. She's using drugs. She's living with a group of drug users in the home of their drug dealer. She thinks, correctly, that her father has abandoned her. She thinks, incorrectly, that I want to grab her and lock her up and beat some sense into her."

A tear dripped down Dolly's cheek.

"All I want to do is separate her from the bad influences in her life and guide her back into a drug-free, happy, productive life," Dolly continued. "She's my baby, Mamma, and your granddaughter. She's been brainwashed by her gang friends that I'm the enemy. You may be the only hope to get through to her 'cause I sure can't right now. Will you help me?"

The speech left Anne sobered and introspective. "How can I get in touch with her?" she asked in a small, quiet voice.

"She's pretty paranoid, but she talked to me. Maybe you could write her a letter?"

Anne Doolittle motioned Dolly to step inside. She shuffled to a drawer and took out a sheet of note paper. Then she fumbled around the drawer, found a ballpoint pen, and began to write. "I'll call you when it's ready," Anne said.

"OK, Mamma," Dolly replied and began to walk slowly out the door. Then she turned and looked into her mother's eyes. "Thank you, Ma," she uttered with a heartfelt sincerity that had been absent for so long in their relationship.

Mothers, she thought. *You can hate 'em for years, but they'll always wanna help their babies.*

Dolly smiled. For the first time in their lives, she and her mother were finding some common ground.

20
Paradise Bound

Fantasia
Saturday morning

O h, damn!" Dolly exclaimed as she raced in the door of
Fantasia's, half an hour late again. Harriet gave her a bored
look. "Is he here yet?" Dolly asked. Shaniqua jerked her
finger in the direction of the small office in the back of the store.

"I'm terribly sorry," she said, throwing her purse into the corner and searching her desk for the report, which was now a full
week overdue. "I was, I mean, I'm just having some temporary dif-
ficulties. If you'll give me just a minute. . . ."

"What in God's green earth is going on with you, Dolly?" the
district manager asked. "Are you just another flash in the pan? Three
months ago, I put my trust in you and made you the manager of
this place. For a few weeks, things seemed headed in the right direction. Now the whole store looks like crap, and sales are going to
hell in a handbasket. And I don't have to tell you that having Melissa quit and take over the competition's store six blocks from here
is giving us a lot of grief. I know those people. They've been after
our management training manuals and inventory control software
for years. Now I find out that Melissa sold us out lock, stock, and
barrel."

"Oh, not Melissa," Dolly protested. "She wasn't dishonest. A
little ditzy, but not a thief."

Her manager rose from his chair, his hands on his hips. "Then show me the manuals and the program CDs," he said. Dolly looked at him with fear in her eyes. She looked at the back shelf for the fat blue-and-white binders. They were gone. In a panic, she ran over to the main inventory computer and searched through the software disk case. Both the program and backup disks were missing.

"You didn't even know they were gone, did you?" he said. "I came here an hour early today, after I saw the window of that other shop down the street. It bears an amazing resemblance to the mirrored upgrade display layout we were going to install here in two weeks. Do you think that's a coincidence?"

Dolly knew it was futile to protest. The crisis with April, and the time it took Dolly to cope with it, had destroyed her work routine. Her frequent absences in the last weeks had taken their toll. Melissa and Harriet were both tired of covering for her late arrivals, long lunches, and sudden departures. They figured that if the boss could leave whenever she wanted, why should they work their tails off? And it was not their job to check another employee's packages or handbag when she left for the day.

"I'm on my way to the North Charleston store," the district manager said. "There's a hard-working girl there who's been with us for fourteen months now. Best sales averages in the district. Everybody in the district sees the sales figures for every shop every week. Everybody knows this place is in a nosedive. She wants your job, and if you don't shape this place up in the next thirty days, you're out and she's in. It's that simple. This is your one and only warning, Dolly. Take it seriously."

"I will, don't worry. By the time you're back next month you'll see the place in tip-top shape. . . ." she said, but the manager was already out the door before she finished her sentence. Dolly collapsed into the office chair, crying. She had worked for twenty years to reach this level and get this job, and now all her success seemed to be slipping through her fingers. Dolly felt powerless, abandoned, betrayed. The tears rolled down her face and arms, smearing the ink of the half-finished sales report. Outside on the sales floor, her staff workers ignored her pain and gossiped at the cash register, making bets on how long it would be till Dolly got the axe.

The telephone rang. "Yeah. Just a minute," said Shaniqua as she put the caller on hold. "Dolly," she yelled, as she waved the handset in the air.

Dolly grabbed a tissue, dried her tears, and tried to choke back her emotions. "Fantasia Lingerie, Dolly speaking," she said, her voice quivering.

"Hi, Beautiful," said the voice on the other end of the line. "It's me, Ron. How 'ya been?"

"Oh, Ron, it's soooo good to hear from you," Dolly said, re-membering that it had probably been three weeks since she'd for-gotten to return his calls. "I've been. . . ." Dolly couldn't hold back her tears. "Oh, Ron, it's been awful. My life is coming apart. I hate it. I hate it!"

"Hey, Dolly baby, it's OK. I had no idea you were going through so much stuff."

"It's OK, Ron. It's not your problem. I'm sorry to dump on you."

"No problem, Dolly. Hey, I just got a reprieve from a condo showing I was stuck with. How about we slip away after you finish up at Fantasia this afternoon and spend a romantic day-and-a-half in that little B&B in Savannah I told you about?"

After the agony of pleading with April, the crow she had to swallow just to talk to her mother, and the grief at work, Dolly was ready for a little TLC and escape. She felt a wave of joy and gratitude flow over her.

"Oh, Ron, I can't think of anything in the world I'd love more right now. I'm off at 2:00 today. I'll call in sick for Captain Willie's tonight and run home to shower and get some things together. Can you pick me up at my place at 3:00?"

"You bet, Beautiful," he said. "Whatever ails you, some cham-pagne and a romantic vacation in Savannah will cure. See you at 3:00."

Ron pushed the "End" button on his cell phone, then "Autodial" and "1." "Caroline? Hi, Beautiful. Yeah it's as bad as I thought. Yeah, the Savannah bunch. The managing partners want to change the damn Phase II subdivision plan again. I gotta run down there this afternoon and meet with the financial people tonight and Saturday. Yeah, I know, and I'm really sorry. They were able to get the general contractor to meet with us on Sunday. Yes, I have to work there Sunday, too. No, it will take most of the day. I'll be back late Sunday night. Yes, I know we were supposed to meet with the caterers and confirm the menu for the rehearsal party, but you go ahead and do that. Whatever is good for you is fine with me. Aww, Honey, I know that I haven't chosen the presents for the groomsmen yet, but we still have three months before the wedding. I promise I'll be available next weekend, no matter what. Yes, promise. Cross my heart. OK. I love you, too, Sweetums. See you Sunday night. Keep the bed warm for me. You know how I get when we haven't made love for a couple of days. I'll make up for being gone as soon as I see you tomorrow night. Give Mamma and Papa Sayles a hug for me. Bye."

21
Cookin' With Gas

C.B.'s apartment
Saturday morning

April shook the sleep out of her eyes, tied her bathrobe, and shuffled into the kitchen. Wendy was pouring a bowl of corn flakes when she arrived. "'Mornin, Wendy-poo," she said. "How ya doin today?"

Wendy answered with a big yawn and a weak smile. "Pretty good, but I'm really tired. We just finished a big batch of stuff yesterday, and it took all day and night to package it. We didn't get back till 5:00 this morning, but I still haven't slept 'cause I was tweaked out all night trying to stay up and finish the packaging. Skank stayed up there at the lab. He volunteered to dig out another pit for burying the residue."

"How much junk is left over after a batch?"

"About five or six pounds of waste for every pound of meth. Mostly sodium hydroxide solution, Freon cans, and a lot of old pillow cases and bed sheets, which are used to strain out the red phosphorus. We usually try to get five pounds of d-meth per run, so the waste stuff builds up pretty quickly. Somebody's always havin' to dig holes to dump it in. As soon as C.B. started talking about needing a new dump site, Skank volunteered to start diggin'. You know how he is. He'll do anything for C.B."

"How often do you go up to the lab?" April asked Wendy as she made herself some toast.

"Usually once a week or so. It takes about three days to make a complete batch, and another day to clean the lab for the next batch.

"How long have you been doing this?" April asked.

"I dunno, a couple of months."

"How come you never told me about it? I mean just 'cause we're best friends and we tell each other *everything*."

"Oh, I don't know. C.B. says it's like a need-to-know basis or something. If he needs you, then you'll know about it. Otherwise, he keeps it secret. You, me, and Skank are the only ones in the group that know about the lab. Anyway, it's sooooooo totally awesome, April. 'Ya get to wear full protective clothing, respiratory masks, goggles, everything we saw in the science books in high school – and could never use in those stupid, pathetic little experiments."

"Full body suits? Are you serious? What for?"

"This is heavy-duty chemistry, Babycakes. We're dealin' with volatile chemicals. There's about a gazillion things that can go big time wrong: chemical fires, toxic gases, you name it. You heard about Boomer, right. Hell, he's the best meth cook on the East Coast and he had three labs blow up on him. He wouldn't even let me inside the lab until I had spent a month doing simple weighing, measuring, and mixing jobs outside the lab while he was training me. While he was doing the real cooking, I spent any free time I had sitting on my butt reading meth cookbooks."

"Cookbooks? There are cookbooks for making meth?"

"Of course there are cookbooks for making meth. And PCP, MDA, Ecstasy, LSD, and everything else. Meth is just a chemical compound. Making a batch of meth is no different than making a batch of any other chemical compound. Just trickier than some.

"Anybody with a library card can learn how to make meth. And anyone can order the books on how to set up a meth lab or cook meth from almost any big internet bookstore, no questions asked.

"All the ingredients are easy to get or manufacture. You can get the basic amino acid tablets you need at any health food store. There are no secrets in the world of chemistry. Every formula for every drug and how to make it has been published in some chemical journal somewhere – maybe even twenty, forty, sixty years ago."

"Wow! If that's true, then why doesn't everybody make their own meth?"

"It takes a pretty sophisticated lab and an experienced cook. Like I said, it's dangerous. A little too much of this or cook that too hot or too long and BOOM!"

"I get the picture," said April. "What are we gonna do today?"

"I dunno. I want a new bathing suit, and I saw a nice one at a shop at Barefoot Landing. There's gonna be a big crowd out there by 1:00. I think I'll go out there this afternoon and boost it."

"Boost it?"

"Borrow it. Make it disappear. Take the five-finger discount."

"Shoplifting?"

"Yes, shoplifting, stupid. It's fun. How do you think I keep my closet full now that Daddy's cut off my Platinum card?"

"You steal all your new stuff?"

"Sure. It's easy. I dress like I don't need to steal it, so nobody pays any attention to me."

"Aren't you afraid you'll get caught?"

"Remember when we were playin' in the pool and the rent-a-cops showed up? Remember the rush you got when we made the run for the car? Was that cool or WHAT?"

"You're insane!" April said.

Wendy stuck her tongue out at April. "Takes one to know one," Wendy replied.

"I'll pass on the Barefoot Landing excursion, thanks. C.B. said he and Skank would be back this afternoon. A friend of mine invited me to cruise Ocean Boulevard and party with him and his friends tonight. Can I borrow your cell tonight? Skank's gonna call me when he gets in."

"Sure, no problem. Later, gator."

22
Damage Control

Myrtle Beach Mall
Saturday afternoon

A w, come on," April said to her friend Suzi as they walked down the mall. "Cheer up. So he dumped you. Boyfriends are a dime a dozen. An ex-boyfriend is just an ex-boyfriend. Come along with us tonight. One of Skank's friends has a cool pickup. We're gonna cruise Ocean Boulevard and give the Spring Break kids a good show. There's gonna be a lot of guys there. If ya wanna hook up with somebody new, that's the place to do it. Then we're gonna go someplace and party."

"All right. Beats watchin' TV. Hey, what are we supposed to be lookin' for?"

"A new shower curtain. The one at the apartment is gross. I tried to clean all the black mold off it but no way. C.B. gave me a few bucks. . . ." April's statement was interrupted by the chirping of the borrowed cell phone in her purse. "Hello," April said. "Yeah, Boomer. No, this is April. How ya doin?" Goose bumps ran down her arms when she heard the tension in Boomer's voice.

"April, where's C.B.?" he said impatiently.

"I don't know, Boomer. I think he went to Charleston to get some parts for his car. What's up?"

"I've got a big fuckin' problem over here. I need to talk to him, like now."

"I don't know where he is, Boomer. Have you paged him? Called his cell phone?"

"Yeah. His phone's off and he won't answer any of his pages."

"Well, what's up? Maybe I can help."

"No, you can't. Skank's been hurt real bad. He needs to get to a hospital, fast. I need C.B. to tell me what to do. Dammit! Where the hell is he?" Boomer asked in a panic.

"What do you mean, 'hurt?' What happened? How bad is it?"

"Bad, real bad. He was digging a disposal pit for some residue. I dunno what happened. There must have been some chemicals left in the containers he threw in the pit. All I know is that he took a break from the work, lit a cigarette, and the whole pit blew up. He's hurt bad. He's got glass cuts and red phosphorus burns all over him. I gotta get him some help, but I don't know where to take him. Any hospital will be able to tell what happened and tie him to a meth lab. I gotta get him some help, quick. He's bleeding pretty bad."

"Bring him back to Myrtle Beach, Boomer. Grand Strand Regional Hospital is the closest to you. Unless you hear from me first, take him to the emergency room. I'll meet you there. Tell 'em it's red phosphorus, and then you can split. They have to treat him, and you don't have to give your name."

"I can't April. No way in hell I'm gonna risk gettin' busted again. Three times, you're out. I've gone to jail twice for production. If they bust me one more time I'm locked up for good. This is C.B.'s operation, so it's his problem. I'm just the hired help. I'll bring Skank to C.B.'s place. It's his job to get him to the hospital. I can't risk it." The phone went dead.

April yelled to Suzi, "Come on. We gotta get back to the apartment and see if C.B.'s there. Boomer's bringin' Skank to the apartment. He's hurt bad. We gotta get him to the hospital."

The two girls ran from the beach and jumped into Suzi's car. April frantically punched C.B.'s numbers into the cell phone. All she got was the maddening recorded message, "I'm sorry, but the customer you are calling is out of the service area or is not available."

The ten minutes it took to get from the mall to the apartment seemed like an eternity to April. As they pulled into the dusty parking lot, they immediately saw C.B.'s orange Charger. "Thank God!" April exclaimed as she fumbled with her keys, unlocked the front door, and burst into the living room.

C.B. Correlli's tall, skinny frame was parked in the recliner, chilling out with a beer as he checked out the centerfold model in his magazine. "Hey girls. What's up?" he said.

Suzi was in shock. April was in tears. She ran to his side, kneeled down beside his chair, and grabbed his arm with both hands. "Where were you? I tried all your numbers to get in touch with you?"

"Huh?" said C.B. "I was hangin' with some guys in Charleston. I forgot to take the cell, and I dropped the beeper in the car. What's the big deal?"

April was sobbing with tears. "It's terrible. There was an explosion at the lab, and Skank got hurt real bad. Boomer said he was all cut up and burned and was bleeding everywhere. He's bringin' him here in the truck right now."

"He's WHAT?"

"Skank's hurt. Bad. The disposal pit blew up in his face. He's all cut up and has red phosphorus burns."

"No, no. Not that," C.B. yelled. "Boomer is bringing him HERE? To this APARTMENT?"

"Yeah. We gotta get him to the hospital. Boomer won't take him there directly. He doesn't want to be seen by anyone at the hospital, 'cause he's afraid they'll link him to the meth lab and bust him."

"Oh, that's great, just fucking great. Skank screws up, and now I'm supposed to play ambulance driver? What happens if the hospital people identify ME? Every cop in Myrtle Beach and Horry County is trying to pin something on me. Forget it. You and Suzi take Skank to the hospital. Suzi's never been to the lab or met Boomer. She can't identify him or testify against us. Skank screwed up. It's his own fault for being such an idiot. He's on his own. I didn't do anything to hurt him, and I'm sure as hell not gonna have him attracting the storm troopers to this place. I'm locking up this joint and stayin' away for a few days. You keep out of the place and do what you have to do with Skank. Did Boomer say if the lab was damaged?"

"The lab? Who cares about the damn lab?" April yelled in disgust. "Skank got hurt really bad making YOUR meth so he could sell it for YOU so that YOU can make money without getting in trouble and you don't even care. He does everything for you and you don't even give a shit. Who cares about the fucking lab? What about the family, C.B.?"

C.B. threw her a dirty look and jumped out of the chair. He stuffed some clothes into a gym bag, shoved the girls out of the apartment, slammed the door shut, locked it, and jumped into the Charger. In moments, he was gone.

April was in shock. "I thought we were a family," she said to her girlfriend. In a few seconds, it dawned on April that she and Suzi were Skank's only hope. "Suzi, get in the car. Boomer won't be here for thirty minutes," she said. "I'm really scared. But I know somebody who can help."

"Who?" Suzi asked, her mascara running from the tears.

"Don't ask. Just drive," April said, pulling the car door shut. "Murrell's Inlet."

April got out Wendy's cell phone and dialed her mother's phone number. "Hi, this is Dolly. We can't come to the phone right now, so leave your name and number, and we'll get back to you. Thanks."

Right, thought April. *There hasn't been a "we" for quite a while now.* She hoped Dolly was just out doing some errands.

April dialed another number. A woman's sultry voice answered. "Fantasia Lingerie, where lace and heaven meet. This is Shaniqua. How can I help you?"

"Hey, Shaniqua. I don't know if you remember me, but I'm Dolly Devereaux's daughter. I gotta get a hold of her. Is she workin' now?"

"No, Baby, she's off this afternoon. She won't be back to work 'til Monday morning. Can I take a message for her?"

"No, thanks." April hung up abruptly and dialed another set of numbers.

"Captain Willie's. All the fresh seafood you can eat for $16.95. How can I help you?"

"Hey, this is April Devereaux, Dolly's daughter. Can I talk to her? It's an emergency."

"I'm sorry, Honey, but she called in sick around noon. She's due back tomorrow night. Wanna. . . ?" April clicked off without saying goodbye.

"There," she said to Suzi. "Turn right. Two doors down." Dolly's Honda was in the parking lot. April was tremendously relieved. "Stop here, Suzi. I'll be right back."

April jumped out of the car and ran up the stairs. She shoved the key in the lock. "Mamma," she frantically called out. "Mamma, where are you? Mamma?"

The apartment was dark and quiet. April raced through each room, looking for her mother. The apartment was empty. There was no one home. When the reality sunk in, April slowly made a full turn around, surveying the empty place in shock. She was all alone. There was no one to help. As if in slow motion, April collapsed to her knees, then slumped onto the living room floor, crying.

"You said you'd be there when I needed you, Mamma," she sobbed. "Where are you? Where the damn hell are you?"

23
Telfair Square

You .... "Oh, yes! Oh! More of that." *Could.* .... "Aaaaaaaah!
"Oh, yeah. Oh, yeah!" *Have had this.* .... "Yes, Ron, Oh! Right
there. Oh, Baby, oh, Baby! I'm gonna – slower, slower, yeah,
like that." *On the beach.* .... "That's perfect. I, I, hoo, hoo, hoo." *Last
time.* .... "Oh, Baby, oh, Baby! Ya-ya-ya-ya-ya."

With every stroke, the posts of the massive cast-iron bed frame
in the elegant nineteenth-century bedroom thumped against the
wall, telegraphing the unmistakable sounds of passion throughout the old mansion. Dolly was pink from her nose to her toes.

The sweat rolled off Ron's brow, dripping directly onto her
glistening breasts. "Oh, Ron. A little more, just a little more." *Now
you see.* .... "Oh, yes. There! There!" *What you.* .... "Oh. Oooh.
Ooooooooh." *Were missing.* .... "Aaiieeyahhhhh!"

Like Dolly, the old bed took a pounding for a few more moments before Ron gasped, shuddered, and collapsed in a panting
heap on top of her. Basking in the afterglow of passion, neither
said a word. Eight hours ago at work, Dolly had been in hell. Now,
as the gentle breeze from the garden outside their room carried in
the scent of magnolia blossoms and the sweet perfume of wisteria
and Confederate jessamine, she was in heaven.

They were still connected as Dolly slowly opened her eyes.

The first sight that greeted her was Ron's sun-bronzed face. The veins in his temples were still pulsing from his athletic performance. Dolly had been right about her guess when they were on the boat. He *was* as powerful in the sack as his boat was in the water. Dolly knew why her four orgasms were so electrifying that night. She hadn't had any in two months, and she had saved all the energy for a better day. She was aware of the silly grin on her face. Today, obviously, was the better day.

As for Ron, she wondered where his potent vitality came from. Was it, as with her, all stored up from lack of use – or was he getting plenty of high-quality practice? At that moment, she didn't much care.

She turned her head on the sweat-soaked pillow and looked back toward the door. It was as though a small tornado had hit the elegant bedroom of their suite. The complimentary bottle of champagne sat in its graceful silver cooler, unopened. Their clothes were strewn everywhere between the door and the bed. Her shoes. His coat. Her blouse. His shirt. Her bra. His undershirt. Her skirt. His shoes. Her panties. His boxers.

He was snoring. The connection had finally withered, and they were two separate people again. Dolly chuckled to herself. *Typical man,* she thought. *But that's OK. He earned it.* She tried to move her left arm, but it had been pinned in the lusty wreckage and — like Ron — had fallen asleep. The pins-and-needles that hit her when she tried to wiggle out from under Ron's body were almost more than her passion-soaked brain could handle.

Ever since they had met at White Lightnin', Dolly had wondered about the man she was dating — and, now, sleeping with. She knew that he was handsome, had a magnetic personality, and seemed to have plenty of money. *So far, so good,* she thought.

But so many things had happened so quickly that she still didn't know many of the most basic things about him. Was he married? Had he been married before? Did he have another girlfriend? Did he have kids? What did he think about the fact that she had a teenaged daughter? What would he think about the mess April was in? Was he looking for a long-term relationship? Marriage? What was his family like? Who were his friends? When would she meet them?

The moment that she had accepted his invitation to spend a romantic weekend at the bed-and-breakfast just off historic Telfair Square in Savannah, Dolly had deliberately stuffed every question she had about Ron and their relationship into the closet. Nothing — absolutely nothing — was going to rob her of this hard-earned vacation from the demands of the real world.

It took almost ten minutes for Dolly to gently extract herself from the bed without waking him. She went to her small travel bag, took out the lace-trimmed negligee she was going to surprise Ron with, and sat on the plush, chintz-covered chair in front of the vanity. She soaked in the sights and smells of the place as if there were no tomorrow. The lace curtains waved gently with the breeze. A thousand diffused shafts of light shimmered mysteriously through the Spanish moss that draped the ancient live oak trees in Telfair Square. Somewhere from the direction of the riverfront, the faint echoes of a saxophone playing the blues made their way to her window. Slowly, her heartbeat returned to normal from the ecstatic frenzy of twenty minutes earlier.

After a quick shower, Dolly brushed her long, blonde hair. She looked across the room at Ron. Groggily, he opened his eyes and searched for Dolly. He found her sitting in front of the vanity, silhouetted against the setting sun.

"You are so beautiful," he said.

Dolly smiled. "You're not half bad-looking yourself, stranger," she said. "But you've made me really hungry."

"Well, come back to bed, then," he said with a wicked grin. "I'm ready for seconds."

"There's plenty of time for that, you horny toad. I'm talking dinner. Get your tush into the shower."

Dolly changed into a blue-and-white-striped sundress that showed off her curves and accentuated her blue eyes. Ron slipped into an Italian knit shirt, white linen slacks, and a blue blazer. When they entered the small elevator, another couple was already headed down. Everyone in the little B&B had heard the noise from the suite on the second floor. The other coupled nodded a hello. The twenty-something woman next to Dolly grinned a silent "I-know-you-just-got-yours-but-mine's-coming-soon" grin at Dolly. Dolly grinned back, half embarrassed that everyone within three blocks probably heard her screaming orgasms and half boasting because someone as hot as Ron was the person giving her those screaming orgasms. The younger man gave Ron an envious glance. Ron just grinned mischievously and looked at the elevator door.

The evening that had begun with passion flowed easily into a delicious night. From the flower-covered wrought iron balcony of their restaurant on Factor's Walk, above the historic Savannah riverfront, they enjoyed a pitcher of Long Island Iced Tea, a mouth-watering meal of seafood bisque, blackened filet mignon, broiled mahi-mahi, and key lime pie. A leisurely fifteen-minute walk through the stately, moonlit streets and lushly flowered squares brought them back to their little inn, where they sipped wine in the living room with another couple before returning to their suite.

There, after finally opening their champagne, they spent the night slowly exploring the bodies that had coupled with such frenzy for the first time earlier that evening. Most of their breakfast took place in the same manner, before they showered, dressed, and went down for a leisurely champagne brunch in the dining room. They exchanged knowing glances and chitchat with the other guests, all of whom were also on romantic getaways.

The afternoon ride back to Myrtle Beach was spent exchanging warm glances and few words. Both Ron and Dolly were still basking in the glow of the moment. As they pulled into the SeaVue Apartments parking lot, Dolly leaned over and kissed Ron gently on the lips. "Will I hear from you soon?"

"As soon as I possibly can, Beautiful. Thank you for such a wonderful weekend," he said.

Dolly took a deep breath and headed up the stairs to her second-story apartment. As soon as she reached the door, she sensed that something was terribly wrong. Her heart fell to her feet as she read the message scrawled on the apartment door in April's Electric Pistachio lipstick: "Liar! Where were you when I needed you?"

24
Vital Signs

Grand Strand Regional Hospital

April had run out of tears. Other than the beeping of the vital sign monitors, Skank's room was quiet. "They've got him pretty heavily doped up," she told Wendy as they sat by the side of his bed. "I've been trying to get them to tell me more about his condition, but they won't say much."

"He looks like a mummy from an old movie. Is he burned a lot?" asked Wendy.

"I really don't know. They say he's in stable condition."

"What does that mean?"

"It means he's probably not going to get worse, but that doesn't mean anything else. He could be pretty bad. Hey, where's Suzi? Didn't she bring him here with you last night?"

"Yeah, but she stayed home today. She had a rough night. She's been having boy problems and then all this happened with Skank. When we left the hospital last night, she was stressing pretty hard so she went and got wasted 'til early this morning with some kids she met at a rave a few weeks ago. Remind me to call her later 'cause she wants to know how Skank's doing."

Just then, a nurse walked in and checked Skank's chart. She smiled at the girls. "How are you two doing?" she asked sympathetically.

"OK," April said. "But can you tell me anything about our friend?"

"Nothing new, I'm afraid. There's been no change for the last eight hours. Dr. Thomas talked to you, right?"

"The E.R. doctor?"

"No, the senior resident. He'll be here in a few minutes. Maybe he can tell you more."

Ten minutes later, a short, stocky physician with a goatee appeared. "He looks like that old psychiatrist, Sigmund Freud, doesn't he?" Wendy whispered to April.

"Who's Sigmund Freud?" April asked.

"Hello, uh, Doctor. . . ." Wendy stammered.

"Thomas. Dr. Thomas. And you are. . . ?"

"Delia," Wendy quickly answered before April got a chance to open her mouth. April gave Wendy a puzzled look, but went along with her.

"Oh, and I'm Anita," April said. "How's he doing, doctor?"

"Well, it looks like he was involved in some dangerous work. To tell you the truth, he's lucky to be alive. He sustained a lot of lacerations from flying glass and metal. What I'm worried about, though, are the chemical burns and the damage to his lungs. Do you two have any idea what he was doing when the explosion occurred?"

Both girls shook their heads.

"Well, he has a combination of injuries that suggest he might have been involved in the manufacture of illegal drugs. Do you know what he did for a living?"

"Uh, no, he's just a guy we met at a party," said Wendy.

"Well, he has inhaled toxic smoke from a red phosphorus chemical fire. When this smoke is inhaled, the acid burns the victim's airways and lungs. That's what happened to your friend here. We're worried about him developing chemical pneumonia. Do you know his real name?"

"No, the kids just call him 'Skank.'"

"Any idea if he has family?"

"No idea. Like we said, we just happened to meet him at a party."

"OK, then," the doctor said. "There's one other person who needs to talk to you. He'll be here in a minute."

As soon as the doctor left the room, Wendy jerked her head toward the door. "Let's get outta here, April. I know the part that's comin'."

April was deep in thought, trying to figure out if there was anything she could do to help Skank. "Huh?" she said.

Wendy grabbed her arm and pulled her through the door. "Move it, Ap — er, Anita, NOW!"

"What the. . . ?" April persisted.

"Move your butt, girl. Follow me, fast." Just as they ducked into the elevator, April looked back toward Skank's room. The doctor had his hand on the doorknob, ready to enter. A Horry County sheriff's deputy was right behind him.

"God, that was close, *Delia*. What's with the names?" April said, panting for breath.

"Better safe than sorry. I didn't think we should tell the doctor our real names, in case he was talking to the cops, which — as you clearly saw — he was. That's one thing you gotta learn, April. You always gotta be on the lookout and you gotta always make sure that you're covering your ass, 'cause you never know. Something as simple as telling a doctor your name could end up being the reason you get busted later."

"Oh, did C.B. tell you that?" April asked in disgust as they stepped into the hospital parking lot.

"Yeah, April, he did. Look, I know he's an asshole for the way he acted about the whole Skank thing, but you gotta admit, when it comes to playing the game, he wins every time. He's the biggest dealer in Myrtle Beach, but even the cops can't touch him. That takes skill, April, and brains. He's really smart, ya know?"

"Yeah, a smart *asshole*."

"Have you heard from him?" asked Wendy.

"C.B.? Like I should care if I ever hear from C.B. again in my whole life?" April spat out the words as though they were pieces of rotten meat. "Our Great Father-Protector-God? Mr. 'We – are – a – family – and – we – take – care – of – each – other?' The guy who refused to take his closest friend to the hospital? The great humanitarian who was more interested in the condition of his fuckin' dope lab than he was about whether Skank was gonna live or die? Is that the C.B. you're talkin' about, Wendy-poo?"

"Don't 'Wendy-poo' me, April. I'm not taking sides, but C.B.'s gotta stay out of jail if we're gonna have anybody we can count on. He's kept us out of a lot of trouble. We get our stuff free if we deal a little. And we have a place to eat and sleep and say what we want without getting hassled. That's more than I can say about my parents. And I bet that's more than you can say about your mother. Where was she when you needed her?"

"Leave my mother out of this. This is about C.B. and how he treated Skank."

"OK, OK, girl. Calm down. I'm not the enemy, remember?"

The two girls got into Wendy's BMW. "Where are we gonna go now?" asked April. "C.B. said not to go back to the apartment. I'm down to twelve bucks. How about you?"

"I've got twenty, but I need to get some gas or we won't be goin' anywhere."

"Where are we gonna crash tonight?"

"First, we get outta here. I don't need any chats with the police. I think I know where we can chill for a few days."

"Where?" said April.

"I've got a dancer friend named Candy. She's got her own place, and she just threw out her last boyfriend. She may let us hole up there for a few days 'til we can come up with another plan.

"Let's get some gas and then go see Candy. She's a pretty cool chick, and she makes serious bucks dancing. I bet she can help us out for a few days 'til things cool down with C.B."

"C.B. can go screw himself."

"He doesn't have to, Honey."

"You should know. You're still one of his harem, aren't you?"

"Since when did you start kicking him out of bed, April?"

"Doesn't it bother you that he screws every chick he meets?"

"Nah," she replied. "As long as I'm gettin' mine on a regular basis, I don't care who gets the table scraps."

"That's not enough for me anymore. I want a real boyfriend. Somebody who'll treat me good and won't screw every girl that catches his eye. I just want a really nice guy. Not somebody who pretends to be nice just so I'll go down on him later or something."

"Good luck, chickie-poo. But I think the last one of them died the day before you were born."

25
Issues and Answers

SeaVue Apartments
Sunday night

An hour after she first saw it, Dolly was still sitting on the floor of her apartment, staring at the message on the door. *If April feels the pain as much as I do right now,* Dolly thought, *I know why she takes drugs.* Dolly's melancholy numbness extended far beyond her mind to her soul. She peered into the depths of her heart and listened for the response. It came only slowly.

For years, Dolly had harbored a deep anger against her mother. Deeds and denials from two decades ago had festered and boiled, only to be stuffed below the surface of her consciousness. Over the years, she thought she had toughened herself against the pain, but pain buried is still pain felt — only at a deeper level.

The realities her daughter faced were now as clear as spring water. April had suffered the agonizing emotional loss of her father, who had ultimately chosen a girlfriend's companionship over his own daughter. Being thrown out of her father's house was the ultimate rejection. How could a complete stranger steal her father's love? How could he abandon the flesh of his flesh for a woman he'd known for only a few months?

April was convinced that her mother had failed her in her hour of need. April had really needed Dolly, and, for whatever reason, Dolly hadn't been there. In retaliation, April had cut herself off from her mother — exactly as Dolly had done with her own mother, Anne, twenty years earlier.

Dolly knew she had only one choice, painful though it might be. She rummaged through her handbag and found the cell phone. After punching the numbers into the keypad, she waited and waited for the phone to be answered. She reached no one. Not even an answering machine. *The hell with it,* she thought, grabbed her keys, locked the door, and strode to the Honda.

The two-and-a-half hour drive down the dusty tobacco and cotton roads gave Dolly plenty of time to collect her thoughts. Nevertheless, none of them brought her any comfort. She had pondered the dilemma for years. *Pondered the dilemma?* It was far more than that. She had condemned her mother to burn in hell a thousand times for what she had — or hadn't — done.

Thirteen. She'd been thirteen that spring and never been kissed. Well, Harry Lucas had kissed her while they were in the back seat of the school bus one day, but that hardly counted. Dolly later found out that three other boys had bet him a quarter apiece that he didn't have the guts to do it — and grab her boobs at the same time.

Her damn boobs. Dolly cursed the assets that helped her earn so many good tips during the eight months she danced on stage after Kenny walked out on her. All the other dancers wanted to know if they were real. Dolly was disgusted. If only they knew how gladly Dolly would have traded hers for a smaller set that attracted less attention from boys — and men. But the strip clubs put no emphasis on small boobs.

But men weren't the issue, Dolly thought as she passed a slow-moving tractor, plodding along the country road with a load of manure in tow. The issue was Anne. Always Anne. Only Anne.

She was thirteen. Anne and Tommy, her boyfriend at the time, had gone out together one Friday night. Dolly knew from experience what to expect from Tommy when he returned. Dolly had tried to get permission to sleep over at her Aunt Clara's house to avoid trouble. Unfortunately, her aunt was out of town, and her refuge wasn't available.

Despite the summer heat, Dolly dressed in extra layers of

clothes. Bra. Undershirt. Buttoned, long-sleeved blouse. Zippered jacket. Panties. Tight-fitting jeans. Leather belt with a big, strong buckle. And to make things even more difficult, she inserted a tampon and strapped on a sanitary napkin stained with ketchup. Her period wasn't even close, but she thought the sight of it might be another deterrent.

Then she waited, sweating in the heat, for the inevitable. By 2:00 A.M., when Anne and Tommy came home, she was drenched in sweat from the combination of Darlington's summer heat and her extra layers of body armor. She waited, trembling, hoping that Tommy was drunk enough to simply have sex with Anne and pass out.

He wasn't. Ten minutes after the thumping of the bed stopped in her mother's room, Dolly's bedroom door opened. There, silhouetted against the light from the hallway, was Tommy, staggering into the room, naked and aroused, a whiskey bottle in one hand.

Anne was nowhere to be seen. Dolly screamed out, "Mamma, Mamma, help!" but Tommy told her she'd better be quiet or he'd really give her something to scream about. Dolly finally got up the courage one day to tell her mother what was going on, but when she did, her mother slapped her across the face.

"You little bitch!" Anne had screamed at her. "Don't you ever tell those horrible lies again about him. It won't bring your father back, Dolly. He's gone and there's not a damn thing you or your lies can do about it." Dolly never tried to tell her about the incidents again.

Two and a half hours after the drive started in Myrtle Beach, it ended in Darlington. Her stepfather's old Ford station wagon was in the driveway. There was hope.

Dolly walked through the gate of the picket fence, past the sun-baked flower garden, and up to the screen door. She knocked. No answer. This wasn't unusual. Henry wasn't in good health and couldn't sprint to the door, even if he wanted to, and Anne was often tending their garden in back or doing other chores.

She rang again. The curtains at the door rustled, and Anne opened the door. "I was expecting you," she said. Dolly was puzzled. She had never thought for a moment that her mother was psychic because if she had been, she would have sensed Dolly's pain.

Anne walked slowly to the back of the house. Dolly followed. Anne took her place at the sink and calmly began washing the lunch dishes. Evidently she expected Dolly to start the conversation, because she didn't.

"Hello, Mamma. I was hopin' that you. . . ."

Anne Doolittle raised her hand, stopping Dolly's speech just as it started. Dolly stood at the steel edge of the worn Formica kitchen table, her mouth open and frozen in mid-sentence, when she heard her mother say, "April was here."

"How'd she get here?"

"Don't know. Somebody dropped her off."

"And?"

"We talked. All afternoon. All night," Anne said in an emotionless voice.

"About what?" Dolly asked in a whisper.

"Me. You. Her. Her father. My first husband. High school. Her friends. Sex. Her boyfriend, C.B. Drugs. Heaven. Sin. God. It was quite a day," Anne said simply.

Dolly was awestruck by the implications. April had shared more in one afternoon with her grandmother than she had in the last five years with her. It made her feel sick to her stomach. And it only increased her anger with her mother. How could Anne get April to open up when she couldn't?

"You're mad about the men I had around me back then, aren't you?"

Dolly was shocked. She had never been able to bring the subject up with her mother — and here Anne was, talking about it without even being prompted.

"I didn't care about the men, Mamma. It was what they did."

"To me or you?"

The concept hit Dolly like a hammer blow. She had never considered anything but her own experiences, her own shame. Her mother's emotions never entered her thoughts.

"I . . . I . . . ." she stammered.

"It's OK, Dolly. I have enough guilt to soak up all the hurt for both of us. You blame me for what they did to you, don't you?"

Dolly was stunned again. Here her mother was, freely discussing all the terrors Dolly had experienced as a girl — and didn't dare speak about.

"I was just a kid, Mamma. How could you let them do those things? I was a virgin. In church the pastor told us we had to stay virgins 'til we married and the Lord sanctified our union. Those men of yours took that away from me. I was only thirteen, Mamma. I was only thirteen," Dolly cried, choking back her tears.

Anne Doolittle turned from the sink and calmly continued to dry the dishes with a towel. Without emotion, she cleaned the plates and carefully put them in the rack.

"I was still young, Dolly, with six mouths to feed. I had to take care of you and five others. The ten-dollar bills those men left behind paid for food for three days if I stretched it right. Sometimes it didn't last. Those were the days we went hungry. Darlington wasn't a big place back then, Dolly. Just a dirt track and some farmers. I thought I was lucky when the race mechanics came around. One night I got $15, and we had a chicken for dinner that week. You probably don't remember. I sure did. I was proud of myself that week."

Dolly's mind raged with confusion and disbelief.

"I knew what was happening to you, Dolly, but I also knew I couldn't do anything. You had it the worst. You had developed physically, and your sisters hadn't yet. You took all the heat off your two younger sisters. I knew the boys would be beaten up or hurt even worse if they knew, because they would have fought with the men. That's why I let them go off wherever they wanted so many nights. They never knew, Dolly. I swear they never knew."

Dolly collapsed at her mother's feet, crying. Anne Doolittle gently ran her fingers through Dolly's hair, trying as best she could to comfort her sobbing, inconsolable daughter.

"There's no better explanation, Dolly. I just did what I had to do to get us all through after your father's death. That's it. Forgive me or don't, but that's the whole story."

"You let them rape me!" Dolly raged. "You let those animals rape me! How can you look at me and tell me all this and act like you don't even care?"

"Of course I care, Dolly. This isn't easy for me, either."

"Good! I want it to be hard. I want it to hurt. I want it to hurt so bad that you feel maybe an ounce of what I felt all those years. I want it to hurt you for twenty years like it's hurt me."

"Goddammit, Dolly! It has hurt me for twenty years! It's hurt me every single day for twenty years! I was wrong. I should've protected my baby. I should've helped you. I should've listened to you. I didn't and I'm sorry, but I can't change the past, Dolly. What do you want me to do? I was a kid, too. I was a stupid kid trying to raise six other kids and I was scared. I was lonely. I was everything I never felt when I was with your father. I missed him so much, Dolly. So much." Anne was now sobbing on the kitchen floor next to Dolly.

"I tried to pretend that all those men were him. Every time they touched me, I tried to close my eyes and pretend that they were your daddy. I denied everything, Dolly. All of it. What they did to me, what they did to you, I denied it all. It was easier for me to live that way. Otherwise, I would have broken down. It's the only thing that kept me goin' and kept me able to raise my kids.

"Every time I took the money or the food or the presents that those men gave me, I felt horrible and cheap. But when I was able to turn around and use them to feed my children, I could justify it to myself and deny that I was letting awful things go on in my home. I hated myself for years for letting those things happen, but I can't live my life like that anymore. I can't hate myself anymore. I'm trying to let go of this hate, and I want you to try with me."

"It's not that easy, Mamma. I denied it, too. I pushed it way down deep inside me when I became a mother. I had to raise April and deal with Kenny, and there was no room in my life for this, so I buried it. But now it's come back up, Mamma, and I can't just let it go. I have to hurt. I have to hate you. I have to get all this out and really let myself feel it before I can let it go, 'cause if I don't, I'm only hiding from it like I did all these years. I don't wanna hide anymore, Mamma. I don't wanna hide. I don't wanna...."

Dolly's sobs grew so heavy that she couldn't speak. The two women held each other on the kitchen floor, sobbing uncontrollably for ten minutes.

When Anne could finally speak, she said, "You hate me, and I have to live with that. It hurts me so bad, Baby, but I understand. I just have to live with it."

"I don't hate you, Mamma. I hate what you let happen to me. I hate those things. I hate those men. I hate the fact that you didn't try to stop it. But I don't hate you. I'm not going to let those men make me hate my own Mamma. I'm not going to let them win. If I hate you, I'm letting them win. I'm letting all the bad things win, and I don't wanna do that. I love you, Mamma. I do. I know you tried the best you could. I know you were scared and confused and you had your back up against the wall and you had to do everything and go through everything all alone. But see, Mamma, I did, too. I was alone and scared, too. We could have gotten through everything if we'd just been scared together instead of all alone. I needed you, Mamma, and you weren't there. And now I realize that you needed me, too."

"I still do, Baby. I need you. I need you to help me get rid of these demons that I have inside. I need to hear you tell me you love me so that I can love myself, too. I need to have a loving, honest relationship with you so that I can live my life in peace."

"I need it too, Mamma. I need it, too." Dolly whispered as she clutched her mother.

"Dolly, Honey, when I talked to April yesterday, I realized so many things. I got jealous of you because you still have a chance to do what I never could. I have to live my life knowing that I didn't help you when you needed me most. I have to wake up every day knowing that I had a chance to save you from something evil, but I didn't. April's in a lot of trouble, Honey. A lot. But you can still help her. Don't give up on her, 'cause if you do, you'll live the rest of your life in the kind of regret that I've had. I don't want that for you."

"I don't either, Mamma. Where is she now?" Dolly asked, still gasping through the tears.

"I don't know, Honey. Her boyfriend threw her out, but she didn't say where she was living. I tried to get here to stay here with me, but she said she had one last friend who could help her."

26
Runway Lights

Nice place, Candy," April said as she toured the condo with
Wendy. *Anything would be nice compared with C.B.'s place,*
she thought. The color-coordinated apartment was filled
with curtains, chairs, and rugs decorated in soft grays, peach, pink,
and slate blue. Silk flower arrangements and framed prints comple-
mented the decor. Everything looked new and well cared for —
just like Candy herself, who was tall, blonde, and very well en-
dowed. The coral-colored tube top left no doubt of that.

"Thanks. What's your name again, Honey?"

"April. April Devereaux."

"Sounds like a stage name."

"Nah, it's my real one," April said. "Is 'Candy' your real name
or a stage name? Or am I supposed to ask that?" April asked with a
perplexed look on her face.

"I dance as 'Candy.' My friends call me Ruth. I was named
after my grandmother. You guys want a Coke or something?"

"No, thanks," they said in unison.

"So, to what do I owe the honor?" Candy asked, motioning
the two teenagers to sit down.

"Well. . . ." Wendy really didn't know where to start. "April
just turned eighteen. She's thinkin' about dancin'. I told her you

could tell her what she needs to know. And, well, I'm sorry to ask, but we sorta need a place to crash for a few days."

"Well, one thing at a time. Just eighteen, huh? Don't you think that's a little early for stripping? That's not too young for the clubs and the guys — they like 'em young — but what about for you? It's a tough life. Not a job for everybody."

"Well, uh, I sorta a need a job and a place to stay. My boyfriend's a jerk and my father's girlfriend won't let me live with him."

"Sounds like me when I was eighteen," Candy said. "Except my father was the jerk and my boyfriend dumped me." The three women laughed in unison. The ice was broken.

"How long have you been dancing?" April asked.

"Two years, off and on, mostly on."

"What does it take to make a lot of money as a dancer?"

"Talent, good physical condition, the right attitude, and assets," Candy said. "What do you think?" she said, nodding in the direction of her breasts.

April blushed. "What do you mean?" she asked.

"Of my assets. Real or silicone?"

"Oh, I'm sure they're real," April replied.

Candy stood, slipped off the tube top and slowly turned around. "$10,000. Best boob doc in L.A. Office right on Rodeo Drive. The same one who did Pamela's and Demi's."

"Wow!" April said.

"How about yours, April? You have a nice set. Good genes or good doctor?"

"They, uh, I, uh, they're mine," said April. "Runs in the family."

"Your mother have big ones, too?"

"Yeah. Grandma, too."

"Ever danced before?" Candy asked.

"No, never," April replied.

"You got rhythm?"

"Huh?"

"Can you feel the music, go with the flow?"

"Oh yeah, that, for sure."

"Well, it's a start. I can loan you some dance training tapes, but if a girl can't feel the music, and can't get off dancing for herself, then she'll never make it work."

"I thought you were supposed to dance for the guys."

"You do, but sometimes the place is almost empty, and sometimes it's full of jerks, and if you can't have fun dancing for yourself, then you'll never last."

"Are you sure you don't want something?" she asked the girls. "I'm going to have a Phillips Head."

"A what?"

"Phillips Head Screwdriver. You know, vodka, orange juice, and pineapple." Candy took a glass to the refrigerator and poured the two juices over several ice cubes. From a liquor cart she poured in a heavy splash of vodka.

"Cheers," she said. "I'm really a little shy at heart, and even though I've been showing it all for two years, it still doesn't come naturally. I was raised a Baptist. I need a little liquid license to get naked and let go. A drink before I go onstage helps."

"Do you make a lot of money?"

"April!" Wendy jumped in. "That's none of your business."

"It's OK, Wendy. She's here to learn about the business. Yeah, Honey, you can make pretty good bucks on a good night. It depends on the crowd, the competition, and the kind of dances you do."

"What do you mean?"

"On a good night, there's plenty of visiting golfers and local regulars — they tip the best — not too many girls, and lots of guys who want premium dances."

"Premium dances?"

"You've never even been inside a club, have you?" Candy said with a laugh.

"Well, no. I only turned eighteen a couple weeks ago. I couldn't go in."

"Of course. Well, here's how you make your money. First is the stage dance. That's the one you do on the raised stage with all the spotlights and special effects. Sometimes you're alone on stage; sometimes there's other girls. Depends on how full the club is and what time of year it is."

"When's the real busy season?"

"Spring and fall, when the golfers are here in full force. A lot of 'em just use golf as an excuse to get away from their wives, do all that male bonding crap, drink like fish, and get laid."

"What about the dancing itself. Do you make it up new each time, or how does it work?"

"No, you do the dance in three sets. Each set is three or four minutes long. The first one is a warm-up. You dance with your whole costume on. The second set, you take off the bottom of the outfit, leaving only your g-string. Most of the girls flash 'em a little boob in the second set, too. The third set, you take off your top and shake your tits."

"How do you get and collect the tips?"

"While you're dancing, you look for eye contact with the guys closest to the stage. The guys that give you eye contact want to see you up close. Or if all the chairs by the stage are taken, and they want to see you up close, they'll walk over to the stage and bring your tip. You go over to them, say hello, ask their names, shake your booty under their noses, tease 'em a little, and then lift up your garter so they can put the tip under it."

"How much do you get?"

"A dollar usually, five if you're lucky."

"Sounds like you'd have to dance all night to make a hundred dollars."

"The stage isn't where the money is, Sweetie. You make your real money doing table dances, couch dances, and working in the V.I.P. rooms when you're not on stage."

"Huh?"

"The table dances are the same as you'd do onstage, but you do it at the guy's table. You stick your assets right in his face and shake it. Ten bucks for three or four minutes. No touching — in a good club, at least. The house gets $3, you keep $7."

"The club takes part of your tips?"

"How do you think the club owners pay for those private jets, girl?"

"What's a couch dance?"

"You take the guy into a private room filled with couches. No door, and a bouncer standing outside, keepin' an eye on things. You dance on his lap and he gropes you for three or four minutes. He pays $25, the house gets $5, and you get $20."

"He gropes you? You mean the guy can actually touch you?"

"Yeah. Tits and ass, but no pussy. And the g-string stays on."

"That's pretty gross."

"Yeah, sure is. But you make $20 in four minutes and still go home a virgin," Candy said with a laugh. "Same as working at a fast food place, but better money." She poured herself another drink.

"What was the other one?"

"The V.I.P. Room. Upstairs. Private rooms with doors, TV, premium sound systems, and personal waitresses to bring the guy drinks. I've seen guys who drop $500 in an hour just for champagne at $250 a bottle. Some guys just like to flash their cash. They can basically have anything they're willing to pay for and the girl is willing to provide."

"How much does the girl make?"

"The V.I.P. rooms cost the guy whatever you agree on. Usually $250 to $300 an hour. The fewer the dancers, the more they can charge. The house gets $50 per room use. You get the rest."

"What does the guy get for his $250 or $300 an hour?"

"That's up to you, babe. But for $250 an hour, the guy's not gonna settle for a kiss or a blow job. He's looking for a real good screw, and for that kind of money, most of the girls will give him anything his little heart desires. If you work the V.I.P. rooms, you can make $800 to $1,000 or more in a night."

"You mean have real sex with the guy, right there?" April said, her eyes wide open. "You really screw guys up there?"

"I wouldn't, of course, but for that kind of money, a lot of the girls are happy to."

"Do you have to do the V.I.P. stuff?" April asked.

"No, you don't have to do anything you don't want to do," Candy said. "On a good night, a girl can make anywhere from $150 to $300 without the V.I.P. rooms."

"That's a relief."

"You gotta tip off the staff, too, but it's not too bad."

"Tip off?"

"Yeah. The most important thing besides the house — they take their cut of the tips right off the top — is the DJ. He's your producer, your promoter. He's the one who decides what music you dance to, what special effects to use, what color lights. He can make you or break you. He gets 10 percent of your tips. Be *real* nice to the DJ — and *never* piss him off. You gotta tip the servers, too, every time they bring you anything. They gotta make a living, too, and they only get $3.35 an hour and tips."

"How much an hour do the dancers earn?"

"Nothin'. Dancers work strictly for tips. Hey, look, it's 4:00. I have to be onstage at 5:00, and it takes me a half hour to do my makeup and get my costume on. If you wanna dance at Fast Fannie's, where I work, I can take you there now. They audition every day from 3:00 to 7:00."

April looked at Wendy. "What do you think, Wendy-poo?"

"It's your call, April."

"If I go, will you come to the audition with me?

"Sure."

"OK, then. I'll go. Thanks, Candy. If you think I can do it, I'll try it. And let's face it, I need the money."

"That's what it's all about, girl," Candy said as she took the last sip of her drink. "That's what it's all about. Get your stuff ready. We'll leave in five minutes."

27
Best–seller List

Monday morning, 8:01 A.M.
Myrtle Beach Police Department

C apt. Steve Hunt's brown eyes turned cold and sharp as he stared down the officer who walked in the door of the squad room a minute after roll call started. "Good morning, Detective Langston. I'm delighted that you could take the time out of your busy morning and join us here. Is the coffee to your satisfaction?" Hunt's withering gaze made it clear that he expected prompt attendance and tight discipline from all of his staff.

The officer nodded curtly, acknowledging the rebuke. "Sorry, sir. It won't happen again."

"We are in full agreement, Detective Langston, or Wal-Mart will have a new applicant as a night security guard. Now that our menu is full, here's the daily specials."

A ripple of muffled chuckles passed through the group of nine men. At one time or another, all of them had experienced Hunt's displeasure, but everyone knew that Steve Hunt was The Man. His arrest record was legendary, his authority was unquestioned, and his orders obeyed instantly.

"Item one. There was an ad in one of the weekly throw-aways that looks like a porn film operator is recruiting future Ginger Lynns and Long Dong Silvers in the Grand Strand. We need a couple of young female undercover agents to apply for the jobs with fake IDs to see if they're recruiting underage kids. Castillo and Rollins, you run the sting. Call S.L.E.D. and see if they have a couple of young female officers who fit the bill and want to volunteer. The job is a low-risk operation and should only last a couple days to a week at most."

With a big smirk on his face, Detective Rollins asked, "Do we get to do the nasty if we get hired?"

"Ain't no girl ever gonna do you, on or off the screen," said his burly, older partner. The rest of the squad broke out into guffaws and good-natured laughter.

"Cut the chatter. We've got work to do. Item two. A casualty showed up at Grand Strand Regional with red phosphorus burns and a lot of lacerations two days ago. Looks like a meth lab blew up somewhere around here. We had no fire reports from the Forest Service, so there probably wasn't a big fire. The guy's street name is Skank. That's about all we could find out about him. He's burned bad, in a coma, and the girls who brought him in split before we could question them.

"One of the girls who brought him in matches the description of an eighteen-year-old small-time user by the name of April Devereaux. She told the hospital that her name was Anita. We busted her and some of her friends a few weeks ago. We think they are tied to a dealer and possible manufacturer named John Anthony Correlli. Street name's 'C.B.,' or 'Cue Ball.' He's bad news from California, with ties to the Hell's Angels and their meth labs."

"A skinny Skinhead dude?" asked Detective Langston. "Mid-twenties. About 6', 165 pounds, tattoos, Doc Martens? Yeah, Skank is a flunkie of his," he commented. "Correlli's on our crystal meth and Ecstasy best-seller list."

"Well, Detective Langston, you *are* good for something, after all," Hunt said. The officers laughed. They knew that Langston had been forgiven.

"Our job is to find the lab — or labs. May be more than one. As you've reported in the last weeks, there seems to be a lot more crank and Ecstasy on the streets lately. Correlli spends too much time in town to be doin' the cooking by himself, so there's probably one or two people helping him make the stuff. He lives up by Seaboard Avenue, but nobody's been at his house since the explosion. His Skinhead dealer-friends seem to have scattered. Anybody heard anything new on the street?"

The officers shook their heads. "OK, then. I'll pass out the pictures and info sheets we have for Correlli and the kids who were busted for possession and intent to distribute. See what you can find out about them. We're not looking to hassle the kids who got busted. They're probably more victims than players. We just want to get them off the street and into some rehab program. It's Correlli and his cooks that we want to put out of business before they hook any more kids. OK. Hit the streets."

Dressed in a golf shirt, slacks, and loafers, Steve Hunt left the building and jumped into his Mustang convertible. He wondered if Dolly had heard anything new about April. He was not happy to know that Dolly's daughter was in such a bad position, but at least it gave him the opportunity to see her again.

As he drove past the T-shirt shops, fast food restaurants and mini-golf parks that lined the road, he remembered his senior prom. *Their* prom. It was the Myrtle Beach Class of 1981. Steve was eighteen. Dolly was almost seventeen. They were in love, but there was something missing; something that made Steve wonder about their future.

Dolly was a bubbly delight to be with. Friendly, cheerful — but often moody. Someplace deep, he sensed even then, there was a place inside her where she hurt a lot. But she never wanted to talk about it. Dolly, way back then anyway, was looking for the fast track to fun.

In her deep-blue sheath prom dress, she had looked like an angel. He hair was up in a bouffant; her eyes sparkled like light-blue diamonds. She gasped when she saw the cymbidium orchid corsage he had bought for her. Steve almost stuck her with the pin as he tried to pin it on. He blushed when his hand grazed her breast as he faltered with the corsage. She only giggled and bent over just a bit so that he could get a glimpse of the present she had in mind for him later that night.

The prom was held in the ballroom on the top floor of the old

Lafayette Hotel, now long gone. Back then, it was a beautiful pink Art Deco building south of the Pavilion near the Second Avenue Pier. Steve and Dolly danced all night to the beach music of The Catalinas, the pulsing disco sounds of Donna Summer and The Bee Gees, the energizing beat of rockers like Eric Clapton, and the sensual ballads of Linda Ronstadt.

They relished every moment spent in each others' arms, but there was always a difference in intensity between them. He liked beach music and Juice Newton; she liked high-energy tracks from Foreigner, Meat Loaf, and Clapton. After the last dance, they went for a long, moonlit walk on the Second Street Pier, then kicked their shoes off and walked down to the beach. Walking turned to kissing, kissing to caressing, and under the pier, his tux and her sheath quickly became part of a passionate blur of flying clothes. There, on the beach, was the first — and last — time they ever made love.

Neither of them had ever talked about that night since. It was as if they both sensed that the match they both wanted so badly and enjoyed so much was not meant to be.

That summer they found themselves involved in new lives. Steve was working two jobs, cramming money away for college. Dolly had hooked up with Kenny Devereaux and was exploring the delights of three-letter chemical toys with names like LSD, PCP, and THC.

Yet as ill-suited as the match had seemed so many years earlier, Steve had never forgotten Dolly's deeply rooted kindness, empathy, compassion — and passion. The fact that fate had thrown them together again in this bizarre, drug-linked fashion had its own irony. Nevertheless, he remembered the old Juice Newton hit, "You Make Me Want To Make You Mine" and thought to himself, *Yeah, she still does.*

Steve pulled into the parking lot in front of Fantasia and strode in. Dolly was ringing up a sale and didn't see him come in. The other girls did, however, and they whispered to her, "Psst. Dolly. It's Steve."

Dolly's face lit up as soon as she saw him. "Shaniqua, can you finish up here for me?" she asked.

"Sure, Baby," she said. Everybody in the shop could see that Dolly was still sweet for Steve.

"Come on back here," Dolly said to her good friend as she pointed to the small office. "You're lookin' great, Steve. Pardon the mess. It's been a madhouse here. I'm fighting to keep my job."

"I thought you just got a promotion a few months ago," Steve said, puzzled.

"That was before April's crash-and-burn, I'm afraid," she replied. "That took so much time that I really let my work go — and they're gonna can me if I can't clean up my act and get this place squared away soon. But enough of my problems. Any news about April?"

"Not right now. Correlli has gone underground for the last week. One of his flunkies was badly burned in a drug lab explosion somewhere around here. A girl matching April's description and another girl brought the guy — what was left of him — to the hospital two days ago. Have you heard from April lately?"

Dolly felt like a hammer blow had hit her chest. "Yes, I have, Steve." She sat down and recounted the scrawled note on the door and her conversation with Anne the next day.

"I can only imagine how tough that must be for you, Dolly," Steve said, putting his arm around her. Dolly shivered with fear but welcomed his physical closeness. "But we really need to talk with April. She — or the other girl she was with — may know something about this drug lab. It's probably Correlli's operation, and it's pumping a lot of new drugs into the streets."

Steve helped Dolly to her feet, then embraced her with a long, firm hug. "Let me know if you hear anything, OK? And anytime you need me or just want to talk, I'm always available. Always," he said, and kissed her on the cheek.

Dolly took a long look into his eyes, leaned forward, and kissed him square on the lips. "You were always my idol, Steve. Nothing about that has ever changed."

28
Failing Grade

Fast Fannie's Gentlemens' Club
North Myrtle Beach

April, this is Kiki Hatchet, the house mother here. Kiki, this is April, and her friend, Wendy. April wants to dance here. Wendy's just here to lend a little immoral support," Candy said, grinning. "Kiki will get you ready for the audition, April. I gotta go dress for success. See ya."

"Thanks, Candy," April said. Her fingers tingled with excitement. She had never been inside a strip club before, never mind take her clothes off in front of strangers.

April looked around the club. To put it mildly, it was huge. The dance floor alone was the size of a small parking lot. Three mini-stages flanked the main dance floor, each with its own lighting system and brass dancing pole. With the exception of the long, wooden bar area and the illuminated disco dance floor, everything was painted black and trimmed with pink-and-green neon. She looked all over to find a clock. There was none. This was obviously a place where time stood still.

Kiki said, "This way, girls," and led them down a dark corridor, trimmed in the same pink and green neon. The hallway twisted and turned. April wondered if she'd ever find her way back out.

"How many dancers work here?" April asked Kiki.

"Depends on the season, Honey. Sometimes twenty-five, sometimes fifty."

"Wow! Fifty girls?"

"Not at the same time, of course. A lot are part-timers who work after school or after their other jobs. Some are here for a week; some for a few months. Some work nights, some afternoons, some only on weekends, and some just work the big golf tournaments. It depends."

At the end of the corridor was a door marked "Private." It was flanked with autographed posters of gorgeous, silicone-enhanced centerfold models-turned-strippers who had danced at the club.

"To Carlos Carrera, the best of the best, XXX OOO Sally," said the autograph on one of the posters. The lipstick from Sally's kiss covered her signature just as wax seals from centuries before had vouched for the signatures of kings and noblemen. April guessed that Carlos was the club owner or manager.

Kiki opened the door and showed April and Wendy inside. There, three young women sat on couches and chairs, waiting to audition. All three wore exotic costumes and six-inch high-heeled shoes. On the right, a tall, red-haired girl wearing a rhinestone-studded cowgirl outfit smoked a cigarette while flipping through the pages of a dancer's magazine. A slender young black woman in a peel-away gold lamé dress sat in the middle, painting her impossibly long fingernails with electric blue polish.

The third girl was a tall, busty blonde. She sat in ordinary walking shorts and peered through a chemical haze with complete indifference while she applied flesh-colored latex cover-up paint to her nipples with a small paintbrush. When the latex dried, she carefully dusted the area with powdered makeup and voila! The paint-covered nipples now looked like real nipples again. She obviously knew the intricacies of the local nudity ordinances, which said that a dancer's nipples had to be covered at all times — but did not specify *with what* they had to be covered. The blonde obviously intended to go to work that same afternoon.

"If this is your first time, watch a couple of the videos to get the hang of it," Kiki said. "Make sure you have all the basic moves — the snake crawl, the electric slide, the hair rub, and the pole tricks — all down pat before you dance for Carlos. He's seen 'em all. You gotta be good to dance here. Where's your costume?"

April's eyes popped wide open. "Costume? I just brought a bikini."

"Oh, God, another one off the turnip truck," Kiki said with an audible sigh. "There," she said, pointing to a small closet door. "Find something in there and use it for the audition. You need a g-string, a top, and a bottom. This is an eight-club, national chain. You gotta have real skill, a minimum of two top-notch outfits with matching shoes, and a full make-up kit if you want to dance here. This ain't no place for country bumpkins or wannabes. You do have a g-string and heels, don't you?" April had only brought the bikini and flats.

April looked at Wendy with despair in her eyes. Wendy turned to the house mother and asked, "Uh, can we go talk to Candy for a minute?"

Kiki rolled her eyes in her sockets and shrugged. "Follow me," she said.

A half hour later, April was in the middle of a full-blown panic attack. The other three girls had been called for their auditions at ten-minute intervals. Each returned through the waiting room, confident or smiling or both. Each looked at her and wished her luck, but the tone of their voices and the looks they gave her didn't inspire any confidence. The busty blonde told her, "Don't worry, Honey, you'll do OK. There's a big golf tournament goin' on. They're short eight girls this week."

April's problem was lack of time. After finding Candy, borrowing a g-string and a pair of shoes, and choosing a costume from the worn-out collection in the closet, April had only ten minutes to look at the training videos and try to learn some of the basic moves and tricks.

"Oh, my God!" she said to Wendy as she tried to mimic some of the moves of the veteran strippers. "I didn't know you had to have a spine made of rubber or be able to do all that stuff. I thought you just pranced around, shook your butt, and took off your clothes. There must be a hundred different moves. And the energy! Some of those girls must work out four hours a day. Do you see those bodies? Did you see how that little one climbed the pole and slid down upside down? Did you see how the brunette could move her boobs? This stuff is real work!"

The housemother opened the door at the far end of the room and called out, "Next!" Wendy and April rose to follow her, but she waved Wendy off. "Dancers only," she said, and motioned for April to follow.

Even the walk down the short hallway to the audition area was painful. Candy's six-inch platform shoes were a full size too small, and the straps bit into her feet. The height and the sharp 45-degree incline of the shoes showed off her calves and butt as they were designed to, but made it hard to balance.

"It's not hard to figure that the damn things were designed by men who don't have to wear them," April had heard Dolly say once.

April hobbled down the hall, praying she'd be able to walk as far as the audition room without falling. The room itself was a small version of the main dance floor, but only about ten by twelve feet in size. At the rear of the room there was a small audio rack system with a CD player and two speakers. The right wall was lined with a small black leather couch and a matching easy chair. The walls were regulation black, with more of the club's signature pink and green neon lights along the wall. In the center of the room was the audition stage, about eight feet square and eighteen inches above floor height. In the center of the stage was a polished brass dancing pole. April shivered with anxiety as she stood just inside the door and looked around.

"Here's her stats, Carlos," said Kiki, handing him a clipboard with April's application. The tall, bronzed Venezuelan-born club manager wore black slacks, a black-and-white polka-dot Italian silk shirt, eelskin loafers, a heavy gold necklace, and a diamond-encrusted Rolex. His black ponytail glistened in the twin shafts of light from the spotlights that illuminated the dance floor from behind the couch. He yawned and glanced at April's application with little interest.

"What's your name, babe?" he asked without looking up.

"April Devereaux, sir," she answered.

"Real or stage name?"

"Real."

"What do you dance under?"

"I'm sorry. What do you. . . . ?"

Carlos Carrera looked over the top of his designer sunglasses. *This won't take long,* he guessed. *And just as well.*

"Your stage name. What's your stage name?"

"I, uh, don't have one yet, sir, uh, Mr. Carrera."

Carlos wagged his head to Kiki. "She looks like a 'Vicky Love,' to me. What'cha think, Kiki?"

"Definitely, boss," Kiki said with a snicker. "Absolutely a Vicky Love."

"You have just been christened 'Vicky Love.' Please strut your stuff for us, Miss Love," Carlos said. He nodded to a hovering waitress in a pink bustier who refilled his champagne glass. Kiki Hatchett pressed the play button on the CD player. Seconds later, Rod Stewart started punching out one of his signature songs, "Do Ya Think I'm Sexy?"

April was shaking uncontrollably as she walked up the two back steps to the stage and made her way to the brass pole. "Go with the beat and have fun," was the advice Candy had given her, and she tried to focus on that.

The first three-minute set seemed like an eternity. She tried to climb up the pole so she could slide down and do a floor crawl but found that she lacked the upper body strength to do so. *God!* She thought. *You really have to be in top physical shape to do this stuff!* Instead, she slid down onto the dance floor in a heap, nearly twisting her ankle in the process. Somehow she managed to rise and regain her balance on the super-high heels and did her best to remember as many of the sexy moves that she could from the tapes.

The second set moved faster, to the sound of Blondie's "Heart of Glass." Turning slowly around and flexing up and down, she gradually peeled off her wrap-around dress and threw it off the stage as sensually as she could. The cool air on her legs made her break out in goose bumps, but she tried to focus on the beat and on the moves. By the time the second set ended, she could already feel painful blisters forming under the straps of her shoes.

"Oh, my God, look," the club manager whispered to his house

mother as he nodded his head in April's direction. From under the tiny triangle of cloth that made up April's g-string, wispy curls of brown hair peeked out. Kiki Hatchett looked, saw what he meant, rolled here eyes, and shook her head. "She didn't even have the sense to shave it."

Within seconds, the third song boomed out of the speakers: "Bad Girls," by Donna Summer. April took a deep breath, wrapped herself around the pole, and hung on for dear life. She knew the moment of truth was at hand.

After several knee bends, shakes, and shimmies, she focused directly on the club manager's bored eyes, slowly spun around three times, and peeled off her top in the process. Her breasts swung free and quickly reacted to the cold air and her fright. Then an amazing thing happened. The freedom of her nudity had a liberating effect on April. She felt her tension subside. *I might could actually get good at this*, she thought as she started to get a genuine feeling for the music. A small surge of confidence welled up inside of her, and she closed her eyes and moved with the flow of the pulsating music.

This must be what Candy was talking about, she thought. *Dance for yourself, not the audience*. A warm feeling started to flow through her. Somehow, she knew, she could get good shoes and outfits and learn the moves. This was going to work. She just knew it.

April's consciousness was jolted back into reality when the music stopped in mid-song. "Thanks for comin' in, kid," said Kiki. April looked around in disbelief. The manager had already left without a word. "Get some experience, learn the ropes, and come back again sometime later if you want. See ya.'"

Holding Candy's red heels in her hand, April ran back down the hall in tears, looking for Wendy. "I didn't make it. They said I'm not good enough, Wendy. Not good enough. I'm not good enough for anybody. Not for my father, not for my mother, and not even good enough for this fuckin' strip club. Oh, God, I wanna die," she said to her girlfriend in tears. "I just fuckin' wanna die. Take me home. Take me somewhere. But take me away from here," she said, sobbing in Wendy's arms.

Wendy held her and comforted her closest friend as best she

could. "Well, chickie-poo, I'm afraid we have a little problem. Candy made up with her boyfriend, and they're not looking for room-mates right now. I think it's time to patch things up with C.B. and hope he'll let us back into his old place. I got a girlfriend named Blue that's a friend of his. She says he's back living there now."

"I don't care. I just don't care. If C.B. will take me back, I'll do anything he wants. Just get me out of here."

29
Twenty-four / Seven

B ad news, boss." Eddie DeMarcos rolled his chair over to Steve Hunt's desk and yawned. "Sorry. Long night." There was no need for an apology, but it was a sign of respect. Hunt knew that his detectives had been up for the last 30 hours working on a drug sting at a big beach party. It had netted only seventeen hits of Ecstasy and a little pot — nothing that would make the morning newspaper. But that's what working vice and narcotics was usually about: small victories.

"We had another Ecstasy-related death last night. A college kid on spring break jumped from the balcony of his hotel and drowned in the pool. The coroner said he had Ecstasy in his system. One of our guys thinks that one of Correlli's dealers may have sold him the stuff. Correlli and his bunch were seen at the site of a rave near there last night. Here's what went down."

Hunt took the Incident Report that DeMarcos handed him. Horry County was no special hotbed of drug activity. Ecstasy was flooding the entire country, and no wonder. It was cheap and easy to get. Packaged like candy, it was easy to hide and use — no straws, no needles. It caused intense feelings and euphoria. It especially intensified the sense of touch. But it literally burned out brain cells, and, in high doses, it could kill with a single use.

"Damn. Did Correlli have anything on him, or was he playing his usual tricks?"

"No, as usual, he was clean. No drugs or cash on him. One of his new kids — a girl named Blue, I think — was probably holding the drugs, but she was clean when we got to her. She was a minor, of course. He's too smart to use an adult to hold the stuff. I dunno who was holding the money. We never did find it."

"Tell me about Blue."

"Must be new on the street. Looked pretty clean and well dressed. Straight cut, electric blue hair and some henna tattoos — typical teenage rebellion stuff. No weird clothes, only a couple of piercings evident, no major permanent tattoos, no needle tracks, and she wasn't very stoned. She smelled like she was smokin' pot but so did half the kids there. We didn't eyeball her smokin', so we didn't have probable cause to test her. We couldn't hold her or get a home phone number out of her. She left with Correlli."

"Did you get anything out of her?"

"Not really. She gave Correlli's address as her residence. By sundown, he'll teach her never to do that again. Show's how new she is to the street life."

"Who else did you take in for questioning?"

"Coupla kids from Surfside, Garden City, and North Myrtle — don't remember their names — and one you mentioned before – April Devereaux. She's evidently hangin' with Correlli again. We busted her for intent a few weeks ago, right?"

"Yeah. At least she has a mother who loves her and is trying to straighten her out. It's a damn shame how many parents just kick 'em out the door the first time they get in trouble. Most of the first-timers are good kids who ran into bad times and met the wrong person when they're vulnerable."

"Yeah. We see plenty of them. Slimebags like Correlli are predators. They're always loooking for new meat."

"No, Eddie, creeps like Correlli are scavengers, not predators. Nature created predators as hunters. They're designed by nature and evolution to seek out their prey and eat it.

"Correlli is a scavenger, like a vulture. He's out searching for sick or wounded animals. When the target shows signs of weakness, the Correllis of the world swoop down on them like roadkill."

"I know what you mean, boss," the detective said. "I had a cousin like that. He got pissed off at his father — the old man was a jerk, but not a real bad jerk — and ran away. Three months later, the Feds found him up in North Carolina, hangin' with a bunch of dope dealers and gunrunners. It doesn't take much for the dealers and gangs to scarf up a kid who's hurtin' and lookin' for some attention and protection."

"Do we have anything recent on Correlli?"

"Not a lot of hard evidence. We know he's distributing and probably has about eight or ten dealers working for him. Some of them — April Devereaux, Wendy Hickson, and this new kid, Blue — live with him. Jimmy Mullins — Skank — that 16-year-old in the coma who was Correlli's flunkie — died in the hospital about a week ago."

"Damn!" Steve blurted out and slammed his fist into his desk. "That's the last kid that Correlli is gonna kill. At least we know a little about him now. OK. If we can find the lab, and tie Correlli to it, we can get him off the street."

"What's the plan, boss?" the detective asked.

"Surveillance. We watch his house. Either Correlli has to go to the lab sometime or somebody from the lab has to bring the drugs to his distribution point. It's Tuesday. He probably brews up a new batch for distribution on Friday and Saturday nights. I want to put Correlli's place under twenty-four-hour surveillance for a week and see what happens. I want to log every time somebody enters and leaves the place, and I want a twenty-four-hour tail on Correlli himself."

"That'll tie up just about the whole department, boss? What about the porno and prostitution stings we got goin'?"

"Nothing's happening with the porno project right now, so we can pull Jack and Tommy off that. The hookers aren't all going on vacation, so that can wait, too. Have one detective stay on each of those cases, and set up rotating shifts for everyone else. Correlli is a menace. I want to string him up by his short hairs. You scope out his apartment and tell me tomorrow how we can stake out the place: people, video, bugs, whatever. We're a little short on probable cause, so we probably won't be able to get a warrant for a bug. But let me know what you can do.

"I'm going to see if I can get one of his dealers to roll over on him. If we had someone inside his operation who could give us information, that would be a huge asset. Give me your surveillance plan tomorrow, Eddie." Steve Hunt slapped his second-in-command on the back. "It's nice to know that all the money the Army spent on your recon training wasn't a complete waste."

"No way, boss," the detective said with an ear-to-ear grin. "This operation's gonna be my kinda fun."

30
The Deal

Law Offices of Jack Marchetti
Myrtle Beach

I 'm only here because Grandma told me to come," April said defiantly. "I'll do whatever I have to do to get this thing over with, but I want out of here the minute we're done and I want *you* out of my face," she barked at her mother.

Dolly was so mad that her ears turned red. "Don't you talk to me that way, you little. . . ." She restrained herself from finishing the sentence, but it was too late.

"Little what," Mamma? Little tramp? You know all about being one of those. Little druggie? You know all about being one of those, too. Little Skinhead White Power neo-Nazi racist? Well, I guess you missed one of three. Better luck next time you grow up. What the hell do you know about my life? What the hell do you know about what I think, or what I feel, or what I need? When were you ever around to find out?"

"Don't you call me names or raise your voice to me, April Devereaux. I'm not the person who caused your problems or threw you out or offered you drugs."

The lawyer knew better than to jump into the middle of a mother-daughter fight. He retreated to the high-backed, plum-colored leather chair at the far end of the small meeting room and patiently waited for catfight to end. But Jack Marchetti wasn't making any killing on defending this little witch on intent to distribute charges, so his tolerance had its limits. After three minutes of high-volume accusations and counter-charges, he calmly pulled out a large, silver-plated police whistle and blew on it full blast. It had the predictable effect. Both women stopped yelling instantly.

"Now that I have your attention, ladies, here are the rules," he said softly.

"One. I ask the questions and you answer me *and only me.*

"Two. The only person you ask a question of is me, not any-one else.

"Three. If either one of you breaks either of the two rules, this meeting is over; I'm not your attorney anymore; you forfeit your entire retainer; and you find yourself another lawyer for April's trial this Friday.

"You now have thirty seconds to consider this set of rules and both say to me, 'Yes, Mr. Marchetti, I understand.' Are we clear?"

April fumed and threw her purse on a chair. Dolly steamed and threw herself into another chair.

"Ladies, what is your decision?" He looked at Dolly first.

"Yes, I understand." He looked at April. She was still fuming, and she peered out the window onto King's Highway.

"April?"

"Yes, dammit, I understand."

"Thank you, ladies," Marchetti said with deliberate civility. "Now that you have chosen not to kill each other, I have some very good news. I've cut a deal with the assistant D.A. on the posses-sion-with-intent-to-distribute charge. If April accepts, the charge will be reduced to simple possession. She'll do community service and enroll in a mandatory drug rehab program. If she stays clean for six months, it means no jail time and nothing permanent goes on her record."

"Screw rehab. I'm no junkie," April muttered.

"And if she rejects the offer," the lawyer interjected, "she gets tried as a drug dealer and could get twenty years in the Women's Correctional Institution in Columbia. The new D.A. just got elected on a tough-on-drugs campaign platform. He'll love having a new conviction this early in his term — especially of a teenage girl — to show that he's really tough on drugs and wasn't kidding during the campaign."

"What do I have to do if I want to get the deal?" April asked in a low, shaky voice. The prospect of twenty years behind bars had a strong effect on her teenage bravado.

"The D.A. and the police know that your friend Anthony Correlli is a major drug manufacturer and distributor. They know that you know a lot of the important details of his operation: the kinds of drugs he makes, where his lab is, who his chemists are, what he sells, and who his dealers are. They want a full, signed statement from you covering every detail of his operation and everyone he's connected with. If they get it by Friday, you get your plea bargain deal. If not, you go on trial as a drug dealer and face hard time with no chance of parole."

"When do you have to have an answer for the D.A.?" Dolly asked.

"I'd like to have it today, but we have 'til Friday, 5:00 P.M. You can't possibly think of turning it down, April. It's the best deal we could possibly expect."

"Of course not, Mr. Marchetti," Dolly said.

"Who the hell do you think you are?" April yelled at Dolly. "I'm eighteen. You don't run my life anymore. You don't decide anything for me anymore. I'm not gonna sell out my friends. They care about me. They take care of me. They don't judge me. And they're my family. I'm not gonna hurt them, and I'm certainly not making any decisions at all until I have time to think about it."

April picked up her purse, burst out of the room, and ran to the curb. As soon as she waved her hand into the air, the thundering dual exhausts of the orange Charger boomed in the distance. In seconds, C.B.'s car screeched to a halt at the curb and April jumped in. Peeling rubber behind them, C.B. shot the car down King's Highway, hung a hard left onto 501, and headed home.

31
Soap Suds

C.B.'s apartment
Myrtle Beach

April stood at the kitchen sink, drying the dishes as Suzi Vetter washed them. "I'm in big trouble, Suzi," April told her. "I know you and me haven't been all that close, but I need someone to talk to. Can I trust you to keep your mouth shut?"

"Yeah, babe. That's OK. We're tight. What's up?"

"I've got big trouble with this intent-to-distribute thing. The trial is Friday. If I don't cop a plea, the ambulance-chaser my mother hired says I could end up doing twenty years. But he sucked egg with the D.A. and cut a deal."

"Damn, girl. What's does the prosecutor want you to do?"

"Roll over on C.B. and everybody he's connected with."

"Damn! Everybody?"

"Everybody."

"What are you going to do?"

"I don't know. I sure as hell don't want to rot in a blue shirt in Columbia for twenty years. But you guys are my family, and I don't want to screw all of you."

"Look, sweetheart, it looks like you don't have a helluva lot of choice. Do what you gotta do. We'll survive. Except for C.B., you're the only one facing hard time. The rest of us are gonna get off with community service and a fine. Let's face it, we'd all be better off if we'd never met C.B. Look what happened to Skank. He'd probably still be alive if C.B. hadn't sucked him in and made him his personal slave."

"I feel so bad for Skank. I cry for him every day. He was so lost. I was with C.B. when he met him. Skank had been sitting on the curb in front of the carousel across from the Pavilion for three days, just staring at the people who went by. All he had was a pair of jeans, a big floppy shirt, and an empty bottle of soda. I don't know how long it had been since he had any food. He had no money, no friends, and his family had kicked him out. He was just sitting there. C.B. took him to a hot dog stand and fed him. He asked me to take care of him at the house. From then on, Skank thought C.B. was God.

"After the explosion, Skank was moaning and bleeding when Boomer dumped him off at C.B.'s and split. There wasn't anything we could do for him, but if C.B. or Boomer had taken him directly to the hospital, maybe he would have pulled through. Skank's gone now, but I'm worried about you and Wendy."

"There's nothin' you can do about Wendy, April. She's been tight with C.B. since Day One. She was his first groupie when he came here from California. Any time any of the other girls wanted a piece or wanted attention, they'd have to make sure Wendy got hers first. And as soon as he found out she was a chemistry whiz, well, ole C.B. started groomin' her to take over the lab. Hell, she loves workin' at the lab more than she loves C.B. She's a damn genius when it comes to chemistry. Heard C.B. braggin' to his dealers that she makes the best meth that ever came out of the place. I even think Boomer is jealous."

"But I've known Wendy since grade school. She's my best friend. I can't leave her — or roll over on C.B. and have her go down with him."

"Ain't nothin' you can do about Wendy, girl. If anybody tries to take away her chemistry playground, she'll punch 'em in the nose. Wendy thinks she made the big time. She's probably gettin' $1,000 to $2,000 a month from C.B., plus all the free candy she wants. And Wendy's the only one in the whole group who really buys all that Skinhead White Power bullshit. The rest of 'em are just in it because of the drugs and the fact that they have nowhere else to go. Wendy's past the point of no return, babe. Don't try to make her any part of your plans. She'll side with C.B. over you any day."

As April listened to Suzi's talk, she stopped drying the dishes and turned progressively more pale. Deep down, she knew that C.B. was incapable of loving anyone, but she had no idea he had such a grip on her best friend. The thought of Wendy working in the same lab that had killed Skank made her blood run cold. She knew that if she copped a plea and rolled over on C.B., Wendy might wind up in prison instead of her. The thought made her sick to her stomach. She wanted to cry, but April could only choke out a cough.

"I'll tell you somethin'. It's a secret, too. You're not the only one leaving. I'm gettin outta here, too. My boyfriend and I got back together, and we decided to live together. We just rented us a trailer in North Myrtle. I've been waitressin' at Easy Rider up there for over a year now. It's a biker bar. Tips are pretty good, and the bikers don't hassle the staff too bad. The guy I work for owns Horsefeathers, the strip club next door. I know they're always lookin' for girls at Horsefeathers. You any good at dancing?"

"Hah!" April laughed. "The first time I auditioned, I fell on my ass and they threw me out," she said.

Suzi laughed. "That's a new one! How'd you fall?"

"My borrowed shoes didn't fit, and I only had ten minutes to practice."

"Well buy some shoes and practice, girl. You don't have to be a rocket scientist to be a stripper. But it does take skill, practice, bein' in good shape, and havin' the right stuff, like good shoes and costumes."

"I don't have the money for all that. The shoes and the outfits will cost almost $250."

"I know a guy who'll lend you the money. It'll cost you twenty percent a week interest, but if you get a dancer job, you can pay him off in a month or two, easy. His name is Joey. Italian guy, long black hair and pierced ears. You can find him at the back of the room at Easy Rider every Saturday night, doin' his business. If you want to make some fast bucks, borrow the money and go for it at Horsefeathers. My guy won't let me dance there because it's a bottomless club. So I just serve drinks at the bar next door. But if I could, I'd dance. I make a hundred a night in tips at Easy Rider. I could make three or four times that next door."

"I gotta have a place to stay."

"We can rent you a room in the trailer. My boyfriend works days at a truck stop on 17. I could use the company."

"Like I said, I don't have any money. I can't pay you any rent now."

"Your credit's good for a few weeks until you get a job. Wanna go for it?"

"You're a doll, Suzi. Thanks. Give me twenty minutes and I'm outta here."

"Me, too, babe. Me, too. C.B. can go screw himself. God! I'd love to see his face when he learns that he just lost two more chicks from his harem."

32
Rolling Over

Capt. Steve Hunt's office
Thursday morning

Ap.pril yawned to cover her nervousness. The sleepless night before left her weak and edgy. She had no idea that the interrogation was going to last so long. It had already been three hours, and it was clear they weren't done yet. She was worried that somehow she'd make a mistake, slip up, and say something stupid that would hurt Wendy.

Dolly was there to give her moral support, but she was not supposed to speak until spoken to.

"OK, Miss Devereaux," said the young female detective who was interviewing her. "Move a little closer to the microphone again, please. Now, we've gone over Correlli's recruiting methods and the people he recruited. We've covered what he sold and where he sold it. Now let's move on to the lab itself. Did Mr. Correlli ever take you to a clandestine drug manufacturing laboratory that he operated?"

"Yes, he did."

"On how many occasions?"

"One."

"When?"

"About a month ago."

"Where is this lab located?"

"Somewhere west of Myrtle Beach, about an hour or so out of town."

"Can you be a little more specific, please?"

"Yeah, sure. But can I have some coffee or somethin'?"

Steve Hunt nodded to the detective, and she left to get April a cup of coffee. Steve said to April, "Coffee's on the way. Let's keep rolling. Where was the lab?"

"I dunno. I was asleep in the back seat of the car most of the time. We went out 501, and after a few minutes, I fell asleep."

Hunt closed his eyes and slowly shook his head from side to side. This interrogation was producing virtually nothing he didn't already know.

"Who was in the car?" He asked. April's mind raced. Who should she name? She remembered the day when she and Wendy bonded as best friends.

It was their tenth grade chemistry class. The teacher paired them to do an experiment to show the effects of low temperature on various solids and liquids. Wendy had been holding a beaker of dry ice in one hand when she slipped on some water on the floor. April intercepted the falling beaker, saving Wendy from the possibility of freezing burns. Both excelled at chemistry, and after the accident, the two forged a lasting lab partnership that turned into a deep friendship. By the end of the year, they were known as "The Chemistry Twins."

"Tell us everything you know, April," Steve said. "If you hold back anything now and it comes out later, the deal is off and you could go directly to trial. Who was in the car with you?"

"Just C.B., Wendy, and me."

"That's Anthony Correlli, Wendy Hickson, and you?"

"Yes."

"Describe the location of the lab."

"It was a trailer in the woods somewhere."

"Please be more specific."

"I don't know where it was. Just out 501 someplace. I was in the back seat, talking to Wendy, and before long, we both fell asleep. C.B. woke us up when we got there. It was dark by then. He was delivering some supplies he'd bought in Georgetown and North Charleston."

"Was there anyone else there at the lab?"

"Yeah, Boomer, the cook."

"Boomer? What was his real name?"

"Just Boomer. That's all I ever heard C.B. call him."

"And what did you and Miss Hickson do at the lab?"

"We just helped C.B. unload the stuff."

"Did either of you work at the lab?" April couldn't bear to think of Wendy being connected with the lab's output. The recent death of the college student who jumped off the balcony after taking C.B.'s drugs had hit the community hard. The pressure on the police to arrest drug dealers was high. Wendy would be roadkill if the police found out she was cooking meth.

"All we did that night was keep C.B. company and help him unload the truck," April said. "Boomer was the cook there. We ate some sandwiches with him and C.B. and drank a few beers and came home."

"By cook, do you mean the manufacturing chemist who ran the lab and made the drugs?"

"Yeah."

"Did he have any help with his work?"

The detective returned with a cup of coffee. April took it and fumbled with the sugar and creamer, using the time to think what to say. Her brain scrambled for the right answer — not a lie, not the whole truth.

"Wendy and I didn't see anybody else there except C.B., and C.B. wasn't a cook. He didn't know how to make the stuff, just how to sell it."

"Do you know if Correlli or this man named 'Boomer' had any help working at the lab?"

"There was one kid, Skank, who helped out sometimes."

"Skank? What was his real name?"

"I didn't know then, but I later learned that his name was Jimmy Mullins."

"What did he do?"

"He was like C.B.'s go-fer. He did anything C.B. wanted. Skank worshipped C.B.," April said. The tears welled up in her eyes. "C.B. told him to dig a pit for the chemical waste. When Skank dumped the stuff in, it blew up." April dissolved in tears over the loss of her young friend. "He was only 16," she said between sobs. "Only 16."

Dolly reached around and held her in her arms. It was the first time they had touched for months. April didn't resist. Her tears flowed and flowed. Dolly looked up at Steve Hunt. She saw the compassion in his eyes.

"Detective, Ms. Devereaux, April, I think that's all we'll need for now. We'll call you if something else comes up. Dolly," Steve said, "stop by my office on the way out."

Dolly nodded, then returned her attention back to her frightened daughter. "You did the right thing, Baby. I'm proud of you. I'll be right with you through all of this. Don't you worry. You and I are family. Real family, not like Correlli and his victims. We'll make it through this."

All April could do was sob. She had just told the police everything they needed to arrest the only people she had talked with, eaten with, laughed with, cried with, and slept with for three years. April knew that with the exception of C.B. himself, the other kids were just like herself. They didn't hate anybody. They didn't want to hurt anybody. They just wanted to ease what pain they could with meth and pot and Ecstasy and share the rest of the pain with people who wouldn't judge them.

Now April had blown the whistle on her only friends. The police would go after them, and they would have to separate and run. She felt like crawling into a hole and pulling it shut.

Dolly left her sitting in a chair in the hall outside Steve's office. She knocked and he waved her in. "I know how hard that was for you in there, Dolly. I'm sorry we had to make her rehash everything, but that's the only way we have to get to Correlli."

"Thanks for your concern, Steve. I know what you're doing for her, and I appreciate it."

"It's my job, Dolly," Steve said. "Sorry that my work has to be a bad part of your life for a while."

"Don't be sorry," Dolly replied. To herself she thought, *It's not the best reunion I could think of for us, but what the heck. At least it brought us into contact again.*

"Hey, April's got an N.A. meeting tonight at 7:00. I'm gonna drop her off at the Community Center and wait for her. You want to grab a hamburger somewhere nearby?"

"Yeah," Steve said. "I'd like to have a hamburger with you."

33
Undress for Success

Tall Pines Mobile Home Park
North Myrtle Beach

T urn, turn, start the peel. Turn, turn, give 'em more of a smile. It's not supposed to look like you're in pain," Suzi yelled to April. "You're supposed to make it look like you're enjoying it. The guys want to think you're taking off all your clothes and showing them all your treasures just because they're such powerful, manly, irresistible studs, not because you're after their wallet."

Both women laughed. The disco beat pounded through the trailer as April worked on her dance moves for the audition. "Shimmy down, shimmy up. That's the stuff. Turn, turn, more peel. Unwrap yourself like you were a Christmas present for all those drunks and morons — oops! — valued clients — you're there to please. Remember, they're at the club to get whatever it is they're not getting at home.

It's all about fantasy, April. Don't ever forget that. Keep the customers in their fantasy world and they'll keep their wallets open. Remind them of their wives and girlfriends and you'll go home broke that night."

April pushed the button on the VCR remote control and the "Erotic Dancing, Part III" tape stopped. "Enough is enough," she said. "I'm either ready or I'm not. Which outfit should I wear? The French maid or the cowgirl?"

"It doesn't matter, Honey. Jack Claymore either likes ya or he doesn't. His switch only has two positions: on and off. Just do your best dance, turn him on, and you got a job."

"What does it take to make him happy?" April asked with a quizzical look in her eye. "What does this guy expect before he hires a girl?"

Suzi headed for the refrigerator to get lunch started. "Depends on his mood, Honey. Depends on his mood. Hey, you know that Kyle said you were lookin' a lot better already. I told you that two weeks of vegetarian living and a little organic gardening would do wonders for you."

April walked to the small mirror on the wall and looked at herself. It was true. Living inside C.B.'s apartment and coming out only at night had given her the complexion and looks of a vampire. Her pale skin was now regaining some of its natural color, and her new tan was making her look, well, almost like a normal person.

Suzi's boyfriend, Kyle, was the first guy April had met in two years who didn't use drugs. He never seemed depressed, and there was no rage in him. Even the arguments he had with Suzi were mild and gentle when compared to the shouting matches that had been so common at C.B.'s. His work at the repair shop was hard and hot, and he came home tired and dirty. But he always had a kiss for Suzi and took a few minutes to listen to her talk about her day before he hit the shower.

At 1:45, April said, "OK, Suzi-Q. Give me a lift over to this joint and I'll see if I can get myself a job and stop being a freeloader."

Suzi picked up her purse and car keys and said, "Let's roll." As soon as they left the driveway, April reached into her purse and retrieved a half-smoked joint. She lit it and took a deep drag. Suzi said "No, thanks" when April offered her a hit. One more drag and the joint was finished. April threw the roach out the window.

Ten minutes later, at the front door of the club, April hopped out. "Good luck, Honey," Suzi said as April stepped out onto the broiling asphalt of the club's deserted parking lot.

"Thanks a million, Suzi," April said, hoisting her costume bag to her shoulder.

You'll need it, Suzi thought as April disappeared through the blacked-out glass of the front door. *There's a price to pay for everything in this world. I hope he's in a mellow mood.* She broke the train of thought and drove away.

April wandered down the hallway of the empty club. She was amazed to see that it was less than a quarter the size of Fast Fannie's — and not nearly as clean. Glasses and bottles from the previous night still lined the edge of the stage. The place smelled like sawdust, beer, and cigarettes.

April continued on until she saw some light coming through a half-opened door. "Hello?" she called out. "I'm here to see Mr. Claymore?"

"In here," said a man with a deep voice. April walked into what turned out to be a crowded office. "Yeah?" he said, without raising his head. A twenty-something man in a light tan suit stood nearby.

"My name's April. . . ."

Jack Claymore raised his hand. "Chill." The short, barrel-chested manager looked up at the liquor salesman and threw a price list back to him. "Whattaya got that's cheaper than the Chardonnay? The price of that stuff is killin' me. Most guys here don't give a damn about wine anyway. They only drink beer and whiskey. The wine's only for the broads."

April took a look around the office, glanced at the club owner, and thought, *I wish I had smoked a whole joint. Maybe two.* The small office was cluttered with papers and magazines. The trash can was overflowing with more paper, and everything smelled of cigarette smoke. Even the screen of the computer on his desktop was yellow with nicotine stains.

"I can get you a pretty good blended white from Italy or Germany for $3.45 a bottle," said the salesman. "You're paying $4.25 for the Chardonnay. Want me to send over a bottle of the white blend to taste, Mr. Claymore?"

"I drink Dom, not that crap. Just send over four cases of the white stuff, the rest of the monthly order as usual, and a case of Dom. And make sure they don't bill me for the Dom."

"Well, er, Mr. Claymore, I'm afraid that the new owners have, uh, tightened up the rules a bit," the salesman said sheepishly. "I'm afraid we can't do the free Dom anymore. We just don't have the profit margins we used to. . . ."

"Bullshit!" Claymore said, exploding like one of the land mines whose name he shared. "Remind your new owners that I've got five clubs that spend three hundred thousand bucks a year with them, and that there are four other fuckin' distributors who'd gladly kick in the Dom Perignon AND kiss my ass for this fuckin' account. End of discussion," Claymore said as he signed the liquor order and threw it at the salesman. "See ya next month." With the conversation terminated, the salesman quickly packed his briefcase and left. Suzi had described her boss accurately. He didn't negotiate.

"Yeah?" he said to April.

"Uh, hello, Mr. Claymore. My name is April. I'm a friend of Suzi Vetter's. I'm here to audition for a dancer job. Where can I change?"

"Follow me," Claymore said as he beckoned her to follow him into a small lounge room behind the office. "Back there," he said, pointing to the door of a bathroom. Inside, there was barely enough room for April to slip out of her jeans, panties, and T-shirt and change into the cowgirl outfit. She wiggled into the "Hot as a Pistol" bikini panties, white leather mini-skirt, and fringed top. Sitting on the john, she strapped on her six-inch red high heels with their built-in strobe lights. Digging into the bottom of her costume bag, she found the custom-burned music CD that Kyle had made for her, took a deep breath, and walked out.

She had the moves. She had the outfit. She had the shoes. She had the music. She had the proper mental attitude. She was ready to do the strip dance of all strip dances for the manager of this club, sleazy though it might be. She was totally prepared this time. She wasn't going to take no for an answer.

Jack Claymore was sitting in a high-backed chair, facing away from her as April walked back into the room. "I'm ready," she said with a big, bright smile, and extended the CD toward the seated manager.

Claymore looked over his shoulder. "Nice outfit. The customers will love it," he said. He swiveled his chair around to face her and looked her in the eyes. He was naked from the waist down, and there was an evil grin on his face. "It's audition time," he said. "Put on the music, lose the costume, and show me how much you want the job."

34
HazMat

Near Galivants Ferry, S.C.
3:00 P.M.

Air Leader to base. We're over Dawsey Swamp, about a mile north of Galivants Ferry and a mile east of the Little PeeDee River. I have the trailer and the orange Charger in sight."

Capt. Steve Hunt keyed the microphone of his tactical field radio. "Roger, Air Leader," he replied to the State Law Enforcement Division helicopter commander. "It was thoughtful of him to paint a Confederate flag on the roof of the car. Makes it a little easier to see through the pine trees, don't you think?"

"10-4 Captain. The black pickup's there, too."

"Thank you Air Leader. We'll take it from here. Base out." *This is a little too easy,* Steve thought to himself. *We've got Correlli and Boomer both right where we want them to be.*

Hunt turned to Maj. John Sharp, his counterpart in the Horry County Sheriff's Department, who was heading the operation. "They're in there, Major," he said.

Maj. Sharp motioned to the joint city-county SWAT team. The seven men spread out as they had rehearsed for the past two days and slowly made their way through the woods until the trailer was in sight.

"McConnell. Bissell."

"Yes, sir?"

"Slip that wireless loudspeaker up there as close as you can. Leakey and Collier, cover them."

"No problem, sir. It will be loud enough to dance to." In ten minutes, the two men returned, smiling.

"OK everybody, listen up," Maj. Sharp said. "Is the loudspeaker in place?"

"Yes, sir. Right next to the tree at the blind corner of the trailer," Sgt. Bissell replied.

"What did you learn from your recon?"

"We saw shadows behind the window shades. Looks like two adults inside, could be more. They have the blinds closed on all the windows and doors, so they can't see anything outside. There's only one exit, through the side door. Unless they have sensors planted — and I don't think they're that high-tech — surrounding the trailer should be fairly straightforward."

"OK. From the cars, we can assume it's probably C.B. Correlli and his chief cook, Marvin Jeeter, the guy they call 'Boomer.' There may be others that we don't know about. Anyone inside should be considered armed and dangerous. And remember, the lab itself is one big bomb waiting to go off. We want to talk them out if it's humanly possible. If the lab goes up, it could easily kill anyone within fifty yards of the place. You heard what those chemicals did to the Mullins kid. Keep your full protective gear on at all times, and keep the radios set to tactical channel 1."

"Yes, sir," the heavily clothed men said in near-unison. "Tac 1."

Inside the trailer, Boomer was lecturing Wendy on the final stages of d-meth production. "Remember, babe, what you have at the end of the run is a mixture of d- and l- isomers. The d- is cool, but the l- is crap. Separate the two and reprocess the l- into d- by oxidizing it and reanimating it."

Outside the trailer, the final stages of the assault were underway. "McConnell and Bissell, take the front, with me. Rollins and Davis, the back, behind the pickup. Sharpshooters, at 45 degree angles off the front entrance: Leakey, to the right; Collier, the left. Fire only on my command, and then only when you have a clear field of fire."

"Yes, sir," said the snipers.

"HazMat, are you ready?"

From a half-mile down the road, the eight-man Hazardous Materials Team responded, "Yes, sir."

"OK, everybody take your positions and sound off," said the SWAT commander. The men started crawling noiselessly into position. After two minutes, all the men signaled their readiness.

Steve Hunt's thoughts momentarily returned to his first visit to Jimmy Mullins in the hospital. In addition to the chemical burns to his lungs, the teenager had suffered external burns on 65 percent of his body. He was covered with sterile ointments and bandage material that would not stick to what little remained of his skin. Tubes and wires and machines were all that was keeping him alive. It was bad enough when Steve saw the kids come into the holding tank, spaced out on Ecstasy or speed. Most of them, at least, would end up someplace where they could recover. The boy in the bandages and the space-age Burn Unit air bed had it a hundred times worse. Jimmy Mullins was literally better off dead.

Reality beckoned Steve back from his reflections. Maj. Sharp turned on the wireless microphone that controlled the camouflaged loudspeaker. A hundred yards in front of them, he couldn't believe his eyes as a young woman casually opened the door, walked down the steps, sat on the bumper of the pickup, and lit a cigarette. She had no idea that two camouflaged officers were hidden behind the other end of the vehicle.

"Rollins and Davis, we just got a break. Did you see her?"

Any whisper would have given them away. The two men nodded their heads in the affirmative. The command came through their earphones. "Exfiltrate her and make sure she doesn't make a sound."

The two men rounded the pickup from opposite sides. One wrapped a heavily gloved hand around her mouth and carried her off quickly down the blind side of the trailer. Steve couldn't believe their good luck. *Now for the rest of them,* he thought.

The loudspeaker barked out commands. "Attention inside the trailer. This is Major John Sharp of the Horry County Sheriff's Office. You are surrounded and under arrest. Drop any weapons and come out the front door with your hands in the air."

Inside the trailer, Boomer yelled, "Sonofabitch!"

"Now what?" said C.B. "There's only one way out of this place. We're fucked!"

"You're fucked," said Boomer. "They don't have shit on you, but I'm dead. They've got two priors on me and a warrant out for attempted murder in New Mexico. If they take me here, I'm gonna fry in New Mexico. Hasta la vista, C.B.," Boomer said as he pulled a .45 automatic pistol out from under a counter. "It's been fun, but I'm outta here."

The massive meth cook grabbed C.B. and said, "You're my insurance. We leave together. Move!" He pointed the .45 at C.B.'s head and said, "You sure as hell don't look like the hero type, but don't change your sorry-ass stripes now."

"Attention inside the trailer," Maj. Sharp yelled again. "Come out with your hands up now." He tensed as he saw the door open two inches.

"I have a hostage," Boomer yelled, and pushed C.B.'s face into the crack of the door, his cheek flattened against the glass. "Back off, put your weapons down, and let us through, or I'll blow this motherfucker's head off first and then start on you," Boomer yelled.

Through a spotting scope, Steve Hunt could see the panic in C.B.'s eyes. Maj. Sharp called out, "You know we can't do that, Boomer. Let him go, put down your weapon, and both of you come out with your hands up"

"I don't fuckin' think so," Boomer said. "Back off, now. We're coming out and getting into the truck. One goddam blade of grass moves and he's fuckin' dead."

The door opened another crack, and Steve Hunt saw the snarl on Boomer's face. "Leakey and Collier, report in," Maj. Sharp whispered into his tactical radio.

"No clear field," said Leakey.

"No clear field," said Collier. "They got a million tubes and bottles right behind them."

"Attention everybody," Sharp said crisply into his radio. "Pay no attention to anything I say over the loudspeakers. All commands will be on Tac 1 only."

"Boomer, let the man go. Make it easy on yourself," Sharp said into the loudspeaker's microphone. "We don't want to hurt you, but you know we can't let you take him anywhere. Put down your weapon."

"Fuck you, man. I'm dead in New Mexico anyway, so it doesn't matter to me. Here or there, somebody's gonna kill me. Might as well be here."

"Boomer, don't hurt him. It will. . . ."

Boomer slowly pushed C.B.'s head through the door, a hammerlock on his throat and the pistol against his skull. "Gimme room, man, we are very definitely drivin' out of here right now," Boomer yelled.

"Leakey and Collier. Can you take him?" said Sharp.

"No clear field," said Leakey. He peered through the powerful telescopic sight. He could see the whites of C.B.'s eyes. "Bad angle."

"No clear field," said Collier. "Bad angle. Wait a minute. . . ."

C.B. was choking from the arm around his neck. He staggered and turned slightly as he stepped onto the porch, the big man welded to his back.

"Don't take him to the car, Boomer. Just put down your weapon now," Maj. Sharp said through the loudspeaker.

Two hand-chosen, 7.62 mm. soft-point rounds lay nestled in front of the firing pins of the two U.S. Army M24 sniper rifles. Two fingers each tightened another half-ounce on the triggers as the snipers tracked their target through their 10x telescopic sights.

The meth cook was a professional criminal. He held his head only a hair's breadth away from that of his hostage as he moved out the door onto the landing. But even professional criminals have no control over the rules of geometry. For every inch the desperate man and his terrified hostage moved forward, one sniper's line of fire worsened and the other's improved.

"Leakey and Collier. Take out the male shooter only. Fire at will." Boomer was two feet, six inches out the door when the line between Collier's rifle intersected the path between Boomer's right ear and the nostril on the far side of his face. Collier squeezed the trigger the last few hundredths of an inch. The single bullet found its mark. Boomer's head exploded like the pumpkin in the annual

Fourth of July fireworks safety commercials on TV.

C.B. ran screaming down the stairs, fell, and writhed on the ground, covered with Boomer's blood, screaming and scared beyond comprehension. "I give up, I give up," he yelled. "Don't shoot, don't shoot."

In two more minutes, the glory part was all over. Wendy shook uncontrollably in the back of the ambulance, scared out of her mind. C.B. bounced around in the back seat of the squad car, his feet shackled and his hands cuffed. The detectives zipped Boomer's corpse into a body bag and hefted it into a police station wagon. Steve Hunt congratulated the Sheriff's Department SWAT Team commander for his good work, and then thanked each of his own men for theirs. The chief of the HazMat team just shook his head and sighed. He knew that his men had a week's worth of tedious, dangerous work ahead of them.

35
One Chicken, Roosting

Dolly poured herself a fourth cup of coffee and rubbed her left ear, which was aching from the hours she'd already spent on the phone, searching for April. One more call and then she'd hit the road again. "Hello, Mamma?"

"Hello, Dolly. Mercy! You sound awfully tired."

"Yes, I sure am, Mamma. But I'm still walking and talking. Have you heard anything at all from April since last week? I'm worried half to death. No, I have no idea at all. I stopped by Kenny's house yesterday, but there was no sign of her. Kenny's neighbor said he went off someplace with his girlfriend. I'm gonna go by again this afternoon, just in case. No, I don't know any of her friends anymore. That's always been the trouble."

"I'm praying for her, Honey," Anne said. "I haven't gotten a letter from her for two weeks. Lately she'd been writing me every week, and I've been writing her back. Ain't it funny how in these days of cell phones and e-mail, a real, honest-to-gosh letter can mean so much?"

"I'm glad you two made the connection again, Mamma. It breaks my heart that she thinks I'm a major problem. All I want to do is help."

"Don't beat yourself over the head with it, Honey. It's not like she and I somehow became the world's closest bosom buddies in the last few months. She still doesn't understand me, and I don't understand her." Then, with warmth in her voice, she continued, "And neither one of us understands you, but we're trying."

"Thanks a lot, Mamma. I really needed to hear that now, when I'm running all around half the Grand Strand, looking for a lost, unemployed, drug-addicted eighteen-year-old daughter. Is there anything else you want to say to cheer me up for the day?"

There was no rancor in Dolly's voice. In fact, this was the most normal conversation she'd had with her mother in years. Issues remained unresolved, but the emotional dam had been broken that day in Darlington when Anne had shared her deepest secrets. Dolly longed for the day when that could happen with herself and April.

"Gotta go, Mamma. Outside of Steve, there's only two people I know who have seen April in the last two weeks. One of 'em – Correlli — won't talk to me. I'm gonna go try and talk to the other one now."

"Good luck, Honey," Anne said. Then, a split-second before Dolly was about to voice an automatic reply and hang up, her mother said, "I love you."

The words hit Dolly like the ringing of a huge church bell.

"I love you." The three words embodied the entire mother-daughter relationship, one that had been eroded over the course of a decade filled with dark, painful secrets, denial, and half-truths.

"I love you." It was as if someone had pulled the plug on all the resentment and anger she had bottled up inside. The pain from years of rancor and recriminations flew out of Dolly's head like bats leaving their dark cave. In its place, Dolly felt her heart swell with warmth and gratitude. After twenty years, she was finally letting go of the hate and the anger. She could feel herself moving on.

"I love you, too, Mamma," she said, her voice quaking. "I really do. But I gotta go. I'll keep you posted."

"OK, Honey. Bye."

"Bye, Mamma."

Dolly sat on the bed, thinking about the impact of the three words on her. Now, she knew her job was even clearer — find the ways to communicate that same love to April.

Sensing its important mission, the old blue Honda started the moment Dolly turned the ignition key. She stopped at C.B.'s apartment on the way out of town. After the police had raided the place, the landlord hauled all of the occupants' personal belongings out of the apartment, dumped them on the curb, and boarded up the door. Anything of value had disappeared overnight. Only the dirty couch, the beanbag chair, and some clothes remained.

The half-hour drive to the county jail in Conway gave Dolly time to think about what to ask Wendy. Dolly had been surprised that Wendy would even talk with her. She had no one else listed on her inmate visitation card, Steve had told her, so maybe it was sheer loneliness that made her willing to talk with Dolly. She had met Wendy many times during April's younger years. Maybe that's the reason she didn't feel threatened. *Who knows?* Dolly thought. *At least she'll talk to me.*

As she neared the prison on Highway 701, the "J. Reuben Long Detention Center" sign was not hard to see. She followed the arrow and pulled into the parking lot. Inside the main building, her purse was visually checked and then run through a metal detector. Then she walked through another metal detector and signed in.

"Name?" said the guard.

"Dolly Devereaux," Dolly replied.

"Picture ID, please."

Dolly fumbled through her purse and extracted her driver's license. She looked around. *These people have friends or family in jail here*, she thought. She could hardly imagine how awful that might be. *Yet here I am, visiting an inmate myself. Lord knows, I never thought I'd ever see the inside of a place like this.*

The guard carefully compared the driver's license photo with Dolly's face. "This says 'Dorothy Anne Devereaux.'"

Dolly thought about her name. "Dorothy" had been inspired by *The Wizard of Oz*, her mother had told her, and "Anne" came from her mother.

"I'm sorry. That's my full name," she told the guard. "Everybody calls me 'Dolly.'"

"Prisoner's name?" the guard asked.

"Wendy Hickson," Dolly replied. The guard typed the name into her computer. "OK. You're on her list. She's in the minimum security building. Visiting hours this afternoon are 12:30 to 3:30. Questions?"

"What do I do now?"

"Take a seat. Next."

It was 12:20. She'd only have to wait for ten minutes. Dolly took a seat on one of the gray fiberglass chairs. She looked around at the three dozen or so people waiting to visit other inmates. Most were black; some were white. Most looked like they lived on the low end of the income scale; a few looked very middle class. Most talked among themselves in quiet voices; some seemed as nervous as she was.

What could she offer Wendy? Dolly thought. *What would Wendy tell her?* Dolly didn't have to wait long to find out.

"Visitors report to the desk," the loudspeaker said. Dolly walked up to the guard.

"First time?" the guard asked. Dolly sensed that the guard knew everything about everybody, and that asking was just a formality. Dolly nodded, "Yes."

"Through that door, down the hall, and look for the sign on the left, 'Visiting Room.'"

"Thanks," she said. The guard pushed a button; the electric door lock buzzed; and Dolly walked down the long, gray corridor to the sign. The visiting room was filled with lunchroom-style metal tables and attached benches — nothing that could be picked up or thrown. She saw no one she recognized. Then she felt a tap on her shoulder.

"What's up, Mrs. D?"

"Mrs. D." was what Wendy had called her for all the years she'd known her. Dolly was appalled at Wendy's appearance. She looked even worse than she had that day at C.B.'s. The tall, blond-haired, blue-eyed little Yuppie-doctor's-daughter-princess was gone. In her place stood a hard-edged young woman with two eyebrow rings, a lower lip stud, and a barbell through her tongue. Her henna-colored hair was cut shorn to within a half-inch of her skull. The transformation came as a complete shock to Dolly.

Wendy was accustomed to the reaction. Indeed, her appearance was part of her rebellion. "Like the hair, huh?" she said with a wry smile.

"Hello, Wendy," Dolly managed to sputter out. "Are you doin' OK?"

"As well as you could expect in a place like this. Take a look around."

Dolly didn't have to look again. She knew what Wendy meant. "I don't know if there's anything I can do to help you, Wendy, but if I can, I will."

"Forget it, Mrs. D. I think I'm gonna get off the hook. They didn't catch me with anything on me when I was up there at the lab, so I'll probably get off with probation. As a mater of fact, they may even spring me in a couple of days for lack of evidence."

"Well, I hope you can make something good out of all of these tragic events, Wendy."

"Like, straighten up, fly right, go back to Daddy, get off drugs, and go off to medical school?"

"I didn't mean. . . . I'm not judging you. . . ."

"You couldn't judge me, Mrs. D. You don't know a thing about me — or April. My mother had this fuckin' Shirley Temple obsession. I was her little play doll. She controlled every waking minute of my life. All she wanted was for me to be the little child beauty queen and kiddie TV star she always wanted to be – but never was.

And Daddy? The wonderful doctor everybody knows and loves? If I wanted to talk to him, I had to call his service so they could beep the Famous Doctor. Then, if I was really lucky, his staff would fit me into his busy schedule for a five-minute consultation.

"You know that rathole where April and I lived with C.B.? Running away from home was like making a prison break. Moving in with C.B. was like a paradise. Living at the fancy house with my parents, with my own big, pink-trimmed bedroom and all the stuffed animals was a hundred times worse than being locked up here."

"Oh, God, Wendy, I didn't know."

"Of course you didn't. But my parents knew — or were supposed to know — and then they condemned me for what happened to me, just like you're doing to April."

"I'm not condemning her for anything, Honey. I just want what's best for her. All I want to do is get in touch with her and ask her to come home."

"If she wanted to be home with you, she'd be there now," Wendy said. "You're the same as all the others. You think that if you have a kid, you can control them and tell them what's right for them and what to do till they die. Well it doesn't work that way, Mrs. D. April is eighteen. She had enough examples of what to do and not do when she was growing up. Now she just wants to run her own life."

"I just want to talk to her, to hold her. Do you have any idea where she is? How to get in touch with her?"

"No idea, Mrs. D. All I can say is that she better not come around her old friends anymore. C.B.'s gonna get out on bail, and he's not the nicest person in the world when people screw him over."

Dolly's heart raced. *What if someone tries to hurt her? It'll be my fault. I pushed so hard for her to give up C.B. and take the plea bargain. Maybe she could've gotten off without it. Maybe the judge would've cut her some slack, sent her to rehab or something. . . .*

"Is she in danger, Wendy?" Dolly asked in grave sincerity. Dolly's voice trembled.

"You never know what some people might do," Wendy said, laughing, in a teasing, taunting voice.

"Dammit, Wendy, this is my daughter we're talking about. Seriously, is she in any danger?"

"Well, not from me. I don't ever wanna see the bitch again, but that's all. C.B.'s gonna figure out that she's the rat, and he's not gonna be happy. Relax, though. Right now he's just gonna want to keep a low profile and stay out of trouble. He's not stupid. He knows what's important, and getting out of jail and staying out is what's important. He's not gonna risk that just to get even with April or to teach her a lesson. If anything happened to her, it would be directly linked to him. The bitch isn't worth that much to him. Ya know, Mrs. D, you can look for April, but even if you find her, she thinks you're a total hypocrite. She doesn't want to talk to you ever again."

"Hypocrite?" Dolly screamed in disbelief. The guard in the room immediately locked her eyes on the two of them. "Hypocrite?" Dolly whispered. "All I ever did for her was love her. I just want what's best for her. The way she's been living sure isn't going to do her any good as she grows up."

Wendy calmly folded her arms and rested them on the table. "Think back, Mrs. D. What were you doing when you were eighteen? From what April told me, you were doin' drugs, knocked up, and livin' with a Deadhead pot farmer. Then after he dumped you, you moved on to being a stripper. And you're sitting here judging me and April? I rest my case, Mrs. D. Guilty as charged of hypocrisy in the first degree. "

Dolly was speechless. Wendy rose and slowly walked away. "End of interview. Don't bother coming back to do me any more favors or to pump me for more information about your darling daughter. I wouldn't be here if she hadn't ratted on us. I don't care whether you find her or not."

"Wendy, why did you want me here? Why, of all people, am I the only person on your visitation list?"

"I guess I just wanted to let you know what a little bitch your daughter is. She fucked everything up for all of us just to save her own ass. We were a family, Mrs. D. You don't do that to family."

"You also don't hold grudges against family, either. A family is supposed to be about forgiveness, Wendy. She never turned you in, you know. She kept your name clean throughout the entire interrogation. She didn't know that you were gonna be at the lab that day. She tried to keep you out of this."

"Whatever. She should've tried a little harder. She should've shut her mouth altogether."

"Is that really why you asked me here, Wendy? To bad-mouth April? You could've done that to anyone. Why me?"

"I guess I just wanted to make sure that the message got back to her."

"I don't even know where she is. You probably have a better chance of speaking to her anytime soon than I do."

"Don't count on it, Mrs. D. Look, your visitation's over. You can go. I shouldn't have put you on my list. It was a mistake."

Dolly got up to leave, then turned around and looked at Wendy. She seemed angry, but so lonely and vulnerable, all at the same time. "Wendy, have you talked to your parents? Do they know what's going on?"

"Fuck 'em. They don't care. They're not like you. They're not stupid enough to think they can change anything. The cops called 'em 'cause one of 'em knows my dad. He said that I wasn't his responsibility 'cause I was eighteen. Outta sight, outta mind, huh, Mrs. D?"

Dolly could see that Wendy was doing her best to hide her distress. She saw her eyes water when she talked about her parents. *My god*, thought Dolly. *I'm probably the only person on her list 'cause her parents won't even come see her and her only friends are in jail. She didn't have anybody else <u>but</u> me to put on that list.* Dolly suddenly felt so sorry for Wendy that she wanted to grab her and hug her, but she didn't dare try.

"Wendy, Honey, I want you to know that I'm here for you. You're April's best friend, and I care about you. If there's anything I can do...."

"Forget it Mrs. D. You and your precious little April have done enough. Y'all are the reason why I'm here, so you can both kiss my ass. G'bye."

36
Vicky Love

Horsefeathers Gentlemens Club
Saturday night

Eight hours after the club opened at 4:00 that afternoon, April's feet and back were killing her. Horsefeathers had a well-earned reputation for being a rowdy place. But the crowd was no worse than usual that night, and April had almost a month's experience under her belt. It had been a rainy afternoon, so the golfers started coming in early, around 5:00. Because the club catered mostly to Redneck Riviera regulars, the tips had been pretty good so far that night. An onstage bachelor party dance alone had netted her $50.

April, who danced as "Vicky Love," was working the first shift with Jessica, a popular dancer from Georgia, and her friend, Fanny. All three dancers were eighteen. Jessica, the veteran of the trio, had been dancing for all of six months, while Fanny had come to work at Horsefeathers the same week as April.

"Shake your booty," Jessica had said to April and slapped her butt as she headed through the glass-beaded curtain onto the stage for her first dance at 4:00 P.M.

"Break a leg," said Fanny, grinding out a cigarette in the ashtray on her overcrowded two-foot section of the dressing room.

Wearing her black-and-white French maid outfit and six-inch, black, stack-heeled shoes, April sashayed onto center stage, making sure to stay clear of the nail head that poked up through the sagging plywood dance floor. *Damn!* she said to herself. *That thing is still there. Somebody's gonna catch a heel on that some night and go flyin' on her butt.* Jack Claymore was never known to waste money on maintenance. April resolved to bring in a hammer the next day and fix it herself.

Any time now, you idiot, she thought, waiting for Walter Hirchinger, a.k.a. Rocket Ronnie, the club's lame-brained DJ, to start her music. As usual, he keyed up the wrong CD for her first song. Her playlist said that she wanted to open with Gloria Gaynor's version of "I Will Survive." It had become April's personal anthem. She loved the song's slow, vampish piano lead-in, which leaped without warning into a high-energy disco beat. It was a dynamite way to light a fire in a slow crowd. Instead, ole Rocket Ronnie cued up Anita Ward's "Ring My Bell," a slow-paced song better suited for late in the night when all the clients were already half drunk and couldn't tell one dancer from the next.

Way to go, Ronnie, she thought as she waved to the brain-dead DJ and smiled at the only two paying customers in the club. One was the bartender's boyfriend; the other was obviously a businessman who'd stopped in for a drink on the way home from work. *Now's the part that Candy had talked about,* she remembered. *Sometimes the place is almost empty, and sometimes it's full of jerks, and if you can't have fun dancing for yourself, then you'll never last.*

As April wrapped herself slowly around the brass pole, she selected the businessman and decided to make his twenty-minute attitude adjustment stop as happy as possible. She fixed her eyes on his and never let them go.

First, she climbed as far up the twelve-foot brass pole as she could, then bent over backwards to show off her ample cleavage to the max. Then, with one leg at a right angle to the pole, she slowly slid to the floor, where she fanned her legs back and forth like a child making an angel in the snow.

Her efforts were not lost on Mr. Businessman, who dumped his cell phone and P.D.A. into his briefcase, closed it, and drew up close to the stage to get the best possible view.

As the second set started, April bored holes through Mr.

Businessman's skull as she peeled off the bodice of her costume and threw it through the air toward the back of the stage. Now that her bare breasts had captured his full attention, she spun on the pole and danced her way over to him. Six feet from him, she dropped to her knees and then got down on all fours. She covered the last six feet between herself and her audience doing a writhing cat crawl on her hands and knees. When she reached the edge of the stage, her face was six inches from his. "Hi there, Honey," she said, rising up on her knees and shaking her assets just inches from his nose. "What's your name?"

"Uh, hi. My name's Andrew."

"Well, hi there, Andrew. Glad you're here. It would be awful lonesome for me if you weren't. Now I'm not supposed to do this, but I like you, so pull up a little closer and lean back." Andrew inched his chair as close as he could to the bar and leaned back. "Remember now, hands on the chair." Andrew knew what was coming. He was happy to comply.

April crawled up to the edge of the stage, placed her hands on the front rail, bent all the way over the stage and let her hair flow into his lap. Then she bent ever further forward and rubbed Andrew's crotch with the top of her skull.

"Whooooooo-eee!" she said with a laugh as she pulled her head up and extended her leg toward her customer. She gracefully pulled the garter away from her thigh, and Andrew slipped a five-dollar bill under it. April kissed him on the head and resumed her dance.

From the DJ booth, Rocket Ronnie's deep, mellow voice boomed out from the sound system, "Put your hands together and please be generous to our feature dancer this hour, Miss Vicky Love, onstage for your total pleasure tonight."

As she started her third set, she was glad to see that a few more men had entered the club. When the music started, she went back to her pole dancing. She writhed, weaved, and bounced across the stage and slowly, teasingly, peeled off the lace-trimmed black mini-skirt. A blast of cold air from the cooling system rolled over the stage. Jets of fog flowed out through vents in the dance floor. Immediately, April felt her whole body break out in goosebumps. She was glad that ole Rocket Ronnie had put on something with a quick tempo for her final set because at Horsefeathers, bottomless dancing could get mighty chilly if the air conditioning system was on the blink and a blast of fog hit you in the wrong place.

As she worked through the end of her routine, two men walked to the edge of the stage with bills in their hands. She gave each of them a good, vigorous show, up close and personal, showing off everything she was born with and everything else that grew out later. She remembered what one of the dancers said in her first days of work: "Show 'em what they came to see, make 'em smile, and they'll take good care of you."

The first one sheepishly held out a bill, and April lifted her garter, accepted the tip, kissed him on the cheek, and moved on. When she moved over to the second man, she sat in front of him, lay back, rolled forward again, and waited for the tip. He took the bill, folded it in half, and held it between his teeth. April obliged by leaning forward and retrieving the bill between her pressed breasts.

In the final minute of the last track, April returned to Andrew the businessman, and gave him a buck-naked visual delight he'd probably never get at home that night. He beamed. *A nice enough guy*, April thought. *Here's his reward for not being grabby.* She beckoned him forward and used both hands to pull his face to her chest, then squeezed her breasts around him.

"You've heard of those power brown-outs and blackouts out West?" she said. "Well, Andrew, you just experienced a pink-out." Pulling back, she said with a grin, "Did you like the view?"

In his bliss, Andrew said nothing. He just slipped another five-dollar bill into her garter, blew her a kiss, picked up his briefcase, and left. April knew she'd sent him home happy.

After her dance was over, April put her costume back on and mingled with the few men in the club. Only one wanted a table dance, and she was glad to oblige. Another wanted her phone number, but she just laughed. Jessica and Fanny each did a set. By 5:00 there were a dozen men in the place, half golfers, and half regulars.

At 6:00 they were joined by Tatiana, a Russian girl the customers loved but the other dancers all hated. Jessica, who rarely if ever said a bad word about anyone or anything, spoke for the rest of the dancers when she described the Russian as "a greedy, nasty, hard-ass, sex-robot bitch."

Fanny agreed. "Underneath her cold, hard exterior beats a heart of stone," she said with a laugh. Among the dancers and staff, it was a well-known fact that Tatiana made most of her considerable income behind the closed doors of the V.I.P. rooms, not the stage.

"She spends a lot more time dancing on pink poles upstairs than on brass poles downstairs," April said. The other dancers laughed in agreement.

By midnight, the place was full of smoke, loud music, cheap perfume, local regulars, rednecks from the sticks, a couple dozen bikers, and an equal number of low-budget, beer-drinking golfers in town on discount golf package tours.

Jessica was onstage in her Dizzy-Daisy-The-Country-Girl outfit. April was working the crowd. After performing a table dance and pocketing the $10, the customer asked her if she'd like a drink. "Sure," April said, flagging down the mini-skirted waitress. "What's your name?" April asked.

"Jim," he said, resting his hand on her knee. The server bent low so the customer could enjoy the view of her push-up bra through her unbuttoned blouse. "Jim Beam straight up for me," he said. "What about you, Vicky?"

"The usual," she said with a smile to the server. She knew that "the usual" for April was a Diet Coke. The drinks came and the customer paid, giving the waitress a ten-dollar tip. She flashed him some more boob and said, "Thanks."

"Vicky, you have a great body and real talent. I really like the way you dance."

"Thanks a lot," April replied, giving him a big smile.

He leaned closer. "I'm only going to be here for tonight, then it's back to Minneapolis," the man said. "It's getting late, and I'm hoping you'd like to come to my place and spend the night," he said, caressing her leg.

"Sorry, Jim," April said. "I have a boyfriend, and he'd be pissed," she said, using one of the standard lines the other girls had taught her to fend off a pushy customer without making him angry. She moved her leg away from his hand.

"I'd really like you to come home with me, Vicky," he continued. "I was thinking like more of a business relationship than a boyfriend one. Say, $300 for the night?" He moved his hand up her leg and continued to caress her.

"Sorry, mister. I don't go home with the customers. House rules. I'd get fired."

"OK. I understand. I don't want to get you in trouble with the boss. How about we go upstairs to the V.I.P. Room? I really want to make it with you, Vicky. How about $300 for just an hour upstairs?"

"Sorry. I'm not your girl. I only dance onstage and here in the main room. If you want to rent a girlfriend tonight, you'll have to find someone else." April shook off his hand, stood up, and left.

"Your loss," he said with a shrug as April walked away. Five minutes later, she saw that he was handing Fanny the same line. It was April's turn to dance again, so she circled to the back of the club.

"Next on stage is the beautiful Miss Vicky Love," said the DJ. "Everybody please show your love and gratitude for Miss Vicky." The first two sets netted her about thirty dollars in tips. Just as the music for her third set ended, she saw a commotion at the front of the club. Four men she'd seen in the club that evening were now wearing shiny gold police badges on their sweatshirts, golf shirts, and Harley Davidson T-shirts. Blue lights from squad cars outside were flashing through the open doors onto the mirrored walls of the club. As April watched, they hauled off three dancers.

"Myrtle Beach vice squad," sobbed Jessica. "They busted Fanny and Tatiana and Cherry Blossom for pink-pole dancing in the V.I.P. Rooms. Oh, crap. Now I gotta go to the damn jail and bail Fanny out tomorrow. Damn! I really needed to get some studying done tomorrow, not make a jailhouse bail bond run to Conway. I have my French 102 finals at Coastal Carolina U. on Monday."

37
Unscrewed

P ass the red wine, Steve," Dolly said. She loved the fact that they were together again that night. La Luna Rosa was fast becoming their favorite place to renew old ties and explore new ones. Dolly wished that Steve had more time to be with her. But with his long hours, Dolly's two jobs, and her search for April, the two old-and-new friends had a hard time matching schedules for anything except brief cell phone calls.

Dinner was delicious, but she sensed that he was holding something back. "What's up with you tonight, Steve? I have a hunch that you have some news for me. Is there something you want to tell me?"

Steve clinked his glass of Chianti with Dolly's. "I do have news, Dolly. All in all, it's pretty good," he said. "One of our guys saw April last night. She's looking, well . . . pretty healthy. He was working a prostitution sting at a strip club called 'Horsefeathers'. . . ."

All the blood drained out of Dolly's face. "Oh, my God, Steve! That's a really scummy club. Bottomless, too. Pleeeeeeeease don't tell me she was busted for selling sex. I guess I can understand stripping. It's not exactly the kind of job a mother would want for her daughter, but hell, I did it. But if she's selling her body. . . ."

"No, Dolly, no. That's the good part. Our vice squad guy propositioned her twice. Because of her arrest for possession with intent, all the vice and narcotics officers have her description, so later he remembered who she was. April — she dances there as 'Vicky Love' — wouldn't go home with him for $300 or screw him in a V.I.P. Room for the same money. She turned him down cold for both. From what he told me, she only dances on stage and in the main lounge. No funny stuff."

Dolly slumped in her chair and started breathing again. All the memories of her own days as a stripper after the divorce from Kenny came flooding back to her. She knew that the better clubs generally enforced the no-touchy-feely laws and kept the staff out of trouble. Vigilant bouncers made sure that no one got seriously out of hand, and they didn't allow intercourse in the V.I.P. rooms.

Dolly — and others — also knew that the strip clubs filled a useful purpose in the Redneck Riviera. They let horny male tourists burn off some testosterone in a relatively controlled environment, much in the way that other cities had unofficially-licensed "red light districts." The thought of some horny guy three times April's age getting a hard-on from watching her daughter dancing naked in front of him made her sick.

She's an adult now, Dolly, she told herself. *Hell, I gave birth when I was her age. She's not doing anything I didn't do. She's just trying to get by, just like everybody else.*

She shook her head in wonderment. "Boy, Steve. Who'd ever think that I would be relieved that the worst thing my eighteen-year-old daughter is doing is dancing completely nude in a sleazy North Myrtle Beach strip club."

Steve couldn't help but laugh. It was true. Dolly laughed, too. *Laughing feels good. Very good. More than very good. Awesome.* Steve had made her laugh. Dolly hadn't laughed in nearly four months. She took both of his hands into hers and squeezed them.

"Hey, big guy," she said to her white knight. "You made my night." She didn't want the joy to end in the restaurant. "Take me home. Your place. You're good for me. I want you close to me all night."

38
Personal Space

Horsefeathers' parking lot
Wednesday night

D olly had been sitting in her car by the back door of Horsefeathers, warmed by pride and nervous as a tight rope-walker, for almost an hour when April finally walked outside. In jeans and a T-shirt, with no makeup, she looked far too young to be dancing nude at an X-rated nightclub. The last part wasn't important to Dolly. All she wanted was for her daughter to know that she was loved.

April looked around for her ride, saw she hadn't yet arrived, and then punched some numbers in her cell phone to see where Suzi was. She didn't notice Dolly's approach until she was just a few yards away.

"Mamma! What the. . . ? How did you. . . ? What are you doing here?"

"Hello, April, Honey. I just wanted to come by and tell you how proud I am of you."

April's ears were turning red with anger. She couldn't imagine how her mother had tracked her down — or why. "What do you think you're doing, barging into my life?"

"I'm your mother, Honey. I love you. I haven't seen you since the plea bargain. You disappeared. I was worried to death."

"Well, now you've seen that I'm alive. Please go away and leave me alone."

"Honey, why are you so angry? I never did anything to hurt you. All I ever did is give you love. Why do you hate me so much?"

April ignored her. "How did you find me?"

This was the question Dolly was afraid of. "My friends in the business heard you were workin' over here."

"Friends? Which friends? There ain't none of your friends workin' here at Horsefeathers." Then it dawned on her. Saturday night. The arrests. The police. Dolly's old boyfriend, Captain Hunt.

"I know. Your spies. Police spies. You got your detective boyfriend to tell the whole damn Myrtle Beach Police Department to look for me. My own mother pulls the strings and sends the cops out after me. You musta wanted to punish me for stripping here, didn't you?"

"No, Honey, no. That wasn't it at all."

"You look at me and see yourself, don't you, Dolly? You look at me and see all the things you screwed up when you were my age."

"No, no, Honey, no. I'm here tonight because I'm proud of you for telling the cop to get lost when he solicited you."

April was on her own railroad track, rolling down the rails. She wasn't interested in Dolly's rhetoric.

"I get it. If they could get me to do something against the law, they'd bust me and I'd be back in jail — where you could come and save me again. You are a real control freak. Man, that's sick."

"I didn't ask them to do anything."

"Yeah, right, Mamma. It was just a big coincidence that the vice cop came into the place I was working, groped me, and asked me twice if I'd fuck him for $300. God! My own mother thinks I'm a whore. Thanks, Mamma, for your big vote of confidence."

Dolly was in shock. The whole situation was spiraling completely out of control.

"No, no, Honey. I didn't have anything to do with that vice squad thing. They do those undercover stings all the time."

"Yeah, right, Mamma. And you just happened to hear about it five minutes after it happened."

"No, Honey, you have it all wrong. Steve told me. . . ."

"Ah!" So it's not 'Captain Hunt' anymore, but 'Steve.' That tells me a lot. Are you screwin' him just to get information on me?"

Dolly reacted from instinct and regretted it instantly. She slapped April across the face and immediately realized what the effect was. "April, Honey, I didn't mean that."

April didn't flinch or move. She looked at her mother with cold contempt. "Now you've told me everything I need to know about you, Mamma, so here's what you need to know about me:

"One: I'm just fine without you meddling in my life.

"Two: I go to my fun little court-ordered Narcotics Anonymous meetings twice a week and drink bad coffee in a smoke-filled room with crackheads, coke whores, and all the other assorted losers, just like the judge and my Mamma told me to.

"Three: I have a steady, legal job that makes me about $2,000 a month, even after I tip off half the people who work in the slimy place.

"Four: I pay for my own food, rent and cell phone every month and even put a few bucks under the mattress every week or two.

"Five: I have friends I like living with and who like me. And they are not druggies or whores, thank you very much.

"Six: I have a grandmother who loves me, doesn't judge me, and doesn't try to run my whole fuckin' life.

"So, Mamma, you can see that my life is just a bowl of cherries and I don't need you to manage it."

The attack reduced Dolly to tears. "No, no, no, April. You have it all wrong. I love you," she said between sobs. "I respect what you're doing with your life. I didn't send the police to spy on you or test you. I only came here to tell you I love you and to ask you to come home."

Suzi Vetter's old Mercury Cougar appeared from around the end of the building and pulled up behind April. "Mamma, meet Suzi. Suzi's an ex-dope fiend friend of mine. She helped save my life, and now she's my best friend." April immediately continued her non-stop monologue, leaving Dolly no time to reply.

"Suzi, meet my mother. She called in the cops to try to bust me and get me fired from my job because she's ashamed that I'm a stripper. But she failed, and I'm still a stripper and a pathetic excuse for a human being.

"Mamma, say goodnight to Suzi, 'cause she and I are goin' home. And don't try to follow us, 'cause we're gonna lose you if you even think about it."

April threw her costume bag into the back seat, stepped into the Cougar, and slammed the door shut for emphasis. Suzi gave her a worried look.

"Drive, Suzi," April said, looking straight ahead. "Just drive."

Shaking with every sob, Dolly stumbled back to her car, opened the door, and collapsed inside. By the time she stopped crying, the parking lot was empty.

39
The Caddie From Hell

What the heck does a topless golf caddie do?" April asked Jessica, her fellow dancer. "Don't you have to carry those heavy bags of golf clubs? Those things must weigh a ton. What was it like when you worked the tournament?"

"Nah. It's a piece of cake. You don't have to carry anything. All you do is drive an electric golf cart around the course for two hours, show the guys your tits, pour them beer, laugh at all their jokes, take the money, and go home alone."

"Sounds simple enough," April said.

"Remember to put a *lot* of sunblock on your boobs," Jessica said. "It *really* hurts if you get sunburn on your boobs."

"How much does it pay?"

"Well, that depends on the auction and the tips."

"Auction?"

"The caddie auction. They hold it at the club a week before the tournament. You go onstage, strut your stuff, and the golfers bid on you."

"Sounds like a horse or slave auction."

"I dunno about that."

"How much do they bid?"

"Depends. One foursome bid $550 for Tatiana this spring, but they knew that for an extra $50 apiece, she'd give 'em all head."

"Tatiana got $450 for two hours' work?"

"No, they supposedly give some to charity. Keeps some of the heat off 'em if they can claim that some of the money goes to charities. A cut goes to the house. Sixty percent goes to the caddie. So Tatiana got $330 for her two hours."

"Do you have to put out for the golfers?"

"No. They can dream, but they can't demand it. Of course, your tips depend on happy campers. . . ."

"Are you gonna do it?" April asked.

"Yeah," she said. "It's not all that bad, and the money is good. They bid $250 for me last time, and I made another $150 in tips, so I got $300 for the two hours."

"$150. That's good tips. Did you have to. . . ?"

Jessica just smiled. April knew when to stop asking questions.

It was 8:00 A.M. Tee time was a magic moment in the life of every serious golfer. It was a special place in time and space, resplendent with beauty and magic. Ron Pawley soaked up the sight of the sun as it sent golden shafts of light through the tall pine and oak trees of the magnificent golf course. His ears picked up the sound of soft rubber tires buzzing down the cart trails; he savored the unique feeling of his cleats biting into the meticulously manicured grass. He heard the gentle laughs of men joking about their prowess on and off the golf course, and the friendly challenges and bets they made about the game to come. Ron hefted his clubs and walked in the direction of the first tee. The golden sun reflected from his irons and sprayed his tanned face with dancing splashes of light.

Then reality sunk in. Ron groaned to himself when he thought of the challenges presented by the day ahead. Of his three golf partners, Frank, from Toronto, was hung over from far, far too much partying the night before at. . . was it Planet Hollywood? Or the beach bar downtown? Or the strip club? He couldn't exactly remember.

Robert, his 45-year-old countryman from some podunk town in rural Ontario, was still half-asleep, the victim of a 20-year-old coke whore who had given him much more than he could handle. The third, Jerry, was a prospective client from New Jersey; the lead dog for a pack of condo time-share investors. He had dropped nearly $1,500 the night before while miraculously surviving three bottles of $250-a-bottle Dom Perignon and the enthusiastically erotic attention of three equally expensive strippers.

To his total amazement, the woozy foursome assembled at the first tee within five minutes of their assigned tee time. Hungover or sober, he knew, golfers were a dedicated bunch. Whatever their condition, they rarely missed their tee times.

They were met at the first tee by their caddie. "Hi. My name's Vicky Love," April said. "Welcome. Tell me your names."

"Hi, Beautiful. I'm Ron."

"Nice to meet you, Ron," she said, shaking his hand.

Ron tried to peer down her buttoned white blouse, tied at the waist. He quickly got to the point. "When do you go topless?"

"One button a hole," April said "Five buttons. Whoever wins the hole gets to undo the button."

"You're outta work today," Frank, said his buddy, Robert. "I guess I'll have to do the honors."

"Hi, I'm Jerry," said the third. "Don't pay any attention to the two foreigners. This is the U.S. of A. We take care of our own. I'll do all the work."

April smiled her best stripper fake smile. "Let's get on with it, gentlemen," she said. Golfers, start your carts!"

The foursome stumbled and mumbled its way through the first hole. Ron, the only one who hadn't spent the whole previous night partying, easily won the par four hole with a single bogey putt. As he slowly unbuttoned the top button of April's blouse, he smiled at her and said, "Hmmm. I like the way this is shaping up."

Frank amazed everyone with a lucky shot off the second tee. His teammates each ran into the sand traps, much to Frank's delight. As he unbuttoned the second button, he ran his hands across her chest.

"Hey, no samples, Honey," April said, pulling away. *This is as bad as late Friday nights at the club*, she thought.

The mid-summer sun had burned through the haze, and the temperature was already in the high 80s. April opened the cooler sitting on the back of the golf cart. "Guys — anyone ready for a beer?" she called.

Frank said, "Hair of the dog. Yeah, Beautiful. Lay one on me." The others looked at Frank, shook their heads in exasperation, laughed, and played on. The beer didn't help his game any. Frank triple-bogeyed the hole.

Jerry's birdie on the par four third hole made him the easy winner. When he returned to the cart, he asked for a beer. April got out, leaned over, and opened the cooler. As she did, Jerry ran his hand down her back and squeezed her butt.

"Hey, guy. Enough of that," April said, handing him the beer. She opened the third button of her shirt herself.

"Hey, that's my job," Jerry complained.

"It is as long as you play nice," April said, trying to keep a cheerful look on her face. She could sense that this was not going to be a fun morning. At least she enjoyed the dancing. It gave her a chance to move, innovate, and express herself. Driving a golf cart for a bunch of hung-over golfers was not turning out to be her cup of tea, money or no money.

"Two buttons to go, guys," said Ron. "And it looks like Miss Vicky here has a lot left to show us. Let's get rollin'."

The fourth hole was a long, par five doglog left. Frank was half-asleep from the beer. Robert and Jerry were both still hung over, and Ron easily took the hole with a single bogey round.

"I'm getting to like this game a lot," he said, unbuttoning the fourth button on April's blouse. "I don't have much imagination. I like to have things laid right out in front of me."

April smiled and gave him a good look. *What the hell*, she thought. *They get to see 'em every night at the club. This is just a two-hour table dance without the table and without the dance.*

"Lookin' good," Frank mumbled, a big smile on his face.

"Way to go, Ron," said Jerry.

As they were waiting for Frank to finish the fourth hole, they looked over at the fifth tee. The caddie was waving her bikini top in circles in the air. Each of the other foursome gave their lively, top-less caddie a big hug and, in turn, was rewarded with a "pink out." April took a deep breath. She knew that now, they were going to expect the same from her.

The fifth hole was also a walk in the park for Ron, who golfed twice a week with clients. "Gather 'round the cart, guys," he called. "It's time for the main event." He beckoned for April to get out of the golf cart and join them at the fifth tee.

As the men formed a circle around her, Ron walked up and started humming the classic burlesque tune, "The Stripper." April swung her hips and shimmied to what passed for the music as Ron undid the last button. April swayed and turned as she started to loosen the knot that held the blouse together. Slowly, teasingly, she undid the tails of the blouse until it fell open, revealing her hand-some chest to the appreciative, if unsteady, audience of four. From a nearby tee, four other golfers also waved and shouted their ap-preciation.

"All riiiight!" said Jerry. "I feel a short put comin' on."

In your dreams, April thought, as she continued her topless dance under the broiling sun. Now she knew why Jessica had been so adamant about putting on lots of sunblock lotion.

"Hey, April, why don't you lose the rest of the outfit, too. Let's say, for an extra hundred. Or if you like, I've got some good coke."

"Looks delicious to me," said Frank as he eyed her breasts. "Mind if I have a little sample, Babe?" he said as he wrapped his arms around April and shoved his face into her cleavage.

"Get off me, you jerk," April yelled with a voice so loud and filled with conviction that the other three golfers froze in mid-laugh. With all her might, she broke loose from Frank's embrace with a single yank. Then she planted her foot in his stomach and pushed hard. The shove sent him sprawling down the slope and into a sand trap.

"What kind of idiots are y'all?" she yelled, grabbing her shirt. "I'm only here for decoration, not use. If you want a whore, rent one. I'm a dancer and an entertainer. I danced and now you've been entertained. Bye."

April walked to one of the golf carts, turned the key, put her foot on the accelerator, and drove back down the cart path, leaving two of her foursome stranded at the sixth tee without clubs, cart, or caddie. Within moments, the event caught the attention of other golfers on nearby holes, who cracked up and guffawed with laughter while pointing to Ron's foursome.

"Yahoo!" April yelled to anyone within earshot as she drove the cart back to the clubhouse. *"Life rocks!"* Grinning ear-to-ear, she put the accelerator pedal to the floor and yelled out for the pure joy of it. Then she drove off the cart path, onto the greens, and headed straight for the clubhouse.

The other golfers at the tournament scattered in confusion when they saw the beautiful, shirt-waving, topless driver and her cart come roaring straight down the center of the fairway. It was clear that she didn't care much about following golf's holy book, *The Official Rules of Golf.*

40
Amen, period.

Richardson-Hall Funeral Chapel
Darlington, S.C.

A nd there isn't a person here who doesn't know that Henry Doolittle was a hard-working farmer and a beloved member of this community. We know he fought a long, hard, painful fight, and that he's in a much better place now," the preacher said. "But I speak for everyone here when I say that we're all going to miss him a great deal. Amen."

"Amen," said Anne, April, and Dolly.

The minister walked from the small podium next to the casket and offered his hand to Anne. Her tears had stopped, but her eyes were red and puffy. He did the same for April and Dolly, then waited in the aisle.

The pallbearers rose and wheeled the casket to the waiting hearse. Anne, Dolly, April, the rest of the family, and their friends and neighbors followed. The three women entered the first black limousine together for the twenty-minute drive to the cemetery. The rest of the funeral cortege stretched out for nearly half a mile behind them.

"Henry was a good man, girls. I want you to know that," Anne said. "I've been lucky. I had two good men in my life: Robert and Henry."

Dolly squeezed her mother's hand. She tried not to think about all the others.

"I wish you could have gotten to know him better," Anne said, looking at Dolly and April. "He loved both of you, even though the cancer made it hard for him to do or say much."

Both of the younger women knew what she was trying to say. Half the message was literal. Neither Dolly nor April had ever made a great effort to get to know Henry, who was, by nature, a quiet and introspective man.

The other message was equally clear. Anne was hurt that the two of them had spent so little time with her over the last years, while her husband was slipping away and her pain was greatest.

"I'm sorry, too, Mamma," Dolly said. "I know how good he was to you. Steady, warm, and always there when you needed him."

Dolly looked out the car window. *I could have used one like that in my life,* Dolly thought.

April thought of her father and stared at her feet. *I wish I could have had a man like that in my life,* she thought.

As the limousine rolled through the bountiful cotton and to-bacco countryside, Dolly looked across the seat at April. She knew the agony the drugs had caused her. She yearned for reassurance that they would never be part of her life again, but there was none.

At least the physical signs were good. Since she started at-tending Narcotics Anonymous meetings twice a week, April had regained about ten pounds of the twenty the drug life had stolen from her slender frame. The dark circles were gone from under her eyes, and she was letting her hair grow out again. Dolly prayed that she'd permanently stopped using drugs, but she also knew that, for a drug addict, there was no such thing as a cure. At any time, a catastrophic relapse was only one pill away.

April was terrified. She had never been to a funeral before. She barely knew her step-grandfather, and didn't know what to do, or say, or ask. She dearly wanted to talk to her grandmother, to comfort her and ask what to do, but there was Dolly, sitting be-tween them.

For the hundredth time, she thought, *there's Mamma, sitting be-tween me and what I want.* She stared at her shoes and hoped no one would talk to her.

Anne was silent for almost ten minutes. "What are you thinkin', Mamma?" Dolly asked.

April was frightened. *What if they ask me the same question? What am I supposed to say?*

"Us," she said, simply. "The three of us. Look at us. The three surviving female generations of this family, scared silly to talk to each other face to face."

"You came out of my body, Dolly. You're my flesh and blood. April, you came out of Dolly's body. You're her flesh and blood. I love you, you love me. She loves me, she loves you. Hell, it's as simple as that stupid purple dinosaur says on ETV."

Dolly and April were shocked. They couldn't guess where Anne was headed. April cringed, her eyes squeezed shut in fear of whatever was coming next.

"Ladies, we're in the burying business today. Henry's going to be gently laid to rest in that big dark hole in the ground, but that casket won't take up the whole space. So let's dump the rest of our painful things into that hole in the ground while it's still open," Anne said. "I think it's high time that we stopped acting like three helpless ninnies and started acting like three grown-ups who love each other. Brace yourselves for the ride, girls, 'cause here we go."

Dolly and April were speechless. Their attention was focused on every word Anne said.

"Dolly, I have a formal apology to make to you," Anne said. I'm sorry I didn't make it many years ago, and I'm half-sorry I'm making it now in front of April, but this opportunity won't last but another ten minutes.

"When you were fifteen, you got pregnant and had to have an abortion. I accused you of having sex with that crazy Zimmerman boy down the road, even though you denied it. Well, I had a pretty good idea that the one who knocked you up was really Chester Lumpkin, a guy I was seein' that summer. You told me it was him, but I didn't believe you. You told me again, and I called you a tramp and a liar. Well, it turned out that ole loudmouthed Chester bragged to his friends about gettin' you pregnant, and confirmed your story."

Dolly's jaw was slack. She couldn't believe her ears, but her heart was pounding so hard she thought she'd explode. She wanted to speak, but Anne held up her hand. She wasn't done yet.

"I will never in the world be able to tell you how evil I feel about callin' you those names and denying the truth. I guess I just couldn't handle the truth back then. And I know that apologizing now can't possibly make up for the hurt or the harm I did to you, but at least I want you to know that you were right, I was wrong, and I am terribly, terribly sorry I did that to you."

"Oh, Mamma," Dolly said, "I. . . ."

Anne cut her off in mid-sentence. "Save it for a few minutes, Sweetie," she said. "We're almost at the cemetery, and I have something to tell April, too."

April gasped, wondering — fearing — what could be ahead.

"April, darlin', I have another confession to make. It's about your father and mother. As you've probably figured out by now, you're a 'love child.' Your Daddy was handsome, funny, and looking for a playmate. Your Mamma wasn't mature enough to turn him down, and that's where you came from. I pressured him to do the right thing and marry Dolly, and he did, but gettin' Kenny to do the right thing for a wife and daughter was like tryin' to pump air into a tire with a big hole in it. Well, he took off and deserted your mother and you shortly after you were born, and no matter what Dolly and I tried, we could not make that man do his part as a father."

April was already in tears, but Anne continued. "Your Mamma has worked like a horse to keep food on the table, and she half killed herself to get Kenny's cooperation to help raise you proper. But your father's got as much responsibility as Hell's got ice cream, and there wasn't a damn thing either one of us could do about it. So when you went lookin' for love from your Daddy, all you got was neglect, and when you was feelin' hurt and wanted comfort from your Mamma, all you got was a note on the door sayin' that she was at one of her two or three jobs, tryin' to pay the rent. You've been blamin' her for everything you never got from Kenny. Honey, as I live and breathe, your mother did everything in the world to help you grow up right, and she loves you to death."

April was incredulous, she desperately wanted her grandmother to stop — and to go on.

"So what I'm sayin, Honey-child, was that you had a complete jerk for a father, and a damn fine mother who never, ever for a moment stopped loving or caring for you. If you gotta blame someone for feeling unloved, blame that dopehead trailer rat, not your mother."

"Mamma," Dolly said, grabbing Anne with both hands and crying uncontrollably.

"Mamma, Grandma," April sobbed, wrapping her arms around both of them.

Anne's voice wavered, but she retained some of her composure. "OK, ladies, let's us have a good cry here in the limo. It's the perfect place. Everybody will think we're doin' it for old Henry. But when we walk out of this car, we're gonna do it hand in hand, as one family of three strong women who love each other and aren't afraid of showing it." At that point, Anne threw in the towel, hugged her two babies, and cried her heart out with them.

Outside the limo, the members of the funeral party looked at the limo and whispered to themselves, lamenting the great grief being expressed inside. Ten minutes later, Anne, Dolly, and April had started to compose themselves. Then an odd thing happened. April looked at her mother, whose mascara was dripping down both cheeks and onto her dress, and giggled. It was the first time she had giggled with her family since she hooked up with C.B. Correlli four years earlier.

Dolly looked down, saw the mascara stains, and giggled, too. Then Anne chimed in, laughing. Soon the new widow and her two fellow mourners were laughing uncontrollably at how awful all of them looked. It took another five minutes for them to compose themselves.

April looked for her purse and found it. She wrote something on the back of half a bank deposit slip and pressed it into Dolly's hand. "So you can call me," she said with a smile, the last tear still running down her cheek.

For the last few moments before they exited the car, Anne sat quietly, composing her thoughts and bracing herself for all the condolences that would inevitably follow. The widows of men who died slow deaths faced a special challenge. Everyone knew that they had suffered for months or years, caring for their sick one and preparing for the inevitable. Then the surviving family members and friends had to weave and bob and guess as best they could what was the right thing to say.

"I'm so sorry for your loss" might be mistaken to mean, "I'm sorry you lost your husband — but no, it never dawned on me that the last three years of being a full-time nurse were hard on you."

God! Anne thought. *No wonder everybody hates funerals. It was easy for the dead ones. They didn't have to guess what to say or do.*

After the casket was lowered, the last words were spoken, and the preacher said the final "Amen," Anne rose to address the mourners.

"I really appreciate y'all being here with me. You are my dearest friends and closest family members, so I'm going to make this a lot easier on all of us. Henry was a real good man to me, and I loved him every moment that he was alive. But the lung cancer he died from took a lot out of me, too. Once they said he was gonna die, he spent every day hopin' it would come fast, so both of us wouldn't suffer any more. It didn't work that way, and the last three years were awful. Now that he's dead and buried, I will remember him every day in my heart. But I've been mourning his death for the last three years since the day the doctor said he'd never recover, and I'm done with my mourning now. If y'all knew Henry at all, you know he liked his whiskey. So y'all come on over to the house and have a drink with me. This here funeral is officially over, period."

41
Job Deficit Disorder

Myrtle Beach Police Department

E ddie. Meth. How long? How much? Who? Where?"
"Seventeen minutes, twenty bucks. Guy cruisin' Ocean Boulevard in a black pickup last night."

"Dan. Ecstasy. How long? How much? Who? Where?"

"Twenty minutes, twenty-five bucks. Stripper, 20s, at the Silver Slipper last night."

"Damn. Is there any city left in America where you can't get narcotics in twenty minutes for twenty bucks anymore?" The staff knew it was a rhetorical question. If there was, they knew that the Redneck Riviera wasn't that place.

Steve Hunt was exasperated. "It's the same as usual. Every month, we send out buyers to check availability and price, and it's always the same damn thing. Here it is, a month since we took out Correlli's lab, and meth is just as easy to get and just as cheap. Where the hell is this new poison coming from? Any new players in town?"

"No," said Detective DeMarcos. "Not that we know of. The Ecstasy still looks like it's coming from the Israeli importing operation in New York. Marijuana, hell, that grows everywhere. South Carolina's gonna be like West Virginia, Tennessee, and Kentucky soon. It's been one of their biggest cash crops for years."

"What about Correlli?" Steve asked. "He made bail. He could be up to anything he wants. He could be back in business again."

"The judge sets bail at a half-million dollars and a slimebag like Correlli can raise it in two days," DeMarcos replied. "He's a veteran, but he doesn't have that much juice. Correlli must have some major backers."

DeMarcos responded, "If he can provide distribution, he can find all the backers he wants to set up more production. Do we have anybody available to tail Correlli?"

"We're spread pretty thin right now, boss. Fall Bike Week ya know. You, us, and 100,000 of our closest and dearest motorcycle friends. That sucks up all the manpower we've got – and the troops from every other division, too."

"I know. God, if we could only tail him for a week or ten days, we might be able to learn something. Every day he's on the street, the likelihood goes up that he's going to get back into production. Do we have anything new on him that could get us a court order for a wiretap?"

"I don't think so. We don't have probable cause for any new charges."

"Well, it hurts to let him roam the streets any way he wants, but it looks like there's nothing we can do right now. OK. Hit the streets. Remember, the Grand Strand is a resort, the powers that be have officially welcomed the bikers here as our guests, and they spend millions of dollars while they're here. Try to keep them from raisin' too much hell but stay out of their faces and don't hassle them."

Fantasia
Friday afternoon

"Fantasia is a business, Ms. Devereaux, not a social service. This shop was doing well in the first month after you took over, but then sales nose-dived."

"I know, I know, but I had really serious problems to deal with."

"Well so do we, Ms. Devereaux. It's called business. It's called profits. It's called jobs. No business equals no profits equals no jobs. You were a logical choice for the job after the last manager took a hike. Your first month was great. Sales way up. Then the problems started. You came in late and left early. You left new employees unsupervised. We gave you a month to get your act together after the problems started. Then we gave you another month. You've been running the shop for four months, and the sales and profits this last month are worse that the one before. I'm sorry about your personal problems. I know you tried to work them out, but they interfered with your work so much that I can't carry you any longer."

Dolly felt her heart sink into her shoes. It was all true, and there wasn't a damn thing she could say in her own defense. She had let down the store chain, the manager who hired her, and the girls who worked for her. The disaster was complete. Case closed.

The district manager reached into his briefcase and retrieved a file folder. He handed her a check. "This is for this week's pay and two weeks' severance pay. Your health insurance covers you until the end of the month. If you want to privatize it, the conversion papers are in the folder. The 401(k) wasn't scheduled to kick in until the first of next month, so there's no paperwork to do there. Your keys, please."

"My keys? You mean I'm fired? Right now? This minute? What will I tell the girls?"

"Yes, it's better if we get this over with quickly, Ms. Devereaux. Don't worry. I'll give them your best wishes. Your keys, please."

In shock, Dolly fumbled with her key ring and removed the door and cash register keys. There was nothing she could say to the man. It was all true. The constant series of crises with April had sucked up large chunks of her work time. Her late arrivals and sudden early departures had created havoc for the rest of the staff. The girls at Fantasia had been glad to see the previous manager go because she was a witch to work with. They all loved Dolly, but a job was a job. Her erratic comings and goings had played havoc with their lives, and they just hoped that the next manager would bring some stability with her.

Dolly left Fantasia in a trance. Numb from the abrupt termination of her job, she could only nod goodbye to Shaniqua, the only clerk on duty. Shaniqua gave her a sad smile and a small wave, but Dolly hardly saw it.

She opened the door of her little Honda and just sat there in the car, the door half open, one foot inside, one on the asphalt. Dolly's mind swam with a dozen conflicting thoughts and worries. The tourist season was winding down. Her job at Captain Willie's was down from six to four nights a week, and the daily tips were down, too. *How am I going to pay the bills? Where am I going to find another day job?* she wondered.

Dolly sat in the car for nearly half an hour, staring at the sign, "Reserved for Manager. Dolly."

I guess they'll change that on Monday, she thought. When the mental fog lifted a little, Dolly knew what she needed that night. She fished in her purse for her cell phone, dialed, and waited.

"Myrtle Beach Police Department administrative line. Is this an emergency?"

Dolly thought, *Well, lady, it is for me, but not for you.* "No, ma'am, routine business."

"How may I direct your call?"

"Detective Steven Hunt, Please."

"One moment please." Dolly waited as the phone clicked over to Steve's extension

"Hello, this is Detective Steven Hunt of the Myrtle Beach Police Vice and Narcotics Division. If this is an emergency, please dial 911 now. I'm away from my desk at the moment. . . ."

Dolly broke into tears when she heard the voice mail message. When she heard the beep, she sobbed into the phone, "Steve, come on over to my place tonight if you can. I just got canned and I could sure use some company."

42
Bright Ideas

SeaVue Apartments
6:00 A.M.

Dolly rubbed her eyes and tried to wake up. Six o'clock in the morning wasn't her favorite time of the day. "Hi there, big guy," Dolly said to Steve as he sat on the edge of the bed, tying the laces on his perfectly shined black shoes. Dolly rubbed the back of his white dress shirt. "Man! Why do you have them put so much starch in your shirts? They supposed to stop bullets or something?"

"Old habit, Dolly. My father never left the house without one."

"'Bet you have six of them, all identical."

"Twelve."

"Come here and let me put some wrinkles in your shirt." She wrapped her arms around him and gave him a kiss.

"Ummmm. . . . I'd love to, Dolly, but roll call is at 7:00 and I have to stop by my place for some stuff before I go to the office."

"I can be very persuasive, Detective. And I have evidence to show you." Dolly straightened up in bed to show off her curves. She ran her fingers through his curly brown hair. "And it's your job to investigate things . . . like these. . . ." She started to peel down the spaghetti strap of her ivory silk camisole.

"Don't torture me, Dolly," Steve said with a smile that reflected true agony. "It's against the law." Steve stood up and finished dressing.

Dolly watched in awe as the new man in her life drank his coffee, gathered his police accessories, and walked with her to the door. As she put her arms around him and kissed him goodbye, she could feel the gun in his shoulder holster.

"I'm working on a present for you," she said as he went out the door.

"I thought you were the present," he said with a laugh.

"I'm the gift that keeps on giving," she said, blowing him a kiss. "But I'm working on something special for you."

"Don't torture me," he said. "What is it?"

"It's not finished yet. You'll just have to come by often and I'll let you know when it's done."

Steve smiled, waved, and then sprinted down the flight of stairs to the parking lot. With a final wave, he opened the door of the big, blue-and-white Myrtle Beach Police cruiser and drove off. Dolly went back to the bed, still warm from their night of rapture and reassurance. She set the clock for 11:00 A.M., made a mental note to call April, and slipped between the sheets. There were important things to do, but they could wait for a couple of hours, she thought. *If I'm going to be unemployed today*, she thought, *I might as well enjoy at least the first few hours of it.*

"Hi, Honey, it's Mamma. Am I callin' too early?" Dolly could hear a sleepy yawn from the other end of the line.

"No, Mamma, it's OK. I was gonna get up in a couple of minutes anyway. What time is it?"

"About noon."

"Oh. OK. How ya doin?" April asked. It was good to hear her mother's voice again after all the sadness, despair, and violence of the past three months.

"Good, Baby. Well, one little itsy-bitsy problem. I got fired yesterday."

"Fired? Aw, Mamma! That's terrible. Where? Fantasia or Captain Willie's?"

"Fantasia. But that's OK. I got a little severance pay and I can find another job. I wasn't callin' about that. I need your help for somethin' real special. Can I come pick you up? We can do a little shopping and then talk about it over lunch."

April was still shaking off her sleepiness. "Uh, sure, Mamma. Give me an hour to get ready. But I have to go onstage at 4:00 this afternoon. Yeah, happy hour. Bummer for customer traffic, but hey — less girls to compete with. OK. See you then. Oh — I better tell you where I live. North Myrtle, off 6th Street South. Look for a big white van with a fifteen-foot-long fiberglass crab crawling on it. Yeah, the seafood delivery truck. It's not real hard to spot. My new boyfriend drives for them. Bye."

"Do I look like Thelma?" April said to her mother.

"Do I look like Louise?" Dolly answered. They both laughed.

"Since when did you open up shop as 'Dolly Devereaux, Ace Detective?'"

"Since I found out that C.B. Correlli is already out on bond and that he's probably got another meth lab up and running."

"That's police work, Mamma. Heck, you're dating the chief of detectives. You should know that."

"Honey, it's Fall Bike Week. They don't have anybody available to keep tabs on that slimeball — or the other dozens of criminals out there. They mostly have to wait 'til something happens."

"So what can we possibly do? We're not the police."

"Keep tabs on Correlli. Watch him. Follow him. See if we can find out anything about what he's up to, who he's hangin' with. You know a lot of them."

"Yeah — and if they spot me or you, C.B. could make one phone call and have either one of us blown away. He's got some close connections with violent people. Mamma. I mean *really* violent people. Guys who kill people just for the fun of it. Why do you think C.B. and the W.A.R. Skins wear those steel-toed boots? It's not to protect their toes from falling bricks. C.B. personally kicked a Korean guy to death in California just because he was dating a white chick."

Dolly was sobered but undaunted. Her eyes were aglow with excitement. "We could go under cover. Wear disguises."

April looked at her mother as if she had just escaped from the South Carolina State Home for the Bewildered.

"Mamma, are you OK? Or did some old 'Charlie's Angels' videos fall off a shelf and hit you on the head?"

"I want to make sure Correlli gets convicted and stays behind bars for the rest of his life. I think you want the same thing. But I can't do it without you, Honey. I don't know his hangouts, his people. You don't have a car or a driver's license. C.B. hurt you and all those other kids he lured into drugs and the Skinhead scene. And he's directly responsible for Skank's death. God only knows who else he'll hurt or kill if we don't help the police get him charged for everything he's doin'. Will you help me?"

April was bewildered. This had all come out of nowhere. Two weeks ago, she still hated her mother. One week ago, at Henry Doolittle's funeral, Anne had brought all their lives into sharp focus. Now, just a week after the funeral, here was her mother — the enemy just two weeks earlier — asking for her help investigating the man she'd trusted and slept with for three years.

"I can't do it without you, Baby," Dolly said again. "Will you help me trail Correlli?"

April thought of all the people whose lives C.B. Correlli had touched. Hers. She thought she was his special girl – until she found out that C.B. slept with all the girls. Then there were the drugs. She thought that free drugs were a fringe benefit of being C.B.'s girlfriend – until he told her she'd have to sell them to keep getting them free. Then there was Wendy, her best friend, whom she loved to be with until she found out that she was C.B.'s favorite, his chief convert, his first courtesan, and his apprentice meth cook.

All the others were just names — except Skank. If it hadn't been for C.B., Skank would still be alive. April's eyes teared up at the thought of how horrible Skank looked when Boomer had dumped him off at the apartment those few weeks before. When April thought of Skank, nothing else mattered.

"OK Mamma, I'll help. I want that bastard to pay for what he did to everybody, especially Skank. But Mamma, you've got to get this Charlie's Angel's dress-up playtime crap out of your head. These people are serious and dangerous. They don't mess around."

"I know, you're right. You know, I went to the jail to see Wendy the day after the meth lab bust...."

"Wendy, oh God, I bet she hates me now. I didn't mean for all that to happen to her."

"Yeah, she's upset with you, April, but you did the right thing."

"I know, I know. I don't want to talk about Wendy right now. This is about C.B."

"Well, that's what I was going to say. She mentioned that he was going to be really angry with you about getting him busted. I asked her if she thought you were in danger, and she said that C.B. wasn't going to do anything to draw attention to himself right now. I just really hope she's right. I don't want to see anything happen to you."

"I think she's right, Mamma. One thing about C.B. is that he's smart as hell. He knows how to play the game. I've never seen him let his guard down. That's why he's been so hard for the police to nail. It took his girlfriend of three years — me — selling him out to finally get him. If he messes up, his whole operation goes down, and that's really bad news for him 'cause he's got people to answer to. Really big people that expect him to keep business going. If they think he's a total screw-up who can't keep himself out of jail, they won't protect him anymore; they won't put up his half mil-lion- dollar bail bonds."

"Who are these 'big people?' Why aren't the cops after them?"

"Geez, Mamma, you're pretty naïve about the drug culture, considering your ex-husband and all. These 'big people' run ev-erything. They're like the drug lords of the whole country. They've got people working everywhere. And those people have people working for them, and those people also have people working for them, and so on all the way down the line.

No matter who you nab, if they're important and valuable enough to the powers that be, they've got somebody powerful above them to get them out of trouble. Hell, some of the 'big people' *are* cops. If you think C.B. was hard to get, you have no idea how im-possible it would be to take down an entire drug ring like the ones these guys run. These kind of people are untouchable. They're richer than the cops, the FBI, or the DEA. Trust me, the cops *are* after them. They have been forever – but they never make much headway."

"I had no idea you were involved in anything like *that*," Dolly gasped.

"I wasn't. Those people don't even know I exist. They're so much further up the food — or drug — chain than me. People like me are nothing to them. C.B. was in a totally different class than any of us. He's for real. Drugs are his profession. Kids like me, we only did it so we could keep using for free. We didn't make any money or anything."

"All right. I get the point. This is serious, I know. I don't want to put us in danger, but I want to do this. I want to help get Correlli. Will you help me?"

"Yeah, Mamma. I'll help. But I don't have a clue in the world about where C.B. is or lives. I only know where he used to hang out. Where do you want us to start?"

"You know that wig shop a few blocks from the Pavilion?"

"You gotta be kidding, Mamma! That nylon junk? Even the cheap hookers won't shop there."

Dolly fired up the Honda. April sighed and fastened her seat belt. She knew Dolly was serious.

43
Shadows

I t's gonna fall off," April said as she readjusted her fifteen-dollar, dirty blonde wig and crouched low in the front seat of the Honda. "I feel like a total idiot. What kind of lunatics are we to think this will do any good?" she asked her mother.

Dolly's brown wig barely contained the ocean of platinum blonde hair beneath it. "Just think of this as some of the 'quality time' we missed out on in the last four years, Honey."

"Yeah, right, Mamma. Quality time, huh? Did C.B. ever get a look at your car? Would he recognize it?"

"I don't think so, Honey. I only talked to Wendy and Skank at the front door of his place that one day I found you, and my car wasn't parked in sight of the door."

"But C.B. went out the back. Could he have seen it?"

"It's possible, Honey, but I doubt it. I was parked behind the strip club. If he was trying to avoid seeing me, I doubt he inventoried the cars in the parking lot on the way out. If we take the alley that leads in to his old place, can we continue by the house and get out to some other street, or is it a dead end?"

"No, it goes through."

"Good. I wouldn't want to get trapped in there."

"I thought you said the place was boarded up and that his stuff was on the street."

"It was — but we have to start someplace. OK. I'll drive the car, you keep the notes. The notebook's in the glove box. Start a new page with today's date and the time. We're about to become the FBI."

Dolly's hands shook as she cautiously turned into the alley leading to C.B. Correlli's old hangout. She tried to look composed so as not to frighten April, but she had no idea how well her act was received. The mercury vapor streetlight from the strip club's back parking lot cast an eerie, greenish glow on the apartment building. The front door of apartment #7 was still boarded up, and there was no sign of life inside.

"Did the police search his place after they arrested Correlli?" Dolly asked.

"They did, but it was pretty quick, from what I heard. Just lookin' for drugs, I think. I wasn't here. I came back that afternoon and found Blue all freaked out."

"Are there any windows we can get in through?"

"What? Are you serious? You're gonna break in?"

"Only if we can't get in an easier way. Do you happen to have a key to the back door, by any chance?"

Good Grief! April thought. *How simple does it get? Yes, I do.* She rummaged through her purse for her keychain. There, with the number 7B clearly stamped into the metal, was just what they needed. She turned to her mother and giggled. Dolly's wig had shifted, and a wisp of blonde hair drooped down the back of her neck. "Some Charlie's Angel you are, Mamma," she said, pointing at the problem with her disguise.

Dolly looked in the car mirror, stuffed the offending hair back into the wig, and laughed.

"Sorry, partner," she said. "It's my first day on the job." Dolly parked the Honda in the club's parking lot. "See if there's a flashlight in the glove box."

"What for?"

"Looking around, of course."

April found the flashlight. "Let's go," she said.

They cautiously unlocked the back door and entered the house. There was little left but dust and trash. The closets were empty, except for a couple of broken clothes hangers.

"Let's check the trash cans," said Dolly.

"You've been watching too many crime TV shows, Mamma," April said. They dumped the contents of the kitchen trash can onto the floor. April screamed as a dozen large cockroaches ran out of the pile and sought the safety of the shadows.

"Nothing here, I guess," said Dolly, after poking through the trash with a piece of a broken yardstick she had found on the floor. "Let's move on."

"Let's get outta here," said April. "We don't know what we're looking for and wouldn't know it if we found it."

"We're looking for anything that will connect anybody to Correlli, girl. Let's check the bathroom and the bedroom and then we can go."

April hugged close to her mother. As they entered the bathroom, another roach scuttled out of their way. Dolly kicked over the bathroom trashcan with her foot and listened. No noise. She poked through the trash with the stick. It contained nothing but crumpled tissue paper, two plastic cups, paper tampon wrappers – and a small, crumpled piece of cardboard. Dolly gingerly rolled it over. It was a business card. Several credit card receipts lay next to it. She picked them up, put them in her pocket, and moved on.

"That's it, Honey," she said. April had been tugging onher sleeve since they entered the place. "Let's get out of here. Lock up and we're gone."

Ten minutes later, Dolly and April sat in a corner booth at Dolly's favorite all-night diner.

"What took you so long, girl?" Dolly asked as April returned from the bathroom. "I thought you'd never come out of there."

"I felt like I had to wash my hands three times to get rid of every trace of that place," April said. "God! How could I ever have lived in that rathole?"

Dolly reached across the table and took her daughter's hand. "You don't ever have to do that again." She reached into her pocket and pulled out the papers. After flattening the folded business card, she read it. It carried the neatly printed name and address of Preston R. Hickson, D.D.S. Printed in the center was the name, "Natalie Bluestein, Dental Assistant."

"Holy cow," said April. "So that's who she is!"

"Who?"

"Blue. The new girl C.B. picked up just before I got busted. Her real name looks like it's Natalie Bluestein, and she worked for Wendy's father. That's why the two of them were so close. I remember now. Blue wanted to get some intern time and become a dental hygienist. She was probably interning at Dr. Hickson's office when she met Wendy."

"Were Blue and Wendy close?"

"Oh, yeah. Blue was also eighteen. She thought Wendy was way cool."

"OK. So let's make up a list of everybody you know who was connected to Correlli. One of them must be able to lead us to him."

April squeezed her eyes shut for a few moments. The thought of reviewing all the associations of the past three years was painful. She looked at her mother. Dolly looked back. April saw the love in her eyes. She pushed aside the pain of recalling and launched into the task.

"Me."

"You. We know you, and you don't know where Correlli is. Next."

"Wendy Hickson."

"So what's with Wendy?"

"Wendy was always very tight with C.B. They let her walk for lack of evidence after they arrested her at the lab. So she's floating around somewhere, probably with him."

"Skank, er, Jimmy Mullins, but he's . . . he's dead. God!" April said as the tears flowed. "I miss that little jerk."

Dolly brushed her tears away. "That's why we have to help find Correlli and whatever he's doing. Otherwise, Jimmy died for nothing."

"Blue. She was never arrested. But she was using and dealing for C.B., so she's probably not very far away.

"Boomer. He's dead. Too bad the police didn't miss and get Correlli," April said. Dolly said nothing. April's anger was understandable.

"Who else?" Dolly asked.

"Suzi. Suzi Vetter. I live with her and her boyfriend. She's a waitress at Easy Rider, next to the place I dance. Suzi's cool, and she doesn't do drugs anymore. Well, a little pot on special occasions, but that's it. She hates C.B., and I'm sure she doesn't know anything."

"Anybody else?"

"Some Hammerskin guy I never met. I don't remember his name. Wendy wanted me to meet him, but I never did. He was from North Carolina, he said. I think he was just passing through, though."

"So who does that leave that we might be able to find?"

"Just C.B., Wendy, and Blue, I guess," April said.

"OK. . . . Now what, I wonder?" Dolly replied. She took sip of her coffee. "C.B.'s probably pretty well underground. The police seized that orange Charger of his, so he'll be harder to spot now."

"I don't know where to look for any of them," said April.

"Neither do I, Sweetie," Dolly said, finishing her coffee. "Neither do I. We'll just have to keep our fingers crossed."

44
Don Ron

Captain Willie's Restaurant
4:00 P.M.

Oh Lord, just give me one easy shift so I can go home and not worry about anybody's problems but my own, Dolly thought. The prayer seemed to be working till 5:00, when the first diners started arriving. Dolly had just finished her side-work in preparation for the evening crowd when she heard someone sobbing in the employee's tiny break room.

When Dolly entered she saw her friend, Darlene, sitting at the small table, her hands cradling her head. The two women had been friends for years but had seen little of each other until Darlene came to work at Willie's the month before. Dolly immediately went to her side, put an arm around her, and asked, "Honey, what's up? What's got you feelin' so bad?"

Her question triggered a whole new round of profound, body-shaking boo-hoos. Dolly's emotional radar was nearly infallible when it came to detecting the source of a woman's tears. Her friend's sobs indicated something worse than the death of a pet, yet less tragic than the loss of a relative or family member. The nature of her sobs meant only one thing to Dolly: Class III boyfriend trouble.

"What's the matter, Baby?"

The question sent Darlene over the top. Her sobbing turned to wailing. "B-b-b-b-baby. I thought I was gonna have a baby."

215

"Aww, Honey, that's. . . ." It suddenly dawned on Dolly that she hadn't talked with Darlene for some time. Since she didn't know much about Darlene's recent history — or even whether she was married or not — it might or might not be bad that she wasn't pregnant, so she clipped the sentence off before she got herself into trouble.

"I was seein' this gorgeous guy. He was the best thing that ever happened to me. He took me on wonderful little trips. Treated me like a queen. I was wild about him. Then he stopped calling. Then my period was late. I sweated it out for weeks. . . ."

The bawling obliterated her words, so Dolly just held her close as she wept and shook. It was no fun to get dumped. That, Dolly knew from long experience. And an unplanned pregnancy was nearly the worst thing that could happen to any woman. Dolly had been there, too.

"I th-th-th-th-thought we had a real thing going," Darlene stuttered through the tears. "Nobody ever treated me so nice before."

"Aww, Honey, I'm real sorry to hear that. You must be feelin' awful."

Darlene burst into another round of tears. *Lord,* Dolly thought, *at this rate, it will be midnight before I get back to work.*

"I don't know what I did, what I said," Darlene blurted out between sobs. "I was always real nice to him. Treated him real good. Then a few weeks ago, he just stopped returning my calls." It dawned on Dolly that she hadn't heard from Ron for a while, either. Weeks, even. Then again, she had been so busy with April's mess. . . .

Darlene's convulsions were starting to diminish. Darlene turned her bloodshot, puffy eyes to her friend and asked, "What am I gonna do, Dolly? He was such a catch."

Something sounded uncomfortably familiar about Darlene's scenario. She and Dolly were about the same age. Both were slender and attractive; both were unmarried and under 40. *Hmmmmm* she thought.

"What do you mean, 'such a catch,' Honey? There's lotsa nice single guys out there," Dolly said, knowing that she was stretching the truth just a teensy-weensy bit.

"Oh, Dolly, you should have seen him," she said. "A real dreamboat. He was in real estate, he said. Tall, nice tan, great body, early or mid-40s. He had a great car, a convertible. . . ."

Bingo! The little light bulb above her head just switched on. *That sonofabitch*, Dolly thought. Obsession kicked in. She had to know more.

"Treated you nice, you say?" Dolly said, fishing for the details she hoped would be coming soon.

"Oh, yeah. I met him at a C&W bar, and he asked me out. We spent the first date cruising the Intracoastal Waterway on his boat. Man, what a big, beautiful boat it was. It was great. He didn't get fresh or anything. I fell for him in a big way."

"How'd it go after that?" Dolly said, her blood pressure rising.

"Well, a couple weeks later, we went out on the boat again, and spent the whole day on the water. It was so romantic. He had this big, fancy lunch all prepared — champagne and everything — and we had a beautiful picnic on the beach of some little island down by Georgetown. Real silverware, crystal, three kinds of cheese, the works. I'd never seen anything like it."

Dammit! Cape Romain. That sonofabitch!

"Sounds very romantic. What happened then?"

Darlene looked into her face. "I couldn't resist him, Dolly. Heck, he was such a doll. We made love on the beach all afternoon. He was wonderful. Awesome, in fact. I never met a guy who could get it on like that before."

"Yup. Sounds like a real special guy," Dolly said. She gritted her teeth and tried to keep her temper in check. "Aww, Honey, that must have been so nice. Did something go wrong after that?"

"No, Dolly," she said, wiping the tears from her eyes with napkins from the chrome napkin dispenser. "Everything seemed just fine. Every few weeks I'd hear from him and we'd go off somewhere and have a beautiful date. I could never get in touch with him during the week because he was really busy with his real estate stuff. I wanted to meet his friends and family and stuff, but we never seemed to get to that. But I didn't care. He was so sweet and attentive. Even drove me to a romantic little place in Savannah one weekend. . . . ."

"THAT BASTARD!" Dolly screamed. The outburst shocked Darlene so thoroughly that she abruptly stopped crying and stared at Dolly, amazed that she could so completely identify with Darlene's pain.

Dolly's ears were red. Her fingers were clenched into fists. One more moment and it seemed as if steam might start blowing out her ears.

"Pretty little bed and breakfast off Telfair Square, I bet."

Darlene was incredulous. "How did you know?"

"Cast iron bed. Lace curtains and chintz–covered chairs. The smell of wisteria in the air. Took you to a garden restaurant on Factor's Walk."

"Ohmigod. Yes!"

"Drove you there and back in a white 450 SL convertible?"

"Dolly!"

"Likes golf. Has a 42-foot boat named the *FunTastic.* Well-stocked bar below. Likes fancy mixed drinks like Singapore Slings and Sex on the Beach. Gets lots of calls on his cell phone, mostly from women he says are clients and wives of clients.... Arrrrrrrgh!"

Now it was Darlene's turn to steam. "That two-timing bastard."

"So, you had a close encounter with Myrtle Beach's All-American Real Estate Playboy, Ronald Huntington Pawley, the Third, did you?"

Darlene gasped. "Y-y-yuh-yes," Darlene blurted out. "How did you, how do you know him?"

"I met him the same way you did. Same place, probably. White Lightnin'?"

"Ohmigod. Yes. When?"

"About three, four months ago."

"I met him there three months ago. First date: Intracoastal Waterway. Second date: champagne picnic on Cape Romain."

"Yes, that was the place, Cape Romain," Darlene blurted.

"Third date: the B&B off Telfair Square in Savannah. The man has a real system. I bet he was screwing us on alternate weekends."

Darlene's tears had long since dried up. Now her eyes were filled with anger. "I'm gonna kill that sonofabitch," she snarled.

"Take a number, Honey. Heck, if that's how he operates, we're probably not alone. This guy is a real bedpost-notcher. He's probably got two, three, four fish on the line all the time. He may even be married. What do we know? Hell, we may have to stand in a long line just for the chance to strangle the bastard. Keep your ear out for anything else you can dig up on him. I'd loooove to cook his goose before he breaks the heart of every other girlfriend of mine."

Harriet, the hostess at Willie's, stuck her head in the door. "Dolly. Darlene. Get busy out there," she yelled. "We've got customers piling up in the lobby. Get a move on."

45
True Blue

W e gotta stop meetin' this way, Mamma," April said with a laugh. "What will the neighbors say?" She nodded to the waitress for a refill of her coffee.

"Well, Honey, I don't think our reputation with the neighbors is in danger of being tarnished. Until recently I was the well-known manager of a lingerie and sex toy shop. You live in a trailer in North Myrtle Beach, and you spend your nights wavin' your naked teenage tush in front of a bunch of drunk rednecks, golfers, and bikers. But there's a bright side to all of this. Our prominent position in the community keeps the attention away from my half-wit brother, your uncle, who joined the Marines and volunteered for Korea just so he wouldn't have to marry his pregnant girlfriend. So, you see, we're doin' the family a big favor being who we are. Between the two of us, we're keepin' Devereaux family reputation safe." Both of them broke out in side-splitting laughter.

After they calmed down a bit, April said, "I have some news. I put out some feelers through Suzi and the dancers about Blue. Suzi told me that a girl who works at Easy Rider heard from a girl who works at a porn video shop that Blue is also working there and dancing at The Paradise Lounge."

"OK. That's a start. Anything else?"

"Well, evidently she's doin' a lot of drugs, and she's workin' the VIP rooms pretty hard. Blue has a real bad self-image thing. She always thought she was worthless, or so Suzi says. She's probably doing the sex thing to get attention and some affection."

"Do you think she'd talk to you, Honey?" Dolly said.

"I don't know. If she's heavy into drugs, she's heavy into pain. Maybe I can help her find a way out — and help find Correlli, too."

Dolly put her hand on April's arm. "That's very, very kind, Honey. I sure didn't have that kind of insight when I was your age – or know what to do with it."

"Thanks, Mamma. Hey, what's up with Grandma? I didn't get a letter from her this week."

"This week? You mean she's still writing you every week? I'll be darned. That's great, Honey."

"Yeah. She's pretty cool. She's decided that I'm gonna learn the family history whether I like it or not, all the way back to England."

"Horse thieves and all?"

"Horse thieves and all. Did you know that when she was born in Darlington, there were still people alive who had been slaves?"

"No, Honey. I never gave that much thought."

"Well she told me that in the 1920s, times were real bad, real hard for her and Grandpa. She said it was because of the boll weevil. It eats all the cotton crop. She said that after the boll weevil came to Darlington, that was the last time she had a store-bought dress for fifteen years. Then she said that the next thing that came was more hard times, in the 1930s. Nobody had any money or work."

"Yes, I remember hearing her tell of the Great Depression."

"Yeah, that's it. The Great Depression."

Tears started to well up in Dolly's eyes. *How easy it is*, she thought, *to think that our own hardships and tragedies are the only important ones in the world.*

"How did I get the honor of being your personal limo driver?" Suzi asked April. "And what part of this lunatic scheme am I supposed to play?"

"Don't worry, Mother Theresa," April said as they pulled into a parking lot across the street from the neon-lit porno store. "I'll only be a few minutes. Wish me luck." Suzi Vetter gave April a hopeful smile and a thumbs-up. April left the car and walked into the X4U Video Arcade.

It wasn't like Blue was hard to spot inside the video store. Even though she was restocking the racks at the back of the place, her height and frizzed-to-the-max, electric-blue hair made her easy to find. The door buzzer made her turn and come to the counter.

"Gotta be eighteen here. Got an ID?" she asked April, her stare blank and emotionless. It had been several months since she and April had seen each other, and that meeting had been brief. In the short time since then, the two of them had switched roles — and appearances.

April shuddered as she saw what three months of partying, sex, and drugs had done to the former Miss Natalie Bluestein, Dental Assistant. Her tanned, pink complexion had paled to the color of dust. She'd added a band-of-thorns tattoo on her arm and dark circles under her eyes and lost not only her beautiful smile but at least ten pounds.

That was the first thing to go when she and her friends started using drugs, April thought. *Their smiles.*

"Whatcha lookin for?" Blue asked her. It was obvious that the answer didn't matter much.

"Lookin' for you, Blue. How'ya doin?"

"Do I know you?" she asked, a suspicious look in her eyes. She looked at April's driver's license. Her eyes shot open. "Whaddaya want?"

"I don't want anything from you, Blue. It's OK," April said, and reached out to reassure her. Blue yanked her hand away. "It's me, April. April Devereaux. We met a few months ago at C.B. Correlli's place."

Blue eyed her with a combination of contempt and amazement. "You are a dead woman. A total, fuckin' dead woman. C.B. said you ratted to the cops on him about the lab. Stay the hell away from me, bitch," Blue spat at April. "You are bad fuckin' news, you and Suzi Vetter. Tell her she's dead, too."

April's mind reeled from the implications. *Would C.B. Correlli really put out a murder contract on me and Suzi? Could he even do it if he wanted to? He was usually so full of bullshit and bravado. . . . Could he really get somebody to kill us?*

"You got it all wrong, Blue. I had to tell the cops about the lab because of Wendy. She was gonna get killed hangin' out at that lab. You saw what happened to Skank. You saw what happened to Boomer. Well, it woulda been a hundred times worse if the whole place had blown up."

Blue scowled angrily at April.

"She was my best friend until she started gettin' so deep into the lab and everything." April said. "He's the one who made her his personal slave and turned her into a drug addict. Wendy was my friend for years. She used to be a real person. We played hopscotch and 'Truth or Dare' together. We did sleepovers and summer camp. We had real fun — fun we could share with other kids and our families."

"Get outta my face. I don't give a damn about what you and Wendy did with your Barbie dolls. She sure doesn't remember. She hates your guts."

"Blue, you don't get it. Wendy used to be a whiz kid in school, just like you. Great on the swimming team when she was a freshman. Lots of friends. Yeah, I know all about her parents. Spoiled Yuppies with too many cars and country clubs and too little time for their daughter. That makes for sad kids — but it doesn't kill them.

"C.B. is a vulture. He goes lookin' for kids who are hurting. C.B. spotted Wendy some day when she was fourteen or fifteen and she was probably thinkin' the world sucked, and everybody hated her and her parents didn't give a damn, and she was worthless and guess what? In ten minutes, she has a new best friend who REALLY understands her. In an hour, she has a new place to hide out away from her parents. In twelve hours, she's high on meth, and in twenty-four hours, if she was before, she's not a virgin anymore.

"Now she's got a cool secret life and she can put up with all the crap at home because she has a place she can run and hide and not deal with the world.

"But then the free drugs end and you gotta start sellin' the stuff if you still want it. And then C.B. finds another chick younger than you, and now you gotta take a number just to get a kiss or a hug or get laid. Sound familiar? I don't know how you and C.B. hooked up, but that's how it happened to me and Suzi."

"Screw you, April," Blue yelled. "Are you some kind of fuckin' evangelist, here to save me from burnin' in Hell? If you leave now and never hassle me again, I'll forget you ever came into this place. Or you can keep running your mouth and I pick up the phone and tell C.B. where to find your sorry ass. Get out!" she yelled.

A tall man wearing a red headband; a yellow, nylon, cutoff muscle shirt; and dirty basketball shoes walked in the door and eyed April with a grin. Then he turned to Blue and said, "Yo, Blue. I need a video," he said, slapping a twenty-dollar and a five-dollar bill onto the counter. "Can ya gimme some personal attention?"

"OUT!" Blue screamed at April. Blue picked up the money, rang up five dollars on the cash register, turned, pocketed the twenty, and walked with the man toward the unmarked door that led to the private porn video viewing rooms. Blue turned to make sure April had gotten the message. "OUT!" she yelled again.

April turned and left, cringing as she thought of the VIP rooms back at Horsefeathers. *Twenty bucks less five for the house. He won't have to wait long for personal attention from Blue,* she thought. *A quickie and then she's off for home, a bite to eat, and then the drive to work and onto the stage.*

46
The Secret

W earing black Nikes, white socks, jeans shorts and a T-shirt that proclaimed, "Don't Trust Boys," April sat at the old pine kitchen table she had come to know well in the past few months. "How old were you when you got married, Grandma?" she asked Anne.

"Not nearly old enough, that's for sure," Anne replied with a knowing smile. "Things were different then, Honey, especially out here in the country. I was sixteen, and Robert was eighteen. Mercy! He was a good-lookin' man."

"Wow, just sixteen, huh? I can't even imagine what it would be like to get married at sixteen. I don't even know if I want to get married at all."

"Well, considering the two main men in your life so far — your father and this Correlli character – that's not a real surprise, Honey," Anne said with a chuckle as she stirred her iced tea with an antique spoon.

"Why are men so rotten?" April asked. It sent a chill down Anne's spine to think that an eighteen-year-old girl could already be so cynical about half of the human race.

Anne continued to stir her tea. "They're not all the same," she

said. "They come in all shapes and sizes and tempers and disposi-
tions. Just like women."

April noticed the odd teaspoon her grandmother was using
to stir her tea. Instead of having a rounded tip, this old spoon was
square.

"Is that some special kind of spoon, Grandma?" she asked.
"Why does it have that funny shape?"

"This was a wedding present from Robert's mother," Anne
explained. "It belonged to her grandmother. Their family used to
own a big cotton plantation with lots of slaves about thirty miles
from here. Then the Civil War came, and they lost their money,
their slaves, the family silver, almost everything. The only family
treasures that survived were a matched set of six silver teaspoons."
She handed the spoon to April.

"See the three little birds on and the stripe on the thing that
looks like a badge? That's the family crest of Robert's great-grand-
father, who came here from England."

"Wow. That's really old, isn't it?"

"Sure is. This teaspoon was made in Charleston when it was
still a British colony. I've been using it to stir my iced tea since
Robert and I got married. When I need to think something over, I
make some iced tea and I sit down and stir it. Give my hands
somethin' to do while I'm thinkin'. That's why the tip of the spoon
is all square. I wore the poor thing flat at the end, I used it so much
for the last thirty, forty years. My mother-in-law did the same thing,
with the same spoon. I picked up the habit from her.

"We learn all sorts of things from our parents and the people
close to us. Some good things, some not so good. Sometimes we're
aware of what we learned. Sometime it takes fifty years to figure it
out."

Anne took a sip of her tea and resumed stirring it. She was in
a reflective mood, temporarily lost in thought. In moments, that
changed.

"Why does my father hate me?" April asked. Anne was taken
aback. She slowly turned her head and saw that April was looking
directly at her, tears filling her eyes.

Anne took April's hands in hers. "Kenny doesn't hate you,

Honey-child. He never learned how to accept love or pass it on to others. Nobody ever taught him how to be a father. It doesn't come naturally to everybody. Most learn enough about it to get along pretty well. Kenny never got much love or affection from his own parents. His father drank a lot. He was a quiet, solitary drunk. When he drank, he just locked himself away from his family. They didn't get much love from him. He also kept a coupla girlfriends on the side. You can imagine that Kenny's mother wasn't very affectionate with the man as a result.

"Kenny grew up in that kind of a home. It's no wonder he went off into the woods and started growing marijuana. He had a father who wasn't around much, and Kenny probably figured that fathers didn't have to be around much. But I do know that he was always lookin' for his father's love and attention — but his daddy never thought he was worth spit. I found out that Kenny started smokin' dope when he was about fourteen — the same age you told me you were when you started gettin' drugs from Correlli."

"If he doesn't hate me, why doesn't he care about me?" April said, the tears now flowing down her cheeks.

Anne was torn between giving April emotional support or information that might help her understand her relationship with her father.

"He doesn't know how, Honey. He just flat doesn't have the skills. His parents didn't care for him very well, so he wasn't able to learn much that was very good to him when he became a father. Parents are the ones kids learn the most from – both good and bad. I know you didn't have the chance to learn much good from your daddy, but you have a real fine Mamma. You've been pretty hard on her, you know."

April stared at Anne. There was deep pain in her grandmother's eyes. She didn't know what to say. Sometimes, April still looked at her mother and saw only the times that Dolly hadn't been there when April needed her. Her unfilled needs were so great that she could only feel her own pain, not the love and care Dolly had provided so much of to help compensate for what Kenny had been unable to give.

"Mamma was pretty hard on you, too, Grandma," April said. Now it was time for Anne to cry.

"It was different between me and your Mamma, Honey. I had a good man for a husband, and Dolly and the others got lots of love and attention from Robert. As a matter of fact, that's where she learned how to love you. Robert was always a-playin' with her, carryin' her around, makin' jokes with her, carvin' little dolls for her outa wood. She was one spoiled little seven-year-old girl when he died. Lord, have mercy! When that tractor rolled over and killed him, she nearly died, too. It's a miracle that little girl didn't actually die from cryin', she was so shook up. We had real hard times after your Grandpa Robert died. Almost no money or food. That's why I prize this old spoon so much. We didn't have any other spoons in the house we were so poor."

"What about Grandpa Henry? He was a real good man, wasn't he? That's what you and all the other people said at the funeral."

"He sure was, Honey, but I was a widow for twelve years before Henry came along. Your Mamma grew up in a dirt-poor family without any proper daddy for almost all the time she needed one.

"I was workin' like crazy to make ends meet, and in those days, no 'nice' guy would even look at a widow with six kids. So the guys who were looking at me just wanted the same things that C.B. Correlli wanted from you: a good time, a servant, and a bed-warmer.

"It wasn't no good way to raise six kids, but there weren't any choices. The food and money the men brought over was the only thing that kept us fed many a night. Things happened between your Mamma and me back then that caused a lot of hurt for both of us. The two of us done buried the hatchet on that now, but the scars are still there. We're workin' on 'em, but even so, it'll take some time to heal."

April's heart felt like someone had opened a valve. Love and gratitude flowed in like a river. She jumped up, ran to her grandmother, and threw her arms around her. "Oh, God, thank you, Grandma," April blurted. "Thank you for helping me understand."

"It's all right, Honey-child," Anne answered, tears flowing down her own cheeks. "It's all right. All this here stuff is gonna come out all right, just you see."

"I still have one thing that's really hurtin' me, Grandma," April said. "I have to make a decision, just like you and Mamma had to make. Someone I love is in trouble, and I don't know what to do."

"Who is it, Honey? What's the trouble?"

"I can't tell you a name, or what the trouble is, Grandma, or you. . . ."

". . .Or you what?" Anne asked. "Or you might tell Dolly? You're an adult woman now, April. I respect you as that. If you're lookin' for help or an opinion, I need more to go on than what you've given me so far. What's been eatin' at ya?"

April was near tears again. "I'm real worried about a friend of mine," she said. "A real friend, not just some Skinhead or somebody I did drugs with. She's in a lot of danger. I think I know what she's doing and what could happen to her, and I have to do something to save her."

"Does she want to be saved?" Anne asked.

The statement had a sobering effect on April. *Who wouldn't want to be saved from being blown up in a methamphetamine lab explosion?* she thought. Then April thought again and answered her own question. *Wendy, the drug-addicted thrill seeker who now hated her guts, and Blue, the drug-addicted Correlli groupie who also hated her guts, that's who.*

"I don't know, Grandma. I just don't know. She doesn't act like she wants my help, but I didn't always act like I wanted any help, either."

"Well, April, if you love her, you've got to do everything you can to save her. But if you can't save her — if she doesn't want to be saved — you've got to accept that."

"If I do what I think is right, they'll probably go to jail," April said, looking into her lap, avoiding her grandmother's eyes. "But if I don't do it, they might both be killed, and soon."

"Do you think either one of your friends will realize that what they are doing is dangerous?"

"No," April replied. "They're all caught up in it. They don't think about the danger, just the thrills and the payoff."

"Do you think they'd be better off alive in jail or dead from what they're doing?"

"Jeez, Grandma. That's what's driving me crazy. Maybe they'd get away with it and just, I don't know, see that they're screwing up and give it all up."

"They sound a lot like you were just a few months ago. How much longer would it have been for you to get to the place where their heads are now?"

"If Skank hadn't died, it wouldn't have been much longer, I guess. I was pretty screwed up."

"Keepin' painful secrets eats you up from the inside, Honey. Now you've seen what it did to me and your Mamma and to you and your Mamma. How would you feel if you told on your friends and they went to jail?"

"Awful, just awful. I was there for three hours, and it almost drove me crazy."

"And how would you feel if you didn't tell, and they got hurt bad or died?"

"Even worse. God! Grandma, I could never forgive myself if they were killed and I could have stopped it."

"Well, Honey, there you have it. Being a grown-up is all about making hard choices. Sounds to me like you know what your two choices are. Now it's time for you to decide which one to take, and you need to do that real soon, or you may lose your chance to do anythin'."

47
Ships Passing

M eeting Steve for a walk up the beach at dusk was the nicest thing Dolly could possibly think of doing then and there. The sun had sunk low in the sky, warm enough to ward off the early fall chill, but gentle enough to enjoy without hats and sunblock. Dolly knew that they would have at least half an hour before the sun sunk behind the wall of high-rise hotels that rubbed shoulders on Ocean Boulevard.

Dolly wanted to hold his hand as they walked, but each time her hand grazed his, he subtly avoided clasping hers — or so she thought. *Maybe he isn't aware of it. Maybe he is just in a state of 'is,' rather than a state of 'moving forward,'* she thought.

Now that Dolly had seen the man Steve both professionally and personally over the course of nearly five months, she wanted to move ahead, get closer, seal the bond. What she got was nothing of substance. Steve was always friendly and ready to meet, talk, and dine, but their second night of passion had also been their last. They had a warm, caring relationship that Dolly was dying to get out of second gear — but Steve, evidently, was not.

Is he seeing someone else? She knew his work schedule in detail, and he didn't have time to date anybody else even if he wanted to.

The spare time he had left over after work, sleep, and visiting his children ruled that out. In fact, he had made a great effort to make time for her, and Dolly made it clear how much she appreciated it.

Is he commitment-phobic? She didn't think so. His first marriage lasted almost ten years. He was certainly no womanizer like Ron Pawley. Her girlfriends said that Steve had dated two women in the past few years. The relationships lasted reasonable periods of time and ended naturally, with no broken hearts or bruised egos.

Is it April? That one worried her. With April's troubled past; her screaming, flaming, emotional issues with her father; her screaming, flaming, emotional issues with her mother; her drug addiction; and her current work as a stripper, Dolly was worried.

Is it me? That one worried her even more. *Was it something I said?* Dolly wondered. *Something I did or didn't do? Maybe I don't measure up in the sack. Am I a lousy lover? Doesn't he like my clothes or perfume? Is it my restaurant job — or something about the old one? Why won't he get closer to me? Am I the liability?*

Then there was the other possibility. *Is it the two of us, the package?* He was a respected member of the community. A college graduate. A Marine Corps officer. An almost-assistant-top-cop in Myrtle Beach. An elder in the Presbyterian Church. What would his friends think if they saw him getting serious with Dolly, the lingerie store clerk, and her daughter, the teenage striptease dancer? What would his colleagues think? His boss? His fellow church members?

Just offshore, a precision formation of pelicans skimmed above the gentle swells of the ocean, only inches separating them from the water. *Just like Steve and me. Inches away and miles apart. But I love this marvelous, warm, caring man. The heck with it,* she thought.

She grabbed his hand as it swung by and squeezed it. Turning her head up to him, she smiled. She wanted him to know that this moment was special. He gave her a warm, non-committal smile, and they continued walking up the beach.

A parallel train of thought was going through Steve's mind. As Dolly squeezed his hand, he felt a pang of guilt. *I love this bubbly, affectionate, good-looking woman. And yet I'm consciously rationing my affection,* he thought. *I'm crazy about her, but I keep her at arm's length all the time. What the heck is wrong with me? Us?* Steve started to mentally run down his list.

She moves too fast. The third time we were together, she asked me to sleep with her. It was great. What a lover. She was marvelous. I'm in great shape, and she wore me out! She couldn't possibly be more erotic. But with how many guys? She seems to go through boyfriends like popcorn. Maybe she's just looking for "Mr. Right," but how can I tell she's not just into short-term relationships and one-nighters?

Steve had reflected on their relationship for the last several months. *Is she with me because she likes me or because she thinks I'll give her inside information and advice?*

He thought about their different perspectives on life. *I'm a long-range planner. I like predictability and stability. I like to know what's coming next. I like to be briefed. I like to be ready for things before they happen. She's spontaneous. She lives in the moment. She's ready to do anything, anytime, anywhere.*

Then there was the dress thing. *I have twelve white shirts, which match five dark-colored suits and dark blazers and slacks which don't clash with the fifteen conservative ties I've been wearing for twelve years. She has a great body — like a fashion model — and likes the latest Western shirts, pants, and boots. She looks and smells great. It really turns me on to see her all dolled up and ready to go out. She must think I'm a total fashion failure.*

Then there was the daughter issue. *April is the most amazing young woman I've ever seen. She got dealt a hand of total crap when she was born. Her mother loved her, cared for her, and doted on her; but her father abandoned her, neglected her, and gave her nothing except neglect and bad examples. She's the daughter of a dope-head marijuana farmer who turned her on to drugs. Is it any wonder she graduated to meth, Ecstasy, and LSD?*

But the reality of April's challenges immediately came to mind. *She's going to N.A. twice a week. She's tested clean so far. But she's working in a drug- and prostitution-infested environment and living with another former drug user. Can she stay off drugs and stay clean? And if she can, for how long?*

Then there was the rest of Dolly's family. *Her mother, Anne, is a wild card, but she and Dolly and April seem to have had a genuine reconciliation. Will it last? And then there's Dolly's brother. . . .*

As the daylight faded, Steve finished up his mental checklist. *The only thing we have in common is that we're both high achievers. Dolly has worked hard to make a better living for herself. Two jobs, sixty hours a week, for as long as I can tell. Then there's me. One job, sixty hours a week, for as long as I can remember.*

Steve looked at Dolly. *Is she the best thing that ever happened to me or a package of trouble?* he asked himself.

Dolly looked at Steve. *Is he the man of my dreams or an unattainable goal?* she asked herself.

Dolly looked at Steve. Steve looked at Dolly. Without a word exchanged, they each squeezed each others' hands and prayed for guidance.

48
She-Crab Creek

Highway 501, Myrtle Beach
Later that afternoon

April and Suzi had to wait less than twenty minutes for Blue to appear. From their vantage point from across the street, April saw Blue get into an old Toyota pickup and drive off towards the Highway 17 Bypass.

"Stay at least three or four cars behind her," she told Suzi. "If she sees us following her, she'll get spooked and head off someplace and hide. If we can stay with her and not be seen, I bet she'll lead us straight to C.B. and Wendy."

"Then what?" Suzi asked. "You think they'll invite us in for dinner? You know, the lost sheep returning to the Correlli family reunion?"

"Just drive," April said. "Hey, she's headed south on the Bypass. Wonder where she's goin?"

Ahead, Blue abruptly turned right and stopped at a gas station mini-mart. "Oh, crap!" Suzi said. "What do we do now?"

"Keep goin', and pull into the parking lot of that hamburger place," April said. "Unless she's already spotted us, she'll just get her gas and stuff and keep on truckin.'"

Sure enough, Blue left the store holding a brown paper bag a few minutes later, pulled out of the gas pump area, and continued on her way.

"So far, so good," April said as Suzi wove in and out of traffic. "Go for it!" April yelled as a light ahead turned yellow. "Run the light if you have to, or we'll lose her."

A car from the turn lane on the right leaned on the horn as Suzi's car ran in front of him. "Thanks a lot, April. You tryin' to get us killed?"

"Nice moves, Babe!" she said, laughing. "You oughta do this for a living." They drove along for nearly twenty minutes until they crossed the South Santee River bridge.

"Look, she's turning left toward the Santee delta. No, look, she's headed — damn! — hang a left — oh, no! How we gonna follow her down a narrow dirt road through the old rice fields without being seen?"

Blue's Toyota disappeared into a nearly invisible dirt road, a trail, really, which led . . . well, April wasn't really sure where it led, but it paralleled the South Santee in the general direction of the Atlantic Ocean.

Suzi braked the car to a halt. "If we can't see her, we can't tell if she stopped or not, and we don't want to run into her. We'll have to go the rest of the way on foot, one of us, at least, and the other can drive behind a ways back. Have a real nice walk, Detective Devereaux."

April stuck out her tongue at Suzi and gently opened the door. She stepped out cautiously and quietly eased the door shut. The trail, she vaguely remembered, led to a small tidal creek where she and her mother had once gone crabbing. For ten minutes, April walked ahead slowly, half-crouched, to keep herself hidden by the underbrush, the thorny vines, and the saw palmettos.

Yard by yard she advanced, beckoning Suzi to follow. A glint ahead made her freeze in her tracks and signal Suzi to stop. Thirty yards ahead she saw Blue get out of her car, carrying her paper bag and a purse.

As April crouched low behind a thicket of vines, she watched Blue pass through what looked like an abandoned shrimp processing plant and down a rickety wharf behind the building. There she boarded a rusting shrimp trawler, which was tied up to the wharf. On the bow was a plaque with the barely visible words, *Alice Anne,* undoubtedly the name of someone once near and dear to an earlier owner. A board on the rotting wharf cracked. Blue nearly lost her balance and must have cried out, because someone appeared on the rear deck of the boat and offered her a hand. April immediately recognized the long, Roman nose of her friend-turned-friend-in-need, Wendy.

Blue made a small, unsteady step onto the boat. The ship's decaying hull seemed barely capable of floating, yet it did. April briefly saw a flash of light reflected from a round shape silhouetted in the window of the wheelhouse. She recognized the outline of C.B.'s shaved skull. She took a final look at the once-proud fishing boat, now rusting into oblivion.

Lousy place to live, April thought. *But the perfect place to hide a drug lab.* As she carefully crept back from the scene, she faced her dilemma: what to do with what she knew. Then, as she reached Suzi's Toyota, the memories of Skank and the Wendy-poo she had once been so close to flowed through her mind, and April began to cry.

The next morning, April twisted Suzi's arm again — not all that hard this time, since playing getaway car driver was an exciting change from waitressing in a biker bar — and the two of them staked out the dirt road that ran off Highway 17. About 10:30 A.M., Blue and C.B. drove up to Highway 17 in an old blue Ford pickup, turned left, and headed towards Charleston.

"Duck!" yelled April as the pickup turned onto the main highway. A minute later, the two girls raised their heads and saw the pickup disappear around a bend in the road.

"God! That was close," said Suzi.

"I knew you'd love it," April said with a grin.

"Do we go in now so you can talk to Wendy?"

"No, Suze," she said. "There's only one way in or out of that boat landing. If C.B. decides to come back soon, we're dead meat. And if Wendy knows that I know where they are hiding out, she'll tell C.B. everything. She's hooked on being a big-fucking-deal meth cook now. We have to wait for Wendy to come out. Then I need to talk to her in some public place. That's my only hope."

Two hours later, they saw the blue pickup approaching and ducked again. The dust on the trail told them that the three drug producers were together again.

"Damn," April said. "How long do we have to wait for Wendy to leave the damn place?" Five hours later, they still had no answer.

"Dammit, April, I've had to pee in the woods three times already, and we ran out of food and Cokes two hours ago. Wendy may be in there for days. I gotta split. I'm on duty tonight."

The words weren't out of her mouth for five seconds before the truck reappeared with a single passenger inside: Wendy.

"Follow that car," April barked out in a mock-police command voice.

"It's a pickup truck, dummy," was the sarcastic reply. April stuck her tongue out at Suzi. Suzi did the same.

"Just drive, detective, drive."

Half an hour later, Wendy made the first of three stops at hardware stores. Suzi was getting more nervous all the time, and April tried to coax her to continue the surveillance. Finally, after visiting an auto parts store, they tailed Wendy to a Chinese restaurant

Suzi had reached her limit. "I gotta go. This is it, April. Call a cab to get home. I gotta go or I could lose my job."

"Go, go, go," she said, and got out of the car. Suzi sped away.

April slowly walked to the door and entered. "May I help you, ma'am?" the hostess said with a slight bow.

"Yes," April answered. "I'm a. . . . My friend, a. . . . I'm meeting a girlfriend, tall, henna-colored hair, alone. . . ."

"Yes, ma'am. Come with me, please." April scanned the room, a little disoriented and a lot nervous.

"Your friend has arrived," the smiling hostess said to Wendy, who was sipping a beer while seated alone in a booth.

"I'm not expecting any . . .YOU!" Wendy barked out, taking the hostess by surprise.

"It's OK," April said to the surprised woman.

"It's NOT OK," Wendy said in return. "This girl isn't with me. Get her out of here."

"Wendy, I've got to talk with you," April said. "And we don't have much time."

Wendy nodded to the confused hostess, who backed away as gracefully and quickly as she could. Wendy ignored April, picked up a large, ceramic soupspoon, and took a sip of the spicy, noodle soup. Then she used her chopsticks, deftly picked up several slippery noodles, and popped them into her mouth.

"What the hell is your problem, April? First you burn C.B. and now you're stalking me. You got a death wish or what?"

"Wendy, you've gotta break loose from him," April said. "Can't you see what's happening to you? The guy you're hangin' with is makin' and sellin' drugs that kill kids like us every month. You saw what happened to Skank. He was workin' for C.B., but C.B. didn't lift a finger to help him when the pit blew up, and now Skank's dead. Boomer was workin' for C.B., and now he's dead, too. Now you're workin' for C.B. in Boomer's old job, and one mistake by you or C.B., and you're dead, too. Can't you see you're gonna end up dead like the rest of them?"

"Get outta my face, April," Wendy said. "I'm at the top of the food chain now. I'm makin' major money. I'm playin' with the best of the best stuff. This is the big league, April. I'm doin' stuff that the guys at Dow Chemical and DuPont don't even get to play with."

"But those guys don't risk their lives every day, Wendy. And the stuff they make goes into things everybody can use. You're making drugs that turn nice kids into addicts so people like Correlli and his bosses can get rich. I have a plan. I have a place for you to live. Give up this shit now and come with me, right now, tonight. I've got contacts who can get you into a drug rehab program, and if you turn state's evidence, they can probably keep you out of jail."

"Oh, I get it. Give up the chemistry I love, give up the fun, give up the money, turn in my friends, and in return you'll cut off my candy, cut off my money, send my friends to jail, and stick me in some fuckin' rehab center with a bunch of lunatics and peeling paint for a year while I make burgers for minimum wage. Yeah, April, that sounds real fuckin' attractive. Fuck you. Get out of here. And if you leave here within thirty seconds and tell nobody that you ever laid eyes on me, I may not tell C.B. that you talked to me. 'Cause if I do, he'll personally kill you. You got it?"

April nodded. "I got it, Wendy. But I still love you, and I still want to help you. Take care of yourself, 'cause C.B. never will."

April rose from the table, left the restaurant and its exotic aromas, and started walking down the road. She knew it was three miles and nearly an hour's walk to Suzi's trailer and her own bed-room. She started walking anyway, welcoming the chance to clear her mind and contemplate the next step in her incomprehensible life.

49
The Plan

The whole operation? A whole batch? A five-kilo run? All by myself?" If Wendy had been any more excited, she'd have needed a tranquilizer to function. She ran to C.B. and threw her arms around his slender frame.

"Jeez, C.B., do you really think I'm ready? I mean, I only did the simple parts of the processing when Boomer was running the lab. You know, I watched him, and he told me all the stuff, and we have all the cookbooks, and most of it's just basic chemistry, but there's some stuff I've never done before, like extracting the d-meth with Freon and the salting and drying stage. You're gonna trust me with the whole operation? I thought for sure you'd bring in another experienced head cook until I finished my training."

C.B. ran his fingers through his short dark-brown hair. He was already preparing for their escape to California by letting his hair and beard grow out.

"No time for that, Wen," he said. "And anyway, Boomer told me weeks ago that this stuff was a snap for you. He said you were the fastest-learning apprentice he ever saw. If you and Blue can't do it, nobody can," C.B. said with a grin, wrapping an arm around each of his two disciples.

"One batch this size will net us a hundred grand. I'm callin' in my markers here, and that will give us another hundred. I think we can make it OK in California on $200,000 until we get back in operation, don't you?"

Both girls giggled. "I'm growin' my hair, and we're gonna have to do a total wardrobe change, too," he said.

"Does this mean I have to lose the blue hair?" asked Blue. "It's my trademark, my identity."

"That's the problem, Babe. Your hair is the first thing the narcs will be looking for. You have forty-eight hours to become a well-dressed Yuppie blonde."

"And me, darlin'? What about me?" Wendy asked.

"Lose the henna. Go for black," C.B. said, giving her a long, wet kiss. "Make it happen, ladies. But don't go to any hair salon for the color change. Buy the stuff in some K-Mart when it's real busy, like at lunch time or 5:30. Only one of you buy the stuff. Wear really plain clothes and sunglasses and keep your hair under cover so nobody takes any notice of you. Do the color changes here on the boat. From now on, we all keep a low profile. It will take a week for Wendy to finish the batch of meth and for my troops to sell it. Then we're outta here and off to California, where we start making meth and Ecstasy."

"Really?" Wendy said, her eyes wide with the possibility of having a new toy to play with.

"For sure, Babe," he said with a wink. "I have an old buddy in Oildale who was a whiz at making MDMA a decade ago. It was the predecessor of Ecstasy — but it gave you a helluva lot better high. Great aphrodisiac. It's a bitch that you can't get the chemicals for MDMA anymore. Oh, well, life's a process of adapting. The bosses think it's gettng too hot for us to keep workin' here. They're gonna get a license from the Hells Angels so we can make it in their territory."

"What do you mean, 'get a license?'"

"The HA's and the Mexican cartel control most of the meth and Ecstasy production on the West Coast. If you want to make either on their turf, you pay them a license fee or they kill you. It's pretty simple."

"I thought you ran our whole show," Wendy said. "Who are 'the bosses' and why do you need any?"

"Everybody needs somebody lookin' out for them, Wen. Somebody up the line with lots of money and power and connections. It's like insurance. Trust me. We've got the best insurance agents of all of 'em."

"Who?" Wendy naively asked.

"That's the question you never ask, Wen. It's like the line from the old spy movies. 'I could tell you, but then I'd have to kill you.'"

Wendy shrugged off the statement as just another example of C.B.'s bragging.

"Hey, I need a hand setting up the lab stuff and hauling in the supplies. Can you and Blue go up to the shrimp plant and get the stuff out of the old cold storage room? I'm gonna set up the initial mixing and heating equipment in the wheelhouse, where there's good ventilation. Bring in that equipment, and the ephedrine, hydriotic acid, and red phosphorus. You can store the chemicals up front on the deck in front of the wheelhouse. Just throw a tarp over them and nobody will know the difference if they stumble in here."

"I love it when you talk dirty, Wen" C.B. said and patted Wendy on the butt. "Ladies, I propose a toast," C.B. said, raising his beer can to theirs. "To better living through chemistry. Our better living, to be specific. Here's to powdered happiness."

50
The Healing

Myrtle Beach

Are you sure you want to do this?" Suzi asked as she drove April north on King's Highway toward the Myrtle Beach Police Department headquarters. April was deep in thought. She hoped she had made the right decision. Ever since she had told her grandmother about her dilemma, she hadn't had a full night's sleep. Grandma Anne's advice made perfect sense but didn't help her to make up her mind.

If April told the police about Correlli, Wendy, Blue, and the boat, Wendy would be busted for being the head cook. The result: her best friend would spend twenty years or more in jail — and hate her forever.

Then again, she could do nothing. But if she made that choice, Wendy was at high risk for being badly hurt or killed in a lab explosion. She had only to think of Skank and shudder at the thought. Either choice would forever end her relationship with Wendy.

The choices had been eating away at her like acid in a tin plate. She knew that the lab was a ticking time bomb, which could go off at any time. Finally, April had made her choice: tell the police everything she had learned about the shrimp boat. The decision had made her sick to her stomach.

Two blocks south of the police station, she screamed to Suzi, "Stop!"

"What the hell. . . . ?"

"Just stop. Pull over to the curb and stop. This thing is freaking me out. I need more time to think," April said. Suzi looked over at her roommate as April began to sob.

"Oh, Suzi, I can't send her to jail. I just can't. Wendy was the best friend I ever had. I can't let her down now. I can't."

"You've done everything you could, April. Wendy had plenty of chances to get out, but let's face it. She's crazy in love with the lab stuff. She doesn't give a shit about C.B. It's the lab that she's in love with. That fuckin' lab is her life, her love, the center of her fucked-up universe. She's God when she's in there, playing with all those dangerous chemicals. It's the thrill of doing a high-wire act. She probably gets higher from running that fuckin' lab than from the meth she makes there."

"I can't do it, Suze. I just can't walk into that cop shop and rat on her. I can't. I just can't give up on her. I'm the only one in the world who gives a rat's ass about her. Her parents have written her off. The cops couldn't care less. I'm all she's got. Just like my Mamma. . . ."

It struck April like a slap on the face. *Just like Dolly never gave up on me. Even after all the grief I gave Dolly, she never gave up on me. Even after I blamed Dolly for all the stuff I should have blamed on Kenny, she took my crap and never gave up on me. She did it for love, just for love.*

April turned slowly to face Suzi, but her mind was racing at a hundred miles an hour. "Take me to my Mamma's place," she said to Suzi. "I need to talk to Mamma."

Fifteen minutes later, Suzi pulled into the SeaVue Apartments parking lot. April hopped out and ran to the driver's side of the car. She stuck her head through the open window and gave Suzi a kiss on the cheek. "Thanks a million, Suzi-Q," she said. "I owe you big-time. Again!"

Suzi wagged her head from side to side in mock dismay and started out the driveway. "VERY big-time," she yelled as she sped away.

April ran up the stairs to Dolly's apartment and let herself in. Dolly was standing in the kitchenette, making a sandwich and a fresh pot of coffee.

"Mamma, oh, Mamma, I love you so much!" she said, embracing her.

"April, Honey, what's happening? What's up? You OK?"

"Yes, I'm OK, Mamma. Really OK. And it's because of you. It's all because of you."

"Oh, Honey, well, I. . . ."

"You don't have to say anything, Mamma. It all just hit me this afternoon, you know, what you've done for me all these years."

Dolly looked at April and smiled. "I just did my job, Honey, that's all. It's what mothers are there for — to take care of their kids, no matter what."

"But I was such a bitch!" April said, the tears streaming from her eyes. "Everything Kenny did wrong, I blamed on you. Everything I did wrong, and you tried to help me with, I blamed on you. And everything you did to help me that I didn't like, I blamed on you. I was so awful to you. I said so many horrible things. Oh, Mamma, forgive me, please forgive me. Now I know that real love is loving someone no matter what they do but always showing them the right thing to do by your example."

Dolly tilted her daughter's chin with her fingers and looked into her tear-filled eyes. "You're the best thing I ever made, Honey. How could you ever think I'd abandon the best thing I ever made?"

"Thank you, Mamma, thank you. Now, thanks to you, I have the chance to show somebody else how much I really love them. And now that I've seen how you did it for me, I know how to do it for them."

Dolly took April's face in her hands. "I don't know who you're talkin' about, Honey, but if they mean that much to you, follow your heart, and do whatever will make God proud of you."

51
Tempting Fate

North Myrtle Beach
Saturday noon

S uzi had worked at Easy Rider until closing on Friday night, so she didn't find the note taped to her bathroom mirror until almost noon the next day. It left more questions unanswered than answered.

"Now I REALLY owe you big-time. I promise I do know how to drive, even though I don't have a license. I'll bring the car back in one piece. I really will. Love XXX OOO April."

Thirty miles to the south, April sat in the underbrush fifty yards from the processing plant, waiting for C.B. to leave. She had been there since eight in the morning, and the mosquitoes and sand fleas were eating her alive. Her legs were beginning to cramp from sitting motionless, and in her haste to carry out her plan, she hadn't brought anything to eat or drink.

Just as she was about to swat a mean-looking blue-bottle fly that had landed on her shoulder, she saw C.B. and Blue carefully walk across the narrow dock, pass through the plant, get into the pickup, and drive off.

Thank God, April thought. *Wendy's alone on the boat. But what if she still won't listen?*

"You've got to do everything you can to save her," she remembered her grandmother saying, "but if you can't save her, you've got to accept that."

Will I be able to accept that, though? she asked herself, fearing that the answer was probably no. *Well, this is it. She either listens or she doesn't.*

She took a deep breath, rose from her hiding place, and stretched her aching legs. They hurt, and she was covered with insect bites. She gingerly walked across the unpaved parking lot, through the plant, and out the back door. Then she turned to the right down the dock, hoping she would make it to the boat before Wendy spotted her.

Ten feet from the stern of the boat, April momentarily saw the movement of a woman's black hair through a window of the boat. Her heart stopped beating for a moment. *Who could that be? What am I getting into?* she thought. *Should I get on the boat — or run like hell?* The woman moved in the direction of the stern — where she could see anyone approaching. April froze in her tracks.

"C.B., did you forget some. . . ." Wendy said, stopping in mid-sentence when she saw April.

"No, Wendy. It's me," April said.

"April? For chrissakes, what are you doing here? Are you an idiot? You can't come here. C.B. will kill you if he finds you here. What the hell do you want?" Wendy said angrily.

April summoned up all her courage. Now was not the time to lose her composure or resolve. "I want you to come with me," she said calmly.

"Um, April, are you feeling, like, a *deja vu* experience right now? It's funny, 'cause I sure am. I feel like this has happened before. Oh, maybe 'cause it happened like just a few days ago," Wendy snapped, her words dripping with sarcasm. "Go away. I told you, I'm not going anywhere, so get the hell out of here. I'm staying here."

"No, Wendy. I'm not going to let you."

"Oh, excuse me? What, are you my mother now? *You're* not going to *let* me? So you've got your life all together now, and you thought you'd just come over here on your high horse and rescue your lost, misdirected ex-best friend. How sweet, April. I'm touched, really. I mean you even tried to rescue me a second time. Wow. That's just great. A real Mother Theresa, huh?" Wendy said, her hands on her hips.

"C.B. and Blue went to the convenience store down the road. He's only gonna be gone a couple of minutes, so why don't you get back up on that high horse of yours and ride right out of here before he comes back and blows your fuckin' head off for being such a sell-out and nearly putting him — and me — in jail for the rest of our lives."

"Wendy, stop it," April said, gingerly walking the remaining ten feet to the boat. "Why do you want to be here so bad? What's so great about all this?" April said, motioning to the rusting hulk. April felt the power of her convictions driving her. She calmly threw a leg over the edge of the boat and stepped onto the rear deck where Wendy was standing.

For whatever reason, Wendy didn't stop her. "You just don't get it, April. I like doing this. I'm really good at it. And I love C.B. more than you ever did. I'm not leaving this and I'm not leaving him. I *like* it here. I *like* being with him. And I also know somebody else who used to like those things until she became holier-than-thou and decided to go on a hypocritical crusade to save everybody from the same things that she did for years. You make me sick, April. Really sick."

"Wendy, you're my best friend. You've been my best friend since grade school. I can't just leave you alone knowing that you could end up in a lot of trouble — or dead." April was beginning to cry. This wasn't going to work. Anne had been right. Some people just don't want to be saved.

"Let's get this straight. I *was* your best friend. *Was* — until you proved to me what a crappy best friend you *were* by betraying me and landing me — your *best* friend — in jail. So, in case I forgot to tell you, you can start referring to me as someone who *was* your best friend, cause, honestly, I really hate you now. So GET OUT!" Wendy screamed.

Just as Wendy screamed, C.B. jumped aboard the boat. "What's wrong, Wen? Who are you. . . . ?" C.B. stopped dead in his tracks when he saw April. "Well, look who had the nerve to come visit us.

April. You little bitch," he said with a chilling laugh. "You've really got some guts, kid. Ya know, sometimes when little tramps like you rat out their ex-boyfriends to the cops, they usually try to steer clear of the guys. You've seen the TV movies and the cop shows, April. You know how violent those nasty old drug dealers can be."

April was shaking with fear but tried not to show it. She didn't want C.B. to think that he could really scare her. *God, he scares the hell out of me, though,* she thought. She knew about his violent history. *He's never laid a hand on me — or any girl — before, though,* she thought, trying to offer herself some reassurance.

C.B. shoved his face inches from April's "What did you come here for, April? Huh? To recruit some more members for your 'I-Was-A-Teenage-Druggie' club?" C.B. snarled.

Swallowing the lump lodged in her throat, April said weakly, "No. Stay out of this, C.B. I came to get Wendy."

"To get her? And take her where? Back to Myrtle Beach so you can hand her over to the cops so they can throw her in jail? Remember, that place you sent me when you sold out the only guy who ever did anything good for you?"

"What were the good things you did for me, C.B.? Get me hooked on drugs? Use me as your personal little whore? Turn me into one of your drug dealers? Oh, you're right. I should worship you like all your other little tramps. Dream on, C.B."

"I gave you a place to stay every time you ran away like a little baby from your dopehead dad and your psycho-bitch mother. I gave you food, drugs, a bed, everything, April. You pissed off the wrong guy."

April knew she should keep her mouth shut and not make him any angrier than he already was, but she had so much of her own anger inside that she couldn't hold back.

"You don't care about us! You never did! None of us! You let Skank die, you bastard!" April was now in tears. "You're so pathetic, C.B. Look at you. You make a living out of ruining innocent kids' lives. You're the most repulsive person I've ever met in my life. You make me wanna puke."

Wendy and Blue stood terrified, immobile, and scared silent as the confrontation unfolded just yards away.

C.B. grabbed April by the throat and slammed her against the wall of the cabin. April's face was contorted with pain and fear.

"I took care of you for three years, April. When your holy Mamma was off working her sleazy jobs, when your dad was off gettin' high and screwin' his girlfriends, I was the only one there for you. I gave you a place to stay, I fed you. This is how you repay me, you little bitch?"

"Yeah, as long as I was in your bed every night and selling your drugs, you were there for me. You're pathetic. It's really sad, C.B. You're so pathetic."

C.B. reached behind his back with his free hand and pulled an ugly, black automatic pistol from under his shirt. "You know what we do with rats, April?" he said as he pressed the gun to her temple. "We kill rats."

April tried to hold back her tears, but it was useless. Tears of hopelessness, fear, and desperation flowed down her cheeks.

How did it come to this? she thought. *This can't be happening to me. Be brave, April. Be brave,* she told herself. *He won't do it. He won't. Be brave.*

"You won't kill me, C.B.," she whispered to him as she looked straight into his cold, angry eyes. He didn't say a word. He knew she was right.

"You won't do it and you know it," she said slightly louder. "If you kill me, it's all over for you, and you know it. They'll all know it was you. Everybody'll know it was you. You'll be finished. They'll fry you in the electric chair and have a party after they've done it."

The adrenaline pulsing through April's veins made her temples throb, but it also gave her courage. "Do you see this Wendy? Blue?" she screamed as C.B. pressed the gun harder into her head. "Do you see this, huh?" Remember this picture. This is what the rest of your life will be like, waiting for this moment to happen to you. Is this what you want? Do you think this is a family, Wendy? Do you, Blue?"

Wendy couldn't believe what was happening right in front of her. Galvanized by fear, Wendy ran behind C.B., and tried to snatch the gun from his hand. The sound of the .45 going off inches from

Wendy's face was deafening. She screamed out, "April!"

C.B. was still clutching April's throat. With his gun hand, he lashed out hard and cracked Wendy across the face with the pistol. The blow sent Wendy reeling to the deck, a wide gash on her forehead spurting blood. April's eyes were the size of half dollars. Fear flowed out every pore of her skin. The gun had been jerked away from her skull, and the bullet had barely missed her head, but the muzzle flash had burned off a two-inch-wide patch of her hair and skin, and the blood flowed profusely from the scalp wound. She crumpled to the deck in shock.

"Get up, both of you," C.B. snarled. "One single word more and I blow you both away and feed you to the crabs. Up! Get up!" he said as he kicked Wendy in the leg. The two girls stumbled to their feet. "Give me that padlock," he yelled to Blue, who was terrified and stood quaking in the far corner of the wheelhouse. "NOW!"

Blue, her hands trembling with fright, handed the lock to C.B. "Start packing up the most critical stuff and putting it out on deck," he said. "I'll move it to the front room of the old plant. We're loadin' the pickup and leavin' as soon as it gets dark." Blue scurried below, as much as to get away from the terrifying scene as to prepare for their escape.

"Up!" he yelled again to April and Wendy. "Get movin'," he said, waving the gun in the direction of the old shrimp processing plant. "Slowly. Either one of you makes a bad move or runs and you're dead."

At the end of the shaky walkway, C.B. said, "In there," pointing to the former cold storage locker. "Open it," he yelled to April, who staggered to comply. She raised the heavy, stainless steel lever that locked the door. It took all her might to open the thick, heavy door, which led to the large, windowless, metal-lined insulated room where the shrimp had once been stored on ice.

"Get in," he said as he pushed the two women inside.

"C.B., don't do this. Just let us go. We won't say nuthin'," April pleaded.

"Coming from you, I don't think that's probably true," Correlli said with a harsh laugh.

Wendy's head pounded like a drum as she fell to the floor. "There's no air in here," she gasped. "How are we gonna breathe?"

"Gee, I don't know," C.B. said as he slammed the door shut and snapped on the padlock. "I'll have to give that some thought."

52
Lifelines

She-Crab Creek
Saturday afternoon

Through the thick, insulated steel door, April and Wendy could barely hear the muffled sounds of movement outside. "C.B. Blue. Let us outta here," they screamed. "We're hurt. We need a doctor. We can't breathe in here."

Their screams went unheeded. C.B. and Blue were too busy moving chemicals and lab equipment off the boat and into the former sales room, which was across the hallway from the large, lightless storage room where Wendy and April lay bleeding.

The fearsome, quiet darkness was pierced by a loud electronic chirping noise. Immediately, both girls realized what was causing it. Wendy still had her cell phone in her pocket. "Thank God!" she said, as she slowly pushed her consciousness through the pain and groped for the phone in her rear pocket.

"Wendy, NO!" April whispered. "Don't answer it! It could be one of C.B.'s friends. We don't want any of them to know we have the phone. Turn the ringer off. Set it vibrate instead. If C.B. comes back, we don't want him hearin' it."

"April. This is our lifeline. Call your mother's boyfriend, the cop."

"Talk into my right ear," April said to her. "I can't hear very well in the left one." She gingerly put her hand to her left ear, praying it would still be attached to her head. She was greeted by intense pain and the wet, sticky feel of blood – but her ear was still there. "Hey, Wendy-poo," she called out through the darkness. "I just did an equipment check. I still got both ears. My head hurts like hell, but I think the bleeding's stopped. And I got all my parts in the right places. All things considered, that's not too bad, right?"

Wendy sobbed nearby on the floor of shrimp locker. April felt Wendy's hand on her foot, then her ankle. She was trying to find her way closer to her friend. She felt Wendy's breath on her face. "It's OK, Wendy-poo. We're together. Friends stick together, right?"

"Right," Wendy said. Through her tears, she told April again, "Call the cop, April. Call him now."

April didn't hesitate. "I'll dial, but you talk to him. I'm not the one in trouble here. If you do the talking, you'll be the one who blows the whistle on C.B. If I make the call, you're the one who will get into more trouble when they come. You talk to them. It will give you a chance at a lot less trouble. C.B. talked you — and us — into all of this shit. My mother and grandmother helped me get out of all this crap. You deserve a second chance, too."

Wendy's head was throbbing with pain, but she realized that, like April, she'd probably live – if she could get the police to capture Correlli before they died of oxygen starvation. "OK, April, I guess you're right. Thanks for the clear thinking. I guess I haven't been doing much of that lately. Go ahead. Make the call. I'll talk."

April couldn't remember Steve Hunt's number, so she called Dolly.

"Hello?" answered Dolly.

"Mamma, I need Steve's number."

"April, you sound awful. What's wrong, honey? Where are you?"

"Mamma, I can't answer any questions now. I don't have time. Just give me Steve's number."

"April, are you in trouble?"

"GIVE ME THE NUMBER!" April yelled in a panic. "We'll talk later."

Dolly knew from the sound of April's voice that she wasn't

messing around. She quickly gave April the number, hung up the phone, and waited anxiously to find out what was going on.

April dialed the number and handed the phone to Wendy.

"This is Captain Steve Hunt."

"Capt. Hunt? I don't know if you remember me, but this is Wendy Hickson, April Devereaux's friend."

Steve was confused. Why would she call him? "Yes, Wendy, I remember. We've met on several occasions, none of them happy ones, though. Is everything OK?"

"No!" she answered as she burst into tears. "I'm with April. You gotta help us. She's been shot by C.B., er, John Correlli. He's holding us hostage in. . . ."

Steve's stomach turned. *Oh, no. No. This can't be happening.* "April's been shot?"

"Yes, she's been shot. She's doing OK right now. She's talking and everything. This is a real emergency. Help us, please!"

"OK, you stay on the line with me, Wendy. Is C.B. still there?"

"Yes, he's right outside the door. We're locked inside a storage room. He could come back any second."

"OK, how bad is April? I don't want to send an ambulance out there without a whole team, but I will if she's in bad shape."

"No, no. Don't do that. She's doing fine. It's just a skin wound. She said the bleeding stopped a couple of minutes ago."

"OK, where are you?"

"We're being held hostage in the old freezer of an abandoned shrimp processing plant. April said to tell you it's on She-Crab Creek, off the South Santee River, south of Highway 17."

Hunt made some feverish notes as she spoke. "Are you in danger right this minute?" he asked.

"Yes, Steve, you gotta come get us right now. We're both hurt. C.B. and a girl named Blue — Natalie Bluestein — are cleaning out a meth lab they set up on an old shrimp boat next to this place. C.B. told me they were leaving for California tonight. But we'll all be dead by then. This room has no lights and no air. It's really hot in here now, Steve, and hard to breathe. We're both feelin' kinda dizzy."

"OK, Wendy, I'm staying with you. Does Correlli know you have a phone in there?"

"No."

"OK, then. How's the battery life on the phone?"

"Let me see. About half. It's got about an hour left."

"OK, that's good," Steve said. "How's the air supply?"

"Nothin' comes in or out. It's a sealed room — an old refrigerated room for shrimp. The walls are metal. The door's almost a foot thick."

"OK. See if you can get him to open the door and give you some new air. Can you hit the door or make noise some way?"

"We've tried, but we'll try again."

"Good. Turn your phone off now and save the battery. We'll need it for later. Here's my direct number. I'm going to hang up now. Put my phone number in your redial memory. But if there's any problems, just call 911 again and they will all know who you are and how to get me immediately."

"OK, Capt. Hunt, but please come get us soon. We don't know if Correlli will give us air or let us die in here. We're scared."

"It's OK, Wendy. We'll get you out. I gotta go now and make some plans. But I promise, we're comin' after you."

53
Airtime

The phone call to Steve had given both girls hope. What they needed now was air and water. April asked Wendy, "What kind of shoes are you wearing?"

"Tennies," she said.

"No good," said April.

"How about you?" Wendy asked.

"Running shoes."

"Damn."

"You got anything hard on you?" April asked. Her breath was coming in pants now. They both knew that the oxygen supply was running low.

"Only the cell phone," Wendy answered.

"Well, I think we better not use that to pound on the door with," April said. "Let's wait till we hear something from outside and then start beating on the door and yelling. We gotta get some air in here," she said.

"Correlli would be happy to let us both die in here," Wendy said.

"Well, maybe our hope is Blue. Maybe she'll see what C.B. did to us and put some pressure on him to avoid murder charges."

"Get real. She's a wimp," Wendy replied. "He scares her shitless. She won't do anything that would piss off C.B."

April tried to find enough air to take a deep breath, but it wasn't there. "If you have a chance to get out of here, Wendy, just go. Don't worry about me. Just go."

"If that door ever comes open again, April, we go out together or not at all," Wendy said. She groped around, found April's hand, and squeezed it.

From outside, the two girls thought they heard something. "April, I think they're outside. Come quick."

April crawled toward Wendy's voice. The two of them felt around with their hands until they found the galvanized tin that covered the door. They both started pounding and yelling. "Help! C.B.! Blue! We're out of air! Help us!"

The exertion of pounding and yelling was almost unbearable. Their lungs burned from lack of oxygen.

"We're dying! Get us outta here! We'll behave! We'll be quiet! Just don't let us die in here! Help!"

To their astonishment, they heard noises from outside. In moments, a shaft of light seared their eyes. The pungent smell of the marsh flooded into the room. Silhouetted against the light stood C.B. with a jug in his hand.

"Dinner is served, ladies," he said as he dropped a gallon of fruit punch and a dozen hot dog rolls onto the metal floor. "I certainly don't want to leave any corpses behind in here when we leave. Not yet, anyway."

"C.B. Let us out. Let us come with you. We'll do anything you want. Just let us out of here," Wendy said.

"Yeah, C.B. We know we screwed up. Just let us out of here and we'll do anything you want. ANYTHING."

"Ladies, I'd be happy to except for one thing: you both disappointed me. You let me down or turned me in. You are the weakest links. Goodbye." He slammed the door shut.

Even with food, water, and a dose of fresh air, the second darkness seemed twice as ominous as the first. The two girls wolfed down the drinks and rolls.

Why did he even bother to bring us food? April wondered. *Maybe*

Blue got to him, she thought. *Maybe he thought that Blue would run off or become a problem if he didn't show some mercy.*

As soon as they had eaten some food, April said, "Call Steve."

Wendy dialed the number. "Steve Hunt," he answered. "Who is this?"

The cell phone crackled with static. "Oh, God!" Wendy thought. "The battery is dying!"

"Tell me your condition," Steve asked.

"Correlli opened the door and gave us food and water. We got some new air. But it looks like the air will only last about an hour," she said. "We were out of energy when he opened the door," Wendy said, taking the cell phone. "You gotta get us outta here fast."

"We're on the way," Steve said. "Hang in there. Wendy, give me a detailed description of where you are and where Correlli is."

"We're in the cold storage room of the processing plant," Wendy replied. "It's the first room on the left when you come in. Down the hall on the left is another room. I don't know what's in there."

"What else is in the building?"

"On the other side of the hall are two other rooms. I think C.B. and Blue are bringing the meth lab stuff to the front room. You know, the chemicals and the equipment."

"Where's the boat?"

"The boat's behind the plant, on a dock that runs along She-Crab Creek. When you go out the back of the plant, the boat's on the right."

"OK, Wendy. Stay calm, stay still. That will cut down on your consumption of oxygen. We're on our way there now, and we have a plan to get you out safely. Turn your phone off now and save the battery. Call me in about a half hour, and we'll tell you what's going to happen."

Both girls were numb with fear and exhaustion. "April," said Wendy. "I'll never forget what you've done for me. You didn't have to come here. My parents never came to visit me — not even to the county jail. I was the fuck-up, the outcast, the one who disgraced them. Dolly was the only one to ever visit me. And I told you to fuck off the last time we met. You risked your life for me anyway. Look what it got you."

"I'd whistle a few bars of 'Together Again,' Wendy-poo, but it hurts too much," said April, whose head was still pounding from the burn wound.

In a flash, April realized the startling irony of her relationship with Wendy. Dolly had refused to give up on her, even when April showed her mother nothing but anger and resentment. Now here was Wendy, expressing the very same emotions to her. Finally, April got the message. At last, she knew why Dolly was so desperate to save her from self-destruction.

"I love you, April," Wendy said, and squeezed April's hand. "You're my best friend. You've always been my best friend. Even when I hated you, you wouldn't give up on me."

"I love you, too, Wendy-poo," April replied. "A lot. 'Cause if I didn't, I'd be shakin' my ass and scarfing up big tips from a roomful of drunk rednecks, golfers, and businessmen right now."

They both giggled, which, they both instantly realized, was pretty absurd, since they were both bleeding, imprisoned, and in mortal fear for their lives.

In the hot, quiet dark, April hugged Wendy close to her. "We're gonna make it, Wendy-poo. We're gonna make it."

54
Poof!

She-Crab Creek
Saturday evening

Dusk had arrived and both C.B. and Blue were near exhaustion. Another three trips to the boat and they'd have all the materials unloaded. "C.B.," Blue asked in a quiet voice. "What are you gonna do with Wendy and April?"

C.B. took a long pull on a hip flask of whiskey. He rarely drank, but the occasion seemed right. "Don't worry about them, Sweet Pea," he said, stroking Blue's no-longer-blue hair. "They'll be OK. I'm gonna give 'em some more air now, and we'll be gone in a few minutes. I already found their car and pulled the distributor wires. We'll be loaded and outta here in a half hour. When we go, I'll let 'em out. We'll be long gone before they can get out to the highway and tell he cops."

"You're not gonna kill them?"

"Hell, no, Sweet Pea. I got better things do with my life – like enjoying you and making you happy." Blue thought of the girls locked in the storeroom. C.B.'s assurances didn't make her feel any better.

C.B. said, "OK, break time's over. Bring up some more stuff. If we don't really need something, just throw it overboard. I'm gonna give our guests a breather and start loading the truck." Blue dutifully walked down the hallway and out onto the dock, where she turned right, avoided the rotted and broken floorboards, and stepped onto the stern of the *Alice Anne*.

Back in the plant, C.B. again unlocked the heavy door. The lack of oxygen had taken its toll. Wendy and April were hardly breathing. "Hey, wake up," C.B. yelled at them, but they barely moved. He went across the hall, grabbed a piece of cardboard, and returned to the storage locker. Using the cardboard as a fan, he waved fresh air into the hot, stinking room.

"Wake up, you idiots," he screamed. "You don't die until I want you to die." Slowly, the air made it into their lungs and the girls showed signs of life. C.B. thought of the time he was wasting. *Maybe I should just lock them up and leave them,* he thought.

As soon as they were breathing again, C.B. slammed the door shut but deliberately didn't lock it. That way, he thought, if they died inside, he could always say that they had never tried to push the inside release lever and escape.

Aboard the *Alice Anne*, Blue brought up a can of chemical waste and leaned over the creek side of the boat to dump it into the water. The moment she bent over the edge, she saw herself staring at two divers in black scuba outfits, each pointing a gun at her face. One put a finger to his mouth. "Not a word or you're dead," he said. "Slowly come over the side and slip into the water. Don't make a sound. We are going to get you out of here alive. Put down the can on the deck quietly and come with us NOW." Blue quickly considered the options, swung her legs over the edge of the boat, and slipped into the arms of the two men in the water.

"Put this in your mouth and breathe naturally," one of the divers said as they strapped a small scuba tank onto her back, put the air hose into her mouth, and slid a scuba mask over her face. Blue did as she was told, and within a few minutes, the police divers had towed her a hundred yards down the twisting creek and were hauling her into a rubber police boat.

Her absence didn't go unnoticed for long. C.B. had backed the pickup truck up to the front of the building and loaded the main gear and supplies. When Blue didn't show up with the rest of the stuff, he went looking for her. The can of chemical waste on the deck freaked him out. Frantically, he searched the boat for his helper.

She was gone without a trace. Just plain gone.

Correlli raced back to the plant, looking for her, but instead he found something quite different. The moment he got to the front entrance to the plant, six powerful floodlights snapped on, turning dusk into broad daylight.

"John Correlli, this is Major John Sharp of the Horry County Sherriff's Department. You're under arrest. Let the two women go and come out immediately with your hands up."

From behind his police cruiser, Steve Hunt said to his colleague, "Let me talk to him. He knows me." The sheriff's officer nodded and handed Steve the bullhorn.

"C.B., this is Captain Steve Hunt of the Myrtle Beach Police Department. We know each other. We don't want to hurt you. We already have Blue. Let April and Wendy go and then come out with your hands up. We don't want to hurt you, and we won't have to if you come out now."

Hunt? thought C.B. to himself. *Dammit, the Devereux broad's boyfriend. Great. Fuckin' great. This is personal to him. This guy wants to hang me.* Then, it occurred to C.B. *Wait, this is personal to him. He's not gonna want to make me mad. I've got April. I've got his girlfriend's daughter and a rich doctor's kid in here.*

"Correlli, let's talk about this. Let me come inside. Go to the window and give me some sign that I can come in and talk to you." Steve looked in the window and saw Correlli with his middle finger pointed straight up in the air.

"OK, I'll take that as a no. Look, I've got my cell phone. Call me. That way we can talk one-on-one." He looked at the window. No middle finger. That was a good sign. Steve yelled his phone number through the bullhorn to C.B. Moments later, his cell phone rang.

"Listen, you bastard," Correlli said into the phone. "I've got your girlfriend's pretty little daughter in here, and I've also got her little friend, you know, Doctor Hickson's daughter, Wendy. If any one of you tries to set foot in this place, I'll kill 'em both. And if you try to shoot me, this whole place will go up in one huge fireball. Yeah, you'll kill me, but they'll both go up in smoke with me. So back the fuck off and go home. If everybody's not gone in fifteen minutes — all the choppers, cars, undercover cops, sharp-shooters, SWAT jerks and all — in fifteen minutes, they're both dead. As soon as you're all gone, I'm leaving with the both of them, and if anyone tries to tail me, by land or air, they're both dead. Don't think I won't do it. I already shot April once, Hunt. Looks like you've got a problem. I've got nothin' to lose here. But you've got quite a bit to lose, don't you? If you wanna play rough, man, I'm ready for you. Get your ass outta here. Now!" With that, Correlli hung up the phone, smiling. *They can't touch me*, he thought to himself.

Inside the storage room, April and Wendy were trying to remain conscious. "Do you hear something?" Wendy asked.

"I dun . . . I uh. . . ."

"The phone. We gotta try the phone." Wendy reached inside her pocket and flipped it open. The light came on. "Thank God!" she said. She punched redial.

The static was bad, but Steve Hunt answered almost immediately. "Who's talking?" he asked.

"Wendy."

"Wendy, we have Blue and she's OK. I just spoke to Correlli on the phone. He's using the two of you as hostages to try to get out of here. We're thinking of using tear gas to get Correlli to come out. Does he have a respirator?"

"Yeah, he does, but he probably doesn't know where it is now. They were gonna unload the boat and bring all the stuff to the front of the plant, then load his truck."

"If we hit him with tear gas, will the gas get through to you?"

"God, I don't know. No, I don't think so. No air gets into this room. We . . . almost . . . died. . . ." The air was almost gone. ". . . twice when he shut us in here. So I think . . . if you use gas . . . outside, we'll be OK . . . in here."

"OK, then, here's what we're going to do. . . ."

The static increased and then the phone went dead. "Oh, shit," said Wendy. "The fuckin' battery died. Now what are we supposed to do?"

"April. April, wake up," she said, shaking her groggy friend. "You gotta wake up. It's almost over. Steve is here. They're gonna rescue us." There was no response. The exertion took its toll on Wendy. The place was as hot as an oven. They were out of air. She slumped onto the floor, her head in April's lap. "You gotta. . . ." she mumbled, and then fell silent.

From his command post behind the bright lights thirty yards from the processing plant, Major John Sharp ran down the final details with his SWAT assault teams.

"All teams: we have two female hostages in the freezer room, the first room to the left. The suspect is in the storage room to the right, which is filled with explosive chemicals. Fire no weapons into the room on the right. However, be aware that the potential for accidental chemical explosions is high and check your protective gear again now.

"Team One: on my command, fire flashbangs into the back room behind Correlli — not into the storage room.

"Team Two: on my command, fire smoke grenades into the hallway only — not into the storage room.

"Sniper Team: if he opens fire, return fire, but only if you have a clean shot which will not penetrate the storage room.

"Hostage Team: charge the building and extract the two female hostages from the first room on the left on my command.

"Fire Team: stand by. Report."

"Team One: we copy. Fire flashbangs in the back room."

"Team Two: we copy. Fire smoke grenades in the hallway."

"Sniper Team: we copy. Return fire only if a clean shot is available."

"Hostage Team: we copy. Extract two female hostages from the first room on the left."

"Fire Team: we copy. Standing by."

"All teams stand by."

"How are the two girls?" Major Sharp asked Steve.

"No idea, commander. Their cell phone went dead a few minutes ago. They've been in that sealed room too long. There's no fresh air supply at all."

"That place may be their coffin if we wait any longer, but it's their bomb shelter if anything goes wrong. OK," said the veteran of twenty-seven hostage situations. "We go now. You get him on the bullhorn to distract him. As soon as you have his attention, we'll launch the assault."

"Yes sir," Steve said, and took the bullhorn in hand. "Attention Anthony Correlli, this is Captain Hunt of the Myrtle Beach Police. I want to come in and talk to you, unarmed, man to man. The phone's not going to do. Let's do this like men, face-to-face. I'm sure we can work something out. Will you let me come in and talk to you?"

There was no sign. "I just want to talk to you, C.B., to see if we can work out something win-win. Wave your hand, throw out a bottle or a stick, or do something to tell me that you can hear me. You don't have to agree to anything except to talk to me. Just do something to show me that you can hear me."

What the fuck, C.B. thought. *He probably wants to negotiate with me in private. He probably doesn't want to show all the other cops how personal this is for him.* He looked around, saw a can of soda nearby, and grabbed it. Crouching low behind chemical cans, he edged close to the hallway door and rolled the can down the short walkway into the parking lot.

"All teams: commence operations," barked Major Sharp into the tactical radio.

C.B. was waiting for Steve Hunt's next statement when he heard the explosions in the room behind him. "What the fuck. . . ?" Smoke filtered into the room from under the doors. Desperately, he groped through the supplies and chemicals, searching for his respirator. He stumbled, got up, stumbled again, and knocked over a large glass bottle of red phosphorus. The moment the chemical was exposed to the air, it was all over.

From the command post a hundred feet away, Steve Hunt was blinded by the powerful explosion. The massive red-orange fireball sent chunks of the roof and dock flying far above them, and blistered the paint of police vehicles fifty feet away.

All the police officers dove for protection from the flaming debris that fell from the sky.

"Fire Team: move in," barked Major Sharp. Immediately, three snorkel tanker trucks from the Myrtle Beach Airport rolled up to the flaming wreckage, pouring chemical foam on the one part of the structure still recognizable: the metal-wrapped cold storage room.

Silver-suited firemen converged on the foam-covered shell. It took three of them to clear the wreckage that blocked the door, but when they yanked it open, they reported on the radio, "Two women inside. Their breathing is shallow, but they're alive. We're bringing them out."

55
Clean White Sheets

Grand Strand Regional Hospital
Two days later

Dolly gazed into the eyes of her daughter, giving thanks to God that she and her friend were not only alive but about to be released from the hospital the next week. She and Steve Hunt stood between the beds that separated April and Wendy.

"The worst place to be ended up being the best place to be, didn't it, Mamma? If C.B. had locked us up any other place, we'd probably both be dead, don't you think?"

"I think we should just be grateful that you both got through it alive, girls," Dolly said.

"I agree," said Wendy from the adjoining bed.

"What happens now?" April asked. "Will Wendy be charged with anything?"

"I can't say for sure, Honey," Steve said, as he turned to look at Wendy. "The fact that you called us from the storage room will have a positive effect, Wendy. But you were still manufacturing meth for C.B. Youll get some kind of break, kid, but you're still facing some pretty stiff charges. Nevertheless, with my testimony, along with April's and Dolly's, you'll get the best deal you can. I'm going to testify that without your phone call, the entire operation would be flourishing in California right now. The fact that you called in while under a death threat from C.B., and the fact that you have no major convictions should work in your favor," he said.

"Thank you, Capt. Hunt. I only did it because. . . ."

Steve raised his hand to cut her off. "You did it, and that's all I have to know," he said. "That took enormous courage, and the source of the courage doesn't really matter," he finished, smiling at April.

"What happened to Blue?" Wendy asked.

"Well, we're not too sure what's going to happen to her. When she was busted, she had an entire bucket of chemicals in her hand that she was about to dump overboard. If that's brought in as evidence — and if I were a prosecutor, I would — she could be in a lot of trouble."

"I don't want to see anythin' bad happen to her. She was barely eighteen. She didn't have a clue about what was really goin' on. She was just like us — young, confused, unsure about herself. Is there anythin' I can do to help?"

"Well, girls, it's really out of your hands now. We'll just have to let the law take care of everything and hope justice is served," said Steve.

"You can't run the world or save people from themselves, girls," Dolly said. "All you can do is set a good example, help where you can, give them love and support, and let them make their own decisions. Sometimes it works, sometimes it doesn't. We can't control anyone else's life. The only life we can control is our own."

"But you kept after me, Mamma. You never stopped trying to get me to straighten up and fly right."

"That's true, Honey, but I always knew that all I could ultimately do was try to be a good mother and a good example. Once you turned eighteen, I didn't have any other control over you. That's just the way it works."

"I'm sorry folks, but visiting hours are over for the day," said the ward nurse. "These girls still need a few days' rest before we let them loose into the world of pizza and fudge brownies."

"Will you come see us again tomorrow, Mrs. D?" Wendy asked with a hopeful look on her face. Dolly was deeply saddened to realize that none of Wendy's family would ever visit her there.

"Sure I will, Honey. I think April's adopted you, so that makes you family now."

Wendy beamed and waved goodbye with her bandaged right hand.

"Bye Mamma. Bye Steve," April said. The four waved to each other as Steve and Dolly walked down the hall.

"Where are we headed now, Captain?" Dolly asked as she squeezed his arm.

"Where would you like to go?" Steve replied.

"The Second Avenue Pier, where you took advantage of me those many years ago."

A fifteen-minute drive and they were walking barefoot on the beach, just as the sun was setting behind the hotels.

"Now just who was that who took advantage of whom?" Steve asked playfully.

"You of me."

"You were hot to trot. You seduced me," he said.

"I was a vulnerable little country girl and you were a big, strong, older man. I was powerless to resist you."

Steve stopped on the beach and put his hands on her shoulders, turning Dolly to face him. "I understand you better now than I did then, Dolly. Back in high school I thought that you were just a wild girl with a need for speed. Now I know that back then, you had your screwed-up home life and your mother's problems holding you back. And I know that Kenny and his drugs were just an escape from all of that."

"Well, Dr. Freud, I've learned a few things about you, too. Like the fact that all those goals you had were your parents' ideas. They taught you to ignore your feelings and just do what you were programmed to do. But I've learned that you've evolved out of the dull, boring robot mold since then. You actually have feelings and moods, almost like a real person," Dolly said.

"What do you mean, 'almost?'" he shot back.

"Real people don't have twelve identical white starched shirts, Bubba," she said with a big laugh. He chuckled.

"Hey, big guy," Dolly said. "We're under the Second Avenue

Pier. Wanna get lucky twice in twenty years?"

"Dolly, I couldn't think of anything nicer," he said, giving her a lingering, sensuous kiss. "But I'm working the night shift tonight. I've got to be on duty in a half hour. I'm off tomorrow night, though. How does dinner at La Luna Rosa tomorrow night sound?"

56
The Wedding

SeaVue Apartments, Murrell's Inlet
Three months later

D olly's skin tingled with excitement in anticipation of the day, night, and next day to come. The weekend had already started, and it promised exquisite pleasures almost too much for Dolly to bear. After the grueling events of the last six months, she was ready for everything good that life had to offer.

She showered and donned the dress she had carefully chosen for the wedding and the trip to follow. She had wanted everything to be perfect: the dress, the earrings, the perfume, and the hat. April couldn't believe that it was all happening. She was looking forward to being part of the ceremony as much as Dolly was.

Two hours before the lavish event, Dolly had checked with Steve and confirmed all the details for the day. The ceremony was at two o'clock. Because the groom was so well-known in the area, the church would be packed with more than two hundred prominent business and professional people and their families from all over the Grand Strand.

There had never been any doubt about who Dolly would choose to drive her to church that day. It had to be Chrissie. Who else had been there to listen to her throughout the years? Who else had the sense of humor to distract Dolly from her deepest fears? Chrissie was the clear choice to get Dolly to the church on time. Chrissie laughed with joy when she heard about the plans and immediately accepted the honor.

"OK, Honey, it's 1:35," Chrissie said, as she opened the door for Dolly and escorted her to her car. During the fifteen-minute drive to the Pawley's Island Community Church, Chrissie's car was full of love, laughter, and an incredible feeling of excitement. It seemed like the drive was over before it had started.

As they pulled into the parking lot of the church, they saw that it was nearly full. "X minus five minutes and counting," Chrissie said to Dolly.

"I love you, Chrissie, you know that," Dolly said. "I could have never pulled this together on such short notice without you."

"It's what true friends are for," Chrissie said, squeezing her hand. "Hey, there she is now."

Darlene, Dolly's other girlfriend, was standing in the parking lot, waiting for them. Chrissie, Dolly, Darlene, and April had a last-minute conference. Chrissie reassured them all. "Our rehearsal went fine. We won't have a problem in the world."

"OK," Chrissie said. "It's time." The four women looked at each other with joyous determination in their eyes as they walked into the church.

"Friends of the bride or groom?" the usher asked with a smile.

"Friends of the bride," Dolly said on behalf of the group. "We'll have to leave early, so put us in the back row, please." She handed the usher a formal, ivory-colored envelope with "Personal for Caroline" written on the front. "This is for the bride. Could you see that she gets it after the ceremony? Thanks." The usher smiled, nodded, and placed the envelope in his inside coat pocket before turning to assist the other last-minute guests.

At precisely two o'clock, a gleaming silver Lincoln Town Car pulled up in front of the church, driven by John Sayles, the bride's father. With joy in his heart, he helped his daughter, Caroline, out of the car while her maid of honor helped with her train. Soon the familiar strains of "The Wedding March" reverberated through the church, and from the anteroom off the altar, Ronald Hunting-ton Pawley, III, and his groomsmen walked out to greet the bride.

From their pew in the back corner, Dolly, Chrissie, Darlene, and April watched as the bride entered and made her stately walk up the aisle. The four women could hardly sit still as the ceremony progressed.

Finally, the moment of reckoning arrived. The minister turned to the congregation and asked, "Is there any good reason why this man and this woman should not be joined in matrimony? If so, speak now, or forever hold your peace."

Dolly looked down the pew at her three companions. They each took a deep breath and rose together.

"I'm afraid there are some good reasons, Reverend. The four of us feel the need to share some important things with Miss Caroline."

Ron Pawley turned as white as his tuxedo shirt. He barked out of the side of his mouth to his best man, "Shut her up and get those four women out of here NOW!" His friend looked back at him in total confusion, since he had no idea what in the world he was supposed to do — or how to do it.

"Miss Caroline, I've heard that you are a fine, upstanding woman, but my friends and I didn't know that you existed until a few months ago. If we had, we would never have accepted all those romantic dates with your fiancé."

The blood started draining out of the bride's face as she listened to the four unknown women in the back pew.

"You must have had a hard time getting all the wedding decisions made with Ron being away on business trips almost every weekend. Well, we were the business he was so busy with," Dolly said. "He sure is a hard-workin' man because he's kept at least three women busy almost every weekend for the last six months.

"When we all put our heads together, we found out that he was winin' and dinin' and screwin' us all silly on alternate weekends. By the way, his favorite place for romancing his girlfriends is a cute little bed-and-breakfast hotel in Savannah, off Telfair Square. So if you're gonna stop there on your honeymoon, don't be surprised if they know him real well."

The shocked bride stood at the altar, her mouth open and her arms hanging loosely at her sides.

"I'm afraid it's true, Miss Caroline," said Darlene. "He took me out on the *FunTastic* on the Waterway, for romantic picnics at Cape Romain, and for dinin' and screwin' in Savannah, just like she said."

Then it was April's turn. "You probably know that he likes golf, Miss Caroline, but the kind he really loves is golf where the caddies are all pretty, young girls — mostly strippers, like me — who he pays to go topless and drive them around the golf course. I know because he hired me as a topless caddie for him and three business friends this summer. But when he offered me money or cocaine to take the rest of my clothes off, I told him what to do with his golf clubs, and I took off."

The church was so still you could hear the buzz of a single mosquito.

Dolly made their closing statement. "Now we know that all of this is comin' as a real shock for you, Miss Caroline, but after we found out what kind of man Ron Pawley is, we felt an obligation to tell you. We know that you probably got a lotta things to do this afternoon, so we're gonna leave now. But in case you want to get in touch with any of us to confirm any of the details, we left our names and phone numbers in a sealed envelope that we gave to the tall, brown-haired usher right there. And if you want to figure out how many other girls he was sleepin' with while he was engaged to you, you can check the captain's logbook on board the *FunTastic*. My friend, here, found our names in there and a notation recording the first day he got lucky with each of us."

Pandemonium broke loose as the four women filed out of their pew and left the church.

The bride screamed, "You two-timing, slimy bastard!" and started beating the groom-to-be over the head with her bouquet. The rest of the bridal party fled in disarray out the nearest door or down the aisle.

When the bridal bouquet had been reduced to a ragged mass of stems, Miss Caroline Anne Sayles shoved Mr. Ronald Huntington Pawley, III, off the altar with a sharp kick from her gleaming white high heels. Pursued by his screaming bride, he fled down the aisle as the congregation gaped in disbelief.

Outside the church, Dolly and her three friends were doubled up with laughter as they witnessed the meltdown of Ron's love life. As they drove away, they saw Ron fleeing the church for his car. The last thing they saw was the bride throwing a shoe at him as he slammed his car door shut and roared out of the parking lot.

"Drive, just drive," Dolly yelled at Chrissie. "Just get us the heck home before I die laughing."

They were still laughing uncontrollably when the two cars pulled into Dolly's parking lot at the SeaVue Apartments. There, in his sparkling red Mustang convertible, Steve Hunt sat waiting.

"What on earth is up with all of you?" he asked the gleeful women.

"Sorry I couldn't be ready earlier," Dolly said to Steve as she gave him a big kiss. "I had to go to a wedding on Pawley's Island."

"Anybody I know?" Steve asked.

"Probably not. Just a guy we knew from way back. We just wanted to pay a courtesy call, meet the bride, and drop off a wedding present." The other three women laughed hysterically.

"What the. . . ?"

"Don't worry about a thing, Steve darlin'. I'll tell you all about it some other time," Dolly said.

She turned to April, Chrissie, and Darlene and hugged and kissed each of them. "Bye, girls. We're off for a romantic weekend," she said, tossing her overnight bag into the car. Steve blushed.

As he turned the car out of the parking lot, he remarked, "You never told me where you wanted to go this weekend, Dolly. Your wish is my command. Where shall it be?"

"Just drive, and take me anywhere you want to go, Honey. The Outer Banks, Charlotte, Charleston, wherever you want, 'cause wherever it is, I know I'm gonna love it. Anywhere, that is, except Savannah."